The Illusion of Simple

The
Illusion
of
Simple

‹›

Charles Forrest Jones

University of Iowa Press
IOWA CITY

University of Iowa Press, Iowa City 52242
Copyright © 2022 by Charles Forrest Jones
www.uipress.uiowa.edu
Printed in the United States of America

Cover design by Derek Thornton, Notch Design
Text design and typesetting by Sara T. Sauers
Printed on acid-free paper

Library of Congress Cataloging-in-Publication Data
Names: Jones, Charles Forrest, 1952– author.
Title: The Illusion of Simple / Charles Forrest Jones.
Description: Iowa City: University of Iowa Press, [2022]
Identifiers: LCCN 2021040667 (print) | LCCN 2021040668 (ebook)
    | ISBN 9781609388317 (paperback) | ISBN 9781609388324
    (ebook)
Subjects: LCGFT: Detective and mystery fiction. | Novels.
Classification: LCC PS3610.O62256 I45 2022 (print) |
    LCC PS3610.O62256 (ebook) | DDC 813/.6—dc23/eng/20211201
LC record available at https://lccn.loc.gov/2021040667
LC ebook record available at https://lccn.loc.gov/2021040668

To Carol

Part 1

‹›

"THE FIRST PULSE to take is your own."

Sheriff Billy Spire faithfully repeats this mantra when arriving at any scene to which he is called. It is a caution against being foolish and rushing in. Or, perhaps more to the point, against losing self-control and hurting someone unnecessarily. It has been a long time since anything like that happened. Still, Sheriff Spire trusts himself far less than he is trusted by the people of Ewing County, Kansas. Better safe than sorry.

Pulling up slowly in the big silver Dodge Ram 1500, he studies the troop of young girls and the tall woman at their center. A skinny man with straight gray chin whiskers stands apart, leaning against the chrome bumper of a well-cared-for eighteen-wheeler. Lit up by its running lights, the vehicle glows like ribbon candy on this late and leaden winter afternoon.

The sheriff looks beyond the group of people on the highway's edge, making sure there is nothing unusual up or down the road, across the

3

sprouting field of winter wheat, or in the distant stand of cottonwoods. Seeing nothing, he veers to the shoulder and swings a lazy U-turn.

He stops, reaches for his notebook and evidence kit. When he looks up, the girls are staring at him. Their faces are filled with alarm as they scoot closer to the woman. One of the smaller ones reaches for her hand.

Billy Spire knows how he looks. He's used to seeing himself through the eyes of others.

<>

Three hours earlier.

Several miles west of Stonewall, Kansas, a red-tailed hawk perches on a telephone pole and watches a coyote tear at something in the highway ditch. The coyote braces its front legs and jerks its head left and right, over and over until that something rips free. He holds his prize haughty and high. Just then a cattle truck roars by, scaring the coyote across a fallow sorghum field toward the safety of a dry riverbed. Halfway there, the animal flushes out a jackrabbit and becomes distracted, dropping his mouthful to give chase in a furious, winding race of death or escape.

The hawk leans forward and lifts off the pole. It hovers for a beat then swoops down to grab the dropped object and carries it to a fat, bare cottonwood limb. Before it can examine its prize, two angry jays rise in ornery objection, flying furiously at the hawk, scolding and pecking. In its panicked retreat, the hawk becomes the second creature to lose the torn object. It tumbles through naked branches and lands in the roots of a fallen tree on the sandy bank of what was once the mighty Arkansas River.

<>

An hour after the hawk dropped its prize, a beat-up surplus school van turns off the highway onto a dirt drive. Its license carries the FI abbreviation for Finney County. The county seat and its largest town, Garden City, lies twenty miles to the west. The van rolls past a small wooden farmhouse very slowly to keep the dust down. The farmhouse door swings open, and a woman in her late fifties wearing blue jeans steps down from the porch.

"There she is, girls," says the van driver. "Wave hello, real nice now."

The nine little girls wave frantically, as if the farmwife is the most glorious thing they have ever seen. The driver, wearing a gray stocking cap over her short black hair, winces sweetly at the exaggerated enthusiasm of her passengers. She stops, rolls down the window, and speaks.

4

"Thank you so much."

"Why, Ayesha, you know you're always welcome. But mercy, what a day. I almost hate to send you out there, cold as it is. Why not just come in for some hot chocolate?"

The delicious offer stirs excited agreement among the girls.

"Yes, ma'am, we will. Afterward. Hot chocolate tastes sweeter when it's earned."

The woman understands. These are girls who lack so much in their lives. Structure, discipline. Commitments made and kept.

"Well, it won't be so bad in the riverbed," she points out. "Sheltered by the embankment and trees."

"We're working on our earth caring badges," Ayesha continues.

"Are you now? That's wonderful." The woman peers at the darkening sky, then adds, "You best get going. That weather isn't going to get any friendlier."

She climbs back on the porch and waves with Kansas dignity, palm high, hand twisting slowly as she watches the van bounce along a set of ruts and park at the edge of the riverbank. She steps back inside, closing the storm door tightly to keep out the cold wind. The woman is an old scout, the legitimate kind, and good church lady. She is glad to provide the girls with a wholesome adventure, never mind the troop's sketchy credentials.

The van comes to a stop where the winter wheat, with its emergent stalks of green, edges up to river scrub. The girls pile out and fumble with zippers and scarves in the icy wind. Their fingers are stupid in the cold.

"You older girls help the little ones." The woman smiles bravely, as if this were all too much fun, the wind-caused tears streaking down her cheeks.

When they are bundled, the troop begins marching to the riverbank. The leader is very tall. The girls follow single file in close order, each using the body in front as a shield against the wind. None of them notice the tufts of white fur blowing past their ankles. The rabbit lost its race with the coyote.

Ayesha Perez is in her early thirties. She has hazel eyes and a golden complexion. Her face is heart-shaped, with a wide forehead and pointed chin. Standing six-foot tall with broad shoulders, narrow hips, and long legs, she has the physique of a runner, which, in fact, she was. Raised in the Fort Riley spillover community of Junction City, she ran track at Bethel College in Newton, a Mennonite school, and she ran very well, graceful stride, her heels kicking almost up to her butt. Arms and legs churning, her head always on a smooth, level plane. She won a lot of medals, which she keeps in the bottom of her sock drawer. For that was then and this is now. She never became an Anabaptist—her stern Baptist grandmother would have spun in her grave—but she graduated college infused with Mennonite ethics, a bristling and impatient commitment to peace and justice. Quick to take offense at any affront to the humanity in others, Perez is powerless against her grandmother's cruel fire and brimstone, against the guilty heartache that rises from her own desires. Inexhaustible in her generosity to those who crave love, especially her needy band of young girls, Ayesha is tired and stingy when it comes to loving herself. Her heart and faith tear against each other.

The troop climbs down into the riverbed, where the wind is quieted by a thick stand of cottonwoods. Ayesha stops to take count and make sure everyone is all right. The girls form a semicircle around her.

"What are those?" one asks, pointing at Ayesha's parka, which is festooned with travel decals.

"They show countries I've visited. This one is Mexico. These are Austria, Greece, Peru, and Sweden. Do you remember these countries? From when we looked at a globe in the library?"

Their mouths say they do, but their blank expressions suggest otherwise.

"We'll have to go back," Ayesha notes with a patient smile.

"What is that silver one?" asks a little girl named Luciana. She wears pink plastic glasses with smudged lenses.

"Which one?"

"Back there."

Ayesha twists and tugs at her coattail. "Oh that. It's duct tape."

The girls all laugh. They knew it was duct tape. Ayesha laughs, too.

"Do you know what, sweethearts? Your coats can have more decals than mine if you dream big and stay in school. Will you do that for me?"

They nod earnestly that they will. Ayesha earnestly nods back at them, but she knows that for many of them, maybe all, the challenges will be too great.

"Onward then." She points her chin down the braided riverbed.

The sky is low and featureless. Without sun, all the color is washed out. The river bottom is silver. The leafless cottonwoods are looming and gray. Wind moans through the branches. Despite the seasonal gloom, the girls are joyous. At the kind attention of a pretty woman. The promise of snacks soon and hot cocoa later. The unburdened freedom to wander, and look, and dream. And maybe pick up a little trash.

After a few minutes, Ayesha stops next to a fallen cottonwood. She breaks off a twig with a smart snap and gestures for the girls to follow suit. They do so with greater and lesser degrees of ease. Some of the smaller girls require two or four sets of helping hands to twist the wood loose from the sinews of bark.

"How do scouts care for the earth?" she asks.

"We leave it better than we found it!" they shout in unison.

"Exactly," Ayesha beams. "Now take off the little side branches and sharpen the end like this."

Ayesha scrapes the end of her stick against a flat stone. When it is sufficiently pointy, she takes a black plastic trash bag from her pocket. Looking around, she spots a crushed, half-buried milk carton. With a quick stab she spears the carton and shakes it off into her bag.

"Let's work for a while, then we'll have a snack."

That's the magic word. Snack. The girls are hungry. They are always hungry. It's one of the conditions of their existence. They have been eyeing the backpack Ayesha carries and are giddy at the prospect of eating.

"Fill it up, girls," she commands. And off they race, tickled and energized that their bellies will soon be filled.

Unfortunately for the Arkansas River and those who care about it, there is no lack of opportunity for the girls. Its fringe of stubborn vegetation is thick with litter. Aluminum cans, plastic bags, Styrofoam, shredded paper, and cloth. Tossed from the highway and blown across fields. The girls stab with their sharp sticks then run back with their pickings. Ayesha extends the plastic trash bag, praising each girl for her contribution.

At a hollow in the bankside, they come upon a ring of scorched rocks. There is a torn blanket and liquor bottles, broken and blackened by fire. Used condoms are scattered about. Even at their young age, the girls know what they are. On the streets where they walk, such things are as common as abandoned shopping carts, as found pennies.

Ayesha cringes. She is not all that comfortable with sexuality. Especially her own. But this is a teachable moment she cannot ignore.

"Isn't this awful, this trash?" she asks sadly. The girls nod, their hearts heavy with her sorrow.

"Do you know how that blanket and glass got here?"

They nod again. They know, probably better than their leader. But Ayesha has a lesson to teach.

The troop stands transfixed. Their faces are shaded with shame and foreboding, as if seeing themselves strewn among the smudged and broken glass.

"It's a pity. No boy is worth this. No boy is more important than the love we hold for ourselves."

"And God's love," Luciana volunteers.

"Yes, that too," Ayesha acknowledges. "So please be careful with yourselves. Love yourselves as much as I love you."

The girls promise they will. But Ayesha Perez knows it's never that simple. Still, she is a person of abiding faith and maybe, just maybe, this talk, this gentle moment in the riverbed will alter the trajectory of one or two. That's enough to hope for. Enough to keep her reaching out again and again and again.

"Now let's eat!" she says, widening her eyes with excitement.

Ayesha leads the girls farther down the riverbed to a tangled shelter of cottonwood roots. She shimmies her body, landing the backpack heavily on the sand. The girls gather around as she pulls out juice boxes and peanut butter and jelly sandwiches wrapped tight in cellophane skins.

As they eat, Luciana settles next to Ayesha. She reaches her lips up to Ayesha's ear.

"Did you go to college?" she whispers.

Ayesha is surprised. Never once, in her three years at La Buena Familia, has any child asked this question.

"Yes, honey, I did."

"Do you think I can go there, too?"

Ayesha draws back to look at the little girl's face. It is serious, determined, and brave. As if she were contemplating climbing Mount Everest or plunging over Niagara Falls in a barrel.

"Yes, Luciana," Ayesha says. "I think you can."

Brown eyes light up behind smudged pink glasses. Luciana will remember this conversation the rest of her life. She will draw upon Ayesha's words for hope, for tenderness, for determination.

A few feet away, a tiny Vietnamese girl wolfs down her drink and sandwich. Her family has so many kids that her parents ran out of conventional names. All they could come up with was their native word for celery. Because that word defies the hard-clipped twang of western Kansas, she soon became known as "Daisy."

Happy and full-bellied, Daisy is keen for mischief. Using her trash stick, she flicks sand onto the other girls' shoes until one of them—a big, thick girl—jumps up and chases her away. Pouting along the opposite bank, Daisy dejectedly jabs her stick into random holes and shadows. The red-tailed hawk watches from a treetop. It has returned several times to look for its fallen prize. It lolls its head side to side. Peering down with one eye as Daisy approaches the object of its interest. When she sees it, and pokes it with her stick, the hawk gives up and flies after something else to seize.

Daisy pries and prods and finally pops the object out of the roots. She bends down to take a close look. It is a fist-sized ball of leather, stained and chewed. Nothing of value, she shrugs. Might as well have some fun. So, lining up like the Tiger Woods she has seen on TV, Daisy takes a long, mighty swing.

The leather clump sails high and hits Luciana on the side of her head. It knocks her pink plastic glasses crooked then falls to the ground. Grim with anger, she sets down her juice and sandwich, she straightens her glasses and carefully aims with the toe of her shoe. Ayesha almost laughs at Luciana's fierce concentration. Yes, of all the girls, Luciana might be the one to make it. She just might.

Fierce though Luciana may be, her aim is errant. She swings too low and sprays a cascade of sand over her nearby mates. They all scream, jump up, and dust off their clothes.

The misdirected clump of leather bounces off someone's shin and in a heartbeat, a dozen girls are whirling around the riverbed. Shouting, giggling, pulling at each other, playing soccer with a leather object of unknown origin. Ayesha protects her food with an outstretched arm. She laughs and shouts encouragement. She knows she should leave them alone at their play. But Perez is a jock and can't resist joining in. Maybe even showing off a little bit. Modeling that girls can be strong, fast, and proud, she races into the middle of the circle. Then stops.

"What is that?" she asks.

The girls freeze and stare, as if seeing the leather object for the first time. Ayesha grabs Daisy's stick. With it and the toe of her shoe, she presses the object into a recognizable shape.

"Jesus," she exclaims.

<>

An eighteen-wheeler rumbles down the highway. The pavement is straight and flat. The driver, a skinny man with straight gray chin whiskers, uses his knees to steer as he thumbs his cell phone for delivery orders. The afternoon is so dismal he has turned on the running lights, a cheery trim of red and gold.

Something suddenly catches the truck driver's eye. He jerks his head up to see a tall woman and group of children running toward the highway waving frantically. The driver drops his phone, hits the brakes, and wrestles the fishtailing trailer to a stop. He throws open the cab door, swings onto the running board, and hollers "What the hell?!"

"We found a hand!" the woman shouts. She points toward a row of cottonwoods lining the river. The driver cranes to see.

"A human hand!" she yells, as if speaking louder will make him understand better. "We were hiking in the riverbed. We found it over there."

The driver continues to squint into the distance.

"What?" he repeats, this time with the uptick of a question.

"Call the goddamned law!" Ayesha shrieks. Then, embarrassed at her foul language in front of the girls, she covers her mouth and adds, "Please."

<>

Billy Spire, sheriff of Ewing County, is forty-eight years old. He has been in office for three terms. Twelve years. He carries two hundred forty pounds on a five-nine frame and carries it well. Shoulders broad as an ax handle and the sweeping, powerful belly of a weightlifter. His head is a pock-marked block of limestone on a bull neck.

As Spire checks his evidence kit under the dome light of the Dodge Ram, the girls study his rough, colorful face. He wears his red hair in a crew cut. His cheeks are sallow. Heavy, purple-green bags sag beneath his eyes. His five o'clock shadow reads almost blue. White scars nick his forehead and brows. Some from sports, more from trouble. His eyes are small and black as the bottom of a well. In every way, Billy Spire's appearance suggests a brutish and plodding intelligence. That, or a serious drinking problem. The truth is he scarcely drinks. Mostly diet cola, which he consumes by the gallon.

Spire swings down from the pickup. As a sign of professional toughness, he almost always wears nothing but shirt sleeves. But there's no fooling anyone today. Not in this wind. He pulls on a quilted nylon jacket and zips it all the way up.

"We found a human hand," the tall woman says.

She looks down upon him from her full height. Working to convey control in front of the girls, her voice is overly calm.

"Who are you?" Spire asks, his voice sounding nasal, resonant and loud. A voice made for hollering.

"My name is Ayesha Perez."

He studies the woman's green parka covered in travel patches, then looks over at the group of girls hovering together.

"And them?"

"We're a girl troop from La Buena Familia in Garden City."

Spire dutifully makes notes in a small spiral notebook.

"Him?" Spire nods at the skinny fellow with chin whiskers.

"He's a truck driver we waved down."

Spire makes another note. The little girls are pressed close to their leader. They stare at the sheriff with open mouths.

"Have you really been to Iceland?" he asks.

"What?"

He points at her parka.

"Does that matter?" she says impatiently.

"No. But I always wanted to go there."

"We found a human hand," Perez reminds him. "Don't you think you should do something?"

"I expect whoever lost that hand has already done something. And if not, well, there's probably no rush in that case, either." He trails off.

"You'd rather stand and talk about Iceland?" Ayesha glares.

"Okay," the sheriff concedes. "Let's go see."

The woman wheels and marches across the field, the little girls running behind her trying to keep up.

Spire looks over at the truck driver, who continues to lean against the fender.

"Guy is driving down the highway, minding his own business, and all hell breaks loose," the driver mutters. "I'll be running late all day."

Spire nods and turns to follow the troop of little girls.

When they get to the spot, the sheriff circles the glove several times, writing in his notebook. Every so often he snaps a picture with his phone.

"That looks very official," Ayesha says coolly. She refuses to own a cell phone. Considers them a force of class division. The rich have all the access and technology that money can buy. The poor struggle to pay bills. They struggle to be heard. They struggle to explain to their children why they cannot have what others take for granted. Ayesha Perez stands with the poor, without a cell phone in her hand.

"They say the best camera is the one you have with you," Spire replies.

"Anyway, this is the only camera we got. Budgets are tight in Ewing County, Kansas."

The sheriff waves his hand over scuff marks in the river bottom. "So, they found it while playing?"

"Yes."

Spire nods and looks over at the girls one more time, studying them for a moment. None of them is wearing a uniform. Or any part of a uniform.

"Girl Scouts you say?"

Perez stiffens at the question.

"I said girl troop."

"What's the difference?" he adds.

"We're unaffiliated," she sniffs.

"Unaffiliated?"

Perez fronts Spire, her back to the troop. Looking down at him, she whispers, "These girls don't have money. Not for dues. Not for uniforms. Not for anything. But they are Americans and deserve the American experience. So, we call them a troop and let it go at that."

Spire nods curtly. Given his thuggish appearance, Perez is not sure he understands.

"Please don't say anything more about it."

"Why would I?" he answers, understanding. He steps around Perez to look at the little girls.

"You all are from Garden City?" he asks.

They nod. He considers them closely. He knows these children. Not individually, not by name, but he knows them. They are the daughters of immigrants. Their families work the packing plants of Garden City, Dodge, and Liberal.

When it comes to processing beef, immigrants have always been the essence who keep the plants running. The jungles of Chicago were manned by eastern Europeans. Same for the neighborhoods of Strawberry Hill in Kansas City. When the big regional beef packers moved farther west, they brought with them refugees seeking freedom and work— Vietnamese, Mexican nationals, Colombians, Hondurans, Panamanians, Somalis. Finding mind-numbing and crippling hours of repetitive motion. Football stadium–sized facilities humming with a million tiny cuts. Twenty minutes from hoof to freezer.

"Are you girls all right?" he asks, eyes sweeping back and forth.

They look to Ayesha Perez for the answer.

"You're okay," she affirms. But the girls do not nod agreement.

"We are afraid of you," Luciana announces.

Spire kneels in front of her.

"Why is that?"

Luciana turns and buries her face in the tall woman's hip.

"You really don't know?" Ayesha asks incredulously. "You lock up people from their community. Many get deported. Especially those who ask for things like fair wages and safe working conditions."

Spire continues crouching and looking at Luciana.

"Well, it's not only me," he says. "But I'm sorry that sometimes has to happen."

It's the best Spire can offer. Ayesha snorts and looks away.

Spire rises and walks over to the twisted clump and kneels down. It's a leather work glove, chewed and deeply stained. Using the tip of his pen and toe of his boot, he pries open the cuff. Inside are splintered white bones and the gristle of torn flesh. He works the fingers and finds them stiff but pliable.

"Whatever happened, happened pretty recent." He takes a plastic bag from his evidence kit and uses tweezers to collect the glove. He records details in his notebook.

"Where did it come from?" one of the girls asks.

"I don't know," Spire answers, twisting a cramp out of his back. "But somebody's probably looking for it. Maybe we should lend a hand."

"Is that supposed to be funny?" Ayesha demands.

"Kind of," he replies.

"Jesus," she says, then stomps to the other side of the riverbank.

The little girls linger, still studying the face of Billy Spire. He grins at them, trying to soften his appearance to look friendly. It doesn't really work. His small eyes recede into narrow crevices beneath scarred brows. Sallow furrows run deep from his cheekbones to his chin. The bulb of his nose is raw and red from too much exposure to harsh conditions.

"He looks like that iguana from the zoo," Luciana says out loud, as if the sheriff weren't standing right there.

The other girls giggle then hurry after Perez.

Spire's grin fades and he shakes his head. He knows what he looks like. He is used to seeing himself through the eyes of others.

<>

Four months earlier, on I-70 at the western edge of Kansas City.

Father Eli Turney has driven past Cabela's sporting goods store probably a dozen times on his way back to Ewing County after visiting his sister in Kansas City.

This time, he would stop.

Turney is six feet four. Three hundred forty pounds the last time he checked, but he hasn't bothered to check in years. He's sixty-two years old. His head is the size of a pumpkin. His features—bright blue eyes, rosy cheeks, a cupid's bow mouth—crowd the center of his face.

Two years prior, the priest had been banished to Ewing County, far west of Kansas City, as the result of an unfortunate incident. His previous church was in a struggling Kansas City parish that had seen better days and a younger population. Despite the difficulties, Father Turney felt blessed in his assignment. He had been raised only a few blocks away, in the family home still occupied by his older sister. The pews were sparsely populated. But among those few were families and friends he had known since childhood.

When Pope Francis was elected, Turney considered it a miracle. The priest identified with the poor, the hurting, the hopeless. He credited the Holy Spirit for moving the College of Cardinals toward a humble man of forgiveness, equity, and stewardship. There could be no other explanation, given the prevailing conservatism of the Catholic Church. And while the pope had changed, the bishop of greater Kansas City was not with him. The bishop remained obsessed with abortion, homosexuality, and activist nuns. He bitterly anguished over Francis and the new directions he proposed.

The bishop was visiting Father Turney's parish to dedicate a new performance center in the church's basement. It was a modest improvement really, a wooden stage centered on an interior wall. Suitable, perhaps, for children's plays and the annual talent show. Still, it was something new. Something suggestive of promise. Something conceived and hand-built by congregation members who puffed with pride and smelled of sawdust.

"My friends," the bishop said into the microphone. An attractive man of middle age, with regular features and an expensive haircut, he waved for people to come close. "This is a glorious occasion. And I am very pleased to make a surprise presentation on behalf of the church elders."

Father Turney looked around suspiciously. He had not been expecting any sort of surprise presentation.

"It is my great honor to dedicate . . ." He stopped and made a show of searching the room. "Father Eli, won't you join me?"

The huge priest shambled forward, looking warily at the congregants.

14

They beamed back at him with delight. The bishop placed his hand on the priest's arm.

"It is my great honor to dedicate this hall in the name of Father Eli Turney. Let it hereafter be known to one and all as Turney Hall."

As the crowd cheered, the large priest fought back tears. He was a sucker for sentiment. Always had been. Turney put his hands up to his neck, signaling that he was too choked up to speak. The trim, handsome bishop smiled radiantly and summoned silence with a regal wave of his hand.

"If I may say a word for my friend who is momentarily . . . distracted. Thank you all on behalf of Father Turney. This is a good man. A man who loves God and all of you. A man who walks in the Lord's presence."

The bishop's kind words broke the dam and Father Turney began shedding tears. His big shoulders shook and every heart in the place melted. The crowd cheered louder.

"So, how about we give this stage a try?" the bishop cheerfully commanded. "Let's hear some music."

A country-western band comprised of parishioners in flannel shirts struck up a song. The uninhibited—small children and old couples—immediately began dancing. By the end of the first tune, everyone was on their feet, clapping and shuffling. Soon the amps were cranked up and the liquor was flowing.

"Catholics know how to party," the bishop chuckled to himself as he glanced at his watch. "I need to check my email."

As the bishop departed the stage, Father Turney waded into a rollicking crowd of well-wishers. Children hugged his massive legs. Gals kissed him on the neck. Someone slapped his back and shoved a tumbler of scotch into his hand. He never had to ask for more. It seemed that after every sip, someone hurried over with a bottle to make sure his glass was not lacking content.

It didn't take long for Father Turney to drink too much. Way too much. The kind of too much that loosens a person's tongue.

During the first musical break, he spotted the bishop leaning against a wall by himself, looking alternately out the window and at his phone. The big priest shook himself loose from his admirers and went over, already unsteady on his feet.

"Thank you so much for coming, Bishop," he enunciated carefully, trying to cover his blossoming inebriation. "I know you're very busy."

"Wouldn't have missed it for the world, Eli. Really. But now I have to scoot." He started toward the door.

"Pope Francis better watch himself," Father Turney blurted out. Maybe it was the liquor speaking.

"What?" The bishop turned with arched eyebrows.

"Better have someone tasting his food." The liquor would not shut up.

"That's funny," the bishop laughed.

"I'm serious," Father Turney replied, wondering if he was slurring his words as much as it seemed. "Those guys are old school."

"What guys?"

"The conservative cardinals."

The bishop squared up to Father Turney. The smile stayed on the lips, but his eyes went dead cold. These were his people, the conservatives. And it was his church threatened by the apostate Francis.

"I'm not sure you're thinking very clearly, Eli," the bishop said in a gentle voice. Gentle in the way a razor is sharp. He looked at the glass in Turney's hand. "Maybe you've had enough."

Father Turney's eyes turned down to study his drink. When he looked back up, the bishop was gone. A fleeting motion out the doorway. Moving fast with anger.

"Fuck me," the priest sighed to himself. Then emptied his glass in one giant gulp.

Two months later, a "long-planned" reorganization was announced. One that contained "exciting new opportunities." That was especially true for Father Turney, who was yanked out of his comfortable suburb and sent to Stonewall, Kansas. A small town to hell and gone from where he was. Out in the middle of the middle of nowhere, southwest of Kansas City.

Father Turney arrived in Ewing County on a blazing hot August afternoon. Outside the town a few lush green irrigated circles of corn and soybeans. Beyond them, a landscape parched and brown. Farmers had begged the county commission to do something, anything, to combat the continuing drought. The only sound that afternoon was the drone of a single engine plane arcing lazily across the sky, releasing crystals of silver iodide in a desperate attempt to seed non-existent clouds into rain. It wasn't working. It rarely did. Still, farmers felt better for the trying.

Father Turney turned off the highway and drove through the center of town. He found a low-slung village of older housing, with grain elevators on the rail spur. He passed the county courthouse, a two-story limestone with tall windows and a concrete façade. The streets were abandoned, empty and silent, not so much as the bark of a dog. Across from the courthouse square an unassuming storefront sign read "Chamber of Commerce." He angled into a parking space and went inside.

"Afternoon," said a middle-aged lady behind a counter. Her honey-colored beehive was piled high, every hair in place. Her fingernails were lacquered white and embedded with glitter. Father Turney surmised that this was a woman with plenty of time.

"Afternoon," the priest smiled back. It was a forced smile. Every atom in his being wanted to go back to his comfortable suburb in Kansas City. "I'm the new priest."

"You are?" the lady beamed. "We've been waiting."

"Are you a parishioner?"

"Oh no." She lowered her voice so nobody else could hear, even though she and the priest were the only people in the building. "Baptist."

"I see," Father Turney nodded, thoughtfully. "Well, we're all God's children."

"You'll do fine here," she said with a wink. "Need directions?"

"No, I can find my way. But I was wondering. What kind of information do you have about Stonewall? Population? Employment? Social services? Anything that might help me know more about this place. These people."

"Now that's a good question," the chamber woman answered, looking around the countertop, drumming her fingernails. "We don't have much of that around here. Tell you the truth, there isn't much interest in Stonewall these days. People who live here know everything there is to know. And people who don't live here? Can't imagine why they would care."

"So, what does the Chamber do?" he asked.

"Precious damn little," she said, still looking. Then she snapped her fingers victoriously and disappeared to a back room, still talking. "I volunteer here a couple of days a week. Just to get out of the house, mostly. Here, take this, why don't you?"

She returned with a well-thumbed telephone book. "There's an information section in front. It includes all of Ewing County. And there's a street map, too." She jabbed a glittery fingernail into a section of off-colored map pages.

"What do I owe you?"

"Not a thing," the lady answered. "Maybe a second opinion if the preacher ever says something I don't like." She cackled with delight.

Phone book in hand, Turney stepped back out into the staggering heat. Across the town square he spotted a diner called Effie's. Though not more than a hundred feet away, he got back into his car and drove, too hot and dispirited to walk. Waiting for a double hamburger and fries, he leafed through the directory of his new hometown.

According to the information section, Ewing County housed 1,232 citizens, almost all in Stonewall. The average age was sixty-four years old. The population was overwhelmingly white. In the yellow pages he found a farm equipment dealer, independent telephone company, rural electric cooperative, grain elevator, one bank, one combination antique store and real-estate dealer, one auto repair garage, half a dozen churches, a liquor store, the Gas-N-Go, and Effie's diner. As in most towns of western Kansas, the local economy serves only to sustain that which has endured. Nothing new.

The government pages listed a school district—largest employer in town—and the county courthouse, with its ancillary volunteer fire department, attorney, title and abstract company. The city council met once a week in a metal Quonset hut next to the self-serve carwash. Finally, there was the Stonewall hospital. Father Turney would later find that it was a rehabbed clothing store, owned and equipped by the county. Staffed by an old Mormon physician, Doc Howard, and his nurse wife whose birth name was June but was known by all as "Mama Doc."

Father Turney tossed down the phone book. He pushed away the plate of half-eaten comfort food.

"Lord help me," he sighed.

<>

This time, driving back to Stonewall after visiting his sister in Kansas City, Father Turney stops at Cabela's.

He pulls off the interstate, finds a parking space, and turns off the engine. The priest drives a tiny Honda Fit. He could have gotten a bigger car to better fit his large frame, but he liked the automobile's opticals so much he knew it was the car for him.

"Have you ever seen a clam bigger than its shell?" he used to love teasing the children back in his former parish. Still smiling from this memory, Turney climbs out of the vehicle, lumbers past exterior displays of fishing boats and four-wheelers, and enters the store through towering wooden doors.

He asks directions from the greeter, then wanders to the back. Past camo clothing and artificial streams stocked with catfish and bass. Past the sprawling diorama of big game and predators. Through a nondescript door, into a small range area where shoppers test bows and arrows. The priest had done a little online research and has a pretty good idea what he's looking for.

"Welcome to Cabela's," chirps a friendly sandy-haired salesman flashing an alligator smile. "How can I help you?"

"I'd like to try a recurve bow."

"Recurve?" the salesman repeats with a skeptical frown.

"That's right."

"Is this for you?"

"Um, a nephew." While Father Turney anticipated the question and had practiced the falsehood, he's still unable to lie with crisp precision.

"He shot much?"

"Never."

"You might want to think about a compound," the salesman says. He gestures toward a rack of possibilities. Turney turns and is confronted by a collection of metal arcs. All struts, tension, and technology, with outsized gears at either end.

"Sights just like a rifle," the salesman says, aiming an imaginary gun. "Nephew will be able to hit the target from the get-go. Only question is how hard."

"No," Father Turney replies. "He's kind of traditional."

Father Turney had researched compounds. But they didn't appeal to him. He wanted something simple and primitive. An honest to God bow with the cleanest and most honest line between his fingers, the arrow, and its target. He spots one on a rack that might be suitable.

"How about that?"

"Heritage Razorback," the salesman coos, alligator smile back in place. "Good mid-range recurve."

The salesman eyes the priest's build. He raises and lowers his arm as if measuring the cut of a sports coat, then pulls parts from off a shelf behind the counter. He starts bolting laminated limbs onto a sinuous wooden riser. As it comes together, the recurve looks like a traditional bow.

Two other men enter. In their early forties, joshing and efficient, they unzip archery bags and begin assembling their compounds. The priest glances over to see that he has been recognized. One of the newcomers approaches, smiling with delight.

"Father Turney! What are you doing here?"

"Oh, Michael. How are you?"

Father Turney hates seeing parishioners in everyday places. Especially former parishioners who remind him of where he was and where he is now.

He used to love being recognized back in the early days. It made the young priest feel important and admired. He rejoiced at the pride in his family's eyes whenever he was approached in public. Then he was no longer simple Eli, the fat kid who broke everything he touched and spilled everything he consumed. He was Father Turney, a being of vestments and grace, leader of prayers that raised glory to the rafters. How he loved to be recognized back then. But times had changed. That early sense of grandeur had worn away, leaving only the desire to be an anonymous human being. Full of uncertainty and honest to his own moods.

"Did you get a chance to read that book I left with your sister?" Michael asks.

Earnest and well-meaning parishioners are forever giving Father Turney earnest and well-meaning books. It is their way of connecting with him. He understands the gesture to be kind, but truth be told, he finds most of it drivel. More than anything he wishes they would just give him the money and let him choose his own reading.

"Yes, I found it quite interesting. Thank you."

"I thought you would," Michael says as he bolts together his own compound bow for target practice. "Especially thoughts on the body of Christ."

I get it, Father Turney thinks. The body of Christ. Lean, strong, organically fed, endowed with divine stamina. Among the well-meaning parishioners, none grate him so much as those flat-bellied men and women who worry about his weight. His body. His risk of diabetes. His affection for fast food. His utter lack of self-discipline.

"Yes," the priest replies. "That was very important."

Michael nods, pleased that his message has been taken in the right spirit.

"And when are you coming back to us?" he asks.

"That's not for me to say," the priest admits with a shrug.

"We miss you," Michael declares. He abruptly shouts "Clear!", and Father Turney and the friend move out of the way.

Michael draws the compound bow and takes dead aim at a bullseye taped to a dense Styrofoam cube about twenty paces away. He pulls the string back until it touches his nose. Steadies for one breath, then triggers the release with a slight twitch of his back muscle. The arrow hits before Father Turney sees it take flight. The point stuck deep into the target's center. Michael looks to the priest for approval.

"Very impressive," Father Turney says.

"Just takes practice," Michael boasts.

"Here you go." The salesman shoves an assembled Razorback into the priest's hands.

"That for you?" Michael asks with a skeptical frown.

"My nephew."

"Didn't know you had a nephew."

"Sort of adopted."

"Oh," Michael nods slowly. "He'd probably like a compound better."

"So I hear."

"Let's give her a try," the salesman urges. He reaches into a cardboard box and hands the priest a wrist guard and shooting glove. "This one pulls thirty pounds."

Father Turney squints at the target, then begins drawing back the string.

"Aim down the barrel of the arrow," the salesman coaches.

At first there is little resistance. But at full extension, the priest's arms begin to tremble.

"Easy now," Michael joins in. "Don't pluck the string. Just release."

Father Turney's tremble becomes an all-out shake. His fingertips fail. The arrow flies free. But instead of going toward the target, it veers upward into a bank of fluorescent lights mid-way down the range. Glass tubes explode, showering the floor with white powder and broken glass. Three of the four men look on in stunned amazement. Father Turney is not at all surprised, given his history of breakage and spilling.

"I'll take it," he says calmly. "And some arrows."

The priest and salesman walk to the cash register as Michael turns to his friend who is still awed by what he has seen.

"Used to be our priest. Out west somewhere now," Michael explains, with a slow, admiring nod. "Fine, fine man."

"Maybe so," the friend answers. "But as an archer, he ain't diddly squat."

Back at the parking lot, Father Turney loads the bow and arrow into the back of the Fit and covers them with a blanket. Winding his way out of the parking lot, he spots a Wendy's down the street.

It's a long drive to Stonewall. Better grab a bite. He orders two burgers and a large chocolate shake from the drive-through window. By the time he gets back to the highway, pointed west, he has dribbled drink all down the front of his shirt.

As Billy Spire finishes writing notes and snapping photos, Ayesha Perez still fumes at the sheriff's terrible joke.

"Maybe we should lend a hand?" she repeats in disbelief. The little girls are bored and getting cold. They wonder if the farmwife still has hot chocolate.

Suddenly, two men loom above them on the riverbank.

"Dispatch called the coffee shop," says the thicker of the two. "Do you need help?"

The thick man looks like a banker, which is exactly what he is. President of the Stonewall Savings and Loan, Owen Middleton is of average height, substantial around the middle, and has soft white hands. He is clean-shaven and wears aviator-style glasses that automatically darken in strong sun. He has a habit of tilting his head at a slight angle when talking to someone. Peering at them with a fixed half-smile, radiating a sort of affable skepticism. On the riverbank squinting into the icy gusts, Middleton wears a parka over his suit and tie. He carries a long-handled ice-scraper, the only weapon he could find in his car. When not in Stonewall, Middleton can usually be found in Topeka, where he serves as a state senator.

Next to Middleton stands a string bean with crooked teeth and hollow cheeks. Leo Ace runs Stonewall's one remaining auto repair shop. He wears grease-stained coveralls and carries a pump shotgun. In his mid-fifties, Ace's Elvis pompadour is plastered with so much fixative it holds rock steady even in the strong wind. He is a packrat savior to rust-bucket pickups and rattletrap jalopies. A self-anointed local historian, Ace can, and too often does, prattle on for hours about the settlement of Ewing County. Or anything else for that matter. As far as anyone can remember, Leo Ace has never had an unspoken thought.

"Sweet Jesus," Ace hollers in his high lonesome voice.

He jumps off the bank and stumbles to his knees. Some of the girls start to giggle. Perez silences them with a stern look. The senator observes and decides to stay where he is.

"What is going on here?" the mechanic continues, unfazed. "What's this about a hand?"

Spire holds out the plastic bag. "Somebody lost a glove. And left their hand inside."

"Where?" Ace bobs and weaves, looking down the riverbed.

"Over there," Ayesha volunteers. "This little girl found it."

Perez nudges Daisy slightly forward. She smiles uncertainly, the way children do when proud before strangers.

"Well good for you, cookie!" Ace bellows, beaming like a yard-art Jesus.

"Her name is Daisy," Ayesha says.

"I was just trying . . ." Ace begins.

"I know what you were trying," Perez interrupts. "And her name is still Daisy."

Spire looks up at Middleton with a slight smile. Between Ace and this prickly woman, justice will have a rough day. The senator shakes his head as slightly as Spire smiles. They are very old friends. They understand each other.

"What do you need us to do, Billy?" Middleton's voice is warm and cultured. It is a voice that hints at great range. From calming conversations over denied loans, to soaring rhetoric about the American spirit and a more perfect union.

Spire runs a palm over his crew cut.

"Look around, I guess. Start with the highway. Owen, you drive east a few miles. Ace, you go west. Call if you find anything. I'll finish up here."

Middleton offers his hand and pulls Ace out of the riverbed. They vanish as quickly as they appeared.

The sheriff turns back to Ayesha Perez. "I can find you at . . ." Spire pauses to consult his notes. "La Buena Familia, right?"

"Yes."

"Then you can go."

The tall woman doesn't move. She stares at him, her brows raised in expectation.

"What?"

"The girls?" Ayesha whispers.

"What about them?"

Perez takes the sheriff's arm in her strong grip. She tilts her head slightly forward.

"Say something to the girls."

"Like what?"

"They don't get a lot of positive feedback. Especially from the law. Would it kill you to say something nice? Something kind?"

Spire straightens. He looks up into Ayesha's eyes while gathering his thoughts. Then he turns to the girls. Their faces are cute. But they are also care-worn. Troubled. Poor.

"I don't know where this is going to lead," he says loudly, as if reading a proclamation in the county square. "But you girls handled it just right. You are brave and smart. Every one of you. My job is to keep people safe. You helped me do that today. Thank you."

"Say 'you're welcome,' girls," Perez instructs. And they do.

An engine roars in the near distance. A mountainous truck with oversized tires churns its way down the dry riverbed. It skids to a stop, spraying gravel onto the girls' shoes. A man wearing hunter-orange coveralls throws open the driver's door. A woman piles out the other side. She looks at the girls, the sheriff, and Perez, then presses her palms against the sides of her face and lets out an eerie howl. The man rushes around and grabs her elbows to keep her from collapsing.

"Remember?" Perez says to the astonished girls. "It's the lady we met earlier. The one with hot cocoa."

They remember. Even though she looks different now. Her face is wet with tears and twisted in horror.

"Oh, lordy. Oh, my children," the farmwife cries. She falls to her knees, grabs a couple of the girls, and hugs them close. "If anything was to happen to you, I just don't know . . ."

She is unable to finish the terrifying thought as more tears pour down her cheeks. The girls allow themselves to be half crushed by the woman's enfolding arms. They smile at their friends. Patient and bemused at the timeless wonder of overwrought adults.

"We're all fine," Perez assures while helping the older woman to her feet. "But we sure could use some of that hot chocolate."

The farmwife sags against the troop leader and tries to smile bravely.

"Yes," she sniffles. "There is plenty for everyone."

"You all climb in the back," her husband commands. He helps his wife into the truck. Perez lifts the girls into the high-riding bed and climbs in after them. The troop cuddles for warmth, with Ayesha Perez at its center. They wave goodbye to the sheriff. He waves back as the truck roars off into the chilly dusk. Soon they will be in the farmhouse, full of hot cocoa and jellied bread.

Spire is left alone in the riverbed listening to the cottonwoods creak and moan around him. The first evening stars play hide-and-seek behind fast-moving silvery clouds. Spire's phone rings.

"Found a truck with a flat tire," Ace bellows, as if he doesn't entirely trust telephonic communications. "About a half a mile west."

"Seen it before?"

"Oh yeah," the mechanic replies. "Russ Haycock."

"Of course," the sheriff says wearily. "Let Owen know where you are. I'll walk from here."

<>

Billy Spire always felt a sense of kinship with Russ Haycock. Though a generation apart, they were equally defined by the hardships of their youth.

Haycock was born and raised in Ewing County, the youngest of eight children. His mother was an impractical little woman who loved movie magazines. She fussed over her hair and wore makeup to scandalous proportions, at least in the opinion of local matrons. She idled away her days dreaming of things she would never have and places she would never see. She took great pride in her flower garden, one of the few pretty things in her life. This was another point of consternation to those who judged the Haycock household in need of less frivolity and more vegetables.

Haycock's father was twenty years older than his wife. A decent enough man, living a life of anxious poverty and too many mouths to feed. Added to those troubles was his own faulty judgment. He just couldn't win for losing. Too poor to pay for medical attention and too proud to ask for help, he ignored his glaucoma until it reduced him to sitting on the porch swing, trying to make out passing shapes through an oversized magnifying glass.

Mrs. Haycock died at thirty-four. Killed by vanity, they said. She was painting her toenails over a spread-out newspaper, little sponge spacers separating each toe, when one of the daughters ran into the house. Warning of a goat in the flower bed. Of course, the girl could have shooed the goat herself but it was way more fun to see her mother in a tizzy. Mrs. Haycock grabbed a broom and went running, balancing on her heels to protect the drying red polish. As she flew through the screen door, her upper body got too far ahead. She fell down the porch stairs and hit her skull on a broken concrete baluster from a rebuilt country bridge. An ornament she thought added elegance to the landscape. The children raced to her side, screaming about the twist in her neck and the way her eyes fluttered. The old man ran back and forth on the porch, frantically trying to see through his glass. Shouting questions that went unanswered as the Haycock children wailed and pleaded.

Mrs. Haycock was buried three days later. When well-meaning people of Stonewall came to visit, they found the old man still sitting on his porch sipping from a bottle of whiskey. They offered kind words, invoking the

Lord and His ways, but there was no comforting the widower. His natural anxiety bloomed into terror of as many hues and varieties as his dead wife's flowers. Deaf to words of faith or restraint, Russ's father reacted in the worst way. The way certain to realize his deepest fears. He filled his nights with brooding sorrow and his days with snarling rage. He shook his fist and cursed the moon. He treated his kids as if they were to blame, which they knew in their hearts they were. He worked them bitterly, berating their best efforts, dismissing their few sweet gestures. He took all they had and gave them nothing in return. He had nothing left to give. Absent Mrs. Haycock's amusing frippery, life on the farm soon lost any of its remaining charms. When the kids were old enough to walk away, they did. Just as surely as sunflowers pivot toward the warming sun.

<>

Winter afternoons end early in western Kansas. The sun flattens as it dips below the horizon, the undersides of streaking clouds shimmer red and purple. Soon it will be dark. Billy Spire takes a 6-cell black Maglite out of the Ram 1500, along with a pair of gloves and wool cap. He starts walking west. It's cold enough for the ground to be frozen, but the highway crew has salted the snow into slush. The clay shoulder is wet and sticky, a slippery muck the locals call "gumbo." The sheriff minds to step carefully only on pavement. There are enough problems at home without tracking gumbo onto the carpet.

He looks down as he walks, raking the Maglite back and forth. A red Lincoln SUV slows next to him and rolls down the window.

"Where is it?" Owen Middleton asks.

"Up there," Spire gestures. A few hundred yards ahead, a vehicle glows in the headlights of Ace's wrecker. It is a pale green pickup, sitting at an odd angle.

"Why are you walking?"

"To search between here and there," Spire answers. He pulls off the wool cap and vigorously scratches his scalp.

"Don't those come in fleece?" Middleton asks. Billy has been allergic to wool since they were kids.

"This one is standard issue."

Billy rolls up the cap's cuff to show a sheriff's insignia. That he would wear something uncomfortable in order to display credentials is, in Owen Middleton's mind, essential to his friend's nature.

"Is it Haycock's hand?"

"Don't know for sure. But bad trouble and Russ Haycock always had a way of finding each other."

"Hey buddy," Middleton sighs. "Hey buddy" is a western Kansas catch-all phrase that means—depending on intonation—anything from "I hear you" to "you betcha" to "Lord help us."

"You go on ahead," the sheriff instructs. "I'll be right there."

<>

When he was eighteen and skinny as a snake, Russ Haycock wore his wavy blond hair slicked back along the sides with a corkscrew curl that dangled down his forehead. In the style of the rockabilly bad boy Jerry Lee Lewis. Haycock's insolent nature showed itself every time he snapped his head to toss the corkscrew back in place. He was almost handsome, but his good looks were betrayed by one unfortunate feature. His eyes all but lacked lashes. In a place of dust storms, pollens, and the smoke of burning fields, Russ Haycock's pale blue eyes were always irritated and red rimmed. So raw and watery that a passing glance made people wince and avert their gaze.

Following a couple of brothers and the path of least resistance, Russ Haycock enlisted in the Army. He spent some time in Vietnam servicing transport vehicles. Changing oil and tires, greasing the bearings. He mustered out honorably and was bouncing around the West Coast when his father died. All eight children were notified of the death. Only Russ was drawn back to the old farmstead. His interest came more from desperation than sentiment. He was flat broke and lacking prospects.

He arrived in Stonewall behind the wheel of a wheezing '55 Oldsmobile. Next to him sat the only worthwhile thing he had to his name. A wife. She was a tiny, exquisitely beautiful Vietnamese girl. Her eyes were wide in amazement at the drear sparsity of western Kansas.

With olive skin, straight black hair worn with bangs, and perfect teeth, Mrs. Haycock was about the prettiest thing Ewing County had ever seen. Russ called her "Honey." Soon, so did everyone else, though never to her face. It wasn't for fear of causing offense. It was because Haycock guarded his wife jealously and would not let anyone else get that close.

Russ's inheritance consisted of fifteen acres with two "improvements": a saggy barn and an old house with a leaky roof and broken windows. His mother's flower beds, once gay with color, were now lifeless, littered with torn shingles and broken glass.

Haycock planned to flip the place. Turn sweat equity into sweet profit, then hightail it back to the coast. His ambitions were modest, but his skills and decision-making abilities were downright humble. His very first step was in the wrong direction. He destroyed that which held the most value. The old house. Russ hadn't many kind memories of that place. Mostly he recalled the townspeople mocking its appearance. So, he set it on fire. Ostensibly to clear the land. When the smoke became visible, the volunteer fire brigade roared up with half of Stonewall right behind.

They found Russ Haycock watching the conflagration. Can of gas at his feet. Butane lighter in his hand. Smirk on his face. Perhaps he thought his neighbors would find it amusing, or amazing, or some other way impressive. They didn't. Every expression read the same. "What is wrong with these people?" The smirk quickly faded.

"Leave her burn, goddammit."

"That house could be saved," argued the fire chief, gnawing on a spit of chewing tobacco. "Or at least scrapped for material."

"You don't even know what I'm thinking. You don't know nothing about me."

"You got that right," the chief agreed with disdain. He whistled through his fingers and waved his men back from the burning structure.

"It's his property. He's got a right."

The firefighters looked at the chief in disbelief. He pointed at Haycock and shook his head. Fires like that didn't come along very often. The men were disappointed to walk away from battle. But they shut off the pumper truck and started rolling up the hoses.

Honey had slipped into the throng of bewildered onlookers who had chased after the siren. She took refuge among them. The women studied her. Even then her beauty was beginning to fade. The twinkle was gone from her dark eyes. Her skin looked dry and her hair less lustrous.

"Poor thang," one woman whispered to another. "She don't understand one bit of what's going on here."

"She'll figure it out soon enough," her friend replied, nodding her head toward Haycock. "Miserable is miserable in any language."

〈〉

Billy Spire sweeps his Maglite over something in the ditch. He stops and studies it as carefully as he can from a distance. It is important to preserve a crime scene. He takes out his notebook and records the exact time and location. The road banks north to accommodate a curve away from the

28

river. Spire stands on the high side, shining his light downward. The road ditch is deep right there. Deeper than it is for miles in either direction.

The body is face up. It is a white male, bald on top with a fringe of dirty gray hair. Unshaven, mouth open, the pale blue eyes stare directly into the flashlight's beam. Across the forehead is a jagged scar. The filthy denim coat flaps in the wind. The right arm is extended, as if the dead man were offering a benediction. But the hand is missing. There is a dark stain across the chest.

"Damn, Haycock," Billy Spire mutters. "Now you went and got yourself killed."

One hundred fifty yards farther down the highway, Ace leans against the abandoned pickup. Spire signals with his flashlight. The mechanic jumps into his wrecker and guns it onto the highway. Middleton makes a lazy turn and follows behind. The sheriff takes out his phone and starts snapping photos. He is careful not to step closer until all conditions have been recorded. But something has already caught the sheriff's eye. While Russ Haycock lies motionless at the bottom of a ditch, some four to six feet off the road, there is no gumbo on the soles of his boots.

<>

In the ashes of the old house, Russ Haycock started building anew. He began with a basement.

It took more than a month to dig by hand. Shirtless, his pale skin burned by the summer sun, he pushed wheelbarrow after wheelbarrow up a two-by-eight ramp. Honey, shaded by a conical straw hat, raked the displaced soil into neat perimeter berms. When the hole was dug and bordered, he boxed in a foundation of lumber and chicken wire. He made a floor of gravel, joists, and plywood. To gain headroom, he set several tiers of cinderblock on top of the berm. Then he laid headers across the span, forming what was intended to be a basement ceiling and first-story floor.

"I tell you, babe, this will be something," he boasted, his arm draped across her shoulders. "They'll all come to see it. Damn if they won't."

"Mmmm," Honey murmured agreeably. But even then she had her doubts. The angles were off kilter. The cinderblock mortar was too sandy and already beginning to crumble.

"You won't even want to leave."

"Oh no," Honey exclaimed. "California."

"Open up your Golden Gates," Russ sang, leering at her. He laughed and roughly tickled until she twisted away.

Soon, the disconnect between Haycock's dreams and realities was apparent to all, except Russ himself. Forsaking plans or even rough drawings—"it's all right here" he would claim, tapping the side of his head—the design was ever-shifting, the process out of sequence.

When he ran out of what little money he had, he went to Stonewall Savings and Loan. Matthew Middleton, Owen's father and founder of the bank, turned him down. Haycock had absolutely nothing to offer as collateral, not even a sound reputation. Despite the banker's best efforts at gentle reasoning, the conversation got ugly. Russ left mad. The kind of mad that would one day lead to harm.

With nothing to work with but rudimentary tools and scavenged building materials, progress was slow. When the cold weather came, Russ and Honey had to take shelter. They slapped a temporary roof of plywood and tarpaper onto the basement and moved in. It was a hard winter. Snowstorms came and went, each bringing a new freeze and thaw. Russ and Honey scrambled to make repairs, jackleg accommodations to survival.

Winter gave way to spring, then summer, then a year, then two years. The Haycock house never rose any higher than those three tiers of cinderblock. It took all he could muster to maintain even that. There was nothing left over for elevation, much less completion. Eventually, Russ piped in a bathroom and kitchen, a well and septic field. He fashioned a wedge-shaped entryway from two-by-fours, Masonite, and a screen door from an abandoned farmhouse.

Haycock was right. The house was "something."

A half-buried cinderblock structure with crude workmanship and a snarl of exposed wires. And they all did come to see it. It became a minor local attraction. A mythical construction. A fable. A morality tale trafficked by gossips. A monument to orneriness and ill-conceived hopes.

<>

"Poor fella," Owen Middleton says with a catch in his voice. Spire looks at his friend. The senator rarely struggles with emotion.

"Poor fellow, my ass," Ace snorts. "Round up everyone mad enough to kill Russ Haycock and we'd have to lock up the whole damn county."

"Mad and murder are two different things," Spire mutters as he snaps more pictures.

"Wonder how he got here?" Owen asks.

"His front passenger tire is flat," the mechanic volunteers. "I guess he started walking and somebody shot him."

30

"Why?" Owen wonders.

"Why not?" Ace answers, his voice rising and sharp. "World is going to hell in a handcart. Punks shooting innocent people just for the fun of it. Not that Russ Haycock was any kind of innocent."

"Billy?" the senator seeks a second opinion.

"Ace is right about one thing, Russ Haycock was never innocent," the sheriff replies. "Still, he was harmless enough when it came right down to it."

"No," Owen corrects. "I'm asking how he got here."

"Doesn't make sense . . ." Spire begins to point out the absence of mud on Haycock's boots. But he stops. More out of habit than distrust. There is advantage in holding back key pieces of evidence. What cops tell too often gets told. And what gets told can damage an investigation. So he sidesteps. "I don't know, maybe Ace is right."

"What did you start to say?" Owen digs. "What doesn't make sense?"

"It doesn't make sense that anyone would shoot Russ Haycock," Spire deflects.

"Bullshit!" the mechanic snorts. "What doesn't make sense is that it took this long."

"So, make up your mind, Ace," the senator purrs in sly derision. "Is it a random shooting or someone with a grudge?"

"Same thing," Ace snaps. He doesn't worry much about inconsistency and regards backing down as a sign of weakness.

Spire presses buttons on his phone and holds it to his ear.

"We need the ambulance. We got a body here. Russ Haycock. That's right. Let's take it to the coroner in Dodge. Have him send any lab samples straight to Peggy Palmer in Great Bend."

Spire presses a button to hang up and silently shakes his head.

"Let's have a look at the pickup while we wait. Ain't much good in standing here, just watching him be dead."

‹›

Russ Haycock and Ewing County never did get along.

He bounced from one venture to the next. One job to another. He opened a vehicle repair shop in the sagging barn. That lasted just long enough to prove his mechanical expertise ended at oil, tires, lubrication, and Army supervision. He took a correspondence course on real estate. But even back then, Stonewall was a slow market. Especially for a salesman who bristled at every imagined slight. He took a job stocking

31

shelves at Rod's Market. Then stormed out when the manager offered a matter-of-fact suggestion that he should face the can labels out, so customers could see what they were buying.

In short, Russ Haycock demanded that others perceive him as he perceived himself. Respectable, intelligent, and honest. But time and again, he proved the old adages. Every villain is the hero of their own story. Every fool, the wisest man they know.

Finally, Haycock turned his attention to constructing an outbuilding on his property. It would house his latest and last business idea: small engine repair and metal salvage. The building would be beautiful. Neat and trim. Painted white with red lettering and a green metal roof.

Once again, realities fell short. Lacking money and materials, Haycock rooted around construction sites and visited derelict houses with a crowbar and hammer. Usually at night. If anyone stopped him, he would angrily throw the purloined items out of his truck bed and snarl, "It sure looks like trash to me."

Most of the time nobody bothered to intervene. Hardly anything he stole was worth the trouble of having to deal with the man.

The ill-gotten goods stubbornly defied neat and trim. The outbuilding rose even more antigoglin than the basement house. Lacking the resources or patience to construct a foundation, he built flat on the ground. Moisture soon radiated up the walls, creating a musty smell that infused every stitch of Haycock's clothes. He never did paint it white. In fact, he didn't paint it at all. Just let it bake in the sun. The wood turned gray, split and splintered. For winter, he made a heating stove out of a split oil drum. For summer he added an exterior bench on the shaded side. Exactly what he was doing out there was anybody's guess. He seemed plenty busy to passersby, furtive and flailing. But not one person in Ewing County could imagine the product of his industry. Or that it would generate even two nickels.

One spring morning, Haycock's wife appeared at the back door of the local men's store, Morris & Sons. Russ waited in his idling green Dodge pickup, far enough down the alley that he wouldn't have to wave hello. She asked in bashful, halting English whether there was any mending she could do. Mr. Morris hadn't seen Honey up close since she first moved to Ewing County. He was shocked at her appearance. She had the look of dead flowers. The hue of her skin had faded from amber to ashen. Her black hair and eyes had lost their luster. Her face was full of worry lines. She was so small and helpless and polite that he couldn't bring himself to say no.

"Let me talk it over with my wife, Mizz Haycock. Can you come back tomorrow?"

He did talk to his wife, who was the store's seamstress. They decided to cut into their profits a little. Enough to make work for Honey and allow more church time for the devout Mrs. Morris.

From that day on, the tiny Vietnamese woman showed up early every morning at Morris & Sons. Then, eventually, the hospital, retirement home, and church thrift shop. She would drop off baskets of neatly folded sewing and take in bundles of new assignments. Over the months, she grew comfortable enough to chat a bit and even take an occasional cup of tea. As months became years, chat expanded to laughter and tea evolved into friendship.

But a certain tension never went away. Her husband continued to wait in the truck, revving the engine and honking the horn if she made him wait too long. The second she appeared in the doorway, he would swoop like a hawk, pausing just long enough for her to jump in. He would pretend to fiddle with the radio in case any of his wife's customers should try to make eye contact and be friendly.

In truth, he didn't have a thing to worry about.

<>

"This old Dodge," Ace exclaims. "Got to hand it to Haycock. I'd of give up on it years ago." He thumps the front fender out of affection, knocking loose a line of body putty in the side panel.

"Guess that ambulance driver takes you pretty serious," Owen Middleton says, looking at the luminous face of his expensive watch.

"They'll be here," the sheriff answers.

The icy wind had gentled.

"Ace, can you pull around to the front end?" Spire asks.

The mechanic swings his wrecker to where its powerful beam illuminates the front end of Russ Haycock's truck. The Dodge was once a vivid green, but forty years in the elements have bleached it pale and ghostly. The square nose is pitted with rust. The front bumper is bent and spray-painted black. There is a piece of composite board where the license plate should be. On one side is a crude skull-and-bones rendering. The other side is blank, as if waiting for thoughts that Haycock could never gather.

In the back window is a peeling decal. Circular in shape, it represents a sheriff's badge. At its center is a sword through a hangman's noose that, in turn, lies upon an open Bible. Text around the margin reads "Posse Comitatus, Est. 1878."

The metal wheels are spray painted white and mounted with thick, knobby tires. The front passenger side is flat. Spire studies the tire. Writes in his notebook. Looks up and down the highway. Ace slaps at himself to keep warm.

"What do you see that I don't?" Middleton asks the sheriff.

"You sure are nosy about this," the mechanic says. As Billy's semi self-appointed deputy, Ace is sensitive about law enforcement turf.

"KBI's budget is coming up," the senator shrugs. "A little street smarts always helps to keep them honest."

"I see pretty much the same as you," the sheriff answers. "A flat tire."

Spire moves around to the highway side and waits for the clouds to open. The moonlight shines through. He stands still for a long time, only his head in motion, swiveling back and forth.

"Look at the road from right here," he finally says, extending his arms as though preparing for an embrace.

"What about it?" Owen asks.

"Be hard to find a spot with a longer view in both directions."

Ace and Middleton look. The truck sits on an elevated curve between two long straight stretches. Hills are distant in the west. Just as far to the east, the highway bends and disappears into a stand of trees.

The sheriff wonders aloud. "If someone was coming from either direction, how long would it take to get to this spot?"

"At normal speed," Ace calculates, "maybe seven, eight minutes."

"That's a long time."

"A long time for what?" Middleton asks.

"I don't know," the sheriff replies. "But if you wanted to do something on the highway and not be seen, you couldn't find a better place."

As they look out on the highway, the ambulance rolls out of the trees, approaching at normal speed.

"Time it, Owen."

Looking again at his expensive watch, the senator fiddles with a button and waits.

"Seven minutes, twenty-seven seconds," he reports as the ambulance pulls to a stop.

"Ain't that what I said," Ace snorts.

"Seven twenty-seven," Spire writes in his notebook.

"Where is he?" the EMT asks through his rolled-down window.

"Follow us," the sheriff says. He starts toward Middleton's red Lincoln. "Owen, can I ride with you?"

"Sure," the banker answers.

The sheriff opens the passenger-side door, then turns and says to Ace, "Haul in the pickup. Don't touch anything you don't have to. I'll come by first thing in the morning."

"I still say it's a random shooting," the mechanic grumbles.

"You might be right," the sheriff replies. Ace is stunned. Billy Spire hardly ever agrees with him. Almost as a matter of principle.

"Hot damn! I'll have to mark this day on my calendar."

"Sometimes even a blind hog finds an acorn," Spire shrugs. "Just keep this under your hat."

<>

The Haycocks usually got back from town by mid-morning.

Russ would carry Honey's baskets down into the basement house and put them on the dining room table. She would make them an early lunch of soup and grilled cheese. Always the same, soup and grilled cheese. The two treasured any constancy they could find.

Her afternoons were spent craned over a sewing machine, a goose-necked lamp providing a bright circle beneath the low ceiling. She listened to the radio, singing softly, making up Vietnamese lyrics to country-western tunes.

He spent his afternoons in the outbuilding doing this and that. Mostly unwinding copper wire from electronics found at the landfill. He, too, listened to the radio, but not to music. He listened to noon-hour commodity reports, as if he had cattle or crops to sell. While listening, he stared out the shed's window and waited. And waited. Waited for something to happen. Anything. As he waited, a movement rose across the Great Plains that would feed Haycock's fury, lift him up, give him community, and fill him with purpose.

Double-digit inflation of the 1970s sent investment capital searching for new ground, including deep, rich soil. Farm acreage shot up in price. Richard Nixon toured Red Square and opened trade with grain-starved China and Russia. Commodity exports rocketed. Using inflated land values to secure loans, farmers doubled down, taking the advice of Earl Butz, Nixon's Secretary of Agriculture—"Get big or get out." Petrodollarengorged international banks loaned billions to drought-ridden third-world nations that, completing the cycle, bought US farm products to feed their hungry masses. American farmers paid off their loans, then took on more debt to finance greater expansion. The greedy swirl of dreams and money was incentivized by generous economic and tax policies.

Ewing County jumped back then. Shiny, new, and big were everywhere, from new-fangled farm equipment to modern school buildings. From hand-tooled cowboy boots to designer pickup trucks. From snowbird retreats in Florida to promising new possibilities for coming generations. It was a tide that lifted all ships. Except for that of Russ Haycock, who bitterly measured the success of others only in terms of how much further he had been left behind.

Then, the deep well of agricultural optimism fell through to a bottomless pit.

Hyper-expanded capacity led to overproduction and plummeting prices. Unsold farm products rotted at grain elevators and shipping terminals. In 1980, President Jimmy Carter took it upon himself to cudgel Russia for invading Afghanistan, using the stick of discontinued grain sales. Sky-high inflation and "supply side" deficits soon drove President Ronald Reagan's Federal Reserve to grab desperately at all manner of fiscal levers. In time it worked. Inflation fell to acceptable levels. To that yin was the yang of tight money and higher interest rates. For an economy built on cheap credit, the farm consequences were as pitiless as debt, as fatal as foreclosure.

Russ perked up as noon commodity reports became somber, then apologetic.

"Well folks, bad news again today... this week ... this month. Cattle and hogs are down. Same for crops. K-State projects lower prices until the economy shakes off this latest hit. Nobody knows when that might happen. Word out of Washington is that Congress is doing what it can to bulk up subsidies. But don't get your hopes up too much. Lot of people are struggling out there. Not all of them wearing bib overalls. Want to make a small fortune farming? Start with a big one."

The people of western Kansas were hurt bad. Farm foreclosures sky-rocketed as did the collapse of agricultural banks. Worry scoured away cheery smiles then etched its way into fearful creases around eyes, at the corners of grim expressions. Most people handled disaster the way most people do. They scramble, pray, and cry on each other's shoulders. They try to hang on, and when worse comes to worst, they pack up and leave in search of something new to believe and hold on to.

But there is always a minority for whom grace and change don't come easy or don't come at all. From those fringes rose furtive conversations, murderous scowls, and mutterings of conspiracy. Connecting dots of their own invention, they eventually concluded that someone was to blame for the suffering in western Kansas. And that someone must be made to pay.

As pain spread throughout Ewing County, Russ Haycock started feeling better. The great calamity befalling others caused him to see his permanent anchorage at the bottom as something admirable. To his way of thinking, he had played it just right. Went slow. Stayed small and conservative. Didn't go around buying fancy new machinery. Not like those fools now going out of business. It was an interpretation that conveniently omitted a key fact. If he had not gone into debt, it was because Stonewall Savings and Loan, in the person of Owen Middleton's father, Matthew, would not lend him a single dime.

Righteousness is a hard thing to enjoy alone. And, except for Honey, Russ Haycock was as alone as a man can be. Absent company, he started talking to the radio. Interjecting his worldview, his cool analysis of all things local to global. One day, the radio started talking back.

KTTL-FM, 100,000 watts strong, broadcast from Dodge City. Sensing that their agitated audience wanted answers, owners Charles and Nellie Babbs supplemented their country/gospel programming with twice daily commentaries from the Reverend William P. Gale, a retired Army colonel based in California. Former aide to General Douglas MacArthur. Mastermind of the Posse Comitatus. Author of its manual on guerilla warfare tactics.

Latin for "power of the county," the Posse respected no authority higher than the county sheriffs. Truth be told, it didn't respect them much either. Members were urged to return driver's licenses, birth certificates, Social Security cards, and all other documents of power-grabbing "Jew-dominated" officialdom. Gale preached that in the grand righting of things, all debts and taxes would disappear. And if that righting didn't come quick enough, there were ways to hurry it along.

"Damned right I'm teaching violence," the self-designated reverend would growl through Haycock's radio. "It's time someone tells you to get violent, Whitey. Start making dossiers, collecting names, addresses, telephone numbers, and car license numbers of every damned Jew rabbi in this land. You get these roadblock locations where you can set up ambushes and get it all working now. Them from bongo bongo land? Just get a .32-caliber gun and begin pumping it at their feet."

"Hey buddy!" Russ rejoiced.

At last, someone understood. He was not alone. Weeks of Gale's commentary brought unfamiliar feelings to the lonely man in his rickety shed. Feelings of loyalty and community and commitment. Feeling so strong that his lashless eyes brimmed with tearful patriotism and he was moved to action.

<>

Owen Middleton starts the red Lincoln. Its heater blasts and the seat warmers immediately take effect.

"What do you think happened out there?" he asks.

"I don't know," Spire says. "There are problems."

"Like what?"

Spire shakes his head. "I need to think this through. Try to make sense of it."

"Sometimes, it helps to talk."

"We'll let Ace do that for now," the sheriff answers. "By the time we get back to Stonewall, he'll have everyone believing Russ Haycock was the victim of a random highway shooting."

"You don't believe it was random?"

"I expect someone will feel guilty or sober up and turn themselves in," Spire replies. "Meanwhile, why upset everyone about a murderer among us? People have enough to worry about."

"So, it's okay with you if Ace spreads false rumors?"

"It is for now."

Spire is ready to change the subject. Saying too much too soon is rarely a good idea. So, he makes a show of examining the Lincoln. The dashboard is a constellation of digits and lights. It has leather upholstery and mahogany trim. All the bells and whistles.

"Sweet ride," he says. "Just like your daddy."

"Family tradition." The senator takes the hint. No more questions.

The Middleton name was, and is, known all over western Kansas. Owen's paternal grandfather was killed in a steam tractor explosion. His widow invested shrewdly, transforming a small insurance policy into lucrative mineral rights. Eventually, needing a place to put all those petrodollars, she bought Stonewall Savings and Loan. Turned it over to her bookish son and took off for the bustling life of Denver. She drove a succession of Town Cars, each bigger and fancier than the last. It became a family trademark. Nobody in Ewing County could recall Matthew Middleton driving anything but a Lincoln. Same for Owen.

Like his son, Matthew Middleton looked like a banker from central casting. Slightly above average in height, with mousy-colored hair and bright pink cheeks. He spoke with a bit of a twang and sported accessories common to that part of Kansas, western-cut suits, cowboy boots, and aviator glasses. But the splash of cowboy was artifice. A good-old-boy presentation, masking a controlled, intellectual, risk-averse businessman. Matthew was unfailingly polite. Generous in support of community efforts. Fussy about the tidiness of his desktop, front yard, and automobile. Keenly interested in barbershop gossip.

The Spire name was also well known across western Kansas, but for different reasons. Billy's old man, Joe Spire, lived the free life of an actual cowboy. Meaning he was free to drift from one dangerous, dirty, low-paying job to another. Which he did at the drop of a hat. Most of those hats were dropped over barroom fights, unpaid rents, police inquiries about domestic violence, even a rustled cow or two. Joe Spire was a hard man. Harder still when fortified by liquor.

Owen learned business at his daddy's knee. The intricacies and interplay of wealth, power, information, and opportunity. He learned how to use money. The advantage of never being desperate or even worried. A man with money can wait for the deal to come to him and set the terms when it arrives. If the terms are at all in doubt, the man with money can smile and walk away.

"The way you want it is the way you get it," Owen's father often preached. "You want something bad, you'll get it just that way. Bad."

Young Billy also learned from his father. He learned to be distrustful, mean, and physically tough. Joe Spire anesthetized failure and arthritis with bottles of cheap whiskey. It loosened aching joints. And brought trouble. Always trouble. Billy took more beatings than he could remember. Most often in retaliation for something said or done in defense of his mother and younger siblings. But sometimes Joe just wanted to see how much punishment the boy could take. In bars or on hay bales, the old man would haul off and wallop Billy to show his drinking buddies what true toughness looked like. The boy would always fight back. No matter how hard the old man hit or threw him, he would spring up, lower his head, and charge. Again and again, until the old man wore out or the kid was just too hurt to keep trying.

While Matthew taught Owen finance and spreadsheets, Joe Spire endowed his son with other assets. A stout powerful body capable of great violence. A capacity for rage. A cruel face to go along with that bitter fury. Advantages that would make Billy Spire legendary. As legendary as Owen Middleton was for his cool judgment and advantaged self-possession.

Owen was born in Stonewall. Billy and his family ended up there after wearing out their welcome in the last town. And the towns before that.

Old Joe had been working at a sawmill near Leoti. Got fired for operating cutting equipment while under the influence. There were rumors about hiring at McQuitty's Feedlot over in Stonewall. Joe showed up and aptly demonstrated the requisite skills. He rode a horse, herded cattle from one pen to another, even lassoed a dead steer and dragged it out for disposal. He was hired on the spot. That afternoon, the family moved into a dilapidated single-wide trailer that rented for next to nothing and was worth even less.

Billy Spire's rise to local prominence began the next morning.

Gabe Jordan, Stonewall High's math teacher and football coach, was keeping an eye on detention students over the lunch hour. It was one of those hot Kansas days when heat shimmers off the asphalt and corn fields are so dry, they rattle.

"Would you look at that," Jordan said in wonder.

The kids turned in their chairs.

Five youngsters were crossing the street into the dirt schoolyard. They were walking with their heads down, single file, sullen and silent, like a prison chain gang sent to bust rocks. Their hair was unkempt, their clothes were as loose and wrinkled as cabbage leaves. The oldest was in front. A stout boy, who Jordan guessed to be about fifteen, hunched forward, leaning into powerful shoulders. Approaching from the opposite direction were three older, larger boys. Town bullies known for picking on anyone who got in their way and going out of their way to get in the way.

"This is bad," Jordan said, reaching into the top drawer of his desk. He grabbed the silver whistle he used for football practice. Handling those three would take all the authority he could muster.

"You keep working," he ordered the students, then crossed the classroom floor with three long strides. As soon as he was out the door, the detention kids raced to windows.

Jogging across the dusty playground, Jordan saw the three toughs affront the oldest kid, who lowered his head into a coiled position and nodded. The smaller children stood back watching, oddly unconcerned. When one of the toughs shoved the stout boy, the coach put the whistle to his lips. But things broke before he got a chance to blow.

Billy jumped forward, grabbed the biggest fellow's shirtfront, and threw a right knee. Hard enough to knock the guy's balls through the roof of his mouth. The tough went down, writhing in the dirt, both hands on his crotch, too hurt to scream. The second bully threw a wild punch that glanced off Billy's forehead. Spire turned on him, crouched, then came up with his forearms. He knocked the second tough flat on his back, then jumped on him with his knees. Hank of hair in each hand, he began pounding his attacker's head against the hard-packed dirt. The third townie started kicking Billy in the ribs, screaming for him to stop before he killed the guy. Billy paid no notice to the kicks or shouts. The earth was a void, containing nothing but himself, his anger, and the punk whose brains he was going to beat out. The younger Spire kids never moved. They never changed expression. They stood back and watched, quiet and impassive, like this was something they saw every day.

The coach shoved the screaming tough out of the way. He locked his hands around Billy's bull neck and pulled with all his might.

"That's enough," he shouted.

But he could not dislodge the young man, and he could not stop the pounding. The second tough was completely out now. His mouth flopped open, his eyes rolled back.

"Quit!" the coach bellowed. But Billy Spire was still beyond hearing. So, Jordan bit his whistle and bent low. He blew as hard as he could right next to the side of Billy's head.

Spire grabbed his ear and hopped to his feet. He spun toward the teacher, bent forward and ready to attack.

"Stop now," Jordan said, hands out to calm. "It's over."

Billy panted and glared at him. With angry eyes and that brutal face, young Spire was the meanest-looking kid Coach Jordan had ever seen.

"Anyone worth hitting once is worth hitting ten times," Billy snarled. It was one of the few pearls of wisdom Joe Spire ever imparted to his son.

"You made your point," the coach said.

The world came back into focus. Two toughs were down. The third, on his knees, was trying to awaken his unconscious friend. Billy figured the coach was right.

In a small town, talents are taken for what they are. Billy Spire had an obvious talent for violence. But it wasn't that he lacked other abilities. While the younger Spire children were dull in class—slow to grasp, in-turned, unreachable—Billy showed a surprising intelligence, given his upbringing and thuggish appearance. His brightness was begrudging. As if there were something unseemly about being smart. As if understanding things that eluded others were more a burden than a gift. He spoke only when he could no longer stand to hear one more wrong math answer, one more garbled misunderstanding of history, one more muddling of basic science. It soon became evident that Billy Spire's rough exterior obscured a fine, even elegant, mind. Of course, the last person to recognize this suppleness of thought was Billy himself. He hadn't been trained to look in that direction. It held no value in the Spire household. Besides, Stonewall High didn't need a resident genius. It needed a fullback and middle linebacker. It wasn't long before Coach Jordan approached the young man about joining the team.

"I have to work after school," Billy replied sullenly. "Over at the feedlot."

"You don't understand, son," Coach Jordan said. "These are hard times. This town, these people, they could sure use something to cheer for."

Billy shook his head. He could not grasp the coach's line of reasoning. Hard times? Hard times were the only kind the Spire family ever knew. They handled it the way they handled it. They kept to themselves, suffered their own pains, never asked of others, never gave in return. When did any town ever care about the Spires? Why should the Spires care about any town?

"We need the money," he said slowly, as if explaining to a dull child.

"Let me ask you this," Jordan persisted. "If you could earn more money *and* play football, would you do it?"

"Maybe," Billy answered suspiciously.

"That's all I need to hear."

Jordan went straight to the man who could make things happen. A man who understood that winning football increases the flow of local dollars. That happy people celebrate. That full bleachers bring customers to diners, gas stations, and liquor stores. That in the middle of the enduring farm crisis, Stonewall, Kansas, was sick and tired of being sick and tired. He went straight to Matthew Middleton.

"I have to tell you," the coach cautioned, "these Spires are a rough crew. Especially the old man. But my goodness. That kid could be good. Really good."

Middleton sat behind his large oak desk, leaning slightly backward in his chair. He peered at the coach through the middle pane of his trifocals, wearing that expression of affable skepticism he would pass to his son.

"I try not to borrow trouble," he said, smiling patiently.

"Look around," the coach said, pointing out the window. "Trouble is already here."

"We'll ride this out. Just like we have before."

"You're not talking to the same people I am."

Middleton wasn't used to abruptness. He found it unattractive.

"I get around," he replied with a faint smile.

"In a shiny red Lincoln."

The banker sat up.

"Hey, more power to you." Coach Jordan taught boys to play football. He knew how to work pride, how to get under a fellow's skin. "But there are a lot of people not so lucky. Can't even remember what it means to be happy. To have fun. To pull together."

The banker settled back in his chair. He regarded the coach for a long, icy silence. Jordan did not avert his eyes.

"I'll look into it," Middleton finally conceded.

"Thank you," the coach said as he stood up. "My wife says I'm too direct. That one day I'll talk myself out of a job."

"Your wife sounds like a very wise person," Middleton interjected, without the slightest glimmer of humor.

Not surprisingly, Stonewall Savings and Loan held a note on the feedlot operation. Like it did on almost every other business in Ewing County. There was no question that Duane McQuitty would take Matthew's call. And take it seriously. Five minutes after hanging up the phone, Duane wandered out to the pens and waved over his newest hire. Joe Spire leaned down from his saddle and listened. He straightened up, shrugged his thick shoulders in disinterested consent, and rode off. It was settled. His kid would play ball and work odd jobs at Stonewall Savings and Loan.

That night, Matthew Middleton knocked on the door of his son's room, walked in, and looked around. Owen was sitting on his bed, working on a coin collection. The young man had more collections of things than most other Stonewall kids had things, period. Comic books, stamps, model airplanes, forty-five records, baseball cards, electric train sets, board games, and on and on. He had a telephone of his own, a record player, a window air conditioner, and a color television. He had little need of friendship. Lots of kids came around, of course, to play with his stuff.

But he would soon grow bored and send them away. He was happiest alone with his bounty.

"Done with homework?"

"I am," the chubby boy answered, as he pressed Liberty dimes into a blue cardboard sleeve.

"Better clean-up for dinner."

"Yes, sir."

"How is football practice going?"

Owen looked up, surprised. In small-town Kansas every able-bodied boy was expected to turn out on Friday night. Even the banker's son. And of course, his parents came to every game for the same reason. It was expected. Although Owen's father regarded football as a required element of small-town life—he, too, had done his civic duty—there was no question about priority. Nothing was to distract from the serious occupation of preparing for college and learning about the bank. Least of all football.

Owen pondered the unexpected question. Truth be told, Owen didn't enjoy playing football. But, like everything else, he managed with cool reason and guile. Slow of foot, weaker than his bulk might suggest, he played a very pragmatic game. He would flinch almost imperceptibly to pull defensive linemen offsides. He would grab opponents by the facemask and drag them to the ground. He would leg whip, horse collar, and hold opponents who threatened to run past him. Sometimes he got whistled, but mostly not. Either way, Owen didn't care. He approached life analytically. He didn't waste a lot of time worrying about ethics or self-doubt. He didn't shake his fist at the moon over what should or shouldn't be. He took things as they were and managed them effectively. He was uncomplicated and smart. A very rare and powerful combination.

"Uh, I guess it's going okay," Owen finally answered.

"I hear there's going to be a new boy on the team."

"Yeah?"

"Supposed to be pretty good."

"That so?" Owen looked at his father in puzzlement. The way kids do when they recognize that something meaningful is being conveyed but have no idea what it is.

"Try to hold your own, will you?" Matthew explained. "We don't want folks thinking the Middletons are nothing but snooty people in shiny cars."

<>

Billy Spire's fierce brutality transformed an otherwise unremarkable group of kids into a formidable football team. His courage spread by infection. He never criticized or goaded. In fact, he rarely spoke. He simply listened intently to the coach, then did his job with bruising efficiency. He was a natural at the sport. His internal furies found the perfect external expression. It often seemed that Billy was fighting a whole other battle in a whole different place at the expense of opposing teams. As Stonewall began to win, then dominate, Billy's teammates—with one exception—found that more than anything, they didn't want to disappoint their leading player. That he gave his all drove them to give more. To set aside their own fright and pain. To crack heads and break spirits.

The single exception was Owen Middleton. To him, Billy Spire was little more than an oddity, certainly nothing worthy of loyalty or even interest. Not like stamps or baseball cards, which were beautiful and would appreciate in value. Sure, winning a football game was better than losing. But either way, what did it matter? Owen didn't dislike his teammate. They just occupied opposite corners of the universe.

As for Billy, he had no use for the pampered daddy's boy. Matthew Middleton picked Owen up every day after practice and stopped by the malt shop on the way home. Joe Spire never showed his face around the football field. He cared about Billy's exploits only to the degree they were helpful when prospecting around the bar for free drinks. It would be fair to say that young Spire disdained the banker's son. Almost as much as he envied him.

Then, one Friday evening their relationship changed.

Stonewall High had its hands full with the Syracuse Bulldogs, led by a big boy named Harold LaVoy. At six-six and two hundred thirty, LaVoy was country strong. Rough in the manner of farm life. Manhandling cattle, horses, and hogs. Teaching them to fear.

LaVoy played on the defensive line. He quickly tagged the banker's son as the weakest link and battered young Middleton. Slapping the earhole of Owen's helmet, knocking him senseless, sending him reeling so far into the backfield that he tripped his own players.

In offset to Owen's failings, Billy kept grinding it out. With his bowling ball center of gravity, pumping knees, and displaced rage, it was nearly impossible for a single player to knock him down. Not even the giant Harold LaVoy could topple him. On his own, Spire kept a win within reach.

By late in the third quarter Owen was hurting, exhausted, and out of tricks. All he had left was dropping to his hands and knees, making himself a stumbling block against Harold LaVoy's bull rush. The big boy soon tired of that tactic. He faked a rush, stopped, drew back his leg, and kicked Owen Middleton in the ribs. The refs missed the penalty. But Matthew Middleton did not. As the quarter ended, Owen, doubled over and spitting blood, struggled off the field. His father climbed down from the bleachers and started toward the Stonewall coach to complain about LaVoy's rough tactics. Then he changed his mind. He would not send a man to do a boy's job. He waved at Billy Spire, who glanced around uncertainly, then jogged over.

"Look at Owen," the father said.

Young Middleton sat on the bench, head down, arms crossed over his ribs, eyes closed in pain. Spire wasn't sure what the banker wanted of him. Even though he worked at the Savings and Loan during every free hour, he had little interaction with Mr. Middleton. He was assigned chores by the lead teller, a ditzy but pleasant woman who seemed to wonder why he was there. Matthew Middleton had never offered anything more than a polite but aloof "hello" or "good job."

"He's hurt," Billy observed.

"Bad," the father clarified.

Billy shook his head. Bad is a relative term. And Owen wasn't hurt that bad by Spire standards.

"Would you say something to him?" Matthew asked.

"Like what?"

"Like he's doing good. Or that you need him out there."

"Is he? Do we?" Billy asked.

"Maybe not," Matthew Middleton admitted. "But help him. Please."

It had never occurred to Billy that a man like Matthew Middleton needed help from anyone. Much less anyone named Spire. The banker gave Billy a slight nudge toward Owen.

"Okay," Billy shrugged.

Owen was still trying to catch his breath.

"He kicked me in the ribs," he wheezed at Billy without being asked.

"Who?"

"LaVoy."

Spire looked across the field. The big kid was standing among his teammates. A head taller than anyone else. He was glaring at the Stonewall sidelines, snorting billows of steam into the frosty fall air.

"He did that?" Spire was truly amazed that someone would dare cheap shot anyone on his team.

"I can't breathe."

"Well," Spire said with a steely look into Middleton's eyes. "Let's go pay him back."

"He's too big." LaVoy was at least seven inches taller than Owen. Nine more than Billy.

"Nah, he's just tall," Billy answered. "You bust him as hard as you can. He'll go down."

"What if he doesn't?"

"I'll take care of that."

The fourth quarter kicked off and the two boys went back onto the field. Owen still cradling his ribs. First play, Middleton set aside his pain and came up fast, spearing LaVoy's facemask with the crown of his helmet. He heard the big boy yelp. Blood dripped off his chinstrap. Owen was about to crack wise when two giant hands grabbed his shoulders and drove him flat onto his back. The little breath held in his bruised lungs was knocked clean out. He was powerless to stop the hands that closed around his throat.

A shadow flew in from the side and Owen's attacker went rolling. Middleton twisted onto one elbow and saw Billy grab LaVoy's facemask. He yanked the big boy's helmet off and started throwing fists at the unprotected head. His jutting knuckles cracked bones and cut skin from the inside out. Both teams jumped into the melee. Referees blew their whistles, coaches raced to pull the boys apart. Up in the stands, parents began roaring at each other over who started the fight and why. As three Bulldogs wrestled Billy off, LaVoy tried to get in one last kick, spikes first. Spire grabbed the ankle and swung his hip into the knee, twisting the joint in a way it was never meant be twisted. There was a snap and a scream. Then Spire bent low and shook his finger.

"Next time pick on somebody your own size," he hollered, then turned and walked toward Owen.

Middleton sat a few feet away, splay-legged and peppered with clods of dirt from all the players, coaches, and refs grappling around him. His chest was heaving, and his mouth hung open with amazement at what he had just seen Spire do. Their eyes met. And Spire started laughing. Owen would never forget. It was the first time he'd ever seen Billy happy. That brutal, almost reptilian face in unburdened joy. Full, complete, and at one with himself. In violence.

Middleton laughed too. He wasn't sure what had just happened. Or why. But it felt clever and powerful. Like "The Monkey and the Cat." Two

Bulldogs jumped Billy, who started laying them to waste. Owen thought about pitching in. But was relieved to have his father intervene. Catching him by the shoulder pads and dragging him off the field.

Things changed after that. On the Monday after the game, Billy Spire stood on a ladder, raking leaves from the bank's rain gutters. Matthew Middleton approached and held something up to the boy.

"What's that?"

"It's a key to the bank."

"Why?"

"In case there's nobody to unlock the door."

"That's never happened."

"And you could spend the night here if it gets . . ." The banker paused, wanting to pick just the right words. "If it gets noisy at home."

The fearless young man suddenly found himself unable to look Mr. Middleton in the eye. There was no escaping his family. No matter what he accomplished anywhere else in life, they were still an embarrassment. He was and always would be one of those Spires.

"It's not that bad," Billy mumbled.

"No. Of course not. But just in case," Matthew assured. "And thank you for helping Owen. Although I'm not sure you needed to go quite that far."

Once again, Billy was perplexed. Where he came from, there was no "too far" in fighting. You beat up on the other guy until you were good and done. Or he beat up on you.

"He won't be kicking anyone for a while," Billy said, defiantly.

"I guess that's right," the banker replied, looking pained, as if he had been injured along with Harold LaVoy. "Anyway, I'd like you to have this."

He extended his hand a little further. Billy took the key.

As Matthew Middleton walked away, young Spire bit at the inside of his lip. He could handle all the physical abuse in the world. Kindness tore him apart.

"And it wouldn't hurt you to smile a little more," the banker added, without looking back. "You scare some of the customers."

There would be bad and worse times at the Spire family's broken-down mobile home. When things were worse, Billy used the key. Mr. Middleton stashed a sleeping bag in the janitor's closet, along with a small refrigerator stocked with soda pop, candy bars, and little cereal boxes. When times were worse, Billy Spire stretched out in the bank's lobby, over a long couch with green leather cushions and curved arms of chromium steel. And there he slept in quiet loneliness.

Russ Haycock heard about the new kid in town. Jesus, it was all anyone could talk about. On the morning swap and shop radio program, at Rod's Market, and in newspapers Honey brought home to cut out shopping coupons. He heard about Billy Spire, but there were bigger things on his mind.

After listening to KTTL for several months, he sent a few dear dollars to the Identity Church of Reverend William P. Gale. As he licked the envelope, Haycock imagined something grand. A sturdy clan of courtly white men. Well-armed, sure. Don't you dare tread on me. At the same time, cowboy chivalrous. A community in which he would be valued.

In actuality, his donation went to a lonely shack on a remote ranch near Mariposa, California. There, the Rev. Gale and his wife, Roxanne, personally went through each envelope, grubbing bills and coins to maintain their threadbare existence.

A couple of weeks later, Russ received a thick manila package. He spilled the contents onto the workbench in his shed and studied each piece intently. All the sermons, propaganda, decals, and certificates. He made a rough frame to display his good standing in the Identity Church and its affiliate, the Posse Comitatus. Never one to hide his light under a bushel basket, he pressed the Posse decal onto the back window of his green pickup. Thereby vetted and authenticated, Russ was eager to locate some brethren. The place to start would be KTTL. Off to Dodge he went.

He found the radio station out on the edge of town at the end of a muddy driveway. In a long blue metal building with chipped paint. The windows were pasted over with rodeo posters and concert flyers. There were only two cars in the lot. Both had seen better days. He had expected so much more. A nicer habitat, a beehive of newsmakers and musicians, big shot businessmen walking around making deals. But there was not a hint of human movement. He rapped lightly on the door. No answer. A little harder, still nothing. Finally, Haycock pounded hard with the heel of his palm. The door flew open.

"Christ almighty! What do you want?" A tall, thin young man stuck his head out, pulling the door close behind him. Haycock craned to see inside, but the young man blocked his view into the dim interior.

"Just to stop by."

"Why?"

"Because I listen to Reverend Gale."

"Christ almighty," the young man repeated. He turned to someone inside. "You hear this? You wanna talk to him?"

"No," a male voice answered.

"Is that Mr. Babbs? Charles Babbs?" Haycock inquired.

"No," the young man snapped. "Mr. Babbs is out right now."

"When will he be back?"

"Dunno. Didn't say."

"Look." Haycock was somewhere between annoyed and confused. "I want to help. I'm with you."

"Hear that? He's with us."

The inside voice grunted.

"Listen," the young man said. "We don't need no help. We're screwing things up just fine on our own. Sponsors pulling ads. FCC on our ass. State officials threatening our license."

"Can I speak to Mr. Babbs?"

"I told you, he's not here."

Haycock stared at the young man, not sure what to say. He thought they would be happy to see him.

"Is there anyone I can talk to?"

"Talk to?"

"Send him to the Lucky 8," shouted the inside voice.

"Mr. Babbs?" Haycock hollered back.

"Try the Lucky 8," the young man said, then slammed the door.

Walking back to his truck, Haycock noticed a rusty steel tower in the distance. It appeared to be one quick breeze from collapse. One hundred thousand watts had seemed so powerful.

Russ asked at a gas station for directions to the bar. The clerk shook his head and pointed to a squat gray-green building down the road. The exterior suggested Wild West revelry, the interior oozed of sullen idleness and cirrhotic livers.

"KTTL sent you here?" the Lucky 8 bartender repeated, then exhaled a lungful of smoke. She was short, sharp featured, with pinched brows as if suffering a headache. "Why?"

"They didn't exactly say."

"Are you one of them?"

"Could be," Haycock invoked mysteriously, hitching up his belt.

"They used to come in here. The fellows you're looking for. Sat over there," she huffed and pointed with her smoke. "But they're gone now. Had to leave. Too much trouble for what they spent."

"Where did they go?"

"Who knows?"

"No idea?"

"Look," she said. "I sometimes see them at the bait shop. Sitting there late at night. In a tan Plymouth Valiant. But don't go near them without a stick. They ain't nice."

"I'm not that nice myself."

The bartender glanced Haycock up and down, clearly unimpressed.

"Well, good luck with that."

Haycock nursed a beer for an hour, then went looking for the bait shop. It was right down the highway. A tan Valiant was parked outside beneath a naked bulb hanging off a flagpole. It was a hot night, cicadas wailed, heat lightning flashed in the dark horizon. Haycock could make out three men in the car. Next to the Valiant a dark Ford sedan faced the opposite direction, its driver slouched against the front fender. Haycock rolled slowly off the highway. He turned on the dome light, so they could see he was like them. White. He stopped, got out, and approached cautiously. Hands out from his sides to show he meant no harm.

"What you want?" asked a voice from the Valiant's back seat.

"I'm with Reverend Gale."

Haycock bent and peered into the car. The three men kept their eyes straight forward, showing only profiles. He straightened and looked over the roof. The Ford fellow had a scraggly beard and white tee shirt. He was smoking a thin cigar, leaning back on his elbows. One heel caught on the hubcap, head bent low to hide his face.

"What's your name?"

"Russ Haycock. Out of Ewing County."

"Well, Russ Haycock out of Ewing County," said the back seat, "if we come across Reverend Gale, we'll sure tell him you said hello." One of the other Valiant men snickered.

"Hey," Haycock growled, crouching to look in the car. "I'm with you. I'm sick of it, too."

"We ain't never heard of no Russ Haycock."

"Well maybe I never heard of you either." Haycock spat in disgust. "I thought there might be somebody serious down here. Guess I was wrong."

"Serious is as serious does."

"What the hell is that supposed to mean?"

"It means come back when we've heard of you."

"You just remember my name," Haycock snarled.

He spat again, got back in the green Dodge, and took off. Spinning tires and spraying gravel.

A rational man might have calmed down on the drive home. Might have realized that secret societies, especially those bent on terrorism, would reasonably be wary of volunteers who appear out of nowhere. As it would turn out, the Valiant was looking in the wrong direction. The Ford man was an undercover agent of the Kansas Bureau of Investigation. But secret societies, especially white supremacists in western Kansas, aren't generally Phi Beta Kappa. The three Valiant men would spend time in prison. Joining all the other would-be somebodies who were not nearly as clever as they imagined.

A rational man would have gone home, climbed in bed with his fine wife, and forgotten the whole damn business. But Russ Haycock was anything but rational. With every mile back to Stonewall, he worked himself into a meaner twist. Shouting out the window about Jewish bankers and becoming known. As if all the lizards, owls, and stars between Dodge City and Stonewall, Kansas, had been wanting to know.

He skidded the Dodge to a stop next to his outbuilding and went inside with a slam of the door. Honey climbed out of bed and peeked out of the basement house, into her husband's shed. She watched her husband throwing things around, destroying his own stuff, indiscriminate in his anger. Then she went back to bed and pulled covers over her head.

Miserable is miserable, in any language.

<>

A few nights later, Joe Spire staggered home drunk. Something set him off, so he began punching holes into the trailer walls. When that stopped being fun, he turned his fists on the family. Billy got ready to fight him off. The two roared and fronted each other. The mother grabbed Billy by the back of his shirt and dragged him toward the door.

"Go away," she hissed. "You only make it worse."

Billy spun and glared at his mother.

"Why do you let him do this?"

She was a quiet and strange woman. Loyal to her husband at the expense of her children. Maybe she couldn't imagine any other way of life. Or didn't know how to get there even if she could. So, she stayed quiet and strange. Standing by her man. Climbing into a whiskey bottle about as much as he did. It was the dearest thing they had in common.

She glared back. Not a glimmer of hope, nor affection in her eyes. Billy stomped out without a word. There was nothing left to say.

Sleeping at the bank that night, Billy dreamt of sheep. A lamb was bleating in distress. The sound was so unnerving the young man stirred, then woke up. He stared at the lobby ceiling for nearly half a minute before it came to him. He still heard bleating. He stood up, wearing only boxers and a sleeping bag across his shoulders. There in the parking lot were two dimly lit figures. A man and a lamb bound together by a short length of rope. The man was slightly stooped, working with something from his pocket. The animal's head was raised up. Its mouth opening and closing as it cried. At first, Billy thought it was his father. The hair on his neck rose in fear. But that made no sense. This person was taller and thinner. The Spires owned no livestock.

Whomever it was moved to the lamb's side and hooked its head in the crook of his arm. As he lifted, the bleating muffled. Then the man slit the lamb's throat. It fell to the ground, the body contorted in shock. Legs flailed around as if to run. A dark pool fanned across the asphalt.

"Hey!" Billy hollered, slapping on the window.

The man was startled by the sound. He bent forward and peered into the bank. Then he turned, ran across the street, and jumped into an old pickup. Pulling on his jeans and sneakers, Spire burst through the front doors and took off after him. It was three o'clock in the morning. Other than a couple barking dogs, the town was dead quiet.

The pickup took off and skidded around a corner. Billy cut between two houses and got almost close enough to slap the tailgate. Close enough to get a clear look at the ghostly green Dodge pickup, racing toward the edge of town, headlights off.

Mr. Middleton pulled into the parking lot a few minutes later. He was wearing pajamas, slippers, and heavy robe.

"Billy," he said, clearly annoyed. "I warned you about setting off the silent alarm."

The young man said nothing. He pointed at the slaughtered lamb.

"Goodness," the banker exclaimed.

A piece of baling wire was twisted onto the animal's shank. It threaded through a thin metal disk, the lid from a soup can. Middleton tore the lid free. "GET OUT!" was scratched in big block letters, along with a crudely rendered Star of David.

"It was that Haycock fella," Billy said.

"What?"

"In an old green Dodge."

"What in the world is that fool thinking?" Mr. Middleton said as he looked around the parking lot, the neighborhood. Completely bewildered.

"I guess he thinks you should get out," Billy answered. He was the kind of kid who recognized a threat for what it was.

"Could you clean this up, Billy? Right now?"

"Yes, sir."

"And not a word to anyone. No bank needs this kind of publicity."

"What about Haycock?"

"I'll take care of it."

"You?" Billy asked in surprise.

"Yes, me," the banker snapped back. "I will take care of it."

"You and whose army?" the young man mumbled.

Mr. Middleton came from the opposite corner of the universe. The corner that is monied and soft. About something like this, he hadn't a clue. But Billy understood. You beat up on the other guy. Or he beats up on you. There is no "too far" about it.

<>

Just after five the next afternoon, Matthew Middleton got up from his desk and headed out the door. Billy was dragging a garden hose back and forth across the parking lot. Washing a line of debris and faint blood stains toward the curb, one traverse at a time. He saw the banker, turned off the spigot, ran to the passenger side of the red Lincoln, and pulled open the door.

"What are you doing?" the older man asked.

"Going with you."

"I don't think so."

"You got a gun?"

"Of course not."

"Then I'm going."

"Thanks, but get out and finish the parking lot," Middleton said with finality.

As soon as the Lincoln disappeared around the corner, Billy sprinted into the bank and grabbed keys from a pegboard. The ditzy lead teller watched in bewilderment as he took off in a repossessed Corvair.

"I have no idea why that kid is even here," she muttered.

It was a hot, dusty afternoon. The sun floated in a blue haze. The Lincoln pulled to a stop in front of the Haycock place. Middleton peered through the windshield. Heat shimmered off the basement house's sheet metal roof. The yard was full of crap. Broken down cars, each surrounded by oil stains and discarded parts. Junk lumber, mounds of worn tires, miscellaneous metal objects, and a rickety construction that barely passed for a shed. Next to it was a pale green pickup. The banker got out. He removed his sport coat to show that he carried no weapon.

Haycock was deep in concentration when Middleton passed the outbuilding window. He was writing a letter to the Reverend Gale. Bragging of what he had done. Suggesting that he, far more than others, was brave to the cause. But at the sight of Matthew's passing shadow, he almost jumped out of his skin. He thought he had gotten away clean. As cleanly as he had stolen the neighbor's lamb. His instinctive response to threat was to grab a hunting rifle.

Middleton was halfway to the basement house when a shot rang out. The bullet hit a fifty-five-gallon drum ten feet away. The banker dove to the ground behind the metal plates of a rusty disker. He swiped the back of his hand over a mouthful of dirt and bleeding lip.

"Haycock!" he shouted. "What are you doing?"

"You got no reason to be here," came a response from the shed. "Jew bastard!"

"What?" Middleton peeked around a limestone rock bracing the disker. "I just want to talk. Were you at my bank last night?"

There was a second shot. Limestone exploded in the banker's face. Between rock dust and blood, Matthew Middleton went blind. But not senseless. There were no other houses within earshot. It was unlikely that Haycock would simply sit there and wait. He would be coming. Middleton patted his white dress shirt and found his fountain pen. He popped off the lid and clinched the barrel in his fist. A pointy nib was not much of a weapon, but it was all he had.

"I was never at your bank," Haycock shouted. "You hear me?"

"I hear. I'll go. But I need help. I can't see."

There came a distant noise. Middleton cocked his head toward the sound. It was the honking of a car. Louder and louder. Closer and closer. He used the end of his necktie to dab at his eyes. But he only hurt himself worse, rubbing in more grit and rock dust. The honking was very close now. Almost right on top of him. Over the engine roar, he heard the scrape of tires across dirt. Then a vehicle crashed into something solid.

Billy Spire had been a quarter mile away when he heard the gunshot and saw Matthew Middleton go down.

"Goddamn you," Spire screamed, pounding on the horn. He wasn't sure who he was cursing. Haycock, for shooting. Or Middleton, for going alone.

He pressed the gas pedal to the floor. The repossessed Corvair, unsafe at any speed, began lolling back and forth across the gravel road. When Billy hit the brakes, the car skidded onto the Haycock property, over a pile of scrap metal, and into the basement house. Its nose stuck into the cinderblock risers like an ax into a stump. The radiator burst and steam spewed into the air. Billy scrambled out and crouched down. A shot was fired from the shed. It went into the back window of the Corvair and straight out the front.

The young man hid behind the car, eyes darting. He gathered to run, searching for the best direction. When the screen door of the basement house creaked open, Billy's blood went cold. A second gun from that position would have a clear shot at Middleton.

"Honey! Get back inside!" Russ Haycock screamed.

"You stop it right now!" the banker demanded. He was a white and wealthy pillar of the community. He insisted on being obeyed. He started to rise.

"Stay down!" Spire yelled.

"Billy?!"

"Stay down!"

"I'm hurt!" Matthew shouted. His tone was more informative than alarmed. "I can't see."

Through wire mesh, Billy could see the outline of a small and slight person cowering behind the screen door. He charged, running low and fast. Hitting with all his might, he knocked down the door and the person it concealed.

Spire rolled to his knees and threw the door aside. He snaked a thick arm around the person's neck. It was Mrs. Haycock, in a flowery cotton shirt and gray slacks. He lifted her in a choke hold. A human shield between him and the shed.

"Shoot again and I'll kill her!"

Mrs. Haycock worked her mouth like a landed catfish. Opening and closing, trying to breathe. Spire tightened his arm.

"Billy!" Middleton hollered.

"You let her go!" Haycock bellowed from the shed.

"Put that gun down or I'll rip her fucking head off."

Haycock came around the side of the shed holding the rifle above his head. Billy eased up enough for Honey to inhale. She looked at her husband, her eyes pleading under straight black bangs. She gasped for air, tears running down her cheeks.

"Don't hurt her," Russ snarled.

"Billy, get out of here!" the banker shouted. But he was looking the wrong way. About twenty-five degrees to the left.

"Drop it," Spire snarled.

Haycock put the rifle on the ground.

"Now back up."

As Haycock moved away, Spire lifted the tiny Asian woman like a rag doll. Her toes danced in the dirt as she hung on to his encircling arm.

"She's turning blue!" Haycock cried.

"So?"

"Let her go!"

"Farther back."

As Haycock retreated, the young man advanced. Then in one quick motion, he dropped Honey and scooped up the gun. Russ rushed to his wife and cradled her against his chest.

"Billy, I can't see," Middleton repeated. He was on his feet now, using his hands to feel the way. His bearings were still off.

"Breathe now, baby," Haycock murmured. "Just breathe."

As air filled her lungs, Honey sagged against her husband, dark eyes fixed on Billy Spire. Haycock stroked his wife's hair and mumbled comforts in a foreign tongue. This was the first time Billy Spire had seen the man up close. His clothes were worn and grimy. His dull brown hair was thinning. A couple of teeth were gone. And there were those terrible red-rimmed eyes.

Spire pointed the muzzle at Russ Haycock's belt line.

"Wait there, Mr. Middleton," the young man called out. He was conscious of the odd formality, given the circumstances, but couldn't think of anything else to call Owen's father. "Let me come to you."

Matthew lifted his chin and swiveled his head back and forth, as if trying to smell Spire's location. When Billy got close enough, he took the older man's hand.

"Son, I'm blind."

Spire turned for a quick glance. The older man's face was full of blood.

His eyes were closed and puffy. Efforts with his tie left a bright red rash from nearly ear to ear. Billy winced. He'd suffered a lot of injuries. Many worse. But he was used to it. Mr. Middleton was not.

"I'll get you to a doctor."

"What about her?" Haycock yelled, still cradling his wife. "She's hurt, too. You hurt her."

"I sure did," Billy agreed. "And I'll hurt her a whole lot worse next time."

"Like hell!" Haycock dropped his wife and rushed.

Spire didn't know old men could move that fast nor hit that hard. Hard enough to knock the rifle out of his hands. Hard enough to send Matthew Middleton spinning into a loop of barbed wire. Hard enough to land Billy flat on his back.

As they rolled around, Haycock reached for a piece of rebar. Billy knew he had to end it. He bit down on the older man's shoulder. His teeth cut through the skin. He clenched and worked his jaw, tearing into muscle and blood. Haycock screamed and tried to squirm away, but there was no getting away from Billy Spire.

The young man released his bite. Haycock clutched the wound. Billy grabbed the first thing handy, a broken music stand. Brandishing it like a baseball bat, he swung for the fences.

Haycock looked up just in time for the metal base to hit him smack on the forehead. His eyes went out of focus. Blood poured from the jagged gash. He toppled straight backward. Out cold. But Billy wasn't done. Not yet. Anyone worth hitting once was worth hitting ten times. He kicked Haycock in the stomach.

"No!" she screamed.

It was the first and only word Honey had uttered that afternoon. Her voice was airy and high. She tried to shield her husband. Billy threw her off and kicked some more. In the ribs. In the face. Anywhere he had a clean shot.

"That's what you get," Billy explained to the unconscious man.

Middleton untangled himself from the barbed wire and staggered toward the sound. He couldn't see what was happening but knew that Russ Haycock went silent, save for the short grunts with every kick. He could imagine the rest.

"Stop, now, you'll kill him!"

"Good!"

Middleton caught the young man in a clumsy bear hug.

"Billy," Middleton said as calmly as he could while being bucked around on the powerful back. "Please stop."

Spire felt the rage and power surge out of his body. As if stopcocks had opened in his feet and all the adrenaline drained onto the ground where Russ Haycock lay bleeding. Mrs. Haycock stretched over him as a guardian. This tiny woman with the gaunt beauty of dead flowers.

"You shouldn't have stopped me," Billy panted. "He tried to kill you."

"He just wanted to scare me."

"What if he comes back?"

"He won't."

Honey looked up at Billy, her eyes full of sorrow. The sadness of a broken woman. With a broken man. In a broken home full of broken dreams. All she had left was privacy and illusion that things weren't so bad, that they might even get better. But now even privacy and illusion were gone. Billy was too young to understand then. He would eventually, with time and familiarity.

"Boo!" he shouted.

Honey buried her face in her husband's chest and trembled. Billy laughed. He picked up the rifle, jacked out the bullets, then smashed it down onto a cottonwood stump. The stock splintered. The bolt assembly shattered into pieces.

"Jesus!" Middleton yelped, ducking from flying parts he could not see.

"You tell him to stay away," Billy said, pointing his finger at Honey Haycock. "Understand?"

The woman nodded submissively. Her head low, her neck bent like a dying swan.

<>

Father Eli Turney struggles with the Razorback. He's supposed to put the string on after assembling the bow, but instead has put it on first. Tension makes it impossible to bolt tight the risers.

"Mother of God," he mutters, then takes the whole thing apart and starts over.

Father Turney is in the garage of the rectory, the house next to and owned by the church. It is where he lives in Stonewall, like the priest before him and the one before that. It's a simple prairie four-over-four. The exterior stucco is a pink-beige, the interior a light gray that some restive soul must have found serene. Or maybe it was just on sale at the paint store. The walls are decorated with images of popes and saints as rendered by congregational artists. Crucifixes of Jesus hang in several rooms, always in anguish, brow torn by thorns. The house is furnished with hand-me-down recliners and Melmac dishes. The only bathroom is upstairs, along with the main bedroom, office, and alcove for a boxy TV that sits on a red plastic milk crate. Across from the TV sits a plaid polyester upholstered sofa that is impervious to everything but dirt and stains. It sags deeply where Father Eli spends much of his time, TV tray close at hand.

Out back, next to the alley, the garage is a crumbling brick cube bounded by overgrown ivy. The structure is good now only for storage, provided the stored thing can withstand weather, which blows in through finger-wide cracks in the walls. Rollers on the sliding door rusted away years ago, leaving only a couple of feet of play. Just enough for the large priest to squeeze through.

Father Turney wheezes during his second effort to put the bow together. He really shouldn't be in the garage. He struggles to breathe under all that weight, which is made worse by pollen and dust. But it is a private place. The windows are opaque with dirt and spider webs. Nobody goes back there, and it is the right dimensions for his purpose.

The second try goes better. The bow comes neatly together. He takes out a cord with rubber cups at each end and fits the cups over the bow tips. Stepping on the dangling loop, he pulls upward, arching the bow enough to slide the string into its notches. When he releases the cord, the bow quivers with taut energy. He nocks an arrow onto the bowstring, right below the bead. As instructed by the salesman with the alligator smile.

He aims from six paces away. Eighteen feet. At a target he made from a cushion and several thicknesses of cardboard, all crammed into a plastic fertilizer bag.

Slowly he pulls the string back until the base of his right thumb touches the corner of his mouth. A consistent draw is key to accuracy. He aims along the arrow shaft. "Shooting the gap," it's called. His front hand starts to tremble. Then the back hand. The string rips free from his fingers as the arrow flies wide and bites into the soft face of deteriorating brick. It sticks for a half beat, then clatters to the concrete floor with the comic pause of a punchline. A chunk of mortar follows and shatters. He looks at what he has done and takes a deep breath.

"Mother of God," he says again.

Father Turney cannot pinpoint the moment his faith diminished. It would be too much to say it has been lost altogether. He still believes in

God, the Church, and his ministry. But while faith lingers, its vividness and clarity have faded over the years. Like the failing eyesight of an old man. Which is pretty much how Eli Turney views himself. Old and failing.

Once full of vigor as a young priest, Father Turney prayed and reached out. He worked on tolerance, school improvement, peace advocacy, and addiction programs. But racism persisted, children fell into poverty and neglect, drugs and war continued to ravage. It was like swimming against a tidal wave. Over time, it seemed more was lost than gained. The effort was exhausting. It weakened then broke his spirit. He took society's failures as a reflection of his own inadequacy.

Noting Father Turney's flagging morale, the bishop—the same one who later exiled Eli to Stonewall—sent him on a "well-deserved vacation" in St. Louis. There, he was advised to dial back the compassion, ease up on empathy. Practice the prayer of serenity. Accept what you can't change. To Eli, the message was "numb thyself." So, he learned to care less and drink more. It worked well. Too well. Eventually, Father Turney numbed to God. Or perhaps God numbed to him. Either way, he concluded that he was of little value to those who sought divinity. He was not exactly an obstacle to the presence of God, but neither was God taking his phone calls.

He thought about quitting his ministry. But he had no other place to go, no other skills to trade on. Retirement age for a priest is seventy. If he was going to make it that long, he knew he would have to adjust his thinking. Thinking. The opposite of faith.

So, he came to think of himself as an entertainer of sorts. A religious song-and-dance man who kept up a rat-a-tat patter while escorting parishioners through the pains of life. He held hands with the dying and sang them liturgical lullabies. He conjured postcards of the afterlife, a comfort to those who mourned. He twirled together dizzy explanations of hurt and hunger. He spun tales of personal anguish into being nearer to the Lord.

In his best moments, he was convinced that sparkles and clever vacuity worked about as well as the truth under most circumstances. In his worst, he was disdainful of himself. Of the razzle dazzle, misdirection, falsity, and fairy tales. Over the years, this worst part of himself came with greater frequency. Or maybe he was just depressed.

Eighteen months after arriving in Stonewall, slumped into the sagging couch one late night channel-surfing, he clicked onto a survival show in which sinewy urban natives endured short, trying visits to hostile environs. It froze him in place, the remote control suspended in his outstretched arm.

The show was so willful. So melodramatic in its bounces between joy and despair. It was so full of life. Breathy with life. Fierce for life. When the show ended, the contestants limped home to their loved ones, affirmed in their existence and renewed in their sense of self.

As the credits rolled, Father Turney teared up. He started to laugh at his own sappiness, but the laughter choked into a sob. He went down to the kitchen and poured himself a big bowl of cereal. He stared out the window, eating alone, weeping in the dark. It occurred to him that priests may not be the hallmarks of healthy maturity. That made him laugh even more. And then cry.

The next morning Father Turney woke up inspired. He was almost ready to flex his muscles or go for a stroll. A walk today, another tomorrow, maybe he could shed a few pounds. There had to be some muscle under all that fat. Maybe even a lot of muscle, to carry so much weight. He wasn't looking for miracles. Just a passing acquaintanceship with his own masculinity. That was when he came upon the idea. The next time he went to Kansas City, he would stop in Cabela's and buy himself a bow.

Which is exactly what he did.

Eli nocks a second arrow. He cheats forward a little, stepping over paint cans and scrap lumber. He sets his feet shoulder-width apart, ninety degrees to the target. This time he will shoot fast. Not allow himself to over aim, overthink, let his muscles lose resolve. He pulls smooth and steady. His thumb touches the corner of the mouth. He releases.

The arrow flies true and hits the target with a satisfying pop. The point digs deep into foam rubber and cardboard. The fletches quiver. The priest lowers the bow and smiles. He looks at his hand and the weapon it holds. He made the right selection. Something simple, arched, and elegant. Something mystical and meditative. Something that might help Eli Turney find whatever remains true in himself.

<>

"You okay, son?" Matthew asked.

"I'm not the one who can't see."

Billy was behind the wheel. Speeding toward the emergency room in Dodge, which was farther away and where fewer people would take notice. No bank needs this kind of publicity.

"That was a helluva thing you did back there," the older man said.

Because the banker could not observe, Billy allowed himself to smile. He and his old man might not be much, but there was nobody better in a fight.

"Stop rubbing your eyes," he scolded, lest his silence be taken for pride. Middleton dropped his hands from his face.

"But you're okay?"

"I'm fine," Billy answered, slightly irritated. Thinking his toughness was in doubt.

"I wouldn't be," Matthew mused.

The ER doctor rinsed the banker's eyes, then tinted them with a viscous yellow lubricant. For a couple of days, Matthew Middleton would view the world through an amber film. Other than that, he was fine. Could even see well enough to drive Billy home.

When the Lincoln nosed into the dirt yard, two of the younger Spires rushed out of the trailer, their faces streaked with tears. Old Joe Spire appeared backlit in the doorway. He bellowed and started after them. Spotting Middleton's car, he glared, turned, and went back inside. If he had learned anything from his hard years, it was not to mess with the rich. They had all kinds of ways of cutting a man down to size.

Billy got out, lifted a sobbing child into either arm, stiffened for battle, and started toward the front door. Middleton lowered his window.

"Sure you're okay?" he asked for the second time.

"I said I'm fine," the boy answered, without turning his head.

<>

Mrs. Middleton gasped when her husband walked into the kitchen. She gently put her hands on the sides of his face.

"Kiln explosion at a loan site," he explained, putting his hands over hers. "Bad way to find out a client isn't insured."

"Which client?" Owen had wandered out of his room for another Coke.

"Doesn't matter," Matthew replied. "But they're lucky it was me. I'm probably the only person in the world who won't sue. I need them in business. They owe us money."

Owen shrugged his shoulders, grabbled a bottle from the refrigerator, and went back to his bedroom. To press more Liberty dimes into their blue sleeves.

<>

A few weeks later, Matthew Middleton glanced up from his desk. Duane McQuitty stood in the doorway, looking as if his dog had died. Coach Jordan was right behind, looking even worse.

"Is it really that bad?" Middleton wondered, half amused. He waved them in. Coach Jordan closed the door for privacy.

"I won't have a thief working for me," Duane howled. "I just won't do it."

McQuitty was, by then, in his early eighties, skinny and brown as a walnut, with a storm of white hair and trembling hands. He wore mother-of-pearl snaps on his shirt and scuffed cowboy boots. Despite his humble appearance, McQuitty was a man of wealth and local esteem. A solid, decent, caring member of the community. Never one to put on airs. And as with many old men, emotions spilled out through his eyes.

"What are we talking about?" Middleton asked, pushing a Kleenex box across his desk.

"Duane just fired Joe Spire," the coach said.

"It kills me, Matthew," the feedlot owner sobbed. "But I seen it with my own eyes."

"What did he steal?"

"Two saddles from the tack room. Worth a few hundred each, easy."

Middleton turned to the coach with that expression of affable skepticism.

"And this involves me how?"

"Billy needs to stay here," Coach Jordan half yelled, as if the banker was being deliberately obtuse. "He needs a place to live."

"You don't have a house?"

"I sure do," Jordan countered. "Full of three teenage daughters."

"What about you, Duane?"

"After I just fired his father? And given how bad I've done with the boy I already got?"

Like many accomplished men, Duane McQuitty fathered a son with elevated self-importance and low work ethics. A son named Melvin McQuitty.

"Matthew, this is about more than just football," the coach said. "Billy is coming out of his shell. Doing well in class. He matters here. People ask after him when he walks down the street."

Middleton rubbed a hand over his face. His eyes were good as new, but tiny scars from the scatter of exploded cinderblock dotted the corners. The banker massaged them with the tips of his fingers.

"I suppose he could stay with us for a while," he finally sighed. "If he wants to. And his parents will allow it."

Duane McQuitty snuffled in gratitude and blew his nose. Coach Jordan sprang to his feet, smiling. The banker knew he had been bested by the coach, once again. But it was okay. When it came to Billy Spire, he was indebted. And Matthew Middleton always honored his debts.

That night, he brought up the possibility over dinner. Mrs. Middleton was a generous woman, maternal toward every child she ever met. Especially Billy, who she had come to see as needy and neglected. Many times, she had seen him walking home alone after football games. What kind of parents wouldn't cheer on their own son? Still, she was vexed.

"Parents just giving their child away?" she despaired. "I can't imagine."

Matthew nodded in solemn understanding. "I'm afraid there are a lot of things about that family you can't imagine," he replied. "Let me talk to the father."

"No," she said clattering the dirty dishes with rising agitation. "If anyone is talking, it will be me and his mother."

Matthew sighed with relief. He had no desire to meet with Joe Spire. Couldn't imagine how to talk to a man like that.

The next day in Rod's Market, Mrs. Middleton came across Billy's mother. Sniffing a day-old bread loaf at Reduction Junction, a rack of discounted wares and food items.

"Why, Mrs. Spire, how nice to see you."

Billy's mother looked up blankly. She didn't get out much and didn't pay a lot of attention when she did. She was, perhaps, the only person in Ewing County who didn't recognize the banker's wife.

"Norma Middleton." Owen's mother extended her hand.

"I'm Annie." But instead of reaching back, Billy's mother clutched the bread to her chest like it was about to be taken away. Her hands were chapped, fingernails dirty and broken.

"Would you like to have a cup of coffee sometime?"

"Why?" Annie blurted, then blushed. She knew what it meant to be polite, but hadn't had a lot of practice lately.

"To talk about Billy."

"What about him?"

"He works at my husband's bank. Matthew thinks he has a bright future."

Annie Spire nodded uncertainly. The name Spire and bright future were seldom associated. At Rod's Market or anyplace else.

"We're leaving town," Annie answered. "As soon as we pack."

Norma imagined that might not take very long.

"Then how about tomorrow morning?" she pressed.

"I need to ask Joe."

Normally, Norma Middleton would have invited Mrs. Spire to the house. That would have been the friendly thing to do. But in this case, it didn't seem like a good idea. It would only draw attention to the gap, the canyon between their circumstances.

"Let's meet at Effie's," she said, as if it were a done deal. "Say nine."

The next morning, Norma dressed down in jeans and a coral pink sweater. Annie dressed up in stretch pants and a floral windbreaker. Even in Effie's, with its worn linoleum floor and cowboy art, Billy's mother obviously felt out of place. Uncertain how to conduct herself, she looked around anxiously, twisting her wedding ring, as if someone might ask her to leave. She was unsure what to eat. The banker's wife realized that Mrs. Spire was worried about having to pay for what she ordered.

"Since I invited you, let me get the check," Norma assured. Annie nodded and lost some of the tension in her shoulders. After they ate, they talked.

"Billy and Joe are like two bull moose," Annie said between sips of coffee. Her stomach full, her guard a little lower. "Joe touches the little ones and Billy is right there. Up in his daddy's face, pounding away. Wins more now than before, but still not very often. Don't know why he can't just worry about his own self."

"Maybe he understands what it's like to be scared and hurt in your own family. Wants to protect them from that. Protect everybody from that."

"I guess." Annie waved the thought away as if it were an abstraction. Pertaining to some other family, time, situation, and crushing carelessness.

"Anyway, that must be awful," Norma concluded. "For you and the other children." She reached across the table for Mrs. Spire's hand. Annie allowed herself to be touched. "Maybe your husband and son need a little vacation from each other."

"We're not vacation kind of people."

"Well, maybe Billy could stay with us a while," Norma continued, as if the idea were just dawning. "Until the school year is over. Until you're settled into a new place."

"So he can play football. Joe guessed you would say that."

"Did he?" Norma drew her hand back. "What else did he guess?"

"Not much." Annie looked around at the walls. Stalling to gather her words.

"What is it?" Norma asked.

"Joe says there's a Chrysler station wagon."

"A Chrysler station wagon?"

"At the bank. He wonders if it's for sale."

"He wonders?"

"Says it's repossessed."

"Then it's for sale," Norma said. Her head tilted back as pity slid toward contempt. "What else does he wonder?"

"Our truck is about worn out. We can't afford no money down. Not right now. But we would sure pay you back right away."

"Maybe we can work something out," Norma answered coolly.

"It would be best for Billy," Annie nodded.

Two days later, a Chrysler station wagon departed from a disheveled mobile home in Stonewall, Kansas. It was so heavily loaded that the rear end nearly dragged on the ground and the front tires barely touched. Billy Spire didn't wave as his family left. He stood and stared, hands deep in his pockets as the younger kids called his name and cried. His parents looked straight ahead. Straight through the windshield and down the road. Searching for fresh possibilities that would inevitably fall victim to old certainties. Even then, Billy understood. There was nothing he could do to alter their fates. He could only save himself. He watched until glowing red taillights disappeared in distant dust.

At a discreet distance, shaded beneath a willow tree, Matthew and Owen waited in the red Lincoln. They waited until Billy Spire was ready to leave.

<>

The morning after Russ Haycock's body was found, Sheriff Spire is the first person in the Ewing County Courthouse, a neo-classical building in the town square, decorated with columns and pediments. A poor sleeper, Billy is almost always the first person to arrive. Today he had woken up at four, ate breakfast, showered, shaved, and drove twenty minutes from his home in rural Ewing County. His wife, Nadine, had gone to bed late as always. She would sleep until mid-morning, if she got out of bed at all.

Spire climbs the black slate steps to his second-floor office. Original to the 1911 courthouse, the steps are slightly concave, worn down by thousands upon thousands of footsteps. Victims and culprits going to trial. Folks paying taxes, registering property, or getting married. Generations of voters gathering in the small rotunda to watch the county clerk post returns on a slate chalkboard. They still gather that way on election night in Ewing County. Sure, they have computers, but tradition is so much nicer. It is Billy's morning ritual to reach down and stroke the concavity of those steps. To connect with citizens, ghosts and living, who make a community over time.

The sheriff's office is at the corner of the building. A small room, it holds an office chair, a bench seat for visitors, and a sprawling oak table cluttered with paperwork. The courthouse was retrofitted in the seventies. AC ducts hang from exposed pipes amid a tangled mass of electrical conduits and communication cables. Ice tray fluorescent lights illuminate the dropped ceiling. Billy hardly ever turns them on. He looks bad enough, even in good light. Instead, he uses a decorative table lamp that might have come from an old lady's library, which, in fact, it did. Left to him by Norma Middleton. Something to remember her by. As if he would ever forget. On the wall is a framed poster of an American flag, inscribed with platitudes about honor and courage. It was put up by the previous sheriff. Spire left it there as a sign of respect. By the time the old sheriff died, he was used to it. So, it stays. Billy Spire does not like change. Next to the poster a clipboard hangs on a nail. Each sheaf of paper detailing an unsolved case.

Spire's window looks down on the county jail, a free-standing brick blockhouse with a metal roof. It features two cells and an office for the sheriff's deputy. When he has one. Right now, that office is full of the county's Christmas decorations. The last deputy took a better job in Oklahoma. The county commission asked Billy to go slow on a new hire out of budget concerns. Slow soon became not at all. For the past three years, the Ewing County Sheriff's Office has been a one-person operation. Since crime—or at least the possibility of crime—never takes a holiday, neither does Billy Spire.

He sets his briefcase on the big wooden table and takes out the Haycock materials. He pulls reporting forms from a file cabinet and starts filling in the boxes. This will take all morning. He grabs a bottle of diet cola from a small refrigerator tucked under the table. Same refrigerator Matthew Middleton provisioned in the bank lobby years ago. Spire twists off the top and empties the soda into a plastic mug. He tries to hide the fact he drinks pop in the morning. Worries others might think less of him if they knew. Which, of course, they do. Ewing County, Kansas, is the narrow kind of place that holds on to peculiarities in others. He takes a deep swig and begins the tedious process of crime reporting.

A little after 8:30, the phone rings.

"Let's get going," Leo Ace shouts over a revving engine. There are other voices in the background. "I got paid work to do."

Spire throws on his coat and starts walking. It's colder than last night. He can see his breath, sparkling diamond-bright in the morning sun. Halfway there, he mindlessly sips at his pop. The act startles him. He meant to leave the mug at the office. He thinks of stashing it in the bushes. But when you're the sheriff of a small Kansas county, every window has eyes.

Ace's Auto Repair is one block south of the courthouse, a gray stucco complex of garage bays and tire racks. Vehicles sprawl at awkward angles from every side. It's one of the few benefits of a dying town. Not much demand when it comes to either parking spots or municipal aesthetics. Only Roy Engel complains. But then he complains about everything. Some of the vehicles wait for repair. More are engaged in a slow-play cannibalism, as parts are taken and reused over time.

After Russ Haycock's venture went belly up, Leo Ace held a pure monopoly on auto repair in Ewing County. Didn't used to be that way. There used to be lots of competition. And lots of customers. At the turn of the last century Stonewall had nearly four times the population. Then came world wars and the rise of machines that did the work of a hundred men, without injury or complaint. The Dust Bowl. The Depression. Great highways that were supposed to bring people in but ended up only taking them away. Now critical mass is on the dying side. Those who remain are aged and aging. They, too, will trickle away. To their kids and hospitals. To graveyards and cemeteries. The houses left behind will eventually fail. Water will rot the wood. Ice and snow will tip the walls. All that remains will sag, then tumble to the ground.

Ace's shop is embroiled in heated argument. There are four persons present. Ace and three old men who are there every morning. Not one of them doing a lick of work. They are fanned out in the office, flopped on chairs and stacks of tires, drinking coffee. Normally they bicker endlessly over things that don't matter. Things completely beyond their control. But this morning is different. They argue about something relevant. About who will conduct Russ Haycock's funeral.

"I'm telling you, he was Baptist."

"Now how do you know that? Did you ever once see him at services?"

"No. But my momma went to church with his daddy."

"His daddy was blind," Ace snaps. "Does that make Russ blind, too?" The other three go quiet, as if Ace has made a point worth pondering.

"What about her?" one finally continues. "Who knows what God she prayed to?" All four are sobered by this comment.

"You remember how he did with her?" they nod.

"Too cheap to pay funeral costs," they remember.

"Well," Ace speaks in his lowest register, the place his voice goes for authority. "It's got to be that new Catholic priest. He hasn't had as much time to be offended."

"New? He's been here two years."

"I know," Ace cranks. "But that's a damn sight less than any of the others."

Ace is right. Someone should get in touch with Father Turney right away. They agree in unison that someone should be the sheriff.

"It's his job, ain't it?" one of the old men says.

"Glad you worked that out," says Billy Spire, who slipped in unnoticed. Not such a trick, given the poor hearing and inattentiveness of old men. He holds the plastic coffee mug casually, low at his side, hoping no one will see.

"What you got there?" An old coot points at Billy's drink and winks at the others. Spire ignores him but slides the mug behind an oil can.

"You're in some kind of hurry about that truck?" he says dryly to Ace.

"I got a transmission to pull."

The pickup floats mid-air on the lift. Spire walks over and puts his hand on the fender, as if to feel its warmth. Ace follows. The peanut gallery trails right behind, walking soft and poker faced. Hoping they will not be noticed.

"Can Ace and I have a few minutes?" Billy asks without turning around.

The three old men shuffle out, muttering that their expertise and sharp eyes should not be so quickly dismissed. When he hears the door click shut, Spire turns back to Ace.

"I suppose by now all of Ewing County thinks Russ Haycock was shot on the highway."

"I'm sure they do," the mechanic answers.

"You tell them?"

"Didn't have to."

Spire nods with solemn understanding.

"That's not the same as saying no."

"Could be any of 'em. The truck driver. Ambulance crew. The lady with the little girls." Ace refuses to back down. "Good news travels fast."

"Murder is good news?" Spire snorts.

"Is in this case," the mechanic replies. He absent-mindedly rotates the suspended vehicle's flat tire.

In fact, the sheriff is pleased that Ace has broadcast his theory on

70

Russ Haycock's random death. Ewing County needs to believe it is safe. For now.

"Damn!" Ace jerks his hand off the tire and starts sucking the base of his palm.

"What?"

"Something bit me." He shows the sheriff a small cut that's bleeding pretty good.

Billy looks at the tire, pointedly less interested in the wound than its cause. Ace makes a show of wrapping his hand in a dirty handkerchief. He hopes the injury will end Billy's scolding over talking too much.

"Right there." Spire points. The two men lean close to examine a broken gray edge, protruding an eighth of an inch from the tire tread. "What is that?"

Ace searches his toolbox for a pair of needle-nose pliers, then stops to look at his bleeding hand.

"I got to get a Band-Aid."

"You stay right here and give me those."

Billy grabs the pliers, gets a good grip, and yanks the thing out. He takes it to the bay window, where the morning sun is strong. It's a piece of metal, about a quarter-inch long. Shiny and roughly triangular. The point is sharp, the edge is hollow ground. There is a slight indentation, the tail-end of a fingernail groove.

"Look like a knife point to you?" Spire asks.

"Yup."

"What is it doing there?"

Ace pulls a pair of oversized reading glasses from his shirt pocket. They make his eyes seem three times too big. He raises and twists Billy's hand in the sunlight, examining the object from every angle.

"Don't know where it came from, but it wasn't there when the truck was rolling. Would have popped out or worn down."

"Got an envelope?"

Ace goes into the office and returns with a used yellow envelope, now smeared with blood. Spire shakes his head in disapproval.

"Told you I needed a Band-Aid," Ace complains.

"Let's air up this tire," the sheriff says.

"Us? You got a turd in your pocket?"

Ace doesn't like to be bossed around. Especially in his own shop. Nonetheless, he switches on the air pump. It hisses and clatters. He fixes the nozzle onto the valve, and they watch as the tire begins to harden with the whiney sound of inflation. When it's full, the two turn their heads and listen. Not a sound. The mechanic grabs a spray bottle of soapy liquid. He slowly spins the tire, spritzing every inch. Again, nothing. No bubbles from escaping air.

"I'll be damned," Ace declares.

"Keep it to yourself," Billy says, then adds a menacing growl. "This time, I mean it."

"I will," Ace answers, looking somber and mystified.

"You better. You got the whole town believing in a random shooting. This comes out, you'll look like a fool."

Billy Spire is confident this secret is safe. The sheriff believes in pragmatism and interests. Good intentions, not so much. Leo Ace will keep mum to protect his own reputation.

"I got to check out the Haycock place," Spire says, looking at his watch.

"When they gonna hire you a new deputy?"

"The next time Ewing County has a population boom."

"That soon, huh?"

Sheriff points at the tire. "Take it off. Put it someplace safe."

"Yes, sir!" Ace's salute is sloppy with sarcasm.

Spire starts for the door. He remembers and goes back for the hidden mug of diet soda.

"You stop by the priest on your way," Ace hollers. "And Emma says to find some proper burying clothes. You hear me, Billy Spire?"

Ace prefers to boss rather than be bossed. Especially in his own damn place.

<>

The repossessed Corvair remained impaled in the basement house for months. Russ left it there in a sort of you-broke-it-now-you-fix-it belligerence. As if anyone cared. To passing and curious neighbors, it was just one more amazing oddity of the Haycock place. Nobody knew how it came to be there. Leading to wild speculation and gales of laughter at the Stonewall barber shop. Only the banker, Matthew Middleton, seemed to find it less than amusing.

He and Billy Spire kept their silence about that afternoon and its violent encounter. The older man, because bad publicity is never good for business. The younger man, because Matthew made him promise.

After the beating, Russ Haycock went quiet. He still had his beefs, no question about that, but they never again took the form of slaughtered lambs or gunshots. He mostly scowled and stayed off to himself, which was not an easy thing to do in a dying town with one gas station. But even five feet away Russ Haycock inhabited an icy floe, adrift in the sea, alone with averted eyes. Bristling and mute.

His silence was in stark contrast to the explosive end of the movement he admired.

In 1983, a man named Gordon Kahl found himself in Medina, North Dakota. Kahl was a father, grandfather, and husband. He was also a leader of the Posse Comitatus, well armed and in violation of parole conditions. He was in Medina to rally sympathizers against Blacks and Jews to further spread the venom of William P. Gale.

Law enforcement set upon Kahl in a roadblock outside of town. Two federal marshals were shot, one died. Kahl escaped to a berm house in Smithville, Arkansas. A local sheriff went inside to look around. Kahl stepped from behind a refrigerator. The two fired simultaneously. The sheriff staggered outside, mortally wounded. The house caught fire and left nothing but ashes, including those of Gordon Kahl. The murder of a marshal and sheriff alarmed authorities across the nation. Walls began closing in on the Posse and its brethren.

They did not go peacefully. In Ulysses, Kansas, there was a call for execution of the Grant County sheriff. Nothing came of it. Maybe because law officers from every corner of the state showed up with body armor and assault rifles. Later described as "jackbooted thugs" by the National Rifle Association, these new ranks of heavy firepower police officers put the lid on extremism. Fast and hard.

At the same time, sensible Kansans went to battle against KTTL. Religious leaders railed against the radio station's bigotry. Dodge City kicked up a fuss about its stained image. Kansas Senator Bob Dole demanded that the Federal Communications Commission investigate. Magazines from *Jet* to *Christian Century* editorialized against the hatred spewing from western Kansas.

In the center of it all sat the teary-eyed and hapless Nellie Babbs, owner of the radio station, sputtering that "this man Gale is only explaining constitutional law." Not for long he wasn't. At least not on KTTL. Sermons from the Identity Church were replaced with fast-patter disk jockeys spinning rock-and-roll. Shortly thereafter, the Reverend Gale was sentenced to federal prison for threats against a judge and the IRS. He died before serving time. Emphysema took away his voice, then his life.

White supremacy never died in western Kansas. It just went into a dark and airless place. Waiting then. Waiting now. But for Russ Haycock, the glory days had come and gone. Leaving him with nothing more than a jagged scar across his forehead.

Eventually, Haycock strung a stout cable between his trailer hitch and the Corvair and slammed his pickup into reverse. Just as one might extract a loose tooth. The car stayed stuck, but its rear bumper ripped off and flew into Russ's pickup. It left a long cut in the side panel. Haycock patched it over with a slather of body putty and spray paint. The fix lasted quite a while. Until the night of his death. When Leo Ace affectionately slapped the old truck's fender.

<>

Owen Middleton agreed to share his bedroom with Billy Spire. His mother made clear that he had no choice. They would move some of his stuff out of the way and bring in a cot.

But Billy would have none of it.

He wasn't part of the Middleton family, nor would he pretend to be. In truth, it humiliated him to be perceived as needy. He made a plywood pallet for himself in the rafters of the attached garage. He dragged up an orange extension cord, reading light, and a foam-rubber mattress. When it was cold, he piled on sleeping bags. When it was hot, he climbed down and slept on the cool concrete floor. Mrs. Middleton fretted terribly about the boy. All by himself out there. With no family.

"I'm going to go out and drag him into the house," she warned her husband, as they readied for bed.

"You'll just embarrass him."

"He's a boy, isn't he? He needs to be hugged. Wished goodnight."

"Maybe so. But that's not what he knows."

"Then he needs to learn better," she despaired.

Billy Spire lived with the Middletons for eighteen months. He took it upon himself to mow the lawn, carry in firewood, and scrape windshields when they frosted over on a cold night. Never once in all that time did Mrs. Middleton see even one item of Billy's dirty clothes. He slid in and out, using the washer and dryer quietly when no one noticed. He would have died before asking a favor.

If Billy was tentative and ghostlike, Owen was bold and confident. His parents held the center of Stonewall's social life. The house was constantly full of politicians, old friends, new friends, representatives of every cause and community good. Billy would squirrel himself away in the breakfast nook, listening with one ear while studying homework or football plays. He was astonished at the hubbub. It was like nothing he knew. Not one outside person, save a few shirttail relatives, ever sat down at the Spire dinner table. Social graces in old Joe's presence were simple and explosively enforced. Eyes down. Eat fast. Shut up. Get out of the way when trouble starts.

More than anything, Billy marveled at how Owen held forth. Throwing out opinions. Laughing without restraint. Demonstrating mastery of all he knew. Telling jokes without the slightest hint of self-consciousness. Billy Spire had never seen anything like it.

Sometimes, Billy tried to imagine what he might say, given an opportunity. But even in fantasy, his thoughts were clumsy, his words inchoate. Even an imagined audience found him thuggish. When laughter from the other room interrupted his daydreams, Billy would take his stuff out to the garage. Up to his garret and the clip-on reading light. Billy Spire could never have shared a room with Owen Middleton. It was impossible. He felt inadequate enough all by himself.

⟨⟩

After high school, Owen and Billy went their separate ways.

Owen took his good grades and family pocketbook to the University of Kansas. He pledged the fraternity to which his father had belonged. Guided by steady hands back in Stonewall, he completed his accounting degree with purpose and efficiency. Struck the perfect balance between service, study, and beer.

In summers, there were internships at Kansas City banks. Learning his craft. Making connections. In winter, Owen and his fraternity brothers would dash to Colorado ski resorts, stopping in Stonewall for a home-cooked meal and paternal insights on commerce and economics.

In his final year at KU, Owen met LeeAnn Croner, a sorority girl from a good family of grain dealers in Salina. She was a bundle of energy with chipmunk cheeks, a gymnast's body, and a half-smiling mouth that could, with snap rapidity, issue stunning insight, well-placed sarcasm, or wild humor. Everyone approved of the match. Owen and LeeAnn both graduated with honors from the School of Business. At least half of Ewing County came to see them walk down the hill. Afterward at the hotel, Owen's grandmother had a valet fetch a car. A brand new, bright red Lincoln. As his parents stood beaming, she gave him the keys and said, "We are very proud of you."

Owen and LeeAnn married in KU's Danforth Chapel. After several assignments in Texas, Owen moved his young family back to Ewing County. To take over Stonewall Savings and Loan. His father wanted to ease up, at least that's what he said. But he and Norma just wanted to have family nearby. The two grandchildren were great kids. Straight and true. Frequently in the local paper, always doing good. They were both in college now at their parents' alma mater. Solid students and illuminati of Greek society.

Billy Spire's high school grades were also good. Even remarkable, given his situation. Strong enough to get into a small college, especially one that needed a middle linebacker. Coach Jordan tried his best to get Billy to apply. Norma Middleton even tricked him into a Dodge City men's store to buy him a suit that he could wear to college visits. Mrs. Middleton was a formidable force who would not let Billy refuse. It was the only gift he ever accepted from the Middletons, other than the reading lamp and refrigerator in his courthouse office. That suit still hangs in his closet, now five sizes too small. It remains among his most treasured possessions.

But there were never any college visits. It did not fit with Billy's understanding of himself. He was a Spire, and no Spire had ever gone to college. That was for other people. People who knew how to dress and act and talk. People with promising futures. He would join the Marines and see what happened. That was what a Spire would do. The Marines took one look at the rough features and low-slung power and assigned him to the Military Police.

Billy was thirty-six when he met his wife-to-be at a roadhouse near Charleston, South Carolina. He and a fellow MP were sitting at a back table, wearing civvies. On the prowl for an AWOL private with a taste for whiskey and line dancing. The other Marine was going on about country-western music. How it was overproduced now, betraying its working-man roots. Billy waved over a busboy.

"Can I hep yew?" the busboy asked. He was a skinny fellow with a crew cut and thin mustache.

"Tell me about her." Billy pointed to a waitress. She had jet-black hair, full lips, and emerald eyes. She was not so much in a bar, as of it. A being of smoke, dim light, sawdust, honkytonk piano, spangles, and yearny sad songs. Loosely held together by a volatile and unreliable fixative, alcohol.

"She's been here a while," he answered. "Sometimes, sings with the band."

"Any good?"

"Good enough, I guess. If you like warbly."

"What's her name."

"Nadine."

"Got a fellow?"

"Sure does. Name of Smirnoff. Can't get enough of the guy."

Billy nodded. His upbringing didn't teach him much, but he understood vodka. Every serious drunk eventually finds their way to vodka. He reached into his shirt pocket for a piece of paper. His eyes went back and forth between the paper and the busboy's face.

"You Jimmy Dell?" he asked.

The crew cut spun and took off. Billy grabbed the kid by the back of his belt. He was still running, but his shoes found no grip on the sawdusted floor. He pumped and flailed but remained in place like a cartoon character. The other MP wrestled him down and slapped on cuffs. Nadine raced over, followed by a clutch of roadhouse regulars who enjoyed a good fight, as both spectators and participants.

"What the hell? You let him go," she demanded.

"Military Police," Billy said, holding up his badge for everyone to see. "Absent without leave."

The crowd dispersed. Ain't nobody going to stand up for an unpatriotic coward. Not in South Carolina.

"It ain't me," Jimmy Dell pleaded. "It's a mistake."

Billy held up the paper for the woman to see. Nadine nodded slowly as she read. There was no mistake.

"What's going to happen?" she asked in a matter-of-fact voice. Life in a bar is familiar with ups and downs.

"He'll go to the brig. And I'll come back and buy you a drink."

She studied Billy's face. He didn't try to hide or soften what she was looking at. He was what he was.

"I drink Smirnoff," she finally said.

"So I hear."

Billy Spire went back to the roadhouse whenever he could after that. He was happy there, admiring people whirl the two-step, watching Nadine wait tables. He loved to hear her sing, which she did when a band's real singer needed to break for a smoke.

Nadine's voice was small and sweet. And warbly indeed. On sad ballads, she cracked her voice as if fighting off tears. For jumpy rockabilly numbers, she hooped and laughed and shimmied her shoulders. Lots of men offered to buy her drinks. She never turned them down. Even slow danced if they offered a double. But if those men wanted anything more than time, she would plop down in the empty chair at Billy's side. Sometimes the men got mad and followed her, demanding more return on their investment. One look at Billy Spire would stop them cold.

Billy made Nadine feel safe. And making her feel safe made him feel good. Like with his brothers and sisters. It was that simple. The give-and-take of safety was as close to love as either Billy or Nadine had ever known.

One weekend, he popped the question.

"How about we get married?"

She looked at him. Her eyes bright, slightly unfocused. She tossed back the half-empty vodka he was guarding for her.

"I'm never going to stop," she warned. "I come from a long line of drinkers. It's what we do. What we've always done. Don't think you're going to change that."

"You're beautiful," he answered. She was beautiful. Beautiful in a way that deceived an ugly man who imagined beauty as its own cure. Beauty could put down the bottle and abandon wild ways. Beauty would one day make her a fine woman and wife. They would own the world together.

"And you're a fool," she answered, shaking her head.

The next Thursday they were married by a Charleston justice of the peace.

Four years later, at the end of his twenty years in the military, Billy and Nadine moved back to Stonewall. Matthew Middleton had suggested that the old sheriff was retiring, and that Billy would be a shoo-in, given his football heroics and MP experience. He said that Mrs. Middleton missed having him nearby. He did, too. That was all Billy needed to hear. Someone missed him. He filed for office. Nobody else challenged. Been there ever since.

At first Nadine seemed to find a home in Ewing County. Getting to know the locals, being known in return. She even sobered up a little, for a while. That faded with the first winter. Maybe the dreary skies got to her. Or the cold north winds. Maybe Nadine had too much fun in her youth. Or maybe not enough. Whatever the cause, the drinking returned, then got heavier. Her gaiety diminished, dissolving into a bitter, unnamable heartache. It has been years since Billy heard her sing. Beauty had betrayed him.

For all his physical power, Sheriff Spire was helpless against his wife's drinking. She shut the door on the world. Spent her days reading magazines and fussing over never-completed craft projects. At the first hint of dusk she filled a highball glass with vodka. One followed the next.

In the early years, Billy tried to cover it up. He tossed empty bottles in dumpsters around Stonewall, attempting to hide the magnitude of her consumption. He bought cases of Smirnoff from out-of-town places where he was just a stranger. He knew it was wrong. Enabling. But he thought it better than having Nadine drive drunk. Maybe he was just ashamed of her.

Of course, keeping secrets in a small town is a fool's game. Especially for an elected official. In time—a very short time, at that—everyone in Stonewall knew about the Spires. That Billy drank diet cola for breakfast out of a plastic mug. That his wife drank vodka by the bottle. Eventually the sheriff decided he was fooling nobody. Might just as well spend local and buy her Smirnoff at the Stonewall liquor store. When the Spires first came back to Stonewall, well-meaning citizens thought it kindly to ask after Nadine. After a while, they stopped asking. Out of politeness.

‹›

Counted first among Owen Middleton's many treasures is a children's book gifted to him by his flamboyant grandmother. A 1919 copy of *Aesop for Children*. Of all the stories, one fascinated him most: "The Monkey and the Cat." As the two animals sit watching a fire, the monkey convinces the cat to reach in and snatch out some roasting chestnuts. He does so with praise, saying to the cat, "You are much more skillful at such things than I." In the end, the feline stooge ends up nursing a singed paw as the clever monkey eats all the chestnuts.

As Billy Spire was settling in as the Ewing County sheriff, Owen Middleton took over Stonewall Savings and Loan. His agenda was growth. Like his father, he was prescient about financial situations. Could sense vulnerabilities and always kept a healthy supply of investment capital on hand. And like his father, Owen never wanted anything "bad." He took things on his own terms, or not at all.

But unlike his father, Owen was ready to make things happen if they didn't happen fast enough on their own. His favorite tactic was the familiar cat's paw. He would get commodity brokers to start rumors about price softening, then buy land from farmers in a weak financial position. Land that might overlay mineral reserves or water rights. He would have Texas megabanks make inquiries about buying small thrifts in western Kansas. Then push those smalls to consolidate with Stonewall as a means of survival. Consolidations cleverly structured toward absorption. He would use piecemeal investors to buy roadside properties. Then get the county to change the zoning from agriculture to commercial in order to profit from highway widening projects. He made a lot of money and Stonewall Savings and Loan opened offices in Liberal, Garden, and Dodge.

Owen's greatest success was in upholding his personal reputation. Everyone loved and admired the banker. He was a chip off the old block. When a seat opened, community leaders urged Owen to run for the state legislature. He was intrigued by the prestige, the power, the access to inside information. And, truly, by the opportunity to do good things for Ewing County. As a memorial to his father, whom, after he died, Owen continued to miss every day.

As Owen grew his empire, Billy Spire grew in a whole other direction. He grew kinder.

He came into the job with the curt attitude of an MP. Treat everyone like a million bucks, but always have a plan to kill them. He carried himself with erect and intimidating dignity. Trading on his body, his face, his enduring reputation for brutality.

But a few days after being sworn in, something happened to change his thinking.

In retrospect, it was a silly thing. Billy was in line at Rod's Market. He was buying a frozen pizza and running late. Nadine would be even more furious than usual. An old woman in front of him could not get her act together. She forgot something and had to go back to the canned food section. She searched her purse for a coupon that was not there. She counted out several dollars in nickels and dimes. Billy shifted from foot to foot, getting more anxious by the minute. Just as he rolled his eyes, the old lady turned to him. Her face lit up with surprise.

"I voted for you," she said with a bright smile.

Billy felt about two inches tall. Not just that he had been impatient, but that he had misunderstood his role. He was not just a cop. He was a man in whom the community had placed their trust. And hope.

Billy promised himself that he would try to be a better person. An admirable person. The effort agreed with him. It made him feel good to be good. No doubt, he could bust heads when necessary and do so with forceful efficiency. And occasionally, his temper still got the best of him. But slowly over time, the sheriff of Ewing County stopped seeing himself as a cruel simplicity. He adopted a mantra to help stay in touch with these better parts of himself.

"The first pulse to take is your own."

Years passed at the Haycock place. Uneventfully, for the most part.

Mrs. Haycock, dutiful and self-contained, mended and tailored clothes. Russ drove her every morning, cataloging a world full of wrongs. From the tax assessor to Ace's scattered car parts, the list was endless. She sat with her hands folded in her lap, listening impassively. His many grievances going in one ear and out the other.

One day she noticed an unexpected spot of blood in her underwear. She said nothing, for doctors cost so much. Soon the spot became a flow, and Mrs. Haycock visited Doc Howard. She was diagnosed with cancer of the uterus.

It was the first and only time Russ allowed townspeople to safely set foot on his property. Most every day, someone would go out there. At first, delivering and collecting baskets of clothing for mending. Later, when Honey could no longer work, they brought eggs, milk, lemonade, casseroles, and pain killers. She welcomed their kindness with a shy smile and tired eyes. She enjoyed their company and laughter, until her energy ran out. Russ stayed hid in his shed. Thankful, perhaps, at the generosity, but incapable of saying so.

One day, the door remained shut and the curtains drawn. Mrs. Haycock had become too weak for visitors. When a town lady's knocking went unanswered, she left the basket of food and medicines on the porch. The next morning, the basket was there but emptied of its contents. The townspeople replenished and returned. This went on for a few weeks. Nobody ever knocked on the door again. Nothing was expected, neither hospitality nor gratitude. The people of Stonewall understood about dying and its indignities. The need to be alone.

Haycock panicked in his wife's last hours, terrified by the sights and sounds and smells. It was late at night. He called Doc Howard to meet him. Then carried her like a baby to his pickup and through the doors of Stonewall hospital. She was a tiny gray bundle. He was wide-eyed and hollering. Doc waved them to a bed and yanked closed the privacy curtain. He touched her gently, listening to her breathing and heart.

"I need to get something," the physician said. "Be right back."

He went into the office and dialed the phone.

"Billy," Doc whispered. "Russ Haycock is here. His wife's about to die. I may need your help."

"I don't know, Doc," the sheriff answered. He held the phone close, so not to disturb Nadine. She was in one of her moods. "We have a history."

"Wait in the parking lot, then. But you be here in case he throws a fit."

The doctor went back to find Haycock bent over his wife. Tucking a blanket close to her side.

"There's nothing I can do but keep her comfortable."

Haycock nodded curtly and kept fussing over his wife. Trying to keep her warm.

"Listen, Russ," Doc said. Nobody had called him by his first name in years. He immediately understood. It was a tenderness that signaled fatality. "Sometimes there is a death rattle. Sounds like they're suffocating. But it's just the muscles letting go. Don't let it frighten you. Nothing can hurt her anymore."

A few minutes later, Honey gasped and shuddered. Haycock scooped her into his arms and sobbed.

"She's gone now," Doc confirmed.

He left Haycock alone and went into his office to certify the death. He was staring at the ceiling, composing his words, when Russ appeared in the doorway.

"Can I take her now?" he asked.

"Where?"

"Home."

"Don't you want to call the mortuary?"

"No," Haycock answered. He went back down the hall, pulled loose the sheets, and swaddled her body.

"Russ. Wait. Won't you let us clean her up?"

Holding her, again, like a baby, Haycock stood before the doctor.

"I can pay a little at a time," he said softly.

"Sure," Doc answered as Haycock brushed past him on his way out the door. "But don't worry about that now."

Billy Spire was parked across the street from the hospital. He saw the door open. Haycock had something in his arms. Doc Howard followed closely behind, gesturing with his hands. He seemed to be pleading.

"Russ, please," he said. "Don't do this to yourself."

Haycock started for the green Dodge, which he had left idling in the middle of the lot with the driver's door wide open. Then, as if his wife's body suddenly gained gravity and mass, Russ's knees went wobbly and caved. He fell, landing with one hand on the ground, the other trying to keep her corpse from harm. He struggled to stand up, crying in a high-pitched, eerie howl. Billy jumped out of his car and jogged to Haycock's side.

"Russ," Spire said, taking the fallen man's arm.

Haycock turned his face upward to face the sheriff who had marked his forehead with an ugly scar. Russ's painful lashless eyes were wild with sorrow, redder than ever. Billy expected him to jerk away. But he didn't. He let the sheriff help him to the pickup. Together, they laid Honey across the bench seat. Haycock climbed behind the wheel and shifted his wife, so her head rested in his lap.

"I'm so sorry," Billy said.

Haycock searched the sheriff's face. Spire seldom fretted about how he looked. But at that moment, he wished he appeared kinder.

"We been alone, together, for so long," Haycock said, strands of white spittle at the corners of his mouth.

Spire nodded. Haycock started the motor and drove away into the darkness, forgetting to turn on his headlights. Doc whistled through his fingers in warning.

"Let him go, Doc," Billy said. "There's not much traffic. And I don't think he can hear you anyway."

Russ Haycock worked through the night with a pick and round-nosed shovel. By dawn, his wife was six feet in the ground. Some of the kind souls who brought food those last few weeks showed up the next morning to counsel Russ. To help him arrange a church service and proper burial. That they were too late was evidenced by the mound of newly turned dirt a dozen paces from the dilapidated house.

Russ hid in the dark of his basement house, listening to comings and goings as word of her death spread through Stonewall. Half of him wanted to scream at the townspeople, telling them to get away and leave her alone. The other half wanted to fall into their arms and weep. Pulled two ways, he did neither. He sat at the kitchen table with his head in his hands.

And though their willingness to help went uncalled upon, the caring people of Stonewall picked wildflowers from neighboring fields and laid them across her grave in pretty bunches. The visual dissonance was lost on no one. Honey Haycock's tender resting place, from which wreckage stretched out in all directions. Still, they humbly dropped to their knees and sent their prayers after her.

<>

The rectory is dark. It's eight-fifteen in the morning, but who knows how late priests sleep. The sheriff doesn't knock. Instead, he sticks a message in the door asking Father Turney to please call later that day.

83

Spire gets back into the 1500 and heads toward the edge of town. It is cold, in the twenties, though the absence of wind makes it seem warmer. The clouds are thin, the sun is trying to break through. It is about eight-thirty when he arrives at the Haycock place. He's surprised to see Owen Middleton's red Lincoln. The senator is leaning against the rear end facing toward the sun, his eyes closed. Spire grabs his notebook and pen. Gets out of the pickup.

"What are you doing here?"

"Couldn't sleep," Middleton says without moving. Rather than the normal suit and tie, he wears jeans, a hooded parka, and a Jayhawks ballcap. "I figured you'd come here this morning. Thought I'd make myself useful."

"How?" the sheriff asks.

"Don't know." The banker opens his eyes and looks at the ground. "I keep seeing his face."

Billy understands how it is to look upon violent death. He's seen a lot of that over the years. But he remembers how it feels to be traumatized. The urgency to do something. To reestablish control. To put the world back in order.

"Well, since you're here, help me look around," Spire consoles.

"I'd like to," Owen replies, looking relieved. "What for?"

"Anything suspicious. And some funeral clothes."

Spire walks to the basement house's triangular entryway. He runs his fingers over discolored shadows on the doorframe. Shadows of hinges torn off under the weight of a furious young man.

"What is it?" Owen asks.

"Just some old damage," Billy answers.

He turns the brass knob. It is unlocked. Typical Ewing County. He cracks the door open. Downstairs is pitch black. They turn their heads to listen. There is a rhythmic, vaguely musical tapping.

"Sheriff's office!" Spire hollers in his cop's voice. Sharp, resonant, and intimidating.

There is no answer.

Taking a fist-length tactical flashlight off his belt, the sheriff starts slowly down the stairs following the beam. Middleton stays directly behind, his hand lightly on Billy's shoulder, peering over the top of him. At the bottom, Spire feels around for a wall switch. A cheap chandelier lights up. It hangs over the dining room table, which has a basket of clothes at one end and an elegant little sewing machine at the other.

Black cast iron with silver plates and flourishes. A spool of red thread sits on the spindle.

"You'd think she just stepped out of the room," Owen marvels.

"Other than this," Billy notes as he drags his fingers over the tabletop. It is covered with dust.

They walk further into the house, treading as lightly as big men can. There is nobody to sneak up on, theirs is quiet reverence for lives now gone. A pine bookcase is filled with western novels, Reader's Digest Condensed Books, and *The Naked Communist* by W. Cleon Skousen. Pretty stones, seashells, and wooden boxes with painted dragons. A framed black-and-white photograph rests on the top shelf. It shows an Asian family sitting on a bamboo bench. Behind them is a velvet curtain tied with a silk cord.

"That's her, isn't it?" Owen says of a little girl, maybe nine years old with sparkling eyes and a guileless smile.

"Yes," Billy answers. "I think so." In fact, he knows. He recognizes her. Can almost feel her weight in the crook of his arm.

A second black-and-white shows Mrs. Haycock in her late teens. She wears a sleeveless blouse and short shorts. Her legs are slender and flirty. Black eyes peek from beneath the bill of a baseball cap. She holds a catcher's mitt and winces in anticipation of a ball thrown from somewhere off frame. Several GIs laugh in the background.

"And that's Haycock?" Owen asks, pointing at one of the amused GIs. The one laughing hardest.

"It is."

Centered among the photos is a wedding portrait. Large and colorful in a gilt plaster frame. The Haycocks sit on a wooden bench before a rose-colored trellis. The backdrop is pastoral with puffy white clouds. The young bride is exquisite. She wears a golden silk dress highlighted with silver doves. Mrs. Haycock looks shyly off camera, perhaps at the photographer. There is something compliant and sweet about her.

"Isn't she a beauty?" Middleton observes.

"She was."

And though his looks are already beginning to pinch and hollow, Russ is still handsome in his dark suit. Blond hair waxed into a flattop, he stares directly into the camera lens. Affrontive and sure. The opposite of compliant, with a wise-guy smirk.

"What life does to a man," the senator observes, shaking his head.

"Or what he does to himself," Billy replies.

"You ever deal with him?"

"Nah. Not really," Spire lies, not sure whether he's protecting Haycock or himself. "I was called here a couple of times. Whatever he was doing, I told him to stop. And he did."

"That easy?"

"Pretty much."

"Ever talk to her?"

"Not that I can recall," Spire lies once again.

"She used to come to the bank," Middleton muses.

"Did she?"

"Yes. Dad would have his clothes taken in or let out, depending on whether his weight was up or down. Always paid more than she asked."

"Your father was a good man."

"The best."

Spire enters the bedroom. The mattress is covered with a ginkgo-patterned quilt. Next to it stands a chest of drawers with brass pull knobs. He opens a couple of drawers and peeks in. They are full of clothes. All hers. Beneath the bed are milky white plastic boxes filled with shoes, purses, and hats. Smelling sharply of moth balls. Her dresses and sweaters hang in one end of the closet.

"Where is he in all this?" Owen wonders, seeing no sign of Haycock's presence.

"Good question."

At the far end of the basement house they hear the continued musical tapping. They follow that sound into the kitchen. The room shows recent use. The leaky faucet drips steadily into a sink half full of water and dirty dishes. The counters are full of plates, pots, and pans. Some clean, most not. The biting, acrid odor of food gone bad fills the air. A Formica table is stacked with cracker boxes, bread wrappers, jars of peanut butter and jelly. Spire opens the ancient, yellowing refrigerator. Its contents are sparse.

"Circle meat, bread, and beer."

"All the essential food groups," Middleton scoffs.

Past the kitchen is a laundry room. The washer is full of clothes, sour with mildew. The dryer is full of fluffed up jeans, shirts, underwear, and socks. Unwashed clothes are on the floor in full outfits. Lying just where Haycock pulled them off.

"Straight into the washer and out of the dryer," Spire notes. "With no regard for color or fabric."

86

Middleton's first impulse is to tease his friend about his domestic competencies. The way he did his own laundry, Owen's mother used to say that Billy would make some woman a great wife. The banker decides to hold his tongue. There is not much to laugh about in the Spire marriage. But Billy knows his friend enough to anticipate a taunt.

"And yes," the sheriff volunteers. "I still do my own laundry. Hers, too."

The adjacent bathroom is filthy. Greasy stains line the sink and tub. Drain baskets full of matted gray hair, mirror splattered with toothpaste and shaving cream. The toilet missing the tank lid. Every flat surface within reach of the commode is covered with magazines. Hunting, fishing, cheap tools from China.

"Where did he sleep?" Owen asks, looking around.

"Must be out there." Spire points straight up.

"Let's go," Owen sighs. "This is about the saddest place I've ever seen."

Spire has seen sadder.

"Just a minute," he says.

The sheriff roots through the dryer and comes out with a pair of double-knit trousers and a plaid cotton shirt. Owen looks skeptical.

"I'm sure I can find him an old suit to wear."

"There will be no visitation," Spire dismisses. "Who would come?"

"Then why bother at all?"

"What he was wearing went to the KBI lab," Billy explains. "Guess Emma Ace thinks a man ought not be bare-assed naked when he meets his Maker."

"Hard to argue with that," Owen concedes.

They turn off lights, climb the stairs, and close the front door. They don't bother to lock it. This is Ewing County.

Outside, the sun has succeeded in breaking through. The morning has turned bright and beautiful. The two men head to Haycock's shed, weaving along paths through wreckage. Middleton notices something off to one side. He wanders over and bends down.

"Will you look at this," he calls.

A few weeks after his wife died, Russ Haycock covered her grave with a concrete marker embedded with pretty features. A large pink conch shell. Glass stoppers from perfume bottles. Plastic buttons and cheap jewelry. Clip-on earrings and hoop bracelets. In the middle, Haycock spelled her name with plastic buttons. "HONEY," it reads, next to the years of her birth and death. Some of the buttons have popped out, others faded with time. Most remain deep hued and vibrant. Below her name and dates, Russ had written "BELOVED WIFE" in thick copper wire, turned green with oxidation.

"Did you ever see anything so heartbreaking?" Owen asks.

"A person who lives by a graveyard can't be crying at every funeral," Billy tersely responds.

Spire is taken aback by his own cold response. But that's the way it sometimes is with cops. They laugh and snarl at things because it's easier than giving in to the alternatives. In Billy's case, the pain and regret over decades-old violence. Over crushing a delicate woman's dignity, even as her husband lay unconscious and bleeding. Billy wishes he had said something nicer in response to Owen. He wishes he had been more gentle with Honey Haycock that day. But there is no taking back things done and said. So, the sheriff maintains the illusion of imperviousness and keeps walking. Because that's just the way it sometimes is with cops.

Owen kindly slaps dust off the grave marker with his Jayhawks ballcap, then follows.

As they approach the shed door, the sheriff freezes. There are two male voices inside. One with an exaggerated nasal twang, the other less affected.

"Radio?" Owen asks.

"I hate that," Billy mutters.

After so many years in law enforcement, Spire is still unsettled when entering the queer space of unexpected death. He thinks there should be some cosmic power, some mystical force of finality, that brings a person's possessions to the same still quiet as has befallen their owner. But the universe doesn't work that way. So, there he is, time and time again, quieting screaming tea kettles, turning off useless headlights, answering the telephone to inform the caller that, no, their buddy will not be coming to poker tonight. Because he's dead. That's why. It makes Spire feel as if he is an ancillary part of the killing process. An unwilling aide to the Grim Reaper. He steps inside and jerks out the radio's plug.

Looking around, it is apparent why so much of the basement house goes unused. This is where Russ Haycock lived his life.

A small refrigerator hums in the corner. Spire looks out the window. His eyes follow a slight rill under which an extension cord snakes across the yard and into the house. Not exactly code, but a functional source of power. There is a worn and overstuffed red couch with a couple of bricks in place of a missing leg. Woolen army blankets spill onto the floor. A table, made of a large wooden cable spool, is piled with snarls of fishing line and yellowed newspapers. A leaky tube of silicone glue is stuck to a pair of neoprene hip waders.

"Bet this belonged to his daddy," the senator says of a magnifying glass missing its screw-in handle.

A waist-high workbench, running the length of the shed, is covered with electric motors in various stages of disassembly. Underneath are cans of screws, nails, paints, lubricants, and adhesives. At the end is an axe handle embedded in a small bucket of concrete.

"Is that a weapon?" Middleton asks.

"Naw." Spire gestures at a parcel of beer cans residing under the bench. Some flattened. Others waiting. "It's Haycock's contribution to recycling technology."

The vent pipe of a squat iron stove juts up through the roof. Spire squints at scorch marks where the pipe touches wood.

"He's lucky there wasn't a fire."

"It would have been a terrible loss," Middleton observes dryly.

There is no wood for the stove. Only a metal trash can full of torn cardboard, empty boxes, and armloads of apparent junk mail.

"Cheap heat," Owen says.

Spire grunts agreement. He starts to turn away when something catches his eye. He pulls a flyer from the trash can. It reads, "Diversity Is a Code Word for White Genocide." Another asks, "White Man, are you sick and tired of the Jews?"

"This crap," Billy grumbles without thinking. "Thought he stopped a long time ago."

"Wish he had," Owen sighs.

Spire empties the trash can onto the shed's plywood floor. At first, the pile of paper is a blur. But then, like someone searching for arrowheads or hieroglyphics, his eyes begin to discern them everywhere. The three Ks. Swastikas. Crosses and crowns. Coiled rattlesnakes. Swords and the letter W. Mixed in are cheap, hand-stapled pamphlets on modifying weapons. Improvising explosives. Silent killing with a knife to the throat.

Spire picks up a paperback book. *The White Man's Bible*.

Middleton looks at his watch.

"You got to go?"

"Soon."

"Okay," the sheriff says. He considers a few more pieces of hate literature. "I'll have to come back."

He leaves to grab a roll of yellow caution tape out of the Ram. Owen helps him loop it twice around the shed. Sealing it shut. As they walk to their vehicles, Billy Spire realizes something. "Why do you wish he had?" he asks.

"Had what?"

"Stopped a long time ago."

"What are you talking about?" Owen looks perplexed.

"I said 'I thought he stopped this crap a long time ago' and you said 'wish he had.'"

"Am I supposed to be glad one of my constituents is a neo-Nazi?" Owen answers, sounding slightly offended.

"No," Billy answers. "But how did you know he'd been into this crap before?"

"Because that's what you said."

Billy muses. He is not sure.

"I'm going to talk to the county commission about getting you a deputy," Owen hastens to add. "You could use some help."

"I sure could," Spire concedes. "That's a true fact."

<>

Eli Turney is surprised how quickly he begins to get into shape. A slight rise from nothing can seem mountainous. Still, he is making progress and it feels good.

He did it by walking. A few more steps every day. He bought training shoes, cotton tee shirts, and sweatpants so large they had to be ordered in the mail. He set aside time in the early morning and after Mass to put that enormous body into motion. At first it was miserable. Every inch hurt, especially his feet, which pressed flat beneath all that weight. Sometimes he wanted to give up. But he never did. Even on the roughest days, he would groan, cry out for God's mercy, get up and go. First, one lap around the house. Then back and forth to his church office. Eventually, up and down the block.

The neighbors were surprised, even alarmed when they first saw the priest out on the sidewalk. Was something wrong? Could they help?

"Just trying to shed a few," he would assure.

Now his efforts are a matter of neighborhood pride. Residents around the rectory are generous with encouragement. Neighbor ladies shout that he is looking good.

"Does that mean I'm good looking?" he asks with a big smile. The ladies giggle and shoo him off in chaste flirtation. He waves back and keeps moving, but with a little more spring to his step.

After an inter-clergy gathering in Garden City, he popped into a sporting goods store. He tried on many styles of wrap-around sunglasses before finding a pair that fit his pumpkin head. They looked sharp and for the first time in his life, Eli Turney felt a little cool. He threw an extra shooting glove into his shopping cart, along with some wax for his bowstring. The clerk rang him up, then handed the priest an extra package.

"What is that?"

"Hunting points. On the house. We're discontinuing this brand."

"I don't hunt."

"Well, you never know, Father. And we got to clear shelf space."

"I can't pay you anything?"

"We try to stay on the right side of the Lord," the clerk winked.

Father Turney smiled appreciatively, paid for the items, and walked out of the store. He tossed the free package into the glove box of the Fit.

After walking every morning in those fancy new shades, the priest goes into the garage for practice. He is getting better. Some days, even pretty good. His arm strength is increasing. His form and eye improving. In fact, the space is getting a little small for his purposes.

One afternoon, Father Turney has a visitor.

"You've just got to go see them," she exclaims.

She is a concerned lady of the church. That's what Eli calls them. A grim busybody with a heart of gold. She is speaking of an older couple isolated in a farmhouse far from town. Never blessed with children, they are all alone. Good Catholics both, though lapsed in recent years because of his health. His heart is giving out. He struggles to breathe.

"They're so lonely. So helpless. It would do them a world of good," she pleads.

"I'll pay a visit," the priest assures.

"I could drive you."

"Oh, that won't be necessary," Turney replies. "I'm sure I can find the way."

There is nothing deadlier than being trapped in a car with a concerned lady of the church. She has opinions and believes the priest would do well to hear them. She scowls with concentration, trying to figure a means of recovering her captive audience.

"Well," she says with prim sensibility. "They don't really know you. It might be best for me to make an introduction."

"You're too kind," he says. "But I find people talk easier when we're alone. Father Confessor, don't you know."

"Well, if you're sure."

"You're too kind," he repeats, ending the conversation.

The day is bright and mild. Kathleen and Larry Hammerschmidt live in the house where he was born. A two-story limestone with a shingle roof. Father Turney called to let them know he was coming. The elderly couple is sitting on the porch swing when he arrives. Kathleen hurries inside to bring tea and cookies on a metal tray. When the priest starts up the steps, Larry summons every measure of his strength to rise and extend his hand in friendship. Congestive heart failure or not, being country polite is what a man must do.

"Please don't stand on my account," Father Turney insists. The old man starts to totter. Turney hurries up the steps to steady the offered hand. The priest is surprised at his own speed and stamina.

Larry plops down into the swing and starts fiddling with the knob of an oxygen tank.

"Couldn't live without it," he gasps.

Kathleen comes through the door with three teacups and a heaping mound of Fig Newtons.

"How did you know?" the priest ribs her. "Those are my favorite."

"Oh, you're just saying that."

"No, it's true," he swears.

It is a truth made quickly evident. The Newton mound shrinks as crumbs accumulate on Eli's paunch.

The three of them have a lovely chat. Full of seasons and hope, luck and gratitude, faith and comfort. Father Turney tells funny stories about his early days in the church. Larry laughs until he chokes and turns slightly blue and Kathleen has to make Turney stop. The priest calms things down, then takes their hands and prays. Kathleen can feel warm love radiating out of Father Turney's massive paws. Her husband's hands are so dry and cold these days.

After prayer, Larry begins nodding off. The priest taps his watch and Kathleen nods. He stands and places his hand on each of their shoulders. He is as big and robust as they are small and frail. He offers a blessing. Razzle dazzle through the pain. The song and dance of mortality. He helps Kathleen walk her groggy husband inside to his recliner.

"Thank you so much, Father Turney," she says at the door.

She taps her head as if to jar loose a memory. Grabs her purse from the kitchen pantry and starts fumbling around in the pocketbook.

"Please. No," Father Turney insists. "It was my pleasure."

She is a poor woman. Larry's medication is so expensive. But she is also pious and proud. She wishes she had money to give and would give generously if she did. But she does not, and it shames her. She searches his face for forgiveness.

"Those Fig Newtons were offering enough," he comforts.

She smiles faintly, not entirely convinced.

"You know what you could do for me?" he asks. "I try to take a walk every day. Missed it this morning, then ate all those cookies. Would you mind if I wandered around your fields for a while? To enjoy the scenery and burn off some calories?"

"Well, no," she answers with bemusement. Walking around fields is little valued by people who own fields to walk around in. She worries the priest is trying to make her feel better, which has the effect of making her feel worse.

"Really," he insists. "I would love to do that."

"Well," she shrugs. "Help yourself. Just be sure to close the gates."

Eli sets out at a moderate pace. It is a pretty spread. The house is surrounded by Dust Bowl conifers, planted to break the scouring winds. The terrain rolls slightly. The streambed is dampened by a thin trickle. Strands of barbed wire stretch from limestone pillar to limestone pillar. Post rocks they're called. Common to that part of Kansas where, before trees were planted, farms rose out of nothing but stone and hard labor.

The fields are contoured and planted. Larry leases his acreage to neighbor farmers, who sow and reap with gargantuan machines. Modern agriculture is vastly efficient. Productivity is high and for that very reason, commodity prices are low. The Hammerschmidts' share is low if close to nothing. Barely enough to keep them in their own home.

In the fields are enormous rolls of hay, banded with a thin green mesh. Lying on their side, they are six feet high and twelve feet long. Dozens of them, scattered, cattle feed waiting for winter. Eli decides to test his emerging strength. He pushes hard, but even against his great bulk, the roll does not budge. He gives it an admiring pat. "You won this time," he says to himself. He slaps it again and a thought occurs. As dense as a wall of cardboard, the hay roll is a perfect archery target.

Turney knocks on the door. Kathleen appears. She looks anxious, perhaps he wants money after all.

"What a beautiful place you have."

She nods, fretfully. There really isn't any money in her pocketbook. None that she can spare. She made a show of getting her purse in hopes that he would do exactly what he did. Let her off the hook.

"I'd like to come back. Maybe this time next week. Check in on you and Larry. Go for a walk. Enjoy the beauty of this place."

"Well sure," she answers. Almost faint with relief, she reaches out and touches his arm. "You're always welcome."

Father Turney waves as he gets into his little Honda Fit.

"Ever seen a clam bigger than its shell?" he asks brightly.

<>

That same time the next week, Eli Turney arrives at the Hammerschmidts' with a battered cardboard guitar case in his car. It is the only thing he could find to hold his bow and arrows. Again, he talks and prays until Larry's eyelids get heavy.

"Well," he says, pushing back from tea, toast, and jam. "I have a sermon to compose. Mind if I take another walk? A little fresh air?"

"Oh no, Father," Kathleen replies. "Take all the time you want. It's a comfort having you near."

Eli removes the guitar case from the Fit. He puts on the wraparound sunglasses and starts walking. When he gets to the hay bales, he opens the case and assembles his bow. There are eight arrows in the quiver clipped to his belt. He uses golf tees to pin plastic coffee cup lids onto a hay roll. He steps off thirty paces and scrapes a line in the dirt.

The first arrow hits six inches left of the target. Eli smiles. Pretty good for this distance. His second shot overcorrects to the right. Soon, the hay bale bristles with seven arrows. All misses, but close. The eighth arrow flies true. There is a satisfying slap when the field point drives through the plastic lid. Eli beams and looks around, as if others might be admiring his marksmanship. Approaching the bale, he grips with a bit of rubber matting to tug the arrows free. Then he goes back to the line in the dirt.

Second round. The bow is up, string nearly at the corner of his mouth when there is a sound. A scuttling behind the hay roll. Father Turney lowers and listens. A thin raccoon drags itself around the side. Wobbling on its feet and frothing at the mouth. Obviously very sick.

He shouts to scare it away. But the poor creature is beyond hearing, beyond fear. Lost in suffering, it rocks up on its back legs and paws at the air, as if trying to scratch death from the sky. Its eyes are dim and weepy.

Turney stops yelling and examines the landscape. He imagines all kinds of predators out there. Coyotes, foxes, and owls. Waiting to attack. To tear and torture and toss, playful as a puppy with a squeak toy. Joyful in ripping the helpless raccoon to pieces.

"Where is mercy?" Eli asks. The animal falls over. It struggles back to its feet and stands panting. Just then, the priest seems to notice the bow in his own hands.

"Who will put that poor thing out of its misery?" he asks.

He strings an arrow and pulls slowly. Sighting along the shaft at the center of the raccoon's chest.

"Aim small, hit small," he repeats, then releases.

The arrow drives straight through the animal's breast, knocking it to the ground. Eli lowers the bow and watches intensely. The raccoon bucks and growls, trying to work the arrow free. But it is well set and within seconds some major artery or organ is compromised. The raccoon falls, gasping for air and held at a grotesque angle by the projection from its chest. There is blood at the mouth. Then it stops.

"Jesus," Eli says. Once again, he looks around as if others are watching. But this time, he is filled with guilt rather than pride.

The priest walks up and nudges the animal's leg with his toe. It's dead. He grabs the arrow near the fletches and pulls it out. The bright metal surface is tinged with red. He wipes it off against the hay bale, then grabs the raccoon by its tail and flings it into a nearby stand of trees. The crows and coyotes will make short work of what they find. But the suffering is over.

He returns the bow and arrows to the guitar case and walks back to the car. As he climbs into the Fit, he sees Kathleen step out onto the porch.

"Father, will you play us a song sometime?"

"Huh?"

She points at the guitar case.

"Oh this?" he responds. What would Kathleen Hammerschmidt think of a fat priest acting like Robin Hood? It wouldn't comport with the image of gravity and grace. It's a priest's job to affirm, not unsettle. So, he offers what she needs, which is different from the truth.

"I use it to carry a snack," he says, patting the guitar case. "Jacket, pencil, paper, and some Bible passages."

"I've got an old valise you could use," she says of his peculiar baggage.

"No, no," Eli answers. "This works fine."

"Well, okay." She laughs, waves, and goes back inside.

As he slowly drives away, Eli watches Kathleen through her kitchen window. She is taking things down from the pantry. Getting ready to cook dinner.

"Forgive me," he says softly. "It was an act of compassion."

Confessing makes Eli Turney feel better. Even if killing a suffering animal is an act of mercy.

<>

It was two months later, the morning after Russ Haycock was found, that Eli Turney woke to find a note on his front door. It said, "Please call Sheriff Spire."

He called the courthouse. Because Billy was still at the Haycock place, the priest was given the home phone number of Emma Ace.

Small towns are like any other social structure, only more so. A few people do most of the heavy lifting. Emma Ace, Leo's wife, is one of those lifters. She is a buxom woman with a strong voice and irrepressible spirit. A locomotive in a floral dress. She volunteered to make a funeral for Russ Haycock.

As disliked as the man may have been, Emma was determined that he should have a good Christian burial. Probably better than he deserved. But what is the purpose of Christianity except to forgive and show the way to those who need forgiveness. She called out orders and Stonewall stirred to action. The Rotary Club paid for a coffin. The embalmer worked at a deep discount, and the Ladies Benevolence Society covered the balance. Old Mr. Morris, Honey's first tailoring customer, drove to the Walmart in Liberal for cut flowers. Father Turney assured Emma that he would be pleased to conduct the service, free of cost and open to her suggestions.

The few Haycock family members who could be located showed no interest in attending. Most were surprised that Russ had still been alive. Not that they cared, one way or the other. With no travelers to wait on, the funeral was scheduled just three days after the body was found. A graveside affair at the Haycock place, where he would be buried next to his wife.

Day of the funeral, Billy Spire watches a bright sun rise in the east. It will be a beautiful morning, one of the few blessings ever associated with the Haycock name. Spire wears his full-dress uniform, badge patches on the shoulders and mirror-polished Sam Browne duty belt. He lovingly picks lint off the pearl-gray campaign Stetson, worn only on formal occasions.

The night before, Billy screwed up his courage and asked Nadine to accompany him. It was one of those times, he said, when her absence would be noticed and tongues would wag. With an election coming next year, it would sure help if she went along.

"I don't ask that much of you," he rested his case.

She'd been drinking, of course. There was a long pause. Spire braced for a blast of temper, but she simply said "okay" and went back to the find-a-word puzzle in her magazine.

Billy is still admiring the rising sun when she comes out of the bathroom.

Nadine's appearance almost puts the sun to shame. Despite so much neglect, so much smoking and alcohol, she is still a very pretty woman when she wants to be. She knows how to apply makeup. How to mask the delicate web of broken blood vessels across her cheeks and the bridge of her nose. She uses moisturizer like a sorceress, rubbing away wrinkles at the corners of her mouth and between her brows. Wrinkles that come from scowling. Dark eye shadow brings out the luminescence of her green eyes. Her black, shoulder-length hair is even more compelling with wisps of gray. She piles it on top of her head and pins it in place with an ebony comb.

Because it is the darkest and therefore most funereal outfit she owns, Nadine wears a fitted charcoal pantsuit. It features a gambling motif. A full house of queens and deuces fan over one breast. Oversized dice tumble across her ribs. A red-and-black roulette wheel spins at the small of her back. She brushes past Billy and stands before the hall mirror, taking a long thoughtful look before going outside. She squints though cigarette smoke.

"Don't you look pretty?" Spire gushes.

"I'm a goddamn mess," she snaps. "Don't know why I let you talk me into this."

She grabs her coat and purse, slams the screen door behind her. Billy takes his turn at the mirror. Puts on the Stetson, adjusts it just so.

"You look nice, too, Billy," he says to himself. "Given what you got to work with."

They ride to the Haycock place in silence, save the unintelligible squawking of Spire's police radio. Nadine cracks the pickup's window to vent her cigarette. Her hands tremble as they flutter between the smoke at her lips and a refugee strand of hair she keeps pushing back into place. Billy would like to touch her arm and comfort her. But he knows that would only make things worse. Upon arriving, they find more than twenty cars already there.

"Good turnout," he observes, shutting off the engine.

"Everybody loves a freak show," she answers.

"No. They're just trying to be decent."

"And what does that make me?"

Spire is not sure what Nadine is asking. Is she the freak on display? Or does she lack decency? Nothing good can come from clarification, so he doesn't try. Such is life on pins and needles. He goes around and opens her door. Together they join a slow procession toward the grave. Billy returns many hellos. Nadine smiles tightly when told how nice it is to see her. Her fingers anxiously dig into her husband's arm.

Using equipment borrowed from Ewing County Public Works, Ace has skimmed the Haycock property free of clutter. It's all in the dump now, being picked over by rodents and birds. Only Haycock's shed still stands. Cordoned off with yellow tape until the sheriff can complete his examination of hate literature.

The mood is semi-somber. It would be far more solemn were the deceased a community pillar. But this was Russ Haycock. People talk out loud, even within earshot of his casket. They are careless about disturbing his slumber. Twenty-four folding chairs face the grave in four rows of six. The front row seats carry paper tent cards marked "RESERVED." Spire wonders for whom.

The grave is a neat rectangle cut deep in the ground. Haycock's casket sits on a wheeled conveyance, which, in turns, rests on an AstroTurf mat. It is an aluminum box with molded corners, metal rails, and thick orange straps at each corner that serve as handholds to lower the coffin. The mound of displaced dirt is almost black with fertility. Best soil in the world, Ewing County likes to boast. A pair of long-handled shovels are stuck into the mound. Each is shiny new and adorned with a black ribbon.

Beyond Russ's grave lies that of his wife. Mr. Morris has adorned her marker with the prettiest bouquet from Walmart. Mourners wander over in twos and threes to look. They marvel at the curiosity of it. Her name in buttons. Russ Haycock's love professed in copper wire. Some onlookers are amused, even charmed. Others disapprove, clucking that the bastard was too cheap to buy her better. All shake their heads at the tragedy of Honey Haycock. A beautiful girl, tiny and perfect, who could have done so much better.

"Billy and Nadine, you're in the front row."

"I'm not so sure," the sheriff begins as he turns to face Emma Ace. Nadine isn't going to like this.

"Well, I am," the forceful woman snorts. "The man had no family. You three found him. That's got to count for something. Now sit."

Because arguing would only cause a bigger scene, the sheriff does what he's told.

"It will be okay," he promises Nadine.

He realizes that this is a terror for her. Now she's up front. Where everyone can stare at her. Study the famous alky. He looks down. Her hands are shaking. He hears an electric edge to her breathing.

"Take a good look, everybody," she mutters. "Pity the poor sheriff. Married to a drunk."

"No," he whispers. Absent any other straws to grasp, Billy Spire falls back on the old hope that beauty can come to its own rescue. "You look nice."

Father Turney emerges from behind Haycock's shed. He slowly ambles up to the wooden podium brought from church. He is dramatically still and quiet, arranging his notes and doing one last mental run through of the words and intonations. The song and dance of passage. The razzamatazz of pain and meaning. He looks up and sees the sheriff is not alone. He has heard of Nadine, and about Nadine, but he has never lain eyes upon her. Her face is rigid with tension. He smiles, trying to radiate welcoming warmth. She looks back, but her expression does not change. He notices fearful tremors in her cheeks.

Owen and LeeAnn Middleton pull themselves away from old friends talking politics. They take chairs next to the Spires. LeeAnn reaches over to pat Nadine's hand.

"How you doin', sugar?" she asks in her sweetest voice.

"I'm doing. Just doing."

"Bless your heart," LeeAnn encourages.

Two men walk out from behind Haycock's shed. The older is wearing an Army uniform. The younger is dressed as a crossing guard and carries an American flag on a wooden pole. Haycock was a veteran, deserving of all the military honors Stonewall could muster on short notice. The older has an accordion braced across his chest. He teaches music at the high school. Looks like Tennessee Ernie Ford in his middle years, with a high forehead and little brush mustache. He squeezes a couple of sad minor chords and the crowd knows to stand.

"'The Battle Hymn of the Republic,' in honor of this fallen soldier," is his invitation to sing along.

The music teacher's booming baritone mixes with the voices of old women and men. They have sung this hymn so many times that they have worn smooth the rough edges and arrived at subtle harmonies. Spire thinks it is just about the loveliest thing he has ever heard.

Emma Ace stands next to the front row, hip against her husband's shoulder. She is unabashed in her caretaking, craning left and right to make sure all is in order. The second row is filled with old ladies cocking their heads to find the proper alignment of their trifocals. Every slight gust ruffles their blue-tinged, downy hair. When the song ends, Emma leans across Ace and whispers to LeeAnn and Nadine.

"Don't they look just like baby birds?" A naturally loud woman, her whisper is as light as an air raid siren.

"You know, Emma, we can hear you," one old lady sniffs.

"Well, that's exactly what you look like," Emma whines. "It's just the cutest thing."

Nadine stares straight ahead, frozen in the kind of fear that can be mistaken for aloofness. Another old lady nods at her, then raises her nose in a school-girl pantomime of snootiness.

"Who is that?" Emma asks about a car coming up the road. She scuttles off to find out.

Kathleen and Larry Hammerschmidt knew Russ Haycock only slightly, but they are inspired by the priest's ongoing attention. He's like kin now. Visiting weekly, holding hands in prayer, walking around their farm for its beauty and inspiration. And so, on this day they decide to display their loyalty by attending the funeral at which he officiates. Because it will be an outdoor ceremony, no offering plate will be passed and Larry can wait in the car, if need be. They are running late because this is not a good day for Larry. He woke up to labored breathing, which worsened when he put on his dress suit. It was thick with mold after years in the closet. He should have stayed home. But insisted on accompanying Kathleen and showing support for Father Turney. It is what a man must do. But doing it took longer than planned, so they arrive late.

"You go on," Larry wheezes to Kathleen, as she parks their old sedan. "We come this far, be sure Father sees we're here."

"Fine. I'll be back as soon as I can."

"Leave it run, so I can have some heat."

Kathleen walks away from the idling sedan, steadied by an arm of the solicitous Mrs. Ace.

Father Turney clears his throat. It will be an odd service. A hodge-podge of Protestantism and Catholicism, reflecting the ecumenical tastes of Emma Ace. She is not particularly religious but loves ceremony. Eli finds the situation amusing and somewhat liberating. A chance to be looser with the form and liturgy. Not something the bishop would condone, but accommodations must be made in little towns.

"Russell Andrew Haycock," he roars. His voice powerful enough to be heard by the next county, the deaf, and the dead. Nadine almost jumps out of her skin.

"No emphysema there," diagnoses Doc Howard.

The priest offers a solid eulogy. One that everyone could admire but no one would remember. He makes a drawn-out analogy of Haycock and a lowly sparrow. Fixed in God's eye despite its drab and luckless life. Then he pivots, without bothering to connect dots, to the familiar conclusion that every death signals the need for course correction among the living. That brevity of time and glory of God impel us to live more fully and love more deeply. Pop, fizz, spin, and move on. The priest nods at the music teacher, who fingers his accordion and prompts keywords to the coming hymn.

"I sing because I'm happy. I sing because I'm free." This song is not familiar to the faithful of Ewing County. They struggle with the melody but forge on as best they can. The crossing guard sings all the louder to offset their timidity. He has a wonderful voice, high and clear and free. After it is done, Father Turney studies the group for a moment and decides something more is needed.

"Would anyone be willing to say a word about Russ Haycock?" he asks.

It is an unimaginable question and catches everyone off guard. Every person in attendance looks down at their feet. The if-you-can't-say-something-nice silence drags on and on. Father Turney feels his face turning red, but not in embarrassment. He's been in this business far too long to be flustered by an awkward moment or two. His face grows crimson in annoyance at a community that cannot think of a single kind thing to say about someone who dwelled among them for decades. The priest will not have it.

He rakes his eyes across the front row. Ace, the Middletons, the Spires.

"I wonder if each of you would offer something, just a word or two, to help us commemorate this man."

It's more than Nadine can bear. She is on her feet and moving. The entire funeral party watches, their eyes and mouths wide open. Staring straight ahead, she tears out the ebony comb and throws it to the ground.

Hair spills down her shoulders as she makes a beeline to the sheriff's pickup. Finding it locked, she turns her back on the whole community and leans against the tailgate. She fishes a cigarette from her purse, lights it, and fills her lungs.

The priest clears his throat and forges ahead.

"Perhaps you might start, Senator Middleton."

Owen compliantly rises. He turns around to be heard.

"I didn't know Mr. Haycock very well," he booms. "But as someone once said, home is where you're part of it and it's part of you. Ewing County is our home and we love it. We may have a character or two. Every town does. But each one becomes part of who we are, what we are, and the love we feel for each other. May he rest in peace."

The crowd is impressed. A campaign speech right off the top of Middleton's head. Father Turney can scarcely keep from rolling his eyes.

"You, dear?" the priest asks Owen's wife.

Owen sits as LeeAnn rises.

"I believe that God has a plan for every one of us," she says with a chipper lilt to her voice. "I didn't know Mr. Haycock either. But I am sure he was a good Christian and that he's gone on to a better place." Some in the crowd wince with skepticism.

"You, sir?"

Leo Ace is a big talker in his shop, surrounded by pals. But this is an actual audience, and they're really listening. He nervously rubs a palm over his lacquered hair. Looking at the grease left on his hand, he is inspired.

"You can tell a lot about a man by his vehicle," he drawls. Several people in the back yell for him to speak up. So, he stands and hollers. "That old truck of his. How Russ Haycock kept it running, I don't know. But he did. And in my book that says something good about a man."

He sits down. The crowd is stunned.

"At least that's something real," Father Turney mutters to himself.

A baby bird sitting in the second row leans forward to Ace's ear. "Leo, if anyone asks you to speak at my funeral. Please don't."

Those nearby snicker. Farther back, they wonder what was so funny.

"And you, sheriff?"

Billy stands and looks at the crowd. He scans the faces of the community. The Rotary Club and Ladies Benevolence Society. Meals on Wheels. Effie and a few enduring main street businesses. The couple who own the farm where the hand was found. And way in the back is an unanticipated, towering presence. Ayesha Perez's shoulders seem even squarer and stronger amid so many stooped with age. His eyes meet hers. He nods his head ever so slightly, in courtly acknowledgment. She responds in kind. Even farther back, hidden behind the pickup, is Nadine. He can see only the crown of her head. Black hair with silver strands. Enveloped in exhalations of smoke.

"Sheriff?" the priest repeats.

Billy starts. "I didn't know him too well. I did have a few encounters with Mr. Haycock over the years. They weren't all good."

"All as in none," one of the old ladies interjects.

"He pitched in the night the cattle died," the sheriff points out. Heads nod. None can deny that he was there. That he pitched in. Billy goes on. "And to tell the truth, there were times when I wasn't much better than him."

The crowd wonders what this means. But it remains a secret between Billy Spire and Matthew Middleton.

"He had different sides, like anyone else I suppose. But I can tell you this. Russ Haycock loved his wife."

Eyes shift to her grave marker and the pretty Walmart bouquet.

"And as far as possible for such a man, he was devoted to her. He wasn't a big success, I'll give you that. But maybe loving her was enough. Who am I to say?"

The crowd is silent and thoughtful. A few heads shake in doubt.

With the windows up and engine idling, Larry Hammerschmidt can hear nothing of the service. But he is happy watching Nadine Spire, who leans against the pickup tailgate a few feet away. She is a female, so Larry leans sideways for a better look. His oxygen hose snags on the gearshift lever, the cannula yanks from his nose. It falls on the floorboard. When he reaches down for it, his body follows his eyes and within seconds he is pinned beneath the dashboard. Bent so he cannot breathe and is fading fast. In panic, he grabs for the car horn. The sound is explosive, loud, and sharp. And right next to Nadine Spire's ears.

The sheriff's wife screams. Not like a human woman, but like a trapped animal. She grabs the sides of her face and slides down into a sitting position. Emma Ace takes off running, holding the hem of her skirt above thick calves. She throws open the car door, pulls Larry up into his seat and reattaches his oxygen line. Then she lifts Nadine up from the ground and cradles her like a child.

"For a big gal with such tiny feet," Ace observes, "my wife can really move."

LeeAnn hurries over and, with Emma's help, bundles Nadine into Owen's red Lincoln. Hopping in herself, she looks over her shoulder and backs the big car onto the road.

"Don't you just hate funerals?" she says in sympathy.

Nadine does not respond. She is stiff with humiliation and stares wordlessly out the windshield. A few silent miles down the road, LeeAnn pops a CD into the player. Hyper-produced country pop.

"I like to sing along," she says to no one, then joins in.

LeeAnn's voice is soft and pleasant. She sang to her children as babies. It comforted them in a way that never wore off, even when they were teenagers. She hopes the same now. She knows Nadine used to sing and prays that music will set a spark in her. Bring out the voice she used to have. But what works for children offers no solace to the sheriff's wife. After a few minutes, LeeAnn gives up trying and turns the music off. When they arrive at her house, Mrs. Spire opens the car door but remains seated.

"I don't know why I let him do that to me," she says, staring straight ahead. A pause extends, as if there are more words to come. But they never do. Finally, Nadine swings her legs out of the car and walks to the porch.

LeeAnn watches Nadine enter the front door. Through the kitchen window, she sees her grab a tall glass from the cabinet, fill it with straight vodka, and take a deep swallow. The woman's shoulders relax. She stares at something a thousand miles away and takes another swig. LeeAnn checks the dashboard clock as she starts to pull away. It is 10:27 in the morning.

Back at the funeral, Kathleen starts the sedan and off they go. Larry smiles wanly and gives thumbs up to the watching, worrying crowd. His wife waits until they are out of sight to scold him for making such a scene.

"I don't know how Father will ever forgive us," Kathleen despairs.

"He has to," her husband cranks. "He's a priest."

When order is restored, the funeral continues. Father Turney breaks the tension with a few funny remarks, then offers a benediction. Everyone says "Amen." He signals the front row, to the men that remain. Come forward and help lower the coffin.

Ace, Owen, and Billy each take hold of an orange tow strap. But there are four straps, and only three of them. Billy somehow finds this bitterly appropriate. Russ Haycock cannot do anything right, even in death. Father Turney rolls back the sleeves of his robe. He has new strength to demonstrate. Just then, a tall person emerges from the crowd.

"I was there, too," Ayesha Perez announces.

Owen, Ace, and Billy nod, as if to confirm that she was present. She grabs the last strap and braces her feet. Billy is grateful for her help. Father Turney rolls his sleeves back down in disappointment. They lower the coffin, slowly and carefully. From sunlight into deep shade. When it touches bottom, they remove the tow straps and stand back.

"We commend his soul to God," Father Turney concludes.

He takes hold of a black-ribboned shovel, steps on the shoulder, and fills the blade. He is pleased at how light the load feels in his hands. He pauses dramatically—timing is the essence of song and dance—then tosses clods onto the aluminum casket. They land with dull finality. Dust to dust.

The mourners form a line. These are sturdy people with calloused hands and spadework in their blood. They have mucked out stables, planted gardens, and cut irrigation ditches. Dug water wells by hand, two hundred feet deep. They are not dainty in their turns. After two cycles, the grave is full. Russ Haycock is buried. The citizens of Ewing County slowly meander back to their vehicles.

"I'm glad you came," Spire says to Ayesha. "Not a lot of people ever bothered with Russ Haycock."

"I somehow feel invested in the guy," she shrugs.

They walk.

"You around the next few days? I'll need to get a statement."

"I have to go to Topeka. Call me next week."

"Will do," he answers.

Because LeeAnn took the Lincoln, Spire drives Owen home in the 1500. They make idle conversation about who was at the funeral and how they looked. They laugh at the old ladies and the flying Emma Ace. Then Owen gets serious.

"Is Nadine going to be okay?"

"I hope."

"She's not getting any better, is she?"

"No. Not better. But not much worse, either."

"If you say so."

"What else am I going to say?"

Billy is relieved to have arrived at Middleton's driveway.

"What's happening at the Statehouse?"

"Interim committee and some sort of cowboy exhibit."

"Sounds fun."

Owen blows out a puff of air to signal insignificance and boredom. But

Billy knows better. His friend is defined by being senator. Loves Topeka and the machinations of state government.

"LeeAnn going?" It's a rhetorical question. LeeAnn had not been to the State Capitol in years.

"Nah. That stuff bores her to tears. If she's sitting in a car for four hours, it will be headed west. To Denver. Friends and shopping."

Billy nods slowly, as if taking in new information.

"How long you gone for?"

"Maybe a few days."

"Safe travels."

Owen Middleton gets out of the pickup. Without looking back, he waves goodbye over his right shoulder.

Billy waves back, knowing that his gesture will not be seen. His affection need not be acknowledged to be certain. He and Owen are bound by time, proximity, and common experience. When that overloaded station wagon abandoned Stonewall, the derelict trailer, and an oldest son, Billy lost his kin. It was his great fortune to be adopted into the Middleton clan, to have that bond with Owen. The two are grown men now, serious in their bearing and responsibilities. Elected officials, they share public service and the higher calling of Matthew Middleton. They are brothers in legacy and aspiration. Brothers in their understanding of and respect for each other. Brothers in everything but blood. Brothers.

Billy starts the pickup and heads home. To gather the pieces of his wife.

Part 2

‹›

THE MORNING AFTER the funeral, Owen Middleton rises before dawn. He shaves, showers, and eats a bowl of cereal while watching morning news. He slips into the bedroom to kiss LeeAnn goodbye. She stirs.

"When are you coming home?"

"Tuesday, I hope."

"Be good," she murmurs, then rolls over and falls back to sleep.

It's a blustery morning. Naked trees shudder and dry gusts of snow skitter across the pavement. The town is just waking up. Lights glow in kitchen windows. Farmers and other early risers drive slowly down dark streets, easing their way to biscuits and gravy at Effie's. They wave at Owen by lifting their index finger from the steering wheel. The senator stops at Gas-N-Go, Stonewall's sole remaining convenience store. He tops off the tank and heads inside for coffee and donuts. Road food for the four-hour drive to Topeka.

"Becca, what are you still doing here?" he brays to the clerk, a young woman with bad skin and a radiant smile. Owen is one of those unbearably cheery people who are especially loud in the morning.

"Where else am I supposed to be?"

"Over in Colby. At JuCo."

"I ain't that smart." She rings up Owen's purchases.

"You don't even know how smart you are."

"I know how smart I'm not. Got the grades to prove it."

"You don't know how to study is all." He takes out his money clip and peels off a couple of bills. "I've been around plenty of intelligent people. So believe me when I say it. You're more than smart enough."

"Smart enough to have a baby at sixteen."

"They got childcare at JuCo. You owe it to that baby to do better."

"It's cold out there." She looks out the frosty windows.

"Don't try to change the subject."

Owen leaves his change on the counter. As she watches him go out the door, Becca sweeps the tip money into her apron and begins to wonder. Childcare at JuCo. Things are hard for a single mom. Still, she has a long life ahead and plenty to dream about.

Back in the Lincoln, Owen makes a slight detour. Topeka is northeast, but he crosses the highway south to McQuitty's Feedlot. It is abandoned now, a ghost town of cattle pens. Dozens of them, each railed by steel pipe. At the center of the property stands a cluster of neglected structures. An office, equipment barn, garage, and a trio of grain siloes connected by rusting chutes and augers.

Middleton sighs at the emptiness. The doors and windows pried open by vagrants seeking warmth. The plastic bags and blue newspaper wrappers caught on the fences. He recalls a time when the feedlot pulsed. Fifty-thousand head and all the people those cattle required. Stonewall prospered in those days. Back when old Duane ran the place.

So much lost in the few years since his death, Middleton laments. Kansas wind and weather are cruel to untended things.

Middleton stops in front of the old office, the only building with any remaining integrity. The door is secured with a padlock and chain. The windows, inlaid with chicken wire, are cracked but still hold.

The senator gets out of the Lincoln and looks around to make sure he's alone. He pulls his coat tight and paces back and forth across the gravel parking lot. Bending low. Searching for footprints, tire tracks, or drag marks. The wind has erased whatever might have been. He goes to the exact spot and detects faint stains, maybe grease and maybe blood.

But unless a person knew exactly where to look and what to look for, any tell-tale signs are beyond discernment. What has happened is now a secret of time.

He climbs back into the Lincoln and swings a wide turn. Heading for the highway and State Capitol.

<>

The cigarettes he chain-smoked left yellow stains on Duane McQuitty's fingers and cancer in his lungs. It was a lingering death. But he never complained. In fact, he spent his last hours saying how lucky he was. Lucky in business. Lucky for the love of his life, his wife, Betsy, who had passed a few years earlier. Lucky to have so many good friends. Those friends felt lucky, too. They came to see him every day. They told stories that made him howl in amusement, face red with pain, thin arms hugging his own chest as if to keep it from tearing open.

When the disease made its final turn toward death, he grew quiet and withdrew to a distant place. He smiled vacantly and sang hymns right up until the end. The people of Ewing County were sure sorry to see him go. Worried, too, about the fate of the feedlot and the people it employed. The focus of anxieties was Duane's sole heir, Melvin.

Melvin McQuitty is a tall man, six-foot-six, who gilds that lily with cowboy boots on two-inch heels. He wears a mullet as tribute to the hair bands of his youth. Business in the front, party in the back. His face is long and thin with a prominent nose and thick lips. He is striking in appearance, but not handsome. At least not to anyone but himself.

"Wish I could buy that man for what he's worth and sell him for what he thinks he's worth," once said a waitress, to whom he gave a toothy smile but no tip. He thought he was being generous.

Melvin has never been known for the quality of his decisions. He is a gambler more than an investor. A being of impulse rather than consideration. He takes risks in the easy way of one with family money. In his desire to take a big allowance and make it bigger, he went heavy into a collagen scientist full of brio and fraudulent claims. He invested in a dish-antennae start up, unaware that better technologies were already being marketed. He sponsored an expedition for a buried steamboat and came up with nothing but mud. When the money was gone, Melvin always went to Duane for more. And Duane always came through. He was powerless to say no. The good people of Ewing County watched and shook their heads.

When the old man died, he left his cash to the community fund and the feedlot to his son. Melvin would have to work for his money. Still, it was a good gig. McQuitty's had reliable annual profit of one hundred thousand dollars. But Melvin figured he could bump one into two by firing the experienced staff and replacing them with a cheaper crew. They were cheap for good reason. They didn't know what they were doing.

Cattle eat silage and leave waste. Lots of it. Mountains of it. Heavy and malodorous. Managed properly, the waste is collected in plastic-lined lagoons, dried and used to fertilize fields. That's how it's supposed to work, in accordance with common sense and environmental regulations. But an operator must stay on top of things. Getting behind at a feedlot is a dangerous game. Melvin McQuitty had little appreciation for either danger or good housekeeping. He siphoned money for personal use at the expense of the caretaking. For weeks then months.

One spring day a heavy rain came, as it does every spring. The pens, deep in excess muck, got sloppy. Cattle sank in their own waste. Some wallowed so deep they had to be lifted with a backhoe and chain. A few died in the process. At a cost of about fifteen hundred dollars per. Melvin was unaffected by the suffering of animals, but financial losses got his attention. So, he stomped into the downpour, climbed on a front loader, and went to work.

"Get out of the way!" he screamed as the crew shuffled cattle and carcasses.

Desperate to give the livestock a place to stand, he started scooping manure out to the plastic-lined lagoon, which, having not been properly emptied, was way past full. With more muck to move and no place to move it, Melvin knocked down the fence and pushed a wall of crap about twenty yards onto the neighbor's land. There was a cracking sound. The front loader tipped perilously. Melvin jumped off and ran.

Abandoned hand-dug wells are common across western Kansas. Testimony to the value of water. Some thirsty settler went out one day with a pick and shovel, guided by need and a dousing stick. Down through flint and substrata. In some layers, the earth is stable. In others, it is sandy and likely to cave. Then, crude wooden braces are lowered and pounded into place. Down into the darkness. As much as two hundred feet. From the bottom of a deep well, a man can see stars, even in the middle of the day. The Kansas motto, "Ad Astra per Aspera, to the stars through difficulties," was never truer than when digging a well. When old gave way to new, the historic wells were covered and, often, forgotten. The abandoned well that Melvin McQuitty broke through was one hundred eighty feet deep, ten in diameter, a hundred twenty years old.

The front loader idled at an angle, headlights shining up into the rain. When it stopped settling, McQuitty gingerly climbed back on and used the bucket and wheels to wiggle free. That's when the damage was done. Removing the dozer blade was like pulling a knife from a wound. Manure poured into the opening. Straight down walls scarred by ancient shovels, through rotting wooden curbs, into the dark aquifer at its bottom.

Melvin had his crew tear up an old wooden shed and cover the hole with siding. He mounded dirt and manure over the top. By daylight, there was nothing left to see, other than a mountain of crap in the field. Which pleased the neighboring landowner not at all.

"Better to ask forgiveness than permission," Melvin exclaimed brightly, hoping spunk and a toothy smile would win the day.

"You may be right," the neighbor grunted. "But most people wouldn't be jackass enough to say it. Just clean this mess up."

"I owe you for this big time."

"Just clean it up."

Melvin grabbed the neighbor's hand and shook it. Neither was aware that one hundred eighty feet below, trouble was forming. In the shape of a plume.

It was soon evident that something was wrong. Stonewall water taps began delivering a disagreeable product. Amber, with an earthy smell. Calls were made, officials descended. Geologists triangulated to the neighboring property. Its owner whistled softly when a caravan of state vehicles pulled up in front of the house. His nervous wife poured coffee as scientists explained the situation and asked if there was anything the neighbor might tell them.

"Melvin McQuitty did make quite a mess out there," he drawled. "By the old abandoned well."

His wife gasped. This was news to her. About a neighbor for whom she had little respect and even less fondness. Her too-lenient husband would get an earful after the others left.

A public meeting was held, complete with maps showing sources and migration. In their curiously objective manner, state scientists did not mention any names. But everyone could follow the directional arrows straight to McQuitty's Feedlot.

Melvin was at that meeting, too. He raised all kinds of absurd possibilities and demanded expensive, time-consuming tests to prove the contamination source. He asked about cleanup funding and implied that the state should pay, since it didn't prevent the pollution in the first place. The townspeople said little. But their faces wore volumes. They were flat out of patience. Stonewall wanted its water back.

Field staff from the Kansas Department of Environment cleaned up the mess. They poured chlorine down the well to kill cattle-borne pathogens, then sealed the opening with a concrete plug. They pumped nearby irrigation wells to divert the expanding plume from city intakes. Farmers cursed at all that water spilling uselessly into road ditches and tailwater pits. Eventually, the taps flowed clean and life went back to normal. The department packed up and went away.

Then it sent Melvin McQuitty a bill. Seventy-five thousand dollars, including remediation costs and penalties. Melvin was outraged. How was it his fault there was an abandoned well? If he was footing the bill, why wasn't he consulted about the cleanup? He could have done it much cheaper. Furious, Melvin called Owen Middleton.

LeeAnn was at the kitchen table, working a crossword, when the phone rang. She listened long enough to recognize the voice, then handed the phone to her husband.

"For you," she said, rolling her eyes.

"I'm sorry, Melvin, but there's not much I can do," the senator kept repeating. It was a lie, of course. He could do plenty if he wanted to. "You might try the Association or Bureau. Good luck."

When he got off the line, LeeAnn looked up from her puzzle.

"Good luck? You wished that fool good luck?"

The senator shrugged. Owen Middleton is a smart politician, and smart politicians are never needlessly rude. Even the worst pest might one day prove useful.

McQuitty followed Owen's advice and called the Farm Association and Livestock Bureau, lobbying agencies in Topeka. When he threw out Middleton's name, they agreed to meet at his earliest convenience. He said that afternoon, jumped in his car, and burned up the highway.

Cautious men in expensive suits, the lobbyists used Melvin's four-hour travel time to assess the situation. They called Owen Middleton, who listened and offered noncommittal answers. He didn't know who was right or wrong but thought the department did a pretty good job fixing the water. He guessed Melvin was a "decent enough fellow most of the time." The lobbyists recognized faint praise when they heard it.

When Melvin arrived in Topeka he was ushered into an oak-paneled office. Therein sat two lawyers, one from the Bureau, the other from the Association. They listened intently to McQuitty's tale of woe, nodded their heads, and looked at one another with furrowed brows.

"Yes, yes," Association mused. "This is a tough one."

"Amen," chimed in Bureau. "If there was a loophole. A wrinkle."

"Can't you just pick up a phone and call someone?" Melvin asked impatiently.

"Not exactly, Mr. McQuitty. No favor is free in Topeka," Association explained. "If we call the governor's office, they're going to want something in return. Like our support on a per-head tax increase."

"Brrrrr," Bureau shuddered, as if hit by an icy wind.

"What about those assholes at Environment?" Melvin snarled.

"Sure," Association chimed in, leaning back in his chair with fingers laced across his stomach. "They'd probably be happy to cooperate. So long as we agree not to oppose some new watershed regulations they're considering."

"Our members see those regulations as the taking of private property rights," Bureau explained. "And you know how touchy that is."

"This is a tough one," Association repeated.

"Amen," sympathized Bureau.

For almost an hour, they said next to nothing. They threw out a few words, then immediately dismissed their own ideas. They droned on about a recalcitrant legislature and run-amok bureaucracy. One of the lawyers reached into his coat pocket and pulled out a chart showing population shifts and their impacts on districting.

"Urban legislators don't give a damn about rural issues," he complained. "Have no idea what we're talking about."

"Well, maybe I ought to run for the legislature," Melvin snorted in disgust.

It was a tactical error, on which the two attorneys quickly jumped.

"You know, Melvin," said Association. "That isn't a half bad idea."

Bureau laughed and slapped the table.

"You ought to do just that. The legislature needs common sense people like you."

Before he knew what hit him, McQuitty had been helped to his feet and escorted toward the door.

"Representative McQuitty," mused one of the attorneys, even as he helped Melvin along. "Sounds pretty good, don't you think?"

"Senator sounds better," gushed the other.

Melvin found himself in the parking lot, not sure where to go nor who to call. He realized he'd been given the bum's rush and that the two attorneys had already forgotten about his troubles. He wasn't that stupid. But he was that powerless. For now.

He looked across 8th Avenue at the Statehouse. Its towering green-copper dome capped by a Native American with a deeply arched back. Aiming an arrow at the North Star.

"Representative McQuitty," he said to himself with bitter determination. "That does sound pretty good."

‹›

As Melvin McQuitty would later tell it, his entry into politics was a matter of divine intervention. God put him in the right place at the right time. All to serve His purpose. The Kansas Department of Environment, contamination plume, and bill for seventy-five thousand dollars got no mention in the narrative.

As soon as he got home, Melvin McQuitty sought out local political mavens for their advice. They were forthcoming, if not enthusiastic. As luck would have it, a venerable legislator was retiring for health reasons. So, Melvin stepped up.

He moved to a farmhouse just inside the district boundary. Got himself two hundred yard signs and a truckload of undocumented workers. Over one single night, his campaign sprung up like a glorious blooming of popular will, albeit lacking any form of permission from owners of the land where the signs were planted. Still, it was enough to scare off any potential challengers.

Senator Owen Middleton was among the first to congratulate McQuitty on election night. Effusive and instructional during the phone conversation, Owen grieved when he hung up. For the well-being of Kansas. For the dignity of elective office. For the diminishment of his own position, simply by association. As if in final comment on the Statehouse decline, the venerable legislator died two days after Melvin won office.

"They ought to dig him up and haul him to Topeka," LeeAnn told her husband after the funeral. "Even dead, he would be a better legislator than Melvin McQuitty."

‹›

Melvin sought appointment to the House Committee on Water and Environment, which did little but rail uselessly against federal regulations and bicker over such banal issues as backflow protection on lawn sprinklers. It was a make-work assignment for the infirm and estranged. When Melvin asked, House leaders snickered and promised that they would try their best. As if they were doing Melvin a big favor.

In fact, Melvin had an angle. The House Committee on Water and Environment did have one meaningful oversight authority. The Kansas Department of Environment. He wasn't sure what to do with that authority but figured its value would be at least seventy-five thousand.

Tradition has it that rookie legislators hold their tongues while learning at the knees of elder politicians. Only after the first year are their opinions welcome. But Melvin could manage no such restraint. It wasn't his nature. He couldn't have kept quiet if he wanted to. And he didn't want to.

He asked unending questions in committee hearings, smiling his toothy smile as if that would cover any multitude of sins. In the process of seeking clarification, he invariably revealed his profound ignorance of all things legislative. He irritated the hell out of those who had better things to do than twiddle their thumbs as staff spoon-fed a freshman legislator one tedious fact at a time. In other words, he irritated everyone.

<>

During an early session meet-and-greet sponsored by the Farm Association and Livestock Bureau, Melvin wandered the banquet hall accepting warm congratulations from cheerful strangers who knew him only by the name tag on his lapel. Its red border indicated that he was newly elected. Sipping scotch and eating eggrolls, he spotted a couple familiar faces.

"Representative McQuitty!" roared the Association attorney, as if he were feeling no pain. In fact, as befits a cautious man in an expensive suit, he was drinking iced tea.

"You did it!" hollered Bureau. He slapped Melvin's shoulder so hard that scotch sloshed out of the plastic cup.

"No thanks to you," Melvin muttered, dabbing at his wrist with a napkin. The two attorneys roared with laughter, trying to make a joke of it.

"Hey, we were your first supporters."

"No kidding, representative, we're thrilled to see you here."

"I bet," Melvin answered dryly.

Bureau looked at Association. The situation required a fix.

"Tell you the truth," Bureau confided, "we wanted to help, but there was just too much on the table right then. You understand, don't you? Sand can drain through an hourglass only one grain at a time."

"I understand," McQuitty grumbled. "There wasn't room for me in your hourglass."

"Well, there sure is now," Association jumped in, looking earnest. "Got any campaign debt? Need a place to stay during the session?"

"No and no," Melvin sniffed.

"How's your feedlot doing?"

The tall man suddenly got very interested. McQuitty's Feedlot was still in operation after the well cave-in, but just barely. Cattlemen paid Melvin to fatten their animals for market. Not put them belly deep in manure, stressed or even dead. They pulled their animals—those that could be moved—and took them elsewhere. Only the weakest remained.

"I can always use more business," Melvin replied.

"We'll look into it," Bureau said, staring at his partner and nodding slowly.

"Hey, you're our guy," Association added with a wink. "Haven't we been with you from the very beginning?"

Within weeks, several thousand cattle arrived at McQuitty's. They came from as far away as a hundred miles, bypassing a dozen closer and better feedlots. They came from big ranches, big enough to suffer a few losses at a substandard feedlot if it meant thickening the relationship with a sitting legislator. Melvin wasn't much. He was new in the Statehouse and not winning any friends fast. But every legislative session has a few issues where one or two votes make a difference. Representative McQuitty might just be a difference maker.

The tall man got the drift.

Kansas has a reputation for clean politics. Nobody would dare show up at the Statehouse with a bag of greenbacks, talking quid pro quo. But doing business, that's a whole other thing. It's free enterprise. Businessmen want to work with those who understand them. Who hold their best interests at heart. They call it added value, and the calculation is straightforward. How might my life—measured in wealth—gain more value by throwing a few cattle at Melvin McQuitty's feedlot?

When it comes time to collect on the investment, the process is lighthanded, almost elegant. Rancher dials up their legislator, makes a little small talk, then asks about pending legislation in a way that makes their interest quite clear. Say, what are you thinking about that inventory write-off bill? Sure would be good for me. They don't threaten or spell out consequences. No need to. Legislators understand bread and butter.

Thus, made aware of the link between the Statehouse and business,

Melvin started looking for additional products to hawk. Testing how far he could go.

Later in that first session, the Association and Bureau were pushing a close and controversial bill. Night before the scheduled vote, Melvin invited the two attorneys out for dinner. His treat. Never before had Representative McQuitty reached for a check, even as an empty gesture.

They met at a steakhouse that featured buxom waitresses in low-cut tops. Had a fine meal of prime rib. Bureau and Association let down their guards and drank bourbon instead of iced tea. There was lots of laughter. Gossip about who was behind the latest slick play. Political games and tawdry affairs. At one point, Owen Middleton's name came up.

"What was that?" Melvin asked.

The two attorneys sobered by degrees. Claimed he had misheard.

"I'll try that Death by Chocolate," Association pivoted.

"And get that waitress to bring us another drink," Bureau said. "I want to see her bend down again."

They laughed, ate, and drank some more. And when the check came, Melvin paid.

As they walked across the parking lot, McQuitty said, "Hey, let me show you something in my car."

He reached into the trunk and took out a nondescript quilt.

"Nice," said Bureau with a quick feel of the fabric.

"Given to me by an aunt," McQuitty claimed. "Look good hanging in one of your offices."

"Family heirloom," Association admired while fingering the quilt. "You wouldn't want to give away something like that."

"No. But I might want to sell it."

The two looked at Melvin. He was stretched to full height. Six-foot-six. Taller in two-inch heels.

"Are you serious?" Bureau asked.

"Do I look serious?" McQuitty's expression was flat and hard.

The two lawyers made eye contact.

"Okay," said one, rubbing his chin. "How much do you think it's worth?"

"Twenty-five hundred."

"Jesus, Melvin, I don't know anything about quilts but that seems awful steep."

"Not for what you're getting," Melvin said. He held out the quilt and shook it as if that were what he was actually selling.

"Take a grand?"

"Nope."

That's how Melvin McQuitty made a twenty-two hundred profit on a three hundred dollar meal.

"Added value," he smiled as they filled out their checks.

<>

A few days later, the Director of the Kansas Department of Environment was testifying before the House Committee on Water and Environment when Representative McQuitty asked a question.

"What are your standards for settling contamination cases?"

"We have a rubric that considers severity of the problem and past violations."

"Has the legislature ever examined that rubric?"

"No, sir. It's an administrative matter."

"Hmmm," Melvin answered with a tight little smile. "That's interesting."

McQuitty had made his point. Message sent. Back off the seventy-five thousand, or I'm going to subject the agency to an ugly oversight review. Endless information hearings, aggrieved witnesses, riled conservatives, bad press, and undermined authority.

Department moralists found even the talk of compromise unprincipled. Representative McQuitty should be treated no differently than any other polluter. Department pragmatists argued greater good. A hostile legislator, even one as ill-regarded and clumsy as Melvin McQuitty, could tie an agency in knots. The director listened to all sides, then went with the pragmatists.

"Better to put this in the past," he reasoned. The department agreed to settle with McQuitty for seven hundred fifty dollars. One percent of the original fine.

The moralists flushed with rage. Anonymous complaints were sent to environmental groups and the EPA. But in time, the kerfuffle died down. Life went on. There are always bigger and more polluted fish to fry.

Melvin never sent in the seven hundred fifty dollars. He doubted the department would bother to come after it. He was right.

<>

Senator Middleton noses the Lincoln into a garage of the Diamond apartment building. A looming Gothic structure within a short walk of the Statehouse. The ground floor houses several businesses beneath a broad green awning. Upstairs are four apartments, each with its own balcony overlooking congested 10th Avenue. There is a dry cleaner on one side, a brake shop on the other, and a Mexican restaurant across the street.

Middleton bought the Diamond in a foreclosure sale. He told LeeAnn it was a good investment. Which it was. But there are other benefits. He keeps the top right apartment for session housing. And personal use.

"Hello?" he coos as he opens the door. Panting slightly from climbing the stairs, he smells her perfume.

"Back here," she answers.

Owen finds her in the living room. Sitting on her feet in an overstuffed chair, wearing a navy-blue dress and stockings. Black pumps lie on the carpet. She's holding a stack of briefing papers and a yellow highlighter. Forty-six years old, she completed her master's degree decades ago and yet still studies like a schoolgirl. Marking passages and writing notes in the margins. A tactile learner, she memorizes through her fingertips. Her name is Muriel Kovak.

"How are you?" he asks, setting his briefcase and overnight bag on the kitchen table.

"Just fine. You?"

"There are some things."

"Things I can help with?"

"No," he answers. "I'm just glad you're here."

Muriel is a Statehouse liaison with the Kansas Health Office. A fine writer, she translates arcane health policies into simple terms that legislators can grasp. More impressively, she makes them feel smart for being able to understand. Making politicians feel smart is the first step toward having them agree.

Muriel makes her home in Wichita, where she lives with her husband. He is an aeronautical engineer, tidy, certain, and blissfully unaware. When the legislature is in session, she keeps a small efficiency apartment in Topeka. But mostly, she is at Owen's. Both are attracted to intelligence, political savvy, and secrets. In other words, to each other.

Muriel is small and sad looking. Her almond-shaped face is oddly gray in hue. She wears heavy, dark liner to make her hazel eyes look larger, more dramatic, and happier. She pencils her thin brows in an arch that seems ever pleading. Her auburn hair is swept back, her nose a little oversized. Somehow, these flawed features combine into a gentle loveliness. A sum greater than its parts. People are drawn to Muriel's warm and sympathetic presence. They want to tell her things. To receive her wisdom and sweet understanding.

Owen Middleton is drawn to other attributes. Muriel is a nurse. Comfortable with her body and sexuality. Comfortable with his. Comfortable with theirs. If LeeAnn Middleton is a ray of sunshine—strong, direct, full of antiseptic good cheer—Muriel is a wisp of smoke. Sinuous and ethereal. She is oddly polite, almost professional, even in the most intimate of moments. To that extent, she is unknowable.

Being far more astute than Muriel's husband in Wichita, LeeAnn Middleton is aware of her husband's inclinations. It didn't take her long to catch on to phone calls and a woman's voice. The new spring in his step.

"Who is she?" LeeAnn asked one night as they were getting ready for bed.

Owen studied her long enough to know it was best not to insult her intelligence or waste her time.

"Just somebody," he answered.

"Is it serious?"

"No."

"Keep it in Topeka," she warned.

"I will."

"Make damn sure you do. I'm going to read in the living room."

She pulled on a robe and took a book from the nightstand. LeeAnn cared. Of course she did. The admission stung, even though it was half expected. Her father cheated. His father cheated. She prayed that family tradition would not include her own son, but wasn't going to hold her breath. Men were men. She would not tear her life apart over something as silly as a fling. Provided it didn't humiliate her or threaten the Middleton world.

<>

"Merlot?" Owen asks Muriel.

"Before five?" She looks at her watch. It's a little after one. Owen is normally a stickler for propriety and self-control. Never a drop before the evening news.

"I'm feeling a little edgy," he answers. "The whole drive, I was looking forward to wine and a hot soak."

"Want company?"

"Yes, I do."

She slowly unfolds her legs. Rises and stretches. Reaches back to unzip her dress as she follows him into the master bath.

Over a couple of years and thanks to help from the Bureau and Association, the McQuitty operation started to come back. Not as many cattle as used to be, but enough. On top of that, Melvin hustled a buck here and there. Mostly using the feedlot's white tanker truck to haul custom loads for farmers and ranchers seeking "added value."

One afternoon as he waited for his favorite barber, the one who knew how to cut a mullet, Melvin started flipping through an agribusiness magazine. It was mostly glossy ads for farm equipment and production chemicals. But there was an article that made him sit up straight. It was about ethanol production in Iowa. How the industry was beset by self-defeating economics. Buying corn to make ethanol caused corn prices to rise. High corn prices pushed production costs beyond any hope of being financially sustainable. The entire enterprise was near collapse.

According to the article, one enterprising Iowan was working on a new twist. A side business to keep the front doors open. Selling mash, the corn solids that remain after alcohol is squeezed out, for cattle feed. Iowa State nutritionists agreed the stuff had remarkable weight-gain value. Pathologists were conducting tests to make sure it was safe. If all checked out, the promise was great. Melvin rolled up the magazine and stuffed it in his pocket.

There was one fledgling ethanol plant in Kansas. Not much more than a deductible hobby for a handful of heavy hitters. A placeholder for when the technology improved or, more importantly, government subsidies tipped the economics.

Melvin wanted mash from that plant. Wanted it bad. He could see possibilities. An early adopter, he would leverage mega-profits into something more. More, and then most. Having people call him for favors, instead of the other way around.

He got up from the barber's chair, fetched the white tanker truck from his feedlot, and drove to the ethanol plant.

"I heard something about that," the manager said, scratching his head. "But hasn't much been proved yet, has it?"

"Enough for me," McQuitty answered.

"I don't know," the manager hesitated. "I'd have to check with some people."

"Mention my name."

"And what is that?"

"Representative Melvin McQuitty," he huffed. "I'll wait in my truck."

A race began. The manager went into his office and started dialing. Melvin pulled out his cell phone and did the same. The manager had the better technical argument. Cattle feed is nothing to mess around with. Melvin had the political leverage, making not-so-vague references to past favors and matters pending. Eventually, he wore down the resistance.

"Okay, okay, Melvin. Just stop calling us."

Two hours later, the plant manager waved McQuitty into the office. An attorney had faxed a stack of liability waivers for the representative to sign.

"I hope you know what you're doing," the manager said, pushing the paperwork across his desk.

"No guts, no glory," the tall legislator replied.

"Isn't that what Custer said?"

McQuitty pulled the white tanker up to the loading dock. The manager and his helper filled its metallic belly with fifteen hundred gallons of corn mash. A yellow-green compote with a sickly sweet odor.

"Smells like money," Melvin smiled.

The next day at the feedlot, he backed up to a steel-pipe pen that held two hundred Angus cattle. When he twisted the stopcock, mash flowed like oatmeal into the feeding trough. He took a hoe and mixed it with regular silage at a proportion of his own invention. Feedlot staff watched with anxious faces. The cattle drifted over and began to eat. They loved the stuff and crowded shoulder to shoulder. Flank to flank. Melvin looked at his watch after about fifteen minutes, which seemed like an appropriately scientific amount of time.

"Drinks all around," he laughed, swinging his arm in a high, wide circle.

"Are you sure?" asked one of the crew with an apologetic smile.

"Sure?" McQuitty asked, eyebrows raised in irritated disbelief. "Sure enough to find someone who knows how to celebrate."

He roared off in a Jeep, spinning his wheels to spray gravel over his workers' boots.

Even as they ate, the feedlot cattle were beginning to die.

<>

After their bath and time together, Owen and Muriel are hungry. The senator calls the Mexican restaurant to order dinner. He throws on a robe and goes out on the balcony. A north wind has come up. It blows cold, but Middleton lingers outside. This is his favorite time of the day. When the colors of sunset, reds and blues and yellows, seductively mute into silver, purple, and black. When life and warmth slide indoors and glow through the windows. When shadows flicker. Intimate, bookish, and sexy. Like Muriel.

A young Latino boy crosses the street with a brown paper sack and aluminum thermos. Owen has worked out a special arrangement. It's illegal to take liquor off site, but the restaurant includes a pitcher of margaritas, and Owen rewards with a hefty tip. He and Muriel sit on living room recliners to eat. A college football game plays on the flat-screen TV. Their attention goes back and forth between the food, the game, and their respective stacks of paperwork. Reports, budgets, and proposed language.

"We on for tomorrow night?" he asks.

"Tomorrow night?"

"'Mythmakers of the American West.' Costumes optional."

Her pause is long. Owen looks up.

"No," she finally answers while scribbling a margin note. "I'm going with Derek. He loves that stuff. Spurs and cowboy hats."

Derek is Muriel's husband. The aeronautical engineer, tidy and unaware.

"Have fun," Owen mumbles.

He holds a budget in his hand but does not read. Instead, his thoughts drift to McQuitty's Feedlot. He feels the onset of heartburn and goes into the bathroom for an antacid. Returning to his recliner, Middleton empties the last of the margaritas into his glass.

"Medicine with that drink probably doesn't make a lot of sense," Muriel muses while highlighting a fiscal note.

"Neither does this budget," Owen replies.

⟨⟩

The first steer stumbled to its knees in just under three hours.

By then, Melvin had scooped up his girlfriend—a tall, laconic woman with straight black hair—and taken her to a restaurant in Dodge City. Waiting to be seated, Melvin noticed a booth full of local cattlemen. He plopped himself down, uninvited, and began talking about a new feed he was testing. One that would change everything. He went on and on while the polite ranchers let their food get cold. McQuitty's girlfriend stood a few feet away, pointedly bored, looking into the distance with arms crossed over her chest.

Melvin's cell rang. He held it to his ear.

"We got one down," a worker shouted.

"What?" Melvin hurried outside so nobody else could hear. The ranchers and girlfriend watched him pace back and forth in front of the plate glass window.

"Looks like this could take a while," said a cattleman to the girlfriend. "Buy you a drink?"

"Why not," she answered, sliding into the booth.

"What about the rest?" McQuitty shouted. Dying animals bellowed in the background.

"Not good. Maybe we should call someone?"

"God no," Melvin yelped. "I'll be there in thirty minutes."

Melvin rapped on the window and gestured frantically to the girlfriend.

"Got to go," she said.

The booth full of ranchers watched with wide-eyed fascination as the couple roared out of the parking lot. The waitress arrived with the glass of scotch.

"Still need this?" she asked.

"Not as much as she does," the rancher replied.

Melvin McQuitty raced down the road, honking at cars to get out of the way. The girlfriend held fast to the window post to keep from bouncing around. She didn't ask him to slow down. She wasn't the type to waste her breath.

All the while, more cattle fell.

Combining animals from different herds creates optimal conditions for the spread of disease. As a preventative, silage is typically dosed with antibiotics. Those medicines work at the edge of toxicity. Irritating the livestock's digestive system to keep intestinal pathogens from taking root. Hogs are packed tighter than cattle and, therefore, require a heavier dosage.

The day before McQuitty took the tanker truck to the ethanol plant, he used it to transfer a load of hog feed. The truck should have been washed out in between trips. Very carefully. But careful was never the tall man's strong suit. Residue from the hog feed was pooled in the bottom. It blended with the load from the ethanol plant. By mixing contaminated mash with medicated silage, Melvin fed his cattle a double dose of antibiotics.

At first, things worked as intended. Intestinal walls were irritated, and pathogens sluffed off. But there was far more antibiotic than the liver could process. With no place to go, the excess lingered in the digestive tract. Cellular walls broke down, tissues weakened, lesions burst. As cattle started dissolving inside, they fought back as best they could. Frothing at the mouth and evacuating from every orifice. They rolled their heads and kicked at pain in their bellies. It was useless.

By the time Melvin arrived at the feedlot, all the mash-fed cattle were dead or dying. More than two hundred animals. A total value of three hundred thousand dollars. The headlights of his Jeep illuminated a ghastly scene of death, hemorrhages, and excrement. His crew stood and stared, their faces full of horror. Melvin swung into action.

"Shit!" he screamed at his cheap workers. "We got to move them. Anyone finds out and we'll be shut down."

"To where?" one worked begged to know. "One or two, maybe. But this is too many. We don't have the equipment. And where would we take them?"

Just then, the sheriff pulled in. In a small town, word travels fast. Especially when it involves feedlot activity in the dark of night. The death moans of cattle. The stink of mass evacuation. Spire got out of his pickup and shined his flashlight.

"What the hell is going on out here?"

Melvin placed himself between the sheriff and dead cattle, trying to block his view.

"It's nothing. Little infection is all. With so many cattle, there are always losses."

Spire swept past the tall legislator. He watched a great black Angus, blood and saliva dripping from its mouth, fall to its knees, roll over, and die.

"Don't bullshit me. I grew up on this feedlot. What's wrong with those cattle."

"I don't know," McQuitty answered. "I honestly don't."

Spire shined the flashlight into the legislator's face, then turned it on the crew. One by one they lowered their eyes, remaining silent. Spire came back to Melvin.

"You call Ag Extension right now."

"I can take care of it."

"Do what I said." Spire squared his shoulders. Melvin saw that he had no choice.

The Agricultural Extension agent from Haskell County drove right over. On his way, he called the Department of Environment. Key staff and the director gathered at the agency, still rubbing sleep out of their eyes. When all were assembled, they got on the speaker phone and called the sheriff's cell.

"Get this cleaned up," Billy growled, handing Melvin his phone.

"Representative McQuitty," the director said with false cheer. "How can we help you?"

"Two hundred dead cattle," Melvin replied. "What do you expect me to do about them?"

"What do we expect?" the director asked. "We have no expectations. We're just responding to an incident report. Explain the situation."

Melvin began spouting disconnected details about a mysterious outbreak. He concluded by demanding that the department tell him how to dispose of his dead cattle. The director pushed the mute button.

"Well?" he asked, looking around the table.

"Like this is our fault?" one of the pragmatists complained.

"The guy just sounds scared to me," sympathized a moralist.

The director unmuted.

"Mitigating contagion possibility is top priority," the director explained. "We'll call you right back."

"You do that," Melvin snarled.

Department discussion broke along familiar lines. The moralists urged compassion. Think how you would feel? In the dark, with all those dead and dying animals? Let's hold his hand and walk him through. The pragmatists argued that Representative McQuitty was a snake, as proven with the contaminated well. No question if he'll bite, only when. Let him figure it out for himself.

The director listened to both sides. He shook his head in frustration.

"Let me call the Livestock Bureau," he said, then added. "I should never have left the private sector."

"Representative McQuitty?" answered the Bureau attorney. He held his hand over the phone so as not to disturb his wife, who was sleeping beneath an overpriced quilt. He listened without comment, then spoke.

"We don't know how to deal with this guy any more than you do. Goodnight."

The director hung up the phone and surveyed his staff. The two camps were each equally certain of their position. Each side predisposed toward bitter resentment should he choose the other. The director dialed the speakerphone.

"Representative McQuitty," he said. His assistant captured every word on a voice recorder. In case the matter should come up in court or committee. "We're not there. It's hard to give good advice on something we haven't seen. But we're committed to working through this together."

The pragmatists slumped in disgust. The moralists leaned in, eager to make good on their altruistic inclinations.

"Well, aren't you just a Lamb of Jesus," Melvin replied acidly.

The moralists leaned back. Maybe this wasn't such a great idea after all.

The department directed McQuitty to keep a few dead cows for forensic purposes. Wrap them in a tarp and keep them isolated. The rest were to be dusted with lye and buried far away from other cattle or livestock.

"Fine," Melvin spat. "Thanks a lot."

That night saw one of the great mobilizations in the history of Ewing County. Right up there with the Grasshopper War of 1938. Rallied by the sheriff to protect their livestock, their livelihoods, and perhaps even their health, the men and women of Stonewall flew into action.

The county held ten landfill acres about a mile from the feedlot, on a rounded hilltop where precipitation would harmlessly run off. The underlying bedrock was as tight as might be hoped for the fractured geology of that area. The county's public works men cut a nice, clean trench into the ground. Eight feet deep. One hundred fifty feet long.

Townspeople scurried to the feedlot, attired in whatever protective gear they could muster. Rubber gloves, raincoats, and plastic ponchos. Surgical masks and cotton kerchiefs. They came in every manner of conveyance, bracing to haul away over three hundred thousand pounds of dead cattle.

Billy Spire was proud of his town the night the cattle died. He talked for years about the heroics he had seen. Even Russ Haycock showed up, drawn by the racket and headlights. He pitched in without comment or complaint, using a heavy tow chain hitched to the Dodge. Hooking dead cows by their hooves and dragging them into a pile for the side-loaders.

And the one person missing should have been leading the effort: Melvin McQuitty. Those who first arrived that night peppered him with questions. Questions he could not or would not answer. Soon tired of the third degree, he stomped into the feedlot office, lowered the blinds, and locked the door.

The truth came out sooner than he did. Emergency 911 received calls from anonymous sources. It didn't take a master detective to make out their identities. Melvin's crew was fearful of getting sick or being held somehow liable. They spilled their guts as completely as did the poisoned cattle. Local health officials announced that a cause had been identified. No need to worry about contagion.

The people of Ewing County had always despised Melvin McQuitty. That night they found he was even worse than imagined. Giving cattle poisonous feed against the cautions of his workers. Hiding behind a locked door even as the entire community cleaned up his grisly mess.

News spread. A television reporter with heavy makeup and a deceptively friendly manner showed up to walk the scar of freshly turned soil. She wandered around town holding out a microphone to anyone who would talk, which was just about everyone. They told harrowing stories complete with dramatic gestures. Big cattle dropping to their knees. Tossing heads as if choking. Dragging the bodies to a mass grave. Every story included Melvin McQuitty's name.

At the Kansas Farm Association and the Livestock Bureau, staff watched their TVs in dismay. Phones started ringing. Bad news affects all Kansas producers. The heavy hitters were not happy.

"What has that idiot done?" they cried. "Inspectors are going to be crawling all over our asses."

The Association and Bureau sent out press releases. The strategy was, of course, to buy time. Tomorrow will bring another news cycle. And it was true. The next day, there was another mass shooting by someone somewhere. Stonewall, Kansas, slipped back into its quiet existence.

Melvin did a lot of calling. To apologize and reassure. But it did no good.

Customers sent trucks to haul their cattle from the feedlot. It was mostly a gesture of contempt, for there was no value to be recovered from McQuitty's. Thousands of animals that never touched the mash were guilty by association. Not even rending plants would take them. Most were sold to Mexico, at pennies on the peso. A few went to small butcher shops, for personal consumption.

The rest were led to the edge of a ditch and shot. Buried where they fell.

⟨⟩

The world continued eating Kansas beef. Cattle prices held steady. Nobody was sanctioned by the Kansas Department of Agriculture, which exists more to promote than regulate. Owners of the ethanol plant shut it down for "a thorough review of operations and hygiene." The plant manager was fired by the same attorney who sent the liability waivers. Someone had to pay. Some poor head had to roll.

There was one other casualty. Representative McQuitty was put out in the cold, Statehouse style.

In the worst form of political punishment, people simply stopped talking to him. He heard nothing. Important meetings would come and go without his knowledge. Nobody sought his counsel and when he sought the counsel of others, he was met with blank stares.

"Gosh, Melvin, I don't know anything about that," claimed fellow legislators.

"I'm in a bit of a rush right now. How about you get a hold of my office and schedule a meeting?" said lobbyists. His calls were never returned.

"The chair wants all requests to go directly through him," replied staff whenever the legislator requested information. Statehouse workers remained unfailingly polite, but even the lowliest among them neither forgot nor forgave how Melvin had treated them. As something between personal servants and enemies of the people.

It was assumed that Melvin would quietly finish his term and go away. No man, not even the representative from Ewing, could long endure the humiliation of being an empty suit wandering aimlessly around marble hallways. Significant only for his insignificance. But predictions of his political death would prove incorrect.

They failed to account for the degree of Melvin's desperation. The feedlot was done. Devoid of cattle and staff. Equipment repossessed by creditors. The county commission didn't even bother to foreclose on the land for back taxes. Their reasoning was simple. Of what value is a seized property in a town already half vacant?

Being a legislator was the only thing McQuitty had left. Period. His days in the Statehouse were torturous and demeaning, but he still got a meager salary, per diem, and free meals at sponsored receptions. So, Melvin stayed, lingering at the rotunda's brass rail hour after hour. Watching the comings and goings. Waiting for something to happen. Something he could use.

Political populations form a bell-curve. Mass at the middle gets things done. Extreme ends try to shape the center. Extremism in the Kansas Legislature consists mainly of conservatives. White men from rural areas who hate government, excluding farm subsidies and anti-abortion regulations, and yearn for a bygone time when power was exclusively in the hands of white Christian males. They have made peace with women's suffrage but prefer females who are biblically subservient to their men. They loathe government schools, taxation, and any ambiguity about either sexual preference or the Second Amendment. They fall on their knees every night and pray. For Kansas and the mercy of God.

The most extreme of the extreme comprise a bloc known as the "Wings." The nickname carries competing interpretations. Among themselves, the Wings fly with the angels. To those who view them as excessive and bothersome, "wing" is a prefix to "nuts."

Anti-school as they may be, the Wings do know how to add. In Christ, all things may be possible. But in Topeka, it takes enough votes. So, they are always on the lookout for new members. Always ready to forgive past sins in order to increase their numbers.

Ostracized and leaning on the rotunda's brass rail, Representative McQuitty watched colleagues come and go in twos and threes. Heads close together in whispered exchanges, passing as if he weren't even there. His toothy, ingratiating smile drew tighter with every day and every eye that shifted to avoid his. Finally, his mouth took an unfamiliar shape. A thin, flat line of bitterness.

One morning, one of the female Wings sidled up to him at the rotunda rail. A big woman with dyed black hair and a sailor-suit dress. She was famous for refusing to ride alone in a car with any man who wasn't her husband. She walked the straight and narrow. Dismissing anyone who didn't as being sadly deficient.

Standing just close enough to hint at familiarity, she joined Melvin in watching the parade of legislators and lobbyists, staff, and reporters. Every single one walking by wordlessly, looking up, looking down, looking at papers in their hands or laces on their shoes. Not looking at Melvin. Or his new companion.

"You, too?" she asked.

"I beg your pardon?"

"Shut out?"

"Just waiting," he claimed, forcing his best smile.

"Waiting for what?" She stared at him with eyes so strong that he had to glance away. Eyes that demanded the truth.

"That's how my father looked when he thought I was lying about homework," he snorted.

"Was he right?"

"Pretty much," Melvin admitted.

Having made her point, the woman fronted him like a schoolteacher would a thick-headed student.

"If you ever get tired of going it alone, come see us."

"I'm not alone," he insisted.

"You keep telling yourself that."

Two House committee chairs walked past. Melvin nodded at them. There was no response. Moving out of earshot, one said something to the other. The two of them glanced back and laughed. Melvin looked down. The lady was still staring at him, with those piercing eyes and now a smug little grin.

The Wings met a few blocks from the Statehouse, in the side room of a combined barbeque joint and Harley-Davidson dealership. Though the room was brightly lit, it was a place of dark frustration. Radical politics and evangelical anger. In this land of blind faith, the one-eyed man is king. Melvin McQuitty was not particularly shrewd, but he did have a natural aptitude for legislative mischief-making. Schemes and provocations flowed from him like a mighty river. He taught his new comrades how to monkey wrench the system.

He would interrupt committee meetings over arcane procedural points from *Robert's Rules of Order.* He would get into shouting matches and goad chairs into losing decorum. Reporters couldn't get enough of his wild quotes, whack-a-mole logic, and rumor mongering. Finicky legislators fought back in the fussy ways of old men. They even introduced legislation declaring Melvin the "state reptile." McQuitty laughed and announced that reptiles eat insects, which was a good thing given the Statehouse's plague of cockroaches.

Turns out that democracy is a delicate thing. A thing of trust and comity. A thing easily disrupted by those so inclined. Soon, the mass at the middle was willing to bend, if that's what it took to keep Wings from frustrating the legislative process. Provocation evolved into power. Irresponsibility morphed into legitimacy.

Ever one to push the envelope, Melvin McQuitty became an early adopter of what would become the Wing's most sacred symbol. He started carrying a gun whenever and wherever there was someone to impress. A snub-nosed thirty-eight with hollow-point bullets and a stag-horn grip. He wore it on a clip-on leather holster tooled with sunflowers and the word "Kansas."

"My, my," cooed the big woman with piercing eyes. "How much did it cost?"

"The price of freedom," Melvin said, patting the pistol.

He'd been waiting for someone to ask.

◇

Owen Middleton hates costume parties.

He prefers a dark suit and tie. But tonight's soiree is hosted by serious players. The Livestock Bureau and Farm Association, in concert with the Rifle Foundation, Life First, and the Kansas Rural Business Chamber. Groups for whom "costumes optional" means costumes mandatory. Either fly the cowboy colors or raise eyebrows. It would not be smart to hold back on this event. And Owen Middleton is always smart.

So, the senator dons a fringed-leather coat and gray slacks with dark piping along the seams. Pointy-toed boots and bolo tie with a cattle skull slide. In a subtle sign of rebellion, he pops on a narrow-brimmed Stetson Open Road hat. An LBJ trademark in a Reaganite crowd.

"Howdy, pardner," he sarcastically says to the reflection of himself. Then turns out the lights and heads for his car.

At one time, the Bureau and Association identified with "country club" Republicans. Men, and they were predominantly men who stood as pillars of their communities. Political moderates who frowned on taxes as a matter of principle but valued roads, infrastructure, schools, and economic incentives. Boosters of the local sports teams and pancake breakfasts. Believers in the greater good, especially when that good overlapped with business interests. In short, they were like Matthew Middleton.

But the farm crisis of the 1980s wiped out that breed. Back when ag incomes plummeted, and Russ Haycock rode the extremist surge. Farms failed, families moved, depopulation began. Large machines offset vanishing workers, then displaced those who tried to hang on. Of the few remaining jobs, most went to undocumented workers who were paid little and complained less. Politics among the survivors got stingy and bitter. The country club shut down for good.

Clear-eyed leaders of the Bureau and Association could see the future. Fewer rural people meant less rural representation in the Kansas Legislature. Less rural representation meant diminished power. Diminished power meant existential crisis.

They responded with a two-pronged strategy.

The first prong was to shake down remaining members. It was simple, really. Invent threats. Not from whole cloth, for that would lack credibility and require imagination. Easier to give a sinister twist to some innocuous thing said or done. "Kansas Department of Environment studies of runoff fertilizer" twists into a "secret plan to fence livestock away from streams and ponds, all at the landowner's expense." Even the most fanciful threat has credibility to those on the edge of suffering. To those who live among empty homes and storefronts.

"Help us help you," the Bureau and Association cajole. "Dig deep and give."

After the money is collected and spent, the organizations declare victory. Wearing grim faces of men home from the front, they announce that they have thwarted government's evil schemes. Your animals can continue to drink freely. It's a beautiful and lucrative thing to stave off something that was never going to happen in the first place.

The second prong was building new coalitions. The organizations began searching for common ground. They started with what they had. Kansas farmers are generally Republican, churchgoers, white, conservative, and gun owners. So, too, are many Kansas urbanites. The rest came easy.

Begin meetings with prayer. Throw some money at anti-abortion literature. Sponsor turkey shoots with guns as door prizes. Share the coded language of "welfare," "Wyandotte County," and "West Coast lifestyles." Cross-pollinate leadership under the big tent of shared values. Close ranks, vote together, and celebrate conservatism.

"Mythmakers of the American West," Owen reads from a banner stretching over the Topeka convention center entryway. "Yee haw."

Owen Middleton hates costume parties.

<>

Middleton arrives exactly thirty minutes after the reception has started. Timed to avoid small talk, which he also hates. He will make himself highly visible during the main presentation. Then leave right after it's over. He hopes Muriel's husband will drive back to Wichita tonight.

He parks the Lincoln, puts on the Stetson, and starts walking. There is a bit of commotion. A crowd is gathered outside the reception hall. None of them are dressed as cowboys. Many have signs protesting manifest destiny, economic enslavement, inequitable imprisonment, and gender bias.

Officers from the Topeka police department have made a soft barricade of themselves, leaving a pathway for invited guests. The protesters are more a flock than mob. A few hoots about costumes and cultural theft, but it is more teasing than taunting. The cops look slightly bored. One cop, older than the rest, chats up a tall woman with square shoulders. As Owen passes, she notices and shouts.

"Hey, I know you."

It takes the senator just a heartbeat for recognition. He has a good memory for faces.

"Miss Perez," he says, stepping over to shake her hand. "What are you doing here?"

"I might ask the same of you." She draws up to her full height and gives him a look of friendly reproachment.

"Like my mama used to say. If someone is nice enough to invite you to a party, you should be nice enough to go."

"But your mama's not here, is she?"

Owen laughs as though Perez has made a brilliant joke and keeps moving.

"That woman is a hero," he calls back to the older policeman with whom she'd been talking. "Helped solve a murder back home."

"Did you?" asks the cop.

"Not really," she answers. "He just talks that way. He's a politician."

Owen passes through double doors into a short entryway. Several other late arrivals are showing their invitations to steely-eyed men in blazers. They make women open their purses and scan men up and down. A public relations flack with gigantic hair, twinkling eyes, and bright red lipstick smiles, compliments, and joshes in a loud, twangy voice.

"That is just *too* sweet," she says to a lady dressed as Sunbonnet Sue.

"Beefus, honey, where did you find a hat big enough for that old noggin of yours?"

"My goodness, Linda. Aren't you sparkly tonight?"

"I hope there's something left to drink," Linda grumbles as security rifles her purse.

"Plenty inside, darlin'." The flack lowers her voice and points to the demonstrators with her eyes. "We just have to be a little careful is all."

"Senator Middleton, isn't this grand?" She busses Owen on the cheek. "I swear, it's like the Oscars or something."

"Too much fun," he agrees.

Inside the hall, Middleton looks around to get his bearings. He takes red wine off a passing tray and searches for a spot where his visibility will be maximized during the short time he plans to stay. The hall is full of people laughing and hugging and whooping over each other's costumery. A cluster of Wings has sequestered themselves off to the side.

"Hope they freeze their asses off," says one of the Wings, a fellow whose eyebrows are thicker than his pencil-thin mustache. He speaks loud enough to be heard beyond his immediate companions.

Middleton drifts over to the window and looks outside. Dusk is giving way to dark. Soon there will be a blanket of stars and the Milky Way. The crowd is huddling beneath parking lot pole lamps. Blue collar union workers with short-cropped hair and heavy canvas coats. Smart and energetic teachers carrying signs about pay raises and smaller class size. A tall, lean man from a progressive think tank roams the Statehouse, trying to educate uninterested legislators about tax policy implications. Mostly, though, the crowd is young and of color. Blacks, Native Americans, and Latinos.

"Why can't they just stay home?" a woman says. She, too, is in the Wing contingency.

A board member from the Association hurries to shake Owen's hand.

"So glad to see you here," he says.

"I wouldn't dare pass this up," Owen answers, truthfully.

Just then, Owen sees Melvin McQuitty on the far side of the room. The man is impossible to miss. Wearing a skinny, blood-red suit with green cacti and golden roadrunners beaded across the lapels, he appears to be a gaudy refugee from the Grand Ole Opry. His great height stretched by ostrich boots and a towering Resistol 7X cowboy hat. All stacked, he must reach nearly seven feet high. He is talking to wives. Saying syrupy things about their legislator husbands, obsequious in his efforts to curry favor. The husbands smile and dredge up vague return compliments, which they will tersely disavow on the ride home.

Owen notices a bulge on McQuitty's hip.

"Is he carrying that pistol?" the senator says out loud.

"Oh yes," the board member answers. "We had the convention center suspend its no-gun policy tonight."

"Doesn't that defeat the purpose of a security check?"

"The Second Amendment is a right, isn't it?"

Middleton is taken aback. Less by McQuitty's being armed than his own impolitic response. Hinting at Second Amendment qualms to a man he barely knows is a failure of self-control. More importantly, he said "that pistol." As if he had seen it before.

"It certainly is," he deflects. "And what a wonderful crowd."

"If Representative McQuitty would loan us that hat," says a familiar voice, "we could plug the ozone hole."

Muriel Kovak stands behind Owen with a man whose arm drapes across her shoulder. Owen takes measure of his lover's husband. The aeronautical engineer is of moderate height and reed slim, as befits a

137

man who bicycles at eight-forty-five every Sunday morning. The senator knows, because that's a safe time to call. He is outfitted in a leather vest and boots festooned with sharp-grinder Spanish spurs. The rowels jingle when he walks.

"I'm Owen Middleton," he says, extending his hand.

"*Senator* Owen Middleton," Muriel clarifies.

"Derek Kovak," the husband cheerfully responds.

Between the two lovers, there is little conversation about life outside Topeka. Once, when LeeAnn found a lump in her breast, Muriel tutored him on cancer and its treatment. Turned out to be nothing. He and Muriel never spoke of it again. Nor of LeeAnn. It just wasn't necessary. Among Owen Middleton's many talents, none is greater than his capacity to compartmentalize. Muriel, too. It is the basis of their relationship.

"Let's look around," she says, taking her husband's elbow and leading him away. His spurs ring with every step.

Middleton hears his name shouted from across the room. He looks for an escape route, but it's too late. Melvin McQuitty is already upon him.

"Nice outfit," the senator remarks.

Melvin ignores the obvious sarcasm and swings to Owen's side. They look in the same direction. Scanning the room. Avoiding direct eye contact.

"Everything okay?" the representative asks.

"Okay?" Owen asks incredulously. "No, everything is not okay. You made sure of that."

A pair of passing female Wings stop to admire McQuitty's costume.

"Hoo-wee," one of them howls. "Melvin, you're shinier than a pickle on a hot fork."

"Ain't I just," the tall man beams.

"Senator Middleton, you be careful standing next to him. That suit looks absolutely radioactive."

"You're right," Owen answers. "I should run away."

The women twitter off in pursuit of smoked bacon on crackers.

"Will Billy Spire be a problem?" Melvin worries.

"Maybe so." The senator is in no mood to calm the representative's fears. Let him take the next round of antacids.

"You'll find a way to outsmart him," Melvin dismisses.

"If I was smart," Owen replies, "I wouldn't be standing here, talking to you."

"Naw," the man drawls. "This makes you look good. Saint Middleton of Ewing County. Patron of lepers and lost causes."

"Melvin, are you going to be right here for a while?"

"I guess so."

"Okay, then. I'm going over there." Middleton moves away.

Melvin launches himself back into the crowd. Seven feet high, in a beaded, blood-red suit. Humanity scrambles out of his way as if fleeing a plague from the Bible. Praying the pestilent representative will just pass on by.

<>

"Mythmakers of the American West" is a small display, little more than an excuse for conservative gatherings. It was developed by a Washington think tank with dark money and big plastic crates. From one of those crates springs a latticework of thin metal tubes that, animated by magnets and clever hinges, expands to the size of a modest kitchen. From other crates come panels with artwork and narrative. The language is eighth-grade accessible. Straightforward, plain-spoken, and sincere.

The last case contains a cast-iron stanchion and Plexiglas box. Within the box is the exhibit's crown jewel. An exact replica of Teddy Roosevelt's Fabrique Nationale M1900 thirty-two caliber semi-automatic pistol. It has a gold inlay and mother-of-pearl grip, just like the real one, which remains permanently secured at NRA headquarters in DC.

Someone politely taps their wineglass with a fork. Voices rise to offset the interruption. The tapping gets a little louder, the crowd gets noisier. Finally, the flack with gigantic hair whistles through her fingers. A handsome man in a western style tuxedo walks up to a podium and clears his throat.

"We are so proud to have you with us tonight," he says. Then, as if it is written into a script, he smiles. Mechanically, like the opening of an automatic garage door. The crowd applauds politely.

"Don't they clean up good?" the flack hollers, clapping toward the crowd.

"My yes," Tuxedo agrees. "Best-looking crowd in America. Or at least here at the convention center." He rolls his eyes toward the gathering outside. "Let's let them know we're having a good time."

The crowd stomps and roars and peeks out the windows.

"Can we take a moment to thank our partners?"

A long procession of organizational leaders appears at the podium. Each recounting battles they have won and troubles on the horizon. The shakedown never ceases.

Food and drinks are cut off during the introductions. Soon, it tests the crowd's patience. They are ready to party. People begin to shuffle and mutter. By the jangling of his spurs, Middleton follows the aeronautical engineer's bored wandering around the "Mythmaker" exhibit. Finally, Tuxedo returns to the mike.

"Let's give them another fine hand for the work they do," he insists. The crowd half-heartedly applauds.

"And for another round of drinks!" The applause becomes sincere.

Outside, a Black man in his mid-forties stands before the demonstrators. He is boyish in build, wearing a black sweater and puffy brown coat. A professor from the University of Kansas, he has recently authored a highly acclaimed book on the carceral state. The millions of citizens, disproportionately of color, locked up in our jails and prisons.

The professor has to yell. There was a megaphone, but the police took it away. Now they stop a crew of young men from lighting a trash-barrel fire.

"It's cold out here," the young men complain.

"Then go home."

"No trouble," pleads a bald Lutheran minister with kind eyes and wire-rim glasses. "Violence will only hurt our cause."

The young men settle down. The policemen glare, pace around a while, then go back to their cars. They sit inside with engines idling and heaters blasting.

The professor quiets the crowd by flapping his hands in small motions, like a goose on the wing. The demonstrators press against each other for warmth.

"This exhibit is meant to be self-guided," Tuxedo explains. "But tonight, we have a special guest. Author of more than twenty books, including *Blackleg Range*, *Hoot Owl Trail*, and *The Mexican Saddle*."

The crowd is impressed. They may not be familiar with the titles, but these are people of the West and champions of its adulation.

"A bonafide cowboy," Tuxedo continues. "The poet *lariat* of Kansas. Rex Cheney."

The author is a robust fellow with a walrus mustache and chaw of tobacco. His voice is a high-pitched wheeze.

"Well, I don't claim to be no expert, but I did read the study guide."

The professor is surprised at the volume of his own voice. The air is clear, the demonstrators have formed a parabola, and he's worked up.

He jerks his thumb at the exhibit hall, where gay colors dance through the windows. This kind of crap really pisses him off.

"Mythmakers? Are you kidding me?"

The crowd moves nearer. This is going to be an earful.

"You want to know what the real myth is?" he shouts. "The real myth is that these were men of the West. Truth is, all three were easterners. Children of privilege. Beneficiaries of this nation's genocide and abuse. Posers who spun tales and painted pretty pictures to whitewash reality."

The author stands next to the introductory "Mythmakers" panel. Owen Wister is dark-eyed and handsome as a movie star. Teenaged Teddy Roosevelt stares balefully from the Harvard boathouse, shirtless and willow slim. Frederic Remington, lumpy as a sack of potatoes, scowls from the back of a little horse.

"Old Freddy don't look too happy, does he?" Walrus observes. "Imagine how that poor pony felt."

At the Wister panel, Walrus points to book covers and TV posters featuring *The Virginian: A Horseman of the Plains*. All are adorned with handsome cowboys, pretty school marms, and the beautiful rugged Wyoming landscape.

"Wister was quite the thing back in 1902. Right up there with Henry James, Mark Twain, and Rudyard Kipling. Must have read *The Virginian* twenty times when I was a kid," the author wheezes.

"This hogwash makes me want to go out and wash my hogs," Muriel whispers. She is close behind Owen. Too close for comfort. Her husband is standing right in front of the author, drinking in every word.

"Not smart," the senator hisses.

"How rude!" she answers with mock indignity.

"Who was the Virginian?" someone asks.

"'When you call me that, smile,'" Walrus says in his best Gary Cooper. He is met with blank stares. He clears his throat and goes on. "The Virginian's name is never mentioned. That's just where he's from. He falls in love with a schoolmarm from Vermont, kills the local villain in a duel, and rides off into the sunset. It's the foundation for most every western made since."

"Hmmm?" Muriel continues. She's enjoying this little game of cat and mouse. "Hero and heroine from the East. Villain from Wyoming. Some mythmaker of the West, that guy."

"You might be happier with the folks outside."

"I might," she agrees, then drifts away.

"*What* he is matters more than *who* he is," Walrus explains. "He is heroic. The West is a hard place. Can bring out the worst in a man. But the Virginian finds bravery and honor. That's the heart of the genre. Overcoming challenges to find our best."

The professor is on a roll.

"The American economy was built on cheap labor."

"No more, no more!" the crowd rolls with him.

"Slaves and immigrant workers."

"No more, no more!"

"Plantation, poor house, and prison. It's all the same."

"No more, no more!"

"And this is what they celebrate? The subjugation of people? The desecration of sacred ground?"

"No more, no more!"

The crowd is getting loud and forceful. The cops start shifting around. Getting out of warm cars and zipping up leather jackets. Trunks open, out come bats and hats.

A clutch of Wings moves to the window. They crane and peer into darkness. Looming over them is the towering representative from Ewing County.

The big-haired flack senses trouble and hurries over.

"It's cold. They'll break up soon," she snorts. "Let's enjoy the evening. My goodness, darlin', you got too much air in that glass. How 'bout I get you a refill?"

Walrus continues. "Now here is Frederic Remington and his *Fight for the Waterhole*."

At the painting's center, horses stand near a cratered pool of water that mirrors a clear blue sky. Cavalrymen ring the periphery, lying on their bellies, Winchesters at the ready. In the background rises a rooster tail of dust. Blurry "savages" circling. Greedy to steal the West's most critical resource. Water.

The same young men as before take a second try at the trash barrel. They toss in crumpled newspaper and light matches. Flames jump. The cops form a line and start toward the protesters. An unauthorized fire will not be tolerated. The Lutheran minister wades back in.

"No trouble. Please, no trouble."

But this time, the young men do not listen. Their blood is up. They circle the fire, daring the cops to come closer.

The older police officer, the one who was chatting earlier with Perez, gestures for the others to hold back. He will try to reason with the protesters. Ayesha emerges from the crowd. Carrying a liter bottle of water, she walks into the circle of young men and douses the fire. The young men moan.

"We're warm enough," she explains. "We need you here tonight. Not sitting in jail."

"Aw man," they whine. But disperse.

"Thank you," says the older cop.

"We're friends, right?" she asks. "Can we keep it friendly?"

"I'll do my best," he promises.

The flack cannot move the Wings away from the window. Tuxedo comes to her support.

"Just ignore them," he directs, with a disdainful expression. "This is what they want. To ruin our evening."

He motions for Walrus to keep the tour moving. The author nods and reads directly from the study guide.

"Remington's studio was in New Rochelle, New York. He often hired local plumbers and firemen to act as models."

"These so-called mythmakers?" the professor roars. "Ever look them up?"

The crowd roars "No!" then laughs at itself. The professor laughs, too.

"We may not have power. We may not have money. But we do have the public library!"

"Read, baby, read!" The crowd laughs again.

The professor opens an earmarked volume.

"Here is your Frederic Remington. 'Jews—Injuns—Chinamen—Italians—Huns, the rubbish of the world which I hate.'"

The laughter of a moment ago is quickly forgotten.

"And Owen Wister? What did he really think about men of the West?" Again, the professor quotes. "'I'm told they are without any moral sense whatever. Perhaps they are—but I wonder how much less they have than poor classes in New York.' He was a card-carrying member of the Immigration Restriction League."

The crowd boos. The mood is getting angry. The cops move closer.

"Somebody ought to go out there and do something," complains the Wing with thick eyebrows and thin mustache. "We can't hardly even hear."

In fact, even those standing right next to the window can hear fine. But fine is not good enough for some. Melvin McQuitty steps back and stands tall. Every Wing eye turns toward him. He is thrilled at the attention, practically vibrating with the expectations of others. He nods bravely. Just like the Virginian. With several long strides, he walks to a full-length window and adopts a manly pose.

Now sensing the room reeling out of control, Walrus puts more volume in his high-pitched wheeze. "Tragedy sent Teddy Roosevelt to the American West. His mother and wife died on the same day. So, he took his broken heart to North Dakota."

Interior light shines off the long window where McQuitty poses, causing it to reflect like a mirror. Melvin can see no further than his own image. Distortion in the glass makes him look even taller and slimmer than he really is. He is pleased at what he sees. To those looking in from outside, the representative practically glows in his suit.

Owen watches McQuitty. He is not sure what the man is doing, but nothing he does ever turns out good. And the Wings look like a posse in the making. It's time to go. He looks for Muriel. Her husband is listening intently to the cowboy author. She stands a little apart, wearing a slight smirk of skepticism. Owen goes to her.

"Those people. They have no respect for their nation," a Wing exclaims.

Walrus looks up from the study guide.

"Those people?" he asks, then pauses to thoughtfully dip more chewing tobacco.

"I love this country," he finally continues. "Where else could an ignorant redneck like me go to college and get an education? And, corny as they are, I believe in cowboy values. I surely do."

"Roll up your pant legs," Muriel mutters as Owen appears at her side.

"But you can't write about the West without learning some of its history. There isn't just one American story. No, sir. And not all of them are filled with the 'better angels of our nature' and 'self-evident truths.' If you weren't born white, some of those angels and truths. Well, they just weren't quite as available. I'm not sure they are yet."

"Well, shut my mouth." Muriel concedes.

"PC crap," someone mutters. The audience looks pensive. The Wings stiffen with resistance. The flack's face goes sour. Tuxedo scowls.

McQuitty remains transfixed by his own image.

"This might be a good time to leave." Owen nods toward Melvin. "That man can ruin a party fast."

Muriel studies McQuitty and agrees. She walks forward and tugs on her husband's arm. He is confused and slightly annoyed. He's enjoying this. She whispers she's not feeling well. He follows her to the door where, as if by chance, they encounter the departing Senator Middleton.

The professor has his back to the building. He's railing on, but senses his audience looking past him. He turns to see the ceiling-to-floor window where Representative McQuitty shimmers against the dark exterior brick. He is an apparition in a crazy suit. Hat as big and gray as a thundercloud. He stands very still. Staring down at them. At least they think he's staring at them. In fact, he sees nobody but himself.

It is then that Melvin makes his move. Copying something he saw in a cowboy movie, he twists his right hip slightly forward, fans out his fingers waist high, then uses his thumb to sweep back the right tail of his coat. And there it is, the thirty-eight in its tooled leather holster. The price of freedom.

"What the hell is he doing?" asks one of the protestors.

"Son-of-a-bitch is taunting us," answers another.

McQuitty is posing for himself. But to those watching, the gun says "shut your mouths, or I'll come out there and shut them for you."

A young man picks up a fist-sized piece of broken sidewalk. His throwing motion is smooth and powerful. The missile arches through the night sky, slow and graceful.

"Oh shit," says the older cop.

As Melvin's window shatters, so does restraint. On both sides.

The crowd jumps. Owen hurries Muriel out the entry hall. Her husband chases after them, spurs ringing frantically. Behind him comes a mob of angry Wings. Through the opposite door charge in wild-eyed protestors. The two forces collide, with the senator, his lover, and her husband caught between.

Owen pushes Muriel against a wall. He bends at the waist and braces his arms around her, holding on to a decorative rail. Muriel's husband is clipped in the forehead with a protest sign. He stumbles backward and tries to catch himself, but the spurs keep rolling beneath his heels. Down he goes, disappearing behind two lumbering combatants, hands at each other's throats.

Muriel buries her face in the senator's chest. He makes himself into a human barricade. Holding the wall fiercely. Bitterly. With all the strength he can muster. As the battle rages, blows land across his back and people fall into his legs.

"Goddamn!" someone yells. Falling and flailing, they grab a handful of Middleton's fringed coat and tear it down the middle.

Attacking protestors from behind, the cops are waling. Nightsticks bust heads, arms, and any other body parts that yield to wood.

At the other end, security men and staffers drag Wings back into the exhibit hall. The flack is in the middle of it, her hair flying in all directions. Tuxedo hides behind her, pointing to what other people should do. Walrus collars Wings two at a time, still sucking on his chewing tobacco. Enjoying himself and keeping careful mental notes that will find their way into a future novel.

Inside the exhibit hall, women shriek at ripped garments and the slightest appearance of blood. Melvin stands a few feet back from the shattered window. Dusting broken glass from his hat and suit. Disconnected from all he has triggered.

It's over almost as fast as it began. Sirens and blue lights fill the winter sky.

Ayesha Perez circulates among those sprawled on the ground outside the exhibit hall. Running her own triage. She guides and, if necessary, carries hurt people to their cars.

"Get out of here," she warns. "If you go to the hospital, tell them you fell at home."

Fully aware that every lingering minute increases her own exposure to nightsticks and jail, she squeezes back into the entry hall, where the most seriously hurt still lie on the floor. Hands covering their heads to ward off a few last kicks from Wings.

Ayesha spots Owen Middleton. He is still braced against the wall, holding a woman who sobs against his shoulder. The senator strokes her hair and whispers.

"Muriel," he pleads. "Muriel, stop. Your husband is right there."

Ayesha knows tenderness when she sees it. And intimacy. Deep intimacy.

Muriel's husband is among the greater casualties of the night. The floor was not a good place to be. He got stomped and kneed all to hell. With several broken fingers, he dangles his hands like a begging dog. A cut across his scalp gushes blood. A cop kneels next to him.

"Take it easy, buddy. You'll be okay."

But Derek does not hear the policeman. He does not feel the pain. He stares at his wife and Owen Middleton. The way she clings to him. The way he touches her. He stares, mouth open in disbelief.

‹ ›

A red-faced cop grabs Perez by the shoulders, pulls her outdoors, and presses her against the rough brick façade.

"Bitch," he spits. Another officer steps up to assist.

"I got this one. You help inside."

"Okay!" The red-faced cop hurries back to throw someone else around.

"You need to get out of here," commands his replacement.

It is the older cop. The one who chatted with her earlier in the evening. The ally from what the police department would later describe as the Second Battle of the Trash Can.

"Look at this!" she shrieks and points to a half dozen people slumped on the ground.

"You need to leave," he repeats.

"This is bullshit!" she yells. Tears come to her eyes. Their presence makes her furious.

"I know," the older cop answers. "I know."

"We didn't want this to happen."

"No, I don't believe you did."

"It was that tall man's fault."

"You're right. But all you're going to do now is get arrested."

Ayesha Perez heeds his advice. She can't help anyone from jail. She disappears into the night. Beneath the blanket of stars and the Milky Way.

‹ ›

In his bathtub at the Diamond, Owen soaks his wounds and checks his phone for news updates. There is a lot of online chatter and speculation. People who weren't there express the greatest certainties. After midnight, he receives a text message.

"Back in Wichita. ER. He's upset."

"Take care of him," Owen messages in return. "He's a good man."

Among Owen Middleton's many talents, none is greater than his capacity to compartmentalize. And when those compartments threaten to breach, he seals them with stone.

147

That same day, a mysterious event vexed Stonewall and Ewing County. It would become the stuff of legend.

It began in the shadow of concrete grain elevators, where two thirsty kids stopped to drink from the city park's pump faucet.

"What's that?" asked the brother.

"What's what?" sniped his impatient older sister. He cupped his hand around his ear. She shut off the water to listen. There came a low, moaning sound from the park's privy.

Earlier that afternoon, a pharmaceutical salesman ate a big lunch in Liberal. It didn't agree with him. He stopped in Stonewall, jumped from his car, and ran into the dilapidated city outhouse. As he was pulling up his trousers, he noticed something was missing. His wallet. He looked in the obvious place and there it was, floating amid that which also floats. He hung his slacks on a nail, pulled off shoes and socks, and lowered himself, feet first, to grab the wallet with his toes. The wooden seat creaked, then snapped in two. Down he went. Back up he came. Choking, stuck, and moaning.

The brother and sister ran to the courthouse, where their mother worked. Alongside the Ewing County Sheriff.

Spire pounded on the outhouse wall. Ace waited by his wrecker in case backup was needed.

"Sheriff's department!"

"It's about time!" came the answer.

They pulled the poor fellow out, trying not to touch him in the process. They hosed him off in a nearby carwash and gave him a pair of insulated coveralls from the wrecker's toolbox. The salesman roared off with even greater dispatch than that with which he arrived. The incident was over. But the story had just begun.

Billy did not make an official report on the outhouse caper. The unlucky salesman had suffered indignities enough. Let his name be forever forgotten. But in his quest for quiet resolution, the sheriff made a fatal mistake. He forgot to swear Ace to secrecy.

By early evening, the story was all over town. The mechanic did everything but use a megaphone. What he described was accurate enough. The devil was in an omission. Ace refused to name the victim. It wasn't out of consideration. It was mischief. When asked, he would get a faraway look in his eyes, his best imitation of a haunted thousand-yard stare. He would pause dramatically, then answer.

"I really can't say. Wouldn't be right. This is such a small town."

Ace never actually said the victim was somebody from Stonewall. But he sure didn't correct the misimpression either. He was having too much fun.

By nightfall, half the people in town were on the list of possibilities. The higher they stood, the more gleeful the speculation. Suspects included the mayor, the three county commissioners, business leaders, Doc Howard, and all but one member of the clergy. Father Turney literally had a tight alibi. Literally. He couldn't get even one massive leg down the outhouse hole, much less two.

The next morning, Sheriff Spire's phone began ringing before he could pop open his first soda.

"Would you please tell Leo Ace that I did not fall into the shitter," the newspaper publisher begged.

"Dammit, Billy, you got to do something about these rumors," screeched Doc Howard.

There was even a confession.

"It was me," said an old farmer from out in the county.

"Really, Walter?" the sheriff doubted.

"Well, it's better than telling my wife the truth."

"Which is?"

"I was playing poker," the farmer answered, his voice soft with shame. "You know how she is about that kind of thing."

"Okay," Spire said of the righteous Mrs. Walt. "If she calls, I'll tell her it was you."

Around ten o'clock, after an unending string of angry calls, Billy walked over to Ace's. The usual suspects were gathered. The mechanic was holding court, describing the blow-by-blow and including a detail new to Billy Spire. Something about a Rolex watch that was worth a bundle to whomever dared dive in for it. The mechanic was bright-eyed and loud. So was the gang. Everyone was having a ball. Stonewall hadn't been this lit up in years.

"There is no Rolex watch," Billy interrupted, glaring at Ace. "We don't need to be pulling more people out of there."

"Who was it then, sheriff?" asked one of the old coots. "We got a right to know."

Ace stared back for at least ten seconds. There was pleading with his eyes. Don't spoil this Billy. Please.

"You got a right?" Spire challenged, brows arched.

149

"What if that person comes in my house?" the man argued. "Wants to sit on our good furniture?"

"I seen your furniture," Ace jumped in. "Wouldn't make no difference if he did."

Everybody laughed. Even the fellow with good furniture.

"Come on, sheriff."

Billy looked at Ace. The mechanic's expression had turned a shade more desperate. Finally, Billy Spire spoke.

"I really can't say. Wouldn't be right. This is such a small town."

The garage exploded in curses and laughter.

"Ain't that what I told you?" Ace howled. Over and over.

Billy Spire shrugged. Sometimes, the best thing a sheriff can do is let the good times roll.

Besides, he had other things on his mind. Amid all the morning calls expressing complaint about outhouse rumors, the sheriff heard from Agent Peggy Palmer of the Kansas Bureau of Investigation. She asked if he might come by the Great Bend office within the next few days. They had something to talk about.

"Lab results in?" Billy asked. But it was too late, there was only the click of Agent Palmer hanging up the phone. The KBI is famously efficient in its use of its time.

〈〉

Owen Middleton eats a breakfast of cold cereal the next morning.

The "riot" is big news in the *Topeka Capital-Journal*. Front page, above the fold, is a color photograph of law enforcement in action. In the foreground, a tall young woman is shoved toward the camera by a grimacing cop. In the chaotic background, the senator finds his own bowed back. The top of Muriel's head is visible on his shoulder. Derek is nowhere to be seen.

On page three, there is a small photo of the flack, her hair in wild disarray. She is quoted as wondering why anyone would want to ruin such a lovely and innocent evening.

"I'm afraid this will be a black eye for Kansas," she frets. "Who would want to send us more art, the way it gets treated here?"

An indignant Wing offers a quote that is pithy but off target "It takes a craftsman to build a barn. Any old jackass can kick it down."

A single protestor is interviewed. The bald Lutheran minister claims a red-clad giant taunted the crowd with a gun. There is no other mention of Melvin McQuitty.

The final paragraph of the article notes, with obvious relief, that "Myth-makers of the American West" remains undamaged. It will be crated to an evangelical rally in Lincoln, Nebraska. Where security will most certainly be on high alert.

Owen puts down the newspaper, loads his cup and bowl into the dishwasher. Time to get dressed and head to the Statehouse.

⟨⟩

The Interim Committee on Rural Economic Development meets in the Old Supreme Court Chamber. Third floor of the Kansas Statehouse. The room is towering and ornate. Twenty-foot ceiling, shaded chandeliers, medallions woven into the carpet. Looming at the north end is the original Supreme Court bench. In the center of the room is a large table for staff. Around that table angles an oaken horseshoe for committee members. At the south end is the visitors' galley, with rows of salmon-colored chairs shaped like fiberglass potato chips. Staring balefully down from the walls are Kansas's earliest chief justices. First among them is Thomas Ewing Jr., for whom Ewing County is named.

The chamber is full when Middleton arrives. His timing is impeccable. Not more than three minutes before the meeting is gaveled to attention. Striding purposefully toward steps leading up to the Supreme bench, the senator bypasses small talk. Last second buttonholing. Rushed introductions to people he doesn't particularly want to meet, but whose names he will now be expected to remember. He extends only the minimum of courtesies as he goes.

"Hey, how ya doing?"

"Yeah, good crowd."

"Nice to see you."

Senator Middleton sits at Supreme elevation because he co-chairs the committee, along with a Big Dog from the House. He's already done his homework and understands the bureaucratese, budgetary bafflegab, and political hype perhaps even better than its authors. Still, he opens his briefcase and holds up a sheaf of stapled pages, as if in last-minute study. It's a mask, really. Peeking over the top edge, Owen scans the room. A noisy, jumbled scene. He focuses on a group in the corner. The Wings.

Judging from their gestures, they are reliving last night's battle. Blow by exaggerated blow. Their preening postures suggest they feel pretty good about themselves. They still got it. Can still clean house, if need be. The one with the eyebrows and mustache hoots and slaps another on the shoulder. The slapped fellow yelps, as if a deep bruise has been reinjured. This causes the other Wings to point and laugh. They're having a good time. All except one. Representative McQuitty is pointedly boxed off to the side. Several Wings have their broad backs to him, shoulder to shoulder in an impassable wall. Melvin shifts from foot to foot, anxious to get in the middle.

Nobody faults the representative for starting the trouble. That was okay. Fine, really. But he had committed an unpardonable sin. When push came to shove, and shove came to punches, Melvin didn't throw in. Not at all. While his Wing brothers engaged in rough and tumble, the tall man dusted his costume. And he was carrying a gun for God's sake. Nobody expects Rambo. But to be a man, a man must throw in.

McQuitty shifts from foot to foot. He pulls up a sleeve and rubs gingerly, as if working slivers of glass out of his arm. None of his colleagues buy the act.

What a mess, Owen thinks. He was counting on Melvin to deliver Wing votes.

The House Big Dog flops down next to Middleton and stares straight ahead. He is onto the senator's tricks. Knows Owen is not actually reading. He discreetly muffles the microphone with his hand.

"Have fun last night?"

"Hey buddy," Owen affirms with a bob of his head. "You?"

Big Dog looks grim. He was there, all right. Dragged a few Wings back into the exhibit hall. Solid guy. Big and gruff. Maybe takes himself a little too seriously but cares deeply about the Statehouse and how it's perceived by the people of Kansas. Wants it to be regarded with respect and dignity and trust.

"This place is going to kill me."

"Don't you dare die until the recommendations are done," Middleton grumbles.

Big Dog taps his watch. It's time. He removes his hand from the microphone. Owen raps the gavel in a steady but insistent beat. Attendees find their chairs.

"This is the Interim Committee on Rural Economic Development," Owen announces. His Statehouse voice is dramatic and sonorous.

Everyone in the room understands that this is both serious politics and a hopeless cause.

Since World War I, Kansas's rural population has been in decline. Many places are past the tipping point. Too many old people dead or leaving for better health care and proximity to their expatriated children. Too few children to make up the loss. A few towns will survive. Hays. Garden City. Colby. But the vast majority are fated to die. If they haven't already. And there is nothing the committee can do to alter that pattern. Any more than it can hold up its hands and deflect a prairie tornado.

Nevertheless, rural eco-devo is serious politics. Always has been. The few people remaining in western Kansas are highly reliable voters. And among the many who have relocated, the family farm is still their blood and marrow. They hold dearly to what once was and are fierce in its preservation. Theirs is the politics of identity, and politicians better pay heed.

They do. Every campaign season brings promises, pledges, and soaring rhetoric about a better tomorrow. And so it was that a few days after his inauguration, the newly elected governor of Kansas called the senator from Ewing County.

"Make me look good, Owen. And don't spend too much money doing it."

Senator Middleton kept one leadership position for himself, gave another to the House Big Dog. Having both chambers invested is the smart play. Helps to defray skepticism and scrutiny. Defraying scrutiny is important, for Owen Middleton has a hidden plan. He is determined that Stonewall will be among the exceptions. One of the small towns that does survive. His determination never takes the form of idle musing.

All the interests are there. Road contractors, truckers, bond underwriters. Chambers of Commerce and manufacturers of center pivots, farm equipment, and metal buildings. Rural hospitals fill an entire row. Behind them sit the pro-lifers, always scouting out anti-abortion opportunities. And, of course, there are the ag groups. The Bureau, Association, and others. It's a full house. Everyone sitting upright in their chairs. Listening intently. Visions of free money dancing like wind-blown wheat.

"There is not a lot of extra cash in the coffers," Big Dog cautions.

The room nods as one. They know. Still, hope springs eternal.

Owen adds a non-verbal comment. He shakes his head as if in grave doubt that *any* funding can be found. In fact, finding money is easy for the senator, given his facility with spreadsheets and eye for detail.

Most bureaucrats are fiscally conservative. Their worst fear is running out of funds in the middle of a project. So, they routinely over-ask and under-spend, leaving small surpluses that accrue in quiet little accounts. Capital improvements. Equipment reserve. Over time, those small accruals add up to healthy balances. Owen Middleton knows where all those balances are hidden. He's never touched them before. Tried to respect tight-fisted management. But now he needs the money. Stonewall needs the money.

"Still," Big Dog concludes, "if we can find a way to do a lot of good for a small investment, I'm sure the governor will listen."

Owen gives the crowd his look of affable skepticism. Don't get your hopes too high, he conveys.

The first eco-devo conferee is a bearish economist from Fort Hays State who shows slide after slide of market sectors over time. There are annual variations, but the trends are not good. Especially for small family farms. They are fewer. What remains is larger and more automated. Commodity prices are undermined by their own efficiency. His voice is as soft as he is large. He blinks thoughtfully and asks for questions.

"What is an incentive?" begins Big Dog to make sure everyone starts on the same page.

"Stimulating economic activity by moving money from one source to another."

"Sounds to me like guvment picking winners and losers," one of the Wings says in a loud stage whisper. Representative McQuitty's ears perk up.

"Do incentives work?" Big Dog continues.

"Some of my friends argue that incentives don't really drive a company's economic decisions. Other things are more important, like access to markets and critical feedstocks, skills and costs of labor. Those skeptics suggest that incentives essentially pay businesses for what they were already going to do."

"At the people's expense," mutters another Wing. The economist half-smiles in agreement.

Lobbyists in the gallery squirm in their chairs. They are greedy for incentives and wish the Fort Hays egghead would shut up. They look pleadingly at Owen and Big Dog.

"Some incentives pay off." The economist points to a chart in his handouts. "But, as indicated by this larger bar, overall results are not very impressive."

"Privatize the profits, socialize the costs," Big Dog whispers to Middleton. "That's what my daddy used to say."

"Your daddy didn't work for this governor," Owen rebuts out the corner of his mouth.

The economist concludes and invites questions.

"Do you have any idea how bad things are out there?" a moderate senator asks. His district includes a major packing plant, which is leaning on him for better roads.

"I know they are bad," the economist answers. Calm, almost bland, he is guiltless. The numbers are to blame.

"How do you know that?"

"I study economic reports."

"How much do you get paid to study economic reports?"

"Is my salary in question here?" the economist asks.

"No. But who are you to attack incentives? Sitting there at Fort Hays with your studies and nice salary. I wonder if you haven't lost touch with people who hurt?"

Melvin studies his fellow Wings. He notes how they lean back in their chairs, arms crossed in defiance. Theirs is the politics of elimination. Fewer programs. Lower taxes. Less government. Desperate for redemption, he jumps in.

"Hold on there."

The packing-plant senator glares at being interrupted, but McQuitty doesn't notice. Or care. "Do incentives work or not?"

"I'm not saying incentives never work," the economist clarifies. "But the track record isn't good."

"Isn't it just tampering with the marketplace? Choosing winners and losers?"

Melvin gives a sidelong glance to his fellow Wings. It seems the morning frost may be melting. They are leaning forward now. Listening closely. Paying attention to his inquisition.

Owen glances at Big Dog. He is scowling. Neither of them like the direction this is going. The committee exists to advance incentives, not bury them. Middleton leans close to the microphone and clears his throat.

"The representative from Ewing County raises many good questions. But I wonder if he would entertain a break for coffee and restrooms."

Melvin is on a roll and doesn't like being stopped. He shoots Middleton a dark look. Owen stares back impassively. The representative recognizes warning in those dull eyes.

"Of course," he responds with a princely bow.

"The chair thanks you. We will reconvene in twenty minutes."

The room comes to its feet as one. The volume rises, as people arch their backs and ask each other what they think so far. Lobbyists hurry into the hallway to argue strategy and counterpoints. The irate packing plant senator rushes to the Big Dog, demanding redress for McQuitty's impertinence.

Melvin stretches to his full height, glancing left and right for encouragement. Somehow, the representative got an egghead liberal to make a case for anti-incentive conservativism. The Wings are impressed. But not enough to end the shun. Other than prayer, shunning is their favorite activity.

Senator Middleton heads to a restroom on another floor, far away from small talk and favor seeking. He checks for texts. Nothing from Muriel, which is a good sign. Now to deal with his colleague from Ewing County. He takes the long way back to the chamber, reading every notice on every wall to forestall a conversation he doesn't want to have.

Near the chamber doorway, Melvin is sipping coffee and standing on the edge of the Wing cluster. They have allowed him to come closer, but not yet join them. The senator takes a deep breath, lowers his head. Winding through milling conferees and salmon-colored chairs, he walks up to the tall legislator and extends his hand.

"I just had to stop it," he beams, speaking loud enough to be heard by nearby Wings. "You had that poor professor out on his feet."

Melvin is taken aback. As is everyone else within earshot.

Topeka is a dynamic of connections. A spinning, kaleidoscopic wonder of who's allied with whom, why, and for how long. Of favors done and backs stabbed. Of interests combined then at odds. In the cloistered world of the Kansas Legislature, every synchronicity generates endless speculation.

And now here is the mighty Senator Middleton. Big as life. Shaking hands with Melvin McQuitty, like they are the best of friends. Everyone with a pulse takes notice. Among them, the Wings are most impressed. Owen Middleton may not share their worldview. But he has power. Real power. The kind of power they crave.

"A minute of your time?" the senator asks.

"Absolutely," Melvin answers with a wink toward his open-mouthed colleagues.

Owen guides the tall man to a vacant corner of the chamber. They stand with their backs to the wall and face the room. Positioned so everyone can see them, but no one can hear.

"Act like I just told you something funny," Owen says.

McQuitty tosses his head and snickers as if the senator has shared a clever insight. Owen grins slightly to complete the charade.

"You need to shut up."

Melvin stiffens slightly. But keeps smiling.

"We need those incentives, Melvin. You and me. And here you're goading that economist into talking against them."

"I was just . . ."

"Trying to get back into favor with your buddies," the senator completes.

McQuitty has nothing left to say. Middleton is exactly right.

"You just sit there and be quiet," Owen says.

Anger flashes across Melvin's face. He quickly forces it into a broad smile. Everyone in the chamber is stealing glances, and not being very coy about it.

"You see them," the senator says. "They're all wondering why Owen Middleton is hanging out with that guy. Every second we stand here together, you gain stature. Understand?"

Melvin nods.

"Try not to waste it."

The balance of the hearing involves a long string of people looking for handouts. They speak of crumbling water treatment plants, decrepit classrooms, and bottomless potholes. They wave statistical charts about waiting times, consumer demand, and work hours lost. They warn of tornadoes, communicable livestock disease, and strains on the power grid. They lay out heart-wrenching tales of childhood morbidity rates and mental health declines.

"More plagues than the Bible," Big Dog mutters.

"And way fewer prophets," Owen replies.

The pleading goes on for hours. Senator Middleton tries to listen, because every speaker went to a lot of trouble preparing comments. And he cares deeply about policy and plight. But his thoughts keep drifting to money. How much and how it will move.

Fifteen million should be plenty. With cooperation from the Secretary of Administration, a notoriously uncooperative man, hidden balances can be shifted to the Kansas Finance Commission, of which Owen is the immediate past chair.

"Any questions, Senator Middleton?" Big Dog is speaking. "Owen?"

It takes the senator a second to reorient. He puts on an air of careful consideration.

"No," he finally answers. "We certainly have a lot to think about."

"The Interim Committee on Rural Economic Development hearing is concluded," Big Dog proclaims with a heavy hit of the gavel. "You all drive safe."

"Hated to wake you up," Big Dog teases after muting the microphone.

"I was dreaming about margaritas," Owen answers.

Chairs shuffle, the room stands and stretches. A reporter approaches in search of a quote.

"Be my guest," Owen says with a courtly bow.

Big Dog is gruffly pleased and combs his hair before stepping in front of the camera.

Out the corner of his eye, Owen sees McQuitty approaching. Wanting more face time. More transfused influence. Middleton grabs his briefcase and disappears out a back door. He hurries from the Statehouse, head down and shoulders hunched. With no Muriel to linger with, he decides to head straight home. Hours alone in the car. Undistracted time to work through details.

Part 3

‹›

A FEW DAYS AFTER THE outhouse caper, a second incident befalls Ewing County. This one not so amusing in either its emergence or consequence.

Judy and Roy Engel are people of steady habit and obsessive yard care. He hand-sharpens his lawnmower blade every week to ensure uniform length and crisp cuts. Fallen leaves are whisked up first thing in the morning and last thing before dusk. Flowers evenly spaced, in pretty little rows. More than nature perfected, this is nature beaten into submission. The Engels are in their mid-eighties. Roy is skinny, with a deeply lined face and chin whiskers. He wears a straw hat in the summer, corduroys and a woolen cap in winter. Judy is matronly plump and makes her own dresses, each with a demure little cape. The design changes only in fabric. Light cottons when it's warm, heavy wool for the cold. This day is blustery and chill.

After morning yard work, they go in for a parsimonious lunch and a

nap. They wake, read the paper, pay the bills, and attend to correspondence. Right at three o'clock, the Engels walk two blocks to the post
office on courthouse square. After depositing the mail, they stop by the
Gas-N-Go for a cup of coffee and donut. They sit at a table in the back
corner, near the soda dispenser and rotating hot dog grill. Occasionally,
they are joined by friends from church with whom they discuss books,
prayer, and the news. Most often, as on the day of the incident, they sit
alone in comfortable silence.

That day, as they get up to leave, Roy slaps his money on the counter.
Becca, the young mother with a bad complexion and radiant smile, is
absorbed in paperwork. Anxiously chewing on a pencil that is already
riddled with teeth marks.

"What you doing there?" Roy asks.

"Oh, nothing," Becca answers, sliding a handful of forms beneath the
counter. At the suggestion of Owen Middleton, she is applying to Colby
Community College. Having such an aspiration embarrasses her. Nobody
in her family ever dared dream of higher education. She shifts the topic.
"Miss Judy, what do you have in the quilt show this year?"

Judy blushes. Her quilts are regionally famous. Precise and dense
affairs, so heavily laden with fabric and thread that they hang a deep sag
into even the heaviest dowel.

"Oh, just a little something," she answers, flapping her wrists as if to
make the whole thing go away.

"Best one she ever made," Roy brags. He opens the door and holds
it for his wife.

"Can't wait to see."

The young woman watches the two old regulars lean into the wind.
Roy pulls his hat down low, lest it be blown away. Judy tightens her coat
and scarf. Then off they go, hand in hand. When they are no longer in
sight, Becca goes back to her application.

It usually takes the Engels about fifteen minutes to walk two blocks
home. The distance is short, but they are never in a rush. They study the
neighbors' yards.

"Isn't that adorable," Judy coos over a ceramic gnome someone set
in their garden.

"Hideous," Roy grumbles. "That's what lazy people do instead of
actually planting something. And look at those trash cans. Why don't
they store those damn things behind the garage?"

"Now, honey," Judy hopelessly frets.

Her thought is interrupted. Roy Engel goes to the ground hard, without warning or provocation.

It is a pit bull. Low slung and powerful. White with black brindle and the distended teats of overbreeding. Roy fights as valiantly as an eighty-something can fight. He hollers and pushes away with his forearm. The dog sinks its massive jaws into the heavy coat sleeve and shakes furiously.

"Stop!" Judy screams. Her arms reach toward her husband even as she is drawn back by fear. "Stop it!"

By then, the teeth are tearing into skin. Brittle bones snap.

As if shot by cannons, two neighbors fly out their doors. Housewives, stout and fearless. One grabs a snow shovel off the porch. The other brandishes the Chinese cleaver she was using to dice onions. They set upon the dog with great fury. Swinging, cursing, slashing, and swinging some more. The dog holds on like death. Until the cleaver severs an artery on its inner thigh. The pit bull yelps, releases, and runs. Bleeding profusely, it drags the cut leg behind. One of the housewives chases after it, still cursing and murderous, but hopelessly outpaced. The wounded animal disappears around the corner.

The torn sleeve of Roy's coat is covered with blood. Some his, some from the dog. He is conscious, but just barely. Sliding into shock. Another neighbor runs out of her house with a blanket and phone. She is already telling the ambulance to hurry.

Undone by it all, Judy's eyes roll back in her head. She topples over and is caught by the third housewife.

"We got two people down," the woman yells into her phone.

Within minutes, Roy Engel is in the back of an ambulance, racing to Stonewall Hospital. The volunteer EMT cuts away Roy's coat and wraps gauze around the bleeding forearm. Judy wobbles on the bench seat next to him. He urges her to bend low, to put her head between her knees. When she tries, she topples forward onto her husband. Roy moans with pain. The EMT is trying his best to hold her up when the doors fly open. Doc and Mama Doc are standing there. She with an oxygen tank, he with a stethoscope draped around his neck. The old physician takes one look and whistles softly.

"Jesus, Roy. What have you done to yourself?"

Back in the street, Billy Spire swings out of his pickup. A dozen witnesses run up, pointing and urgent.

"Give me a minute," he says, looking up and down the street. *The first pulse to take is your own,* he thinks to himself. He pulls a small spiral notebook from his pocket, jots down the date and time.

"Okay," he says. "What happened?"

They all agree it was a dog. Either a pit bull, boxer, Rottweiler, or mutt of undiscernible breeding. It was white, or gray, or brown, or some combination of all three. Nobody ever saw the dog before, unless it was that spotted mutt abandoned out at the dump. Roy didn't do anything to provoke the attack. He was just looking at that yard troll. Or maybe he threw something. Truth be told, nobody was looking out the window until Judy screamed. Why would they be? All agree the wounded animal ran around the corner. In unison, they point to the trail of blood.

"Got it," Billy finishes scribbling. "Now you all go back inside. There's a wounded animal out here. I'll let you know when it's safe."

"You're not going alone," says the housewife, still brandishing the Chinese cleaver in her hand. Spire wishes Ace were around to help with the neighbors. But the mechanic is out on the highway, fixing a flat.

"I'll be fine."

The neighbors push back.

"We're going with you."

"Appreciate it," Spire assures. "I really do. But I don't want to have to worry about anyone but myself."

Spire takes a shotgun from his truck. He jacks in a shell and starts following the trail of crimson, glowing against the white residue of road salt. Within half a block, a pickup rolls up behind him. The vigilant neighbors will not be denied. An old man drives, the two housewives are standing in the bed, peering over the cab roof. One still carries the Chinese cleaver, the other has traded her snow shovel for a hunting rifle. The sheriff glares back over his shoulder.

"What are you going to do, Billy Spire?" the old man hollers out the window. "Arrest us for driving on a public street?"

Billy doesn't acknowledge them. He doesn't want to encourage. But he is grateful for their company, for their caring.

Of all the familiar streets in Stonewall, Kansas, this one is even more so. Billy has been over these very steps hundreds of times. He could walk them with his eyes closed. It was the way the Spire kids went to school.

At the end of the street, the blood trail goes left, and there it is. The decrepit single-wide trailer in which the Spire family once and briefly lived. In a barren dirt lot off to itself, as if the other houses, themselves nothing to brag about, had given it the cold shoulder. The trailer sat empty for some time, but there are new residents. Speckles of blood head toward its steps. Spire's eyes are restless. Scanning left and right. Shotgun at the ready.

Billy hasn't been inside the trailer for decades. He went there once soon after his family took off, to find some sense of them in familiar smells and worn furniture. But its dark interior and echoes of anger made him feel even lonelier. So he left and never went back. And though he drives by the trailer nearly every day, for Stonewall is such a small place, it still makes Billy's heart twist. Wondering what became of the little brothers and sisters who have drifted so far beyond his reach.

The place has bent further with time. Hardly a straight line or right angle to be found. Plywood covers broken windows. Bald tires are scattered across the roof to muffle the rattle of sheet-metal in the wind. Smoke rises from the stovepipe. It's still occupied, unimaginable as that may seem even among the poor and weary of Ewing County.

Movement down the street catches the sheriff's eye. A car turns right and disappears. It is an old Chevy Caprice, modified to ride low on its frame. The muffler is bad.

Spire pauses in front of the trailer to map his approach. The pickup full of neighbors stops a few yards back at the edge of the road. The women search in all directions from their lookout. Spire climbs the steps and knocks.

The door opens. A young Latino man with short-cropped hair leans out. He wears saggy jeans and a black tee shirt. He yawns widely and squints into daylight. Spire suspects the young man is faking. There are no sleep scars, no jet hair, too few wrinkles in his clothes.

"What's your name?"

"Dominguez," he answers.

"First or last."

"Cruz Dominguez." The young man squints at the truck full of neighbors. "What's going on?"

"Dog attacked an old man just around the corner. Blood leads to your door."

"Somebody was hurt?" The kid looks concerned. Or maybe he is trying to look concerned.

"Yes," the sheriff answers.

"Oh man. What a drag. But we got no dog here."

"Mind if I look for myself?"

"Do I have a choice?" the young man scowls.

"Not when there's imminent danger."

"Then I guess you can look." He nods at the shotgun. "But that stays outside. My little sister, she's scared of guns."

Spire walks back to the truck, hands his weapon to the housewife holding the cleaver.

"I'm coming with you," she says.

"Me, too," chimes the one with the hunting rifle.

"No, you're not. Neither of you."

Spire returns to the steps. Cruz Dominguez waves him inside with exaggerated gallantry and a contemptuous sneer. The sheriff steps through the door and pauses for his eyes to adjust. It is dim in there, just as depressing as Billy recalls. There is a woodstove in the middle of the living room, its chimney crudely vented through the ceiling. Dirty dishes are stacked on the counters. Worn rugs lie over worn rugs to insulate the thin floor. The threadbare couch and chair smell of extended use and marijuana. The only light comes from a plastic chandelier above the dining table. Two of the three bulbs are burned out.

"Is it always this dark in here?" the sheriff asks.

"What is there to see?"

There is a rustling in the far end of the trailer. Spire palms his handgun. A little girl appears. She is about nine years old, wearing Hello Kitty pajamas and smudged glasses with pink plastic frames. Half asleep, she leans against the young man. When she realizes that Spire is a cop, she starts to cry.

"No, baby." He pets her hair. "It's nothing, nada."

"I know you," Billy says in the kind voice he uses to comfort children. "Your name is Luciana. We met at the river. Don't you remember?"

The little girl nods.

"What river? What are you talking about?" There is a tense edge to the young man's questions.

Crouching to eye level, the sheriff looks at Luciana in sympathy. He is sorry that she is frightened. Sorry she lives in this sad, hopeless place. Sorry that she is an innocent child with no control. Sorry at a depth known only by those who have lived in the same place and walked the same streets.

"She was with her girl troop. La Buena Familia."

"He said we were brave and smart," Luciana tells her brother, looking up and still leaning against his legs.

"Okay, so you know her," dismisses the young man. "You still don't see no dog."

"Not in this room," Spire answers. "You and your sister stay right where you are. Do not move."

At one end of the trailer is the master bedroom. It is just as worn but a little neater than the living room. On the built-in vanity are school pictures of Cruz and Luciana. He is high-school aged, even thinner than now and just beginning to show facial hair. She looks the same. Could be this year's photo. She grins awkwardly, the way kids do when they're told to smile.

The bed is made. Cheap paisley spread with fitted corners. Above the headboard are two nails where Old Joe Spire used to set his lever-action rifle. Between the nails hangs a wooden crucifix.

The sheriff sighs. A crown of thorns. Agony. Permanent conditions of that dwelling, no matter who the occupant. He goes to the other end of the trailer. Cruz glares as he passes. Luciana looks at the floor.

The back bedroom, from which the little girl emerged, is only slightly larger than the single bed it contains. Billy used to sleep with his brothers and sisters in that tight space, all of them tumbled together like a pile of puppies. This room is cluttered but trying to be cheerful. The closet is full of glittery clothes and bright sneakers. The bed is overrun with stuffed animals. Photos of boy bands are taped to the walls.

"Who else lives here?" Spire asks loudly.

"Just us and our parents," Cruz answers. The sheriff can hear him creeping closer.

"I told you to stay where you are."

The movement stops.

Spire spots a black nylon gym bag under the bed. Out of place amid all the shimmers and pastels. Billy sweeps aside some stuffed animals and sets the gym bag on the bed. It contains marijuana, packed loose in small baggies. With them is a leather billfold, full of money. Comes to seven hundred eighty dollars. He stuffs the cash and dope in the cargo pockets of his trousers. Closes the bag and carries it with him to the living room.

"And you sleep where?" Spire asks.

"Here. There. Wherever I lay my head." The young man stares at the nylon bag.

Spire crouches in front of Luciana.

"Honey, was there a dog?"

"I already told you, man. No dog."

"I'm asking her."

Luciana looks over the sheriff's shoulder at her brother. Cruz shakes his head, so she does the same. Spire stands and turns.

"And that blood on your doorstep?"

The young man thinks. Or pretends to think.

"Oh yeah," he recalls. "Me and a buddy had an argument. Got a little out of hand. He ended up with a bloody nose."

"And left a trail all down the street?"

"I don't know where he went."

"You got a name? I could arrest him for assault."

"No, man, we're good. Besides I only know him as Paco. Just some dude passing through."

"Car drove away from here a few minutes ago. Chevy. Lowered. Bad muffler. Who was that?"

"Chevy? Bad muffler?" the young man shrugs. "Don't know nothing about it."

"Honey, can I speak to your brother alone?"

Luciana blinks behind her smudged glasses.

"Go back to your bedroom," Cruz gently urges.

When Luciana is gone, Spire holds up the gym bag. The young man shifts uncomfortably. His eyes go to the door, but there is no way around the brutal-looking sheriff.

"This yours?" Billy asks, opening the zipper.

"No, man. I swear. It belongs to Paco."

"Hidden where your little sister sleeps?"

"I don't know how it even got there."

"How do you think she would do in foster care? And your parents, they got papers?"

Cruz falls silent. He stares fearfully into the eyes of Billy Spire, whose cruel face is even crueler with disdain.

"I'd lock you up but for that little girl." The sheriff does not mention Ayesha Perez, but he still hears her words. *Would it kill you to do something kind?* "So, I'm going to give you a break."

He opens the bag and turns it upside down. There is nothing left to fall out.

The young man looks panicked.

"Somebody is not going to be very happy, are they?"

"They're bad."

"Then if I was you, I'd leave and not come back."

"You're gonna keep it for yourself?" Cruz asks.

"It will be at the courthouse. Waiting for someone to come prove ownership."

The young man glares defiantly. He's been shaken down before. Many times.

"One last question," the sheriff persists. "And you better get it right. The Chevy with the bad muffler. Where did it go?"

"Dodge, I think."

"Why?"

"There's a vet who treats fighting dogs. Cash only, no questions."

"Dog belongs to you?"

"No, man. Someone I know."

"Then you might try to know better people."

Billy Spire walks out the door. The waiting neighbors perk up.

"No dog," the sheriff announces.

"Billy," argues the old man driving the pickup. "It didn't go anyplace but that trailer."

The neighbors, blinded by indignation, fail to notice the additional volume in his pockets.

"Maybe so," Billy answers. "But who knows why a hurt animal runs one direction or the other?"

"I don't see any trails other than the one we followed," the cleaver woman observes.

"No dog," Billy repeats.

"You should chase them off anyway," the rifle woman adds.

"Why?"

"Because nothing good comes out of a place like that."

Spire stares into the distance, as if he can see through houses, trees, and parked cars. All the way back to earlier generations of neighbors who surely said the same thing about his family. About him. The legacy of the trailer may remain, but the dog is gone. Cruz will be on the run. And there is no reason the little girl should suffer.

"Well, that trailer is not much. Never has been," he concedes. "But for some people, it's all they got."

The old man neighbor snorts.

"I wouldn't worry too much about that dog," Billy Spire concludes. "I'm guessing it's a long way off by now. And probably dead."

"And what about that family?"

"Poor people like that move around. They'll be gone soon enough. Just wait."

But it would turn out that Ewing County had run flat out of patience.

<>

The morning after the dog attack, rumors bounce through the halls of Stonewall High. Most are not accurate.

"The old man lost his arm."

In fact, Roy Engel's arm is seriously damaged. Radius and ulna cracked. More than fifty stitches. But it remains attached and will go with Roy to the grave.

"Had to helicopter him out to save his life."

He was whisked out of town. But not by a helicopter. By a late-model Honda CRV. Their daughter came and took them to her home in Hays. More out of concern for her mother than her dad. Roy is a fount of endless complaints, even in the best of circumstances. And Judy was terribly shaken by the attack. Appalled at being so useless, as if there were anything she could have done.

"Dog belongs to some Mexican thug who laughed at what happened."

This rumor was harder to dispel. The truth was warped by too many narratives.

Like most of western Kansas, Ewing County is full of conservative white people. Conservative, meaning they don't like change. But change has come to western Kansas with heartless insistence. White families stream away. Latino families trickle in. Reactions run the gamut.

Some folks just don't like people of color. Any color. Black. Latino. Asian. They miss the world of their youth. White, God-fearing, and male dominated. Bowling leagues and bridge games. A community bonded together. If, that is, you were white, God-fearing, and male-dominated. These people wish all the "coloreds" would just go away and leave them alone with their memories.

Others think, sure, it would be nice if things could go back to how they were. But that isn't going to happen. We need to be realistic. Population is essential to survival. No people. No schools. No hospital. No shops. No future. They understand that different cultures bring problems. All those languages to accommodate. Fights that erupt when brown boys try to hold hands with white girls. They understand, but what's the alternative? There is no choice but to let them come. Still, those folks should stay in their part of town. Just as we stay in ours.

Some value Latino workers. Farmers, construction firms, roofers, packing plants. All depend on cheap workers who take jobs no white man would touch. Plus, Latinos bring a strong work ethic and mechanical skills. Wouldn't trade them for local labor, even if it were available.

Which it's not. And if problems arise? Immigration services is a just phone call away.

Liberals and clergy do not always agree, not on things like gays and abortion. But when it comes to immigrants, their hearts are equally open. Liberals perceive that we are all strangers in a strange land. There, but for the mercy. The clergy have pews to fill and gospel to preach. Latinos arrive as people of family and faith. Children of God. Shall we gather by the river?

These positions are not fixed. Perspectives and alignments change. Day to day, love to love, injury to injury, situation to situation. Like spinning neutrons and protons of identity. Sometimes in frictionless orbits. Sometimes in rude explosions. The day after Roy Engel was hurt, Stonewall High is reeling toward the latter. School staff tries to keep the lid on. They walk the halls, smiling and friendly, watching bathrooms and the blind corners of stairwells. The principal calls Billy Spire.

"Would you mind hanging around here today? Driving the perimeter? Letting everyone know you're close? No trouble so far, and we'd like to keep it that way."

It is at lunch and in the cafeteria that things go critical. Turns out that the grownups are looking in the wrong direction. After all, who would suspect the nerds?

As usual, they are sitting off by themselves. Absorbed by video games and alternative realities. Two boys are engrossed in some sort of gothic board game, inscrutable to the uninitiated. After thinking about it forever, one finally moves his piece.

"You can't do that," says a brown boy. The only one in the group.

"Why not?" a white boy asks defensively. This is no trifling matter. It's taken him four minutes to think this through.

"Because you can't wait to take a wizard."

"Bullshit."

"Has to be the next turn. Read the rules."

"I have read them," white boy snaps. "But maybe the Mexican version is different."

The brown boy, who actually is from Panama, has tried so very hard to fit in. So hard, in fact, that he has broken off from the other Latino kids, from the perilous trajectories that are too often the only trajectories available. Now, he is on an island by himself. Alone among whites. His emotions well up, threatening either tears or trouble.

"Kiss my ass," he says, voice rising.

The white boy's grandpa was one of the few people in town who would talk to Russ Haycock. Not that they were friends. Haycock wasn't a friendly man. They were more like associates, drawn together by shared perceptions. The grandpa also has a decal in his back window that reads "Posse Comitatus, Est. 1878." The white boy usually skews away from his racist grandfather. Unless he's pissed off.

"Why don't you go back to where you come from? And take that dog with you."

"Fuck you," brown boy replies.

"Hey guys, it's only a game," cries a sisterly nerd in a raspberry beret. She is too late.

"Fucking beaner," white boy yells as he flips over the board. Game pieces go flying. The phys ed teacher and principal notice commotion on the far side of the cafeteria.

In the hierarchy of Stonewall High insults, "beaner" is near the top. Fighting serious. The entire nerd community is stunned into silence.

"Stop this right now," the sisterly one scolds. "You two are friends."

"Fuck this," brown boy says. He stomps off and angrily dumps his cafeteria dishes onto the conveyer belt. The silverware clatters loud enough to disturb a nearby table of white jocks as they design football plays on a napkin.

"Hey, man, keep it down," one snaps.

"Screw you," brown boy answers. PE teacher and principal start running.

One of the jocks stands up and barrels forward, fists clenched. It's a mistake. Brown boy grew up in Panama City, where every kid aspires to be Roberto Duran. National hero with Hands of Stone. He meets the barreling athlete with a combination of short, brutal punches. The jock is stunned. Blood begins spewing from his nose. The two adults swoop in like hawks. Like the highway patrol. Jock is pulled one direction, brown boy the other. They are out of there. Dragged by their collars to the administrative office.

The only remaining cafeteria sound is the sisterly nerd's quiet weeping. A young English teacher, trim and cool, puts her arm around the girl's shoulders. The remaining jocks head to the weight room, to blow off steam in a bench-press contest. White nerd drops to his hands and knees. Crawling after scattered game pieces, hoping to be invisible. But before long he, too, ends up in the principal's office.

Alerted by a secretary, Billy Spire wheels into the parking lot and stomps into the school building. He listens to all accounts then takes the principal aside.

"I think we need a town meeting. Talk us down a little."

"Amen," the principal agrees.

‹›

A note is sent home with every student, inviting parents to a community gathering. Tomorrow night. Staff and teachers spread the word. The principal personally invites local leaders. The clergy, Doc Howard, city commission, and other elected officials. The next morning, phone calls—ranging from curious to alarmed—start rolling in. School staff has been carefully prepped on how to answer questions.

"Community" and "whole" and "unity" are words of the day.

The next night, Ewing County assembles at the scene of the crime. In the cafeteria, with its chipped linoleum floor, banged up steel counters, and rows of nicked dining tables. Tall windows line the west wall. The meeting will not start for an hour, but old people like to give themselves plenty of time. The front table fills with the same baby bird ladies who were at Haycock's funeral.

"My, doesn't this place look grand?" one coos.

"Not really," another cranks. She taps her fingernail on a gray composite tabletop. Someone has defiled it with a crude picture of a penis that remains apparent, even after many scrubbings.

"Oh well," says the first, cheerfully. "Ain't like we never seen one of those before."

Girls and boys from the pep club help with the seating. They wear crimson and gray tee shirts that read, "Go Wolves!" They offer their elbows and walk their guests slowly. Very slowly. Even slower than needed. Rough old farmers and their wives are amused at such coddling.

The pep club kids know all the elders by name. Half of them are kin. In Stonewall, just about every person in town shows up for the senior prom. And not just to watch. They drink punch and dance right along with the graduating class. Old couples do jaunty little two-steps. Small kids jump and wiggle. The actual graduates, all dolled up, bump and grind like they've seen on TV shows. Dancing cool, until snatched by some old aunt or little nephew. Then they two-step or wiggle with beaming smiles.

The sheriff arrives early, too. To serve as a calming, or intimidating, presence. Whichever is required. Walking in through the main hallway, his boot heels click upon freshly waxed tile. He stops to look at himself.

The top shelf of the school's trophy cabinet is reserved for Billy Spire, and Billy Spire alone. He remains Stonewall High's only athlete to attain Kansas-wide honors. All State in football. Runner up for Player of the Year. There is an oak plaque, its brass plate engraved with his name. Next to it is an eight-by-ten glossy of the young man in action. Spire has his back to the camera, his jersey number, fifty-one, fully visible. His explosive tackle sends an opposing player flying up, back, and away. Arms forever flailing mid-air.

"You're still the man," says a voice behind him. It is Owen Middleton.

"And that's still my better side," Billy says, tapping the glass case to indicate his broad back and powerful butt.

"Well," Owen patiently explains, "small children walk this hall every day. We wouldn't want them to have nightmares, would we."

Spire chuckles, then notices Owen's jacket and tie.

"Announcing for governor?"

"I could do better than the one we got." Owen is half kidding. He and the governor are friends, even allies. It's a smart partnership to nurture. And he's half not kidding. Middletons are raised to be confident. "But no, I'm not announcing anything. Speaking engagement in Garden City. Can only stay a minute."

"Lucky you."

"I'd rather be here, but this has been on my calendar for months. Can't cancel this late."

In truth, what the senator can't do is get out of there fast enough. This is the kind of volatile situation Owen avoids at all costs. Emotions may get fierce. Sides may be taken. Resentments may linger. Not good for a senator who strives to stay on good terms with everyone. Always.

<>

The crowd is relieved to see Billy and Owen. The sheriff will keep things under control. The senator will say exactly the right words. Butter wouldn't melt in his mouth. Hellos ring from every corner. The baby bird ladies twitter and hold out their hands for the two electeds to shake. They do, with gentleness and familiarity. Calling each lady by name. The principal rushes to greet the pair.

"Thanks for being here."

"I can only stay a minute," Middleton preempts.

There is a fuss in the entryway. Fathers of the jock and brown boy have arrived at the same time. The white father looks heavy and strong.

174

The brown father, ropy and tough. They square to each other as their sons hang back, looking sheepishly at the ground. Spire moves over and steps between them.

"Nice to see you, fellows." His brick-wall presence holds them apart.

"My kid has a broken nose," white father snarls.

"Good," brown father answers.

Billy turns so the audience cannot hear and speaks softly.

"This is over right now," he says. "Unless you need me to finish it."

The sheriff looks back and forth between the two. His forehead is furrowed, as if daring to be challenged. There is not one hint of play in his eyes.

"Billy, I got to stand up for my boy," white father pleads.

"You and your boy both need to learn how to stay sitting down," Spire answers.

He turns to the brown father.

"And yours is pretty handy with his fists."

"When he has to be," the father brags.

"You didn't *have to be* yesterday, did you?" Spire asks the boy.

"I guess not," brown boy replies.

"And how do you feel today?"

"Terrible."

"Yes," Billy agrees. "That's how it feels."

The kid says nothing, but Spire sees his eyes dampen with remorse. The kind of remorse that's ready to listen.

"I used to love fighting and hurting people." The sheriff smiles ruefully. "Nobody dared treat me with disrespect. Wouldn't tolerate it. Then, when I became an MP, I threw a smartass kid across a room. He was shoplifting at the PX. He landed on a metal chair and broke his back. Ended up in a wheelchair. As far as I was concerned, the kid just had bad luck. In the wrong place at the wrong time."

The two boys and their fathers listen silently. But their expressions change as thoughts shift from anger to consequence.

"A few weeks later, I was waiting in the emergency room while they stitched up an AWOL I arrested. I wandered into the PT lab, and there was the kid I hurt. He was trying to stand up. Had metal braces on his legs and two nurses lifting him. It wasn't working. In spite of all his heart and effort, it was something he would never do again. Stand on his own two feet. The punishment I doled out . . . it didn't fit the crime."

"Did you feel bad?" asks jock.

"I felt lost and hateful toward myself," Spire admits. "On my next leave, I came back here to talk to an old friend. Tell him what I'd done."

"What did he say?"

"He told me that I was good at violence, but that violence was not good for me. Would only take me further and further from the best in myself. That if I was happy being feared, I might as well keep on doing what I was doing. But if I wanted true respect, I needed to find the better angels of my nature. Those were the words Mr. Middleton used, 'better angels.' Just like Lincoln. I didn't know 'better angels' actually existed. Especially in me. But I decided to give it a try. To be a better person."

"What happened to the guy in the wheelchair?" the white boy asks.

"He got a lung infection and died. Never left the hospital."

The fathers and sons are taken aback. They look at each other in sorrow.

"Do you still feel bad?" one asks.

"Forever," Billy answers.

More people shuffle into the cafeteria. The sheriff looks around, then addresses the two fathers.

"Why don't you do us all a favor? You don't have to sit together. But don't sit too far apart, either."

The fathers choose seats next to one another. The sons pause before following. Jock has a bandage across his nose and blackened eyes. Brown boy mutters "Sorry." Jock shrugs "It happens." The sheriff nods. The past is the past.

A few minutes later, four more people enter the cafeteria.

They are led by Luciana, in her still smudged pink plastic glasses. She wears sparkly shoes, red stretch pants, and a Minnie Mouse tee shirt that runs tight across her belly. Her furry coat is folded in the arms of a woman who is obviously her mother. Same round, sweet face. The mother wears high-waisted jeans and a sparkly clip in her hair. Behind them trails the father. He looks like Cruz, only shorter and thicker. Clean shaven with a crew cut. The parents are of indeterminant age. They move like younger people, lithe and quick. Their teeth are bright. But their skin has been aged by too much sun, too much worry, and too many hard times.

Behind the father appears Ayesha Perez. She holds her head high, towering over Luciana and her parents, radiating defiant confidence. She spots Billy and herds the Dominguez family in his direction. All eyes follow.

"That's them," blurts a mother in the crowd. "She's in my daughter's class. The dog came from their trailer."

Curious glances harden into stern glares.

"Sheriff Spire. You spoke with Luciana yesterday?" Perez talks loud, wanting to be overheard.

"Yes, I did," Billy replies. He speaks softly, hoping for a more private conversation. The whole town doesn't need to be in on this.

"I'm not sure that was appropriate," Ayesha continues, pointedly ignoring the sheriff's hint at discretion.

"If this is what you want," Spire shrugs, raising his voice to match hers. "I was attempting to locate a dangerous dog. It had already damn near killed an old man."

"And you went after a Latino family because . . ."

"Because the dog was cut, and its blood led right to their front door."

Ayesha flinches a tiny bit. Obviously, this is news to her. The sheriff is not surprised that Cruz Dominguez omitted a few key details. Perez motions the couple to her side.

"People have been driving by their trailer since yesterday. Mostly they shout. But some even get out and stare. Luciana's parents are afraid for their little girl."

"There are a lot of knuckleheads out there." Now Spire is glad to raise his volume. He wants the entire cafeteria to hear. "People need to mind their own business. I catch anyone snooping around that trailer, they'll be sorry."

Collectively, the crowd looks a little embarrassed.

Ayesha Perez leans back and self-consciously tugs the collar of her shirt. Her standard approach of indignation has been thrown off by new facts and unexpected cooperation. She is not sure what to do next. The sheriff senses her momentary confusion. He gently takes her arm and leads her to a corner where they can continue the conversation. Quietly. The Dominguez family stays where they are, uncertain as to what to do. Perez waves for them to come over.

The principal decides it's time to start. He taps the microphone and asks if people can hear. They can. But they are trying to eavesdrop on the sheriff's conversation and don't appreciate being distracted. He keeps tapping and repeating "one, two, three."

"I need to ask about your son," the sheriff says to the parents.

The father looks concerned and says something in Spanish to his wife. Mr. Dominguez is hiding his right hand behind the small of his back. Tucking it into his belt.

"I'm Billy Spire." The sheriff reaches out to shake.

The father reluctantly does the same. But instead of shaking Mr. Dominguez's hand, Billy grasps and examines it, with little regard for subtlety. There, on the base of the thumb is a tattoo. Five dots, like the face of a die. Four in the corners, one in the center. Four walls with a prisoner in the middle. The mark of one who has spent time in jail.

"I'm trying to do better," the father says.

Billy stares hard into the man's eyes.

Cops have uniquely powerful roles in public service. They decide who is the victim and who is the villain. Who deserves help, and who deserves to be tuned up with a nightstick. Often, that decision is instantaneous. Based on intuition and flickers of emotion. The face of Mr. Dominguez is steady, honest, and sorrowful. Spire decides to believe him.

"Your son?" he asks. "Dogfighting? Dope?"

"Maybe."

"And you let him live with you?"

"He is my son," Dominguez again acknowledges. "I did bad things, too. Worse than him. People stood by me. Helped me change. I hope he will change, too."

Perez butts in.

"These people have no control over their adult son. They should not suffer for what he does."

"I wish justice were that perfect," Spire sighs.

Once again, the tall woman is surprised. Most white people, and even more cops, are eager to blame parents with dark skin for failings of their kids. Just as most white parents are blind to the fact that their children are just as guilty. But scrutinized less, seldom pulled over, and rarely prosecuted.

"You have an interesting take on things," Perez says.

"Yeah, well," Billy muses. "I lived in that trailer myself when I was a child. It was bad then. Worse now."

An enormous figure looms up behind them.

"Father Turney," Spire says. "This is Ayesha Perez and the Dominguez family. Would you mind sitting with them?"

Something is obviously going on. There is tension in the room and a lot of eyes staring in their direction. But the priest doesn't need an explanation right now. Blessed are the peacemakers. He gestures toward a row of empty chairs. Luciana's tiny parents take seats and stare forward. Blank and obdurate as stone.

"After you," Father Turney says to Ayesha, extending his arm and a kind smile. She takes his elbow and smiles back.

Billy watches. She shows a warmth that he has not seen before. A smile that lights up her face and softens her eyes. He wishes he looked as kindly as the priest. But he is used to seeing himself through the eyes of others.

The principal finally stops tapping and testing.

"Thank you for joining us, everybody. Shall we get started? Let me introduce . . ."

One of the baby bird ladies frantically waves her handkerchief. The principal goes over and bends down. She whispers in his ear. He nods and goes back to the microphone.

"Please rise for the Pledge of Allegiance," he announces with an expression of restored formality. The room shuffles to its feet.

The Dominguez parents do the best they can with the words, hands over their hearts. Luciana knows the pledge perfectly. She recites it with confidence and passion. Father Turney smiles down on her and recites right along. Perez stands. But she remains silent, right arm dangling at her side. Like a flag in stale air.

The principal introduces Doc Howard, who hitches up his trousers and peers over the top of half-moon reading glasses.

"Listen, with all these federal laws, I can't disclose too much about Roy's condition. But we talked this afternoon and he's doing fine. Will be home in no time." Doc pauses for comic effect, then adds, "His daughter hopes sooner than that."

The room twitters with laughter. Everybody knows Roy Engel.

"Now, Sheriff Spire," the principal continues. "What can you tell us about the investigation?"

Spire walks to the podium, where he asks and answers his own questions.

"Where did the dog come from? Wish I could tell you, but I don't know. Where did it go? There have been no further sightings."

"What about that trailer?!" someone shouts. "What you gonna do about those people?"

"I searched the trailer," he answers. "There was no evidence of a dog."

"What about the blood?" says the old man who followed in the pickup.

"Ask them right there." The woman whose daughter is in Luciana's class is standing and pointing.

Mr. Dominguez looks tense and combative. Father Turney now understands why Spire asked him to sit with the family. He drapes a huge, comforting arm over the father's shoulder and rests his fingertip on the wife's arm. He is there. With them. They are not alone.

"I have, and there is no evidence," the sheriff states.

Even as he speaks, Spire can hear Owen Middleton's voice. "You're being too direct, too impolitic, too confrontive. The next election is always right around the corner." Nevertheless, the sheriff makes his stand.

"I'll not harass that family. They have rights, too."

More than a few people groan. Ayesha nods ever so slightly at Billy. It is a nod of respect.

"Goddamn Mexicans," someone hollers.

Those who don't like people of color, any color, grunt their agreement. Liberals and the clergy gasp in outrage. Pragmatists and employers shoot killing looks at the principal. Get this under control. Now.

"Thank you, sheriff," the principal breaks in, then addresses the room. "And thank the rest of you for expressing yourselves. The first step to improvement is candor."

"Yes," twitters a liberal baby bird lady. "Thanks to all you rednecks for sharing your bigotry with us."

The principal invites a panel to the front of the room. A farm lobbyist will testify to the importance of immigrant labor. A sociologist from Garden City Community College will blur the divides of citizenship and race. A Latino judge from Dodge will tell the heart-warming story of his ascension to the bench. Replete with a constellation of multi-cultural mentors.

Spire goes to the back of the room, trying to figure out who shouted. He wants to pull them aside and underscore his warning. Stay away from that family. A siren wails in the distance. Simultaneously, his cell phone buzzes. He steps into the hallway and takes the call.

"The trailer is on fire," dispatch shouts. "You better get over there."

<>

Spire steps back into the cafeteria. He walks at normal speed to the Dominguez family and motions to the father. Luciana sees and whispers to her mother. Both their round, sweet faces go taut with worry. Billy motions again, but the father doesn't know what to do. He is afraid to move away from his wife and daughter. Not with this crowd.

"I'll stay with them," Father Turney leans over and assures.

"You, too," Billy addresses Ayesha. "Right now, please."

There are murmurs at tall west windows about a distant glow.

Perez takes Dominguez by the arm and tugs him gently toward the aisle. By now, most people are trying to see what's going on out the window. Or watching Billy Spire escort Ayesha and Luciana's father to the door. Few are listening to the lobbyist and his argument that racism is not good for business.

Once outside, Spire jogs toward the 1500. Dominguez follows. Perez, who still runs with grace and speed, flies ahead. They hop into the truck. The sheriff has it moving before the doors slam shut.

"Is there anyone in the trailer?"

"Qué?"

"Your trailer," Spire yells. "Is anyone inside?"

"No."

"You're sure?"

"Yes."

"Sheriff!" Perez shouts as she bounces around the back seat. "What the hell?!"

Gravel flies as they skid around a corner.

"Goddamn it!" Billy roars through the windshield.

Before them are undulating red lights. The trailer is engulfed in flames. Purple, orange, fifteen feet high. Volunteer firemen roll out canvas hoses and wriggle into their safety gear. Spire skids to a stop. All three jump out.

"There's nobody in there!" the sheriff bellows at the captain. It's the same captain who tried to stop Haycock from burning down his house. He is bent and gray now, but nobody else wants the job.

"Who said there was?" the captain huffs, never taking his eyes off the fire.

"I was afraid . . ." the sheriff begins, but the firefighter cuts him off.

"This is arson. Not murder."

"That can't be." Billy Spire cannot fathom such a thing in his own community.

The captain regards the comment as a personal affront. He watches the volunteer force scurry and scramble. His face glows cherry red in the reflection of nearby flames.

"Look at the windows," he answers in a bored tone of voice. He is one of those men who has seen everything twice.

Spire thinks back three days. Then, the broken and leaky windows were covered with plywood. That's why it was so dark inside. Now, the plywood lies on the ground and flames jump through the openings they used to cover.

"Increased ventilation to feed the fire," explains the captain. "And this hot? This fast? Dollars to donuts accelerants are involved."

Mr. Dominguez stands a few feet away. His hands at the sides of his face. Everything they own is in there. Everything but the clothes on their backs. The fact that the family possesses so little makes the loss that much more tragic. Ayesha's arm is around his shoulders. Holding him up and back from trying to rescue things that are already beyond hope. With nothing to save, the firefighting mission shifts to keeping embers from jumping from trees to bushes to neighboring homes.

"Who would do such a thing?" Spire wonders.

"That's your department. But I'm guessing there are at least two people involved."

"Why do you say that?"

"They broke in. Knocked out the plywood. Splashed accelerants and lit the fire. Then got away. Possible for one person? Maybe. But more possible for two."

"Keep this between us," Spire says.

Chief cuts his eyes to the sheriff. They glint with indignation.

"Think you're the only one who knows what he's doing out here?" He fishes around his turnout coat for a pack of cigarettes. Retreats to the firetruck's bumper for a contemplative smoke.

Within minutes, all of Stonewall arrives and forms a wide semicircle in front of the burning trailer. The fire is furious. Towering and taunting. The flames are mostly yellow. But they turn red and blue and even black, as different materials are engulfed. Couches, linoleum, electronics, and tires on the roof. The metal siding sings in distress. One end of the trailer slumps, then collapses in a burst of sparks.

At the center of the semicircle stand five people. Shoulder to shoulder with the crowd, but worlds apart. The three Dominguezes cling to each other. The little girl wails pitifully over her clothes and the suffering of stuffed animals. Her parents are too stunned to cry. Too hurt to express pain, they just watch. Ayesha Perez puts her hands on the shoulders of Luciana and her mother. Beside her, the huge priest steps in to reassure the father.

"You'll stay with me tonight," he says. "Tomorrow, we'll find you another place. A better place. Clothes and other things, too. The congregation will help. You are not alone."

Mr. Dominguez knows that comfort is being offered. He doesn't want to seem ungrateful and bobs his head mechanically, like a spring-loaded toy. But it is so hard for him to focus. He is blinded by loss. Deafened by the crackling fire.

As the trailer is consumed, eyes shyly peek at the family. Once seen as threatening, they now appear only tiny and pathetic. The anger from earlier that evening rises and dissipates like ash into the night sky. The whole community now feels only sorrow. Those poor, poor people. Who had so little, and now have nothing.

The positions around race are not fixed in western Kansas. Perspectives and alignments change. Day to day, love to love, injury to injury, situation to situation.

<>

As ashes drift into the air over Stonewall, Owen Middleton works the Garden City Rotary Club. He moves from table to table, making eye contact and shaking hands. He remembers everyone's first names and uses them generously. He refers to goofy adventures back when they were young and hints at enduring friendships and shared secrets. His attention is welcomed by all, even those with whom he has only a passing acquaintance. Everyone wants to be a friend of Senator Middleton.

After dinner, he takes the podium.

"I bring you greetings from Topeka. Where the high road of integrity has never seen a traffic jam."

The room twitters. It is a well-worn pattern. Owen tells a few corny jokes, crowd responds with giggles and groans. But it's part of Middleton's charm. He's as comfortable as an old shoe. An embedded force. The very stuff of status quo.

"But we're still better than Washington, DC, where the opposite of *prog*ress is *Cong*ress."

Then he slides into legislative priorities and budgetary concerns, quoting figure after figure off the top of his head. Like Muriel Kovak, Middleton is strong at presenting complex issues in easily understood terms. And because they understand, the Rotarians feel intelligent and engaged. They feel at one with Owen Middleton, standing with him on an elevated plain. It is a wonderful sensation. After a few thoughts on municipal planning grants and the transfer of surplus tactical weapons to local SWAT units, the senator sets the hook.

"I'm about done. But let me update you about the Interim Committee on Rural Economic Development."

Some old joker in the room applauds.

"You're a fan of the committee?" Owen asks.

"No, I'm just glad you're about done."

The room breaks out in laughter. Middleton roars hardest of all, to show that he doesn't take himself too seriously. After the mirth runs its course, he clears his throat and continues.

"We've been doing lots of work. Nothing I can report tonight. But look for news soon. Big news."

Smiles are replaced with puzzlement.

"Not even a hint?" the Rotary president asks.

"Okay," Middleton replies. "But it doesn't leave the room."

Everyone is instantly intrigued. The group goes pin-drop quiet. This is Middleton's way of pulling them on board. It's not *my* secret, it's *our* secret. And, by extension, it's not *my* project, it's *our* project.

"One of the nation's largest internet retail operators is looking to build a new distribution center. Very high tech. Huge equipment investments. Lots of good jobs."

Owen pauses dramatically. He knows how to pitch a sale.

"And?" the president pleads.

"And. Western Kansas has low-cost land and fine highways. We're at the geographic center of the US. Quick release in every direction."

Eyes light up. This *is* big news.

"Which company?" they all wonder.

Middleton holds up his palms to ward off the question.

"I can't say anything else. Already told you more than I should. Deals like this are very, very delicate."

The entire Rotary nods in silent agreement. They understand. Or they think they understand. Or maybe they don't understand at all, but since everyone else has gone silent, so will they.

"Let's keep this our secret," Owen winks.

They all promise they won't say a word. But, of course they will. Cautiously at first. Then openly. Owen knows this. It wouldn't do him much good if they didn't. His goal is to slow-build the kind of local support that can be transformed into political energy.

"Let's give Senator Middleton a nice hand," the president gushes.

The applause is lusty and truly felt. The club secretary snaps a photo for the newsletter.

It takes the senator half an hour to get out of the place. Everybody wants a second handshake. To invite him for lunch or pass along greetings from old friends. To offer or solicit advice. To linger in his presence.

<>

Leaving the Rotarians behind, Owen steers his red Lincoln toward the edge of Ewing County.

Melvin McQuitty's house is back from the highway, down a long drive lined with juniper trees. It is a one-story rancher. Rock façade covers the bottom four feet. Above that is brown tongue-and-groove siding and a green metal roof. Light glows from the windows where Melvin has been standing for twenty minutes. Waiting and watching. He sees Middleton's headlights and steps out onto the porch.

"Welcome to Casa McQuitty."

"Melvin," Owen responds with a curt nod as he gets out of the Lincoln.

It annoys the senator to be there. More than annoys, it worries him. Any engagement with the representative is fraught with risk. But he is too far in to get out now. Too committed to the project, to the people of Stonewall. He takes a briefcase from the back seat.

The interior is beautifully appointed thanks to Duane, who bought quality and took care of it. The art-and-crafts furnishings are heavy and graceful, with the golden glow of fumed oak.

A tall woman is reading in a Stickley rocker. Same girlfriend from the night the cattle died, but her black hair is now streaked with blue highlights. She offers Owen a wan smile then, wordlessly, retreats to the bedroom.

"Thank you, darlin'," Melvin says as she closes the door behind her.

Middleton looks around the house and chooses to sit at the kitchen table. It has an enamel top and chromium legs. A bottle of bourbon waits on the counter, next to an empty tumbler. Melvin's glass is half full.

"Pour you one?"

"This is not a social call."

"Suit yourself." The representative provides himself with another healthy pour and dash of tap water.

"So, tell me, Melvin," Owen asks. "You ever been married?"

"Nope."

"I didn't think so."

"Does that matter?"

"Not to me," the senator replies. "Just wondering how a tomcat like you, with a taste for liquor, finds himself running with the Wings?"

Melvin swirls his bourbon and ponders the question.

"In politics and Jesus all things are possible."

Owen officiously opens his briefcase, removes binders of paperwork, and organizes them into neat piles.

"Are we that different?" the tall man wonders.

"Not even the same species."

"But here we are together." McQuitty sits and slouches in his chair like an indolent teenager. "And don't it feel good?"

"No," Owen replies.

Turns out that setting up an offshore bank account is pretty much like the local savings and loan. Present proper identification and deposit an initial amount. Middleton explains a few arcane matters, such as nation banks and exchange rates. The representative listens without much apparent understanding and even less bother.

"If you say so," he answers to every suggestion. "You're the banker."

Discussion turns to transfer logistics. Moving hundreds of thousands from Account A to Account B. The trick is to do so anonymously. Owen has friends at other banks. On occasion, he's helped them skirt the law. Now it's their turn to do a favor. A dummy corporation will be registered in Delaware, which is very protective of investor privacy.

"What do you want to call the company?"

Melvin thinks and answers, "MM Industries."

"Too obvious."

"Then you tell me."

"Don't exhaust yourself," Owen says, voice dripping with acid.

"Well, give me a suggestion."

Middleton looks around the house, searching for an idea. There is shag carpet, furniture, venetian blinds, a bookcase. Something on the top shelf catches the senator's eye. It is Melvin's snub-nosed Smith and Wesson, in the tooled-leather holster.

With every passing day, Middleton has become more haunted by what happened at the feedlot that night. During waking hours, he can crowd the images into remote compartments. But when asleep, drifting and dreaming, there is no control. The visions appear. The blood. The man's face twisted in pain and fury. Too often, Owen wakes to the sound of his own voice. Sobbing.

"How about Manslaughter Investments?" Middleton suggests.

"You trying to be funny?" The man sits up in his chair.

"Funny? No."

"You said we should never talk about it."

"Sorry. Forgot."

It gratifies Owen to see Melvin squirm. To wipe that stupid smirk off his face. Why should the senator be haunted alone? Melvin shoves back from the table and goes for more alcohol. Owen lets tense silence ride for forty-five seconds past uncomfortable.

"How about Frontier Investments?" he finally suggests. "Western. Wide open."

"'*New* Frontier,'" McQuitty improves. "It's a name that moves forward. I don't walk the same ground as my daddy."

"New Frontier it is."

Several hours pass. Melvin is rubbing his eyes. The senator starts sweeping papers back into the briefcase.

"That's it?"

"That's it." Middleton rises to leave.

Until this evening, Melvin McQuitty has not understood Owen Middleton's remarkable abilities. The depth of his knowledge. The sweep of his vision. His patient, relentless attention to detail. The representative is awed, exhausted, and more than a little buzzed from bourbon. Unmoored, he slips on emotion, fancying there might be other opportunities to work together. Maybe even to become friends. Or, at the very least, friendly.

"Thank you, Owen," he says, reaching out.

"Just don't fuck it up," Middleton replies, ignoring the extended hand.

The man's affectionate little pipe dream suffers the same fate as the *Titanic.* Ripped open by an iceberg.

Driving home, stars scatter across a black sky that is pitiless in its distance and disregard. Owen is overtaken by loneliness. LeeAnn is in Denver visiting friends. Shopping and having fun. There has been no word from Muriel, for which he is both grateful and all the more lonely. He turns on a podcast about neoliberalism. The political movement positing that humanity exists to serve the marketplace. Not the other way around.

He arrives at a house that is empty and cold. The senator will take a hot soak in the tub, with a glass of wine and crossword puzzle. Then go to bed. And wait for nightmares to come.

<>

The morning after the fire, Billy Spire starts for Great Bend. He has an appointment at the KBI regional office.

Before leaving town, he looks for Leo Ace. The air is acrid from the smell of smoke. Tensions are down, but not out. Someone needs to keep an eye on Ewing County in his absence. He calls the shop, no answer. Calls the house. Emma says he's at morning Kiwanis, which meets at Effie's diner. The same place where Norma Middleton ransomed young Billy Spire for the price of a used station wagon. The linoleum floors and cowboy motif are worn but otherwise unchanged. Spire arrives to find more vehicles than usual in the angled parking.

"Must be a program," he surmises.

Programs are a big deal at morning Kiwanis. A welcome break from the usual fare of old men and a few old women complaining about weather, politics, and any notion of increasing membership dues. Billy's curiosity is mildly aroused. Who is it this time? The options are limited. Either Ag Extension talking about a coming pestilence. Mama Doc offering free blood pressure tests. Or Stonewall High's barbershop quartet singing for uniforms and travel money.

Spire steps into the meeting room. A towering figure in a military uniform is addressing the Kiwanians. His face looks familiar. Billy spots Ace and slides into an adjacent chair. The military man continues talking but greets the sheriff with a polite nod.

"Who is that?" Billy whispers.

"You don't recognize him?"

"Should I?"

"Oh yeah," Ace answers.

Spire studies the face and shakes his head.

"Wonder how he got that limp."

Billy Spire takes the hint and his blood runs cold. Not from fear. But from shame.

"That's Harold LaVoy?"

"*Major* Harold LaVoy."

"I better go. No sense ruining a good Kiwanis meeting." Spire gets up.

"Don't leave, sheriff," the major interrupts himself. "I was hoping to see you here."

The sheriff sits down and wonders why the Army man was hoping to see him. He comes up with a few reasons, most of them bad.

Major LaVoy's briefing was obviously prepared for a more sophisticated audience. Maybe even top brass. He discusses the Asian Pivot from Middle East to the Far East. From oil to trade. From land forces to Navy. He explains China's "One Belt/One Road" initiative and the threat it represents to US influence. He goes over the military's mission creep from kinetic force to nation building. From warriors to city managers. It all sounds very important, but the audience is completely lost amid acronyms and enormities.

"The Army motto is 'This We'll Defend,'" LaVoy concludes. "Wherever and whatever that takes, that's just what we'll do. Any questions?"

The room is a volume of blank stares. Finally, Leo Ace waves his hand. No sense letting an opportunity go to waste.

"No!" several voices warn.

But it's too late. Major LaVoy has already acknowledged the mechanic. The other Kiwanians prop their elbows on the table and set their chins into their palms. They know what's coming, and this will take a while.

"It all goes back to the Civil War," the mechanic begins, apropos of not much.

But Leo Ace is determined to educate every soul who comes within the sound of his voice about the history of Ewing County, Kansas. Whether that soul wants to be educated or not. And once started, there's no use trying to stop him. Every way has been tried. Many times. He either drones on, undaunted. Or engages in a nasty squabble over being interrupted and then drones on, undaunted. Not privy to this underlying dynamic, the major listens with an expression of respectful appreciation. They all feel sorry for him. The rigors of military life have not prepared him for this level of abuse.

Ace starts with Thomas A. Ewing, the county's namesake and issuer of General Order Number 11, which evacuated four Missouri counties along the Kansas border. This, of course, was done in retaliation for Quantrill's raid of Lawrence, Kansas, on August 21, 1863.

"One hundred eighty-nine men and boys were murdered in the streets," the mechanic points out with a rueful shake of his head.

Then, as luck would have it, one of the first settlers of Ewing County was a Virginian and a southerner by sympathies. He named the town Stonewall, after the rock fence that edged his property. Or so he said.

"Most people figured the real inspiration was 'Stonewall' Jackson, who was accidentally shot by his own troops. Battle of Chancellorsville. May 2nd, 1863."

Ace is fifteen minutes into his lecture by this point.

"Get it? Stonewall? Ewing County? No wonder we've been fighting ourselves ever since."

By now, nobody is even pretending to listen. The major is looking at his wristwatch. Several of the older Kiwanians are fighting sleep. Heads tipping forward, then jerking back. Billy fiddles with his phone. Effie has refilled coffee cups three times by now. That's enough. She collects the dirty dishes, making way more noise than necessary. She snatches Ace's coffee cup right out of his hand, then wipes the table with a rag.

"Stay a little longer and you can join us for lunch," the old lady huffs.

"Mr. Ace," the major finally interrupts, standing up and tugging straight his uniform jacket. "I have studied with brilliant historians at Fort Leavenworth. Faculty of the Command and General Staff College. Your grasp of American history is second to none."

Ace's eyes brim with tears. He clears his throat. He has a lot more to say.

"I wish I didn't have to leave," LaVoy preempts. "Sheriff, I wonder if I could have a minute of your time?"

Billy nods, not sure what to expect. When he was younger, he would have braced for a fight. But he and Harold LaVoy are too old for that sort of thing. Too old and too dignified. As they walk into the main part of Effie's diner, which is mostly vacant now, the sheriff struggles with what to say.

"Your leg," he finally decides. "I'm sorry. Wish I could take it back. I was just an angry kid back then."

Spire's broad shoulders round with shame. His hard eyes and brutal face go soft with remorse.

"You did me a favor," the major answers. "I was never going to make it as a football player. Too slow. But that's all I cared about. Then you knocked me out for the rest of the season. I couldn't even help around the farm. My dad said, 'If you can't do anything else, you damn well better study.' I did. My grades came up. And eventually, I got admitted to West Point."

Ace has joined them. He looks on with amazement. Could that be mist in the sheriff's eyes? Wait until the fellows hear about this.

"Do you remember a man named Matthew Middleton?" the major asks. "A banker?"

"Yes. I remember him," Billy answers.

"He called our congressman, told him I could never afford college. Said I should be considered for West Point. That I had a lot of promise and patriotism."

"He was a good man."

190

"Apparently so. I never met him." The major searches Billy's face. "I have no idea why he took an interest in me. I sent him a letter once, thanking him. Hoping he might explain. His answer was kind and encouraging. But didn't offer a clue."

Billy recalls that night. When Matthew Middleton asked Billy to help Owen and unleashed the vicious fury of a lost boy. And now, he understands that Mr. Middleton had atoned. For Billy's cruelty. For LaVoy's broken knee. For his own regret. Spire wonders whether to explain. But remains silent. Who is he to reveal the secrets of a good man?

"He did things like that. You are not alone."

"Well, it was a blessing I can never repay," LaVoy concludes wistfully.

"I'm sure he's looking down smiling," Spire answers. "You look great in that uniform."

"And you look about the same," the major replies with a chuckle. He studies Spire with a half-smile and furrowed brow. "I have traveled the world and seen serious combat. I have never met a more intimidating person."

"I'm not sure whether that's an insult or compliment," Billy replies.

Ace grabs the major's arm.

"Ever hear the Fort Leavenworth story about a young corporal dressing down a private he caught writing instead of keeping watch?"

"Ace," Billy groans.

"Dwight D. Eisenhower and F. Scott Fitzgerald. I swear it's true."

"Leave the poor man alone."

"You know, Major LaVoy," Ace says, glaring at the sheriff. "Sometimes I wish Billy Spire had been born smart, instead of so darn good-looking."

"Just keep an eye on things while I'm gone, will you Ace?" Spire wheels and pushes out the door.

He makes it all the way to the car before laughing.

⟨⟩

The Kansas Bureau of Investigation maintains a regional office in Great Bend. A town on the edge of Cheyenne Bottoms, a vast marshy bird sanctuary on the Great Central Flyway. Year round, the Bottoms are filled with magnificent plumage. In drab contrast, the KBI sits on a nondescript back street of tire shops, light manufacturing, and Pistol Pete's Nuts & Bolts. Enclosed by a chain-link fence, the compound's most notable feature is a tall communication tower. A needle-thin metal latticework rising seventy feet high.

Spire parks in front of a low, tan building that has been cheaply retrofitted into a law enforcement center. He presses the doorbell and is buzzed in.

Special Agent Peggy Palmer greets him with a welcoming smile.

She is of middle height, trim and fit with short-cropped hair and square-framed glasses. Her face is pinched and leathery. She wears khaki slacks and a navy blazer. She is bright, well-educated, tough, and the mother of three.

She has a famous sense of humor. Once, a convict sent her an obscene Christmas card, warning that he would be released from jail on January 1. She immediately drove to the prison and met with its warden. She showed him the card and talked him into adding nine months to the man's sentence. Then she walked out onto the prison yard. All alone. The only woman to ever do so. Every rifle on the wall was aimed for her protection, but still. She was a woman, alone. She walked straight up to the dumbfounded jailbird and said, "Thank you for the Christmas card. I got you a little something, too."

She directs the sheriff toward her office. "Heard you had a little excitement last night," she says.

"Fire chief call you?"

"Facebook," the agent chuckles. "It's how we get all our intelligence."

They settle into Palmer's office. She offers him coffee. He would prefer diet soda but asks for water instead.

"How's the wife?" Peggy Palmer regrets the words as soon as they leave her mouth. She knows how Nadine is. Everyone does. It was just thoughtless, innocent patter.

"About the same. She has the bottle and it has her."

"I'm sorry. I didn't mean to . . ."

"It's okay," Billy states flatly. "I'm sheriff of a small town. People don't have much else to talk about."

"So, regarding Haycock." The agent is eager to move past this embarrassing moment. Into the traditional game of cat and mouse.

KBI has deep respect for county sheriffs. It absolutely does. But local sheriffs are chosen by politics, rather than qualifications. Not like KBI agents who rise through the meritocracy via education and accomplishment. And, being politicians, county sheriffs are naturally averse to ruffling feathers. Even those that deserve to be. So, local sheriffs are great. No doubt about that. And KBI holds them in the highest regard, you bet. But they can be a little soft. A little on the amateurish side. Present company excluded. Maybe.

"Afraid I don't have a thing for you right now," Palmer says. "The lab promised us something this morning. But so far, nada."

Spire nods his head slowly.

"They're moving into a new facility. Will be great in the long run. But the transition is driving us crazy."

Spire nods again. Slow and dubious.

County sheriffs have enormous respect for the KBI. Absolutely. The agents are brilliant, and the science is remarkable. Couldn't do without them. But there is something. A smugness. The KBI training includes a course called "Advanced Arrogance." Sitting in their plush offices second guessing, while sheriffs work the streets. And when they do get involved, look out. Here come the SWAT teams, flash bombs, and assault rifles. KBI is a model law enforcement organization, as any Kansas sheriff will attest. But they sure make a lot of unnecessary messes, both physical and political. Messes that county sheriffs are left to clean up.

"So, you couldn't call me?" Spire sniffs. "There are other things I might be doing this morning."

"Wanted to talk anyway," she answers.

"About what?"

"Chatter."

"What kind of chatter?"

"Tell me about your fire."

Within the deep mutual respect, there is time-honored sport to KBI/sheriff cooperation. Each side is determined to get more intelligence than they give. To uncover more than they reveal. It's more than a sport. It's a tradition, really. And if law enforcement respects anything, it's tradition.

"Why do you care?" Spire counters.

"Maybe I don't. That's why I'm asking."

"Fire chief suspects arson," Spire answers. "Someone tore plywood off the windows. Accelerants may have been used."

"That everything?"

"We'll know more after the investigation."

The answer is technically correct, but Spire leaves out the dog attack, Cruz Dominguez, the lowered Chevy, the veterinarian in Dodge City, and the chief's speculation that more than one person is involved. He needs to know he's getting, before giving more.

"We have experience with arson fires," Palmer says, leaning back in her chair. She is a master of the war-story technique. Anecdotes that seem to lead nowhere. Until they do.

"Arson fires come in two types. The first is spur of the moment. We had a guy kill his girlfriend in a fit of anger. Tried to cover by setting her apartment on fire. No merit badge there. Lot of smoke but not much flame. The body got singed, but not enough to hide a crushed skull. Turns out that setting a proper fire takes knowledge and preparation.

"The other type is planned. Professor at K-State was separated from his wife. She wanted his money, he wanted her dead. Studied for weeks on the internet, then went to her house in a Tyvek suit. Knocks her on the head, cuts her throat. Splashes paint thinner all around and opens the stove valves. Drives down the road and waits for the joint to blow sky high."

"Heard about it." KBI agents love to talk about their cases. The ones they solve. Billy grows a little fidgety. "Tell me something I don't know."

Palmer smiles patiently and continues.

"Guy drives back to Manhattan. Drops gym bag in a Dairy Queen dumpster. Her family thought he was a prince. Right up until our forensics people searched his computer. Point is, serious arson takes forethought."

"Good work."

"Yeah," Palmer muses. "Good work. But sad story. She seemed like a perfectly nice woman. Anyway, it leads to a question. Accelerants. Torn plywood. Does your fire captain think more than one person is involved?"

Damn. Agent Palmer is good at her job. She brought the story back around and caught him hiding information. So, according to the unwritten rules, he's obliged to fess up.

"Yeah. Come to think of it, he did raise that possibility. Said it was unlikely that one person could have broken in, knocked out windows, and set the fire. More probable there were two."

Peggy Palmer nods slowly. Knowingly. Smugly.

"How are things otherwise?" she asks.

"Otherwise?"

"Any tension these days?"

"No more than usual," Spire replies while brushing a little smudge off his slacks.

"Even after the dog attack?"

Damn. Caught again.

"Oh, there was a little fuss at the high school. All fine now." Spire makes a show of gazing out the window. Letting her know that being jacked around makes him itchy.

Peggy Palmer motions to the door. Billy closes it. She leans forward over her desk, pointedly taking him into her confidence. There will, of course, be a price to pay.

"About that chatter. We keep hearing about KKK types. Trying to intimidate immigrants, illegals, anyone who isn't white."

"Is that new?" The sheriff plays less than impressed.

"Not new. But getting bolder now."

"Now?" Spire stretches the word into a question.

"Now that they seem to have mainstream sympathy. Maybe support."

Agent Palmer purses her lips and stares deeply into Billy's eyes. As if she can see his innermost thoughts.

"Don't know anything about that," he responds.

"Tell me about Melvin McQuitty."

There it is, the price the sheriff must pay to hear more.

"McQuitty?" he answers blankly.

"Isn't he one of yours?"

"He's from Ewing County, if that's what you mean. But I've never thought of him as 'one of mine.' We don't run in the same circles. Never have."

"I just thought you might know something about him," she replies coyly. As if it were only a social question.

"Such as?"

"Who he associates with?"

"I really don't know." Billy is getting a bit testy. He's willing to pay a price, if its value and implications are clear. So far, she's taken a lot. Given nothing.

Palmer senses she's losing the sheriff of Ewing County.

"He's part of a group of legislators, call themselves the Wings," she offers, reeling him back in a little. "They've done nothing wrong or illegal, at least as far as we know. But they keep unusual company. Extreme company. Would you know anything about that?"

Billy rubs his chin. He has a five o'clock shadow at ten-eighteen in the morning.

"Like I said, McQuitty and I don't run in the same circles."

"And no uptick in extreme activities?"

"Not that I know of."

"And last night's fire?"

"Still under investigation."

Palmer rubs her hands as if they hurt. As if she is washing them without water. All the time, she studies Spire.

"Well, Ewing County may be very lucky. And unusual. There are gatherings all over western Kansas. Hidden under rocks and in bars. Too disorganized to be considered cells. Random malcontents connected by hate websites and literature. We keep an eye on them. Always have. Mostly they brag about what they're going to do, but don't."

"Same as it ever was."

"Sometimes the same gets real different, real fast. Last week, we took in four fellows who were conspiring to blow up an apartment building full of packing-plant Somalis. Inspired by McVeigh and Nichols. Trying to touch off the revolution."

"And you think McQuitty is somehow involved?"

"I didn't say that." She holds up her hands in denial. She would never imply such a thing about a sitting legislator. And he better not ever suggest she did.

"Kind of sounded that way," he observes.

Palmer had said something that could be used against her, not that Spire ever would. Still, he has her over the barrel now. The special agent sighs but honors the tradition. Score one for the sheriff.

"He crosses paths with that type fairly often. At town meetings and speeches. Parades, gun shows. The Pancake Race. Always off to one side. Talking. About what, we're not sure."

"Maybe you should ask him."

"Come on, Billy," she scolds.

KBI never asks unless it already has the answers. Until then, they pretend they know more than they actually do. Cat and mouse.

"I can guess how Melvin would answer," Spire volunteers. "He would wave his arms and scream about government overreach."

"I hear he's a little self-serving," she says with a conspiratorial smile.

"Has to be," Spire replies. "Ain't nobody else going to do him any favors."

"I thought he was big with the Wings."

"So I hear," the sheriff bluffs.

In truth, he has heard nothing of the sort and has no clue who the Wings are. Topeka is a company town, crawling with KBI agents. Like all state agencies, it spends countless hours watching the Capitol. Mapping coalitions that might affect its budget or authority. As far as the sheriff of Ewing County is concerned, Topeka is on the other side of the world. Nevertheless, when dealing with the KBI, no self-respecting sheriff would admit not knowing something of importance.

"What else have you heard?"

"Nothing," he says in a way that suggests maybe something. "Nobody tells me a thing."

"Not even your friend, Middleton?"

Peggy Palmer is not the only person paying attention. Billy Spire doesn't miss much either. She has just implied that Owen has some play in this situation.

"We don't talk about the legislature," Billy answers.

"That true?"

"Bores me to death." He's not going to say more until he understands the implications. Melvin McQuitty is one thing. Owen Middleton is his friend.

"Anything more you can tell me?" she asks. One last open-ended question to see what it evokes.

"Not a thing," he says.

"Thank you, Billy," the agent concludes with a quick look at her watch.

"And thank you, Peggy." They stand and shake hands.

"Let me know if you need anything else."

"Haycock's lab work would be nice," he digs.

She walks him out the security door.

"Be careful," Peggy says as they reach Spire's truck. "These people are armed to the teeth and think Jesus is on their side. Matthew 10:16, 'I am sending you out like sheep among wolves. Therefore, be as shrewd as snakes.'" She pauses, then concludes. "The verse actually ends 'and as innocent as doves.' But they usually ignore that part."

"I'll keep a look out," Spire replies, attempting to pop wide his small eyes. "And say, I have something that might interest you."

He reaches into the truck bed and lifts out a heavy cardboard box. Plops it down on the sidewalk.

"What's that?"

He pulls open the flaps to reveal tomes of hate literature and weapons catalogs.

"Where did that come from?"

"Russ Haycock's shed."

Palmer thought she had the jump on Spire. Now, it appears he had her figured out all along. In fact, it is pure coincidence. Billy was taking the box to Great Bend for recycling. Didn't want to dump a box of hate literature anywhere in Ewing County. Prying eyes would surely rummage through anything left by the sheriff. Why shame a dead man whose name was already too associated with shame?

"Damn, Sheriff Spire," she says with admiration. "You're good."

It was a fine game. Each gave some, got some back. The deep respect and collaboration between KBI and local government is reaffirmed. Absolutely.

<>

Leaving KBI, Spire heads southwest to Garden City.

He arrives at a forlorn few blocks between the business district and railroad tracks. In the shadow of massive decrepit concrete grain elevators, skyscrapers of the plains, standing gray against the blue sky. He stops at a one-time gas station, now converted into office space. The small parking lot features opposing concrete islands where fuel pumps used to be. On the islands are two pole lamps, bowing toward each other like novitiates. Across the street, customers go in and out of a newer gas station. A featureless cube of neon and white sheet metal.

The old repair bays still have original doors of roll-up glass panes. The inside has been converted into a combination classroom and play area. Spire sees a preschool-aged girl at an easel, drawing with crayon on a large white pad. Two other children sit in tiny chairs on a spiral throw rug, listening to an older woman read. Around the periphery of the space are mismatched filing cabinets and worn tables piled with toys, hats, scarves, and unopened loaves of bread.

In the adjacent room, where the office used to be, a large plate glass window is obscured by a dusty venetian blind. Across the half-story above the office is a yellowed canvas banner with red lettering that reads "La Buena Familia."

The sheriff is there to get a statement from Ayesha Perez. He doesn't expect much, but someday he might have to make a case to the county prosecutor, a nervous man who chain-smokes cigarettes and fixates on anything and everything that might go wrong. The prosecutor claims that the law demands painstaking exactitude, but Spire thinks he's just plain lazy. Hoping cases brought to him will go away, and looking for any excuse to make that happen. So, Billy is there to cross and dot, just in case Haycock's killer is discovered. To remove as many pins and needles as he can from the prosecutor's tortured mind. In other words, to make him do his job.

He pushes open the door. She looks up and is surprised to see him.

"Miss Perez," he says with a hint of a courtly bow. "May I have a few minutes of your time?"

"You were supposed to call first," Perez scolds. She is sitting at a school-teacher's desk. A substantial construction, dignified though nicked and stained from coffee cups.

"I was passing through."

Billy Spire prefers interviewing people who haven't had time to prepare.

<>

Back in Stonewall, the usual suspects are gathered at Ace's for their daily fare of political bickering and health complaints. They sprawl on stacks of tires and metal folding chairs. The mechanic is working under the hydraulic lift. Servicing a four-door Ford and streaming his consciousness over the morning's program by Harold LaVoy.

"Those boys at the Pentagon got their heads on straight. But what about all those earthquakes from fracking? That's what we should worry about. Who's going to pay for damaged houses? We are. That's who. I love my country, but I can't afford my government."

He rolls a funnel under the car to catch a stream of grimy black oil.

"Jesus, Carl. When was the last time you changed this?" Carl starts to defend himself, but Ace has already moved on. "It's the Golden Rule, I tell you. Whoever has the gold makes the rules. If I were president for just one day. Just one day. I'd carpet-bomb those terrorists. That's for sure, if I were president for just one day."

"We'll see what we can do about that," one fellow drawls, winking at the others.

"About what?" Ace has lost track of his own ramblings.

"About making you president for one day."

The fellows snicker. The phone rings.

"You think I'm kidding?" Ace snipes as he ducks out from under the car. He wipes his hands and picks up the receiver. As usual, everyone listens. The mechanic's face turns stony hard.

"Okay. How many? What kind of car? Where's Father Turney? Okay. Okay. Be right there." He hangs up the phone.

"Kid from the burned trailer and a couple of his thug buddies are at Father Turney's. Asking about his parents and sister."

"You want company, Ace?"

"Maybe so," he answers. Then after a second's thought adds, "Yes, I do."

The mechanic tugs at a reel of keys attached to his belt and unlocks the metal door of a storage room. There, behind boxes of motor oil, is a small arsenal. Pump-action shotgun. Thirty-aught-six. Four-ten twenty-two over under. Thirty-eight revolver. All loaded and ready. Ace hands out the weapons. A couple of the fellows wave them away. They prefer their own firearms, which are out in their vehicles. Guns are never far from reach in western Kansas.

These are seven old men. Among them, Ace is the youngest at sixty-six. They are elderly but not incompetent. They have hunted all their lives. They are steady aims and not the least bit bashful about killing. Animals, at least. Two go with Ace in the wrecker. The other four follow in a Chrysler sedan that has seen better days. They arrive to see two men facing each other on the rectory porch. The smaller one appears agitated.

"Who burned our house?" Cruz Dominguez asks, rocking from foot to foot and gesturing aggressively with his hands.

Father Turney had been working out when the doorbell rang. Lying on the floor, watching Dr. Phil, and doing sit-ups. He wears a baggy gray track suit.

"You need to calm down, son." The priest is sweating, breathing hard.

"Answer me." Cruz mistakenly interprets Turney's exertion for fear.

"Nobody knows," says Father Turney. "Maybe you?"

There had been speculation, even as the trailer burned.

"You think I did this?" the kid howls.

"I don't know. Did you?"

Cruz moves up on the priest, trying to crowd him against the wall. The larger man holds his ground, and the attempt at intimidation serves only to contrast their great difference in height and mass. Eli is still feeling those sit-ups, still feeling flushed and muscular.

"My family. Where are they now?" the young man snarls.

"They're safe."

"Where?"

"I can't tell you that, son."

Luciana and her parents are in the last place imaginable. They are at the home of Roy and Judy Engel, whom their beleaguered daughter hastened to bring back from Hays. Father Turney made the arrangements based on symbiotic needs. Roy and his gardens would need tending. Judy, aid and comfort. The Dominguez family, a place to live. Both families are people of Catholic faith and good will. It was simple. But before agreeing to any of it, the Engels' daughter insisted on two conditions. No brother. No dog. If either shows up, the deal is off.

Cruz continues to shout, alarming two young men who wait in the low-slung, old model Chevy. Its motor idles noisily. The muffler is bad.

They get out and lean against the side panel. Watching in a casual way, as if to indicate disinterested awareness. Their shoulders are hunched forward, hands deep in the pockets of their saggy jeans. It's nippy out, but they're both in tee shirts.

The priest notices their movement. He doesn't know that a neighbor has called 911. That Billy Spire is out of town. Or that Ace and his antiquarian posse are racing his way.

"They are with friends of the church," Father Turney tells the young man. "That's all I can say."

"Take me to them."

"I can't."

"Why not?"

"Was it your dog?" Eli asks.

"What's a dog got to do with this?"

"Was it your dog?"

"Yes." It's hard to lie to a man of the cloth.

"Fighting dog?"

"Oh man, dogs do what they do."

"You have quite a reputation."

Cruz's eyes glimmer with proud defiance.

"A reputation that is not helpful to your parents or sister. Do them a favor. Leave them alone for a while."

The young man bellows in anger. Demanding to see his family.

Thinking they might be inside the rectory, he tries to shove Father Turney out of the way. But the great priest is immovable, and the thin young man is thrown back by his own force. He falls off the porch and lands flat on his back. On a concrete sidewalk that has no give. The wind is knocked out of his body. He rolls and croaks and gasps. His two friends push off the Chevy and start toward the priest.

A wrecker and sedan skid around the corner and screech to a halt. The old men jump out, to the extent that old men can jump, with guns in hand. Cruz's friends retreat to the far side of the Chevy and reach under their shirts. The priest holds up his hands and rushes into the yard. Into the line of fire between the two combatant parties.

In western movies, like Owen Wister's *The Virginian*, the verb is "pull." As in, the cowboy "pulled" his gun. The actor is the cowboy. The gun an inanimate object under the cowboy's power. But in real life, it's just the opposite. The gun is the actor. It pulls its holder toward trouble with great force. A sensible person would stay away from a rough bar at night.

But the gun says, "You don't need to be afraid, let's go in there." Sensible person would ignore an asshole riding the tailgate. Gun says, "You don't have to put up with that shit." Two groups of men fixing to shoot it out in a small Kansas town would stop and wonder why. Guns say, "Shoot first and ask later." And that's just what both sides are pulled to do.

"Stop!" the priest roars, hands poised as if parting the seas. "Put away those fucking guns."

The combatants are shocked to hear a priest curse. He is massive with will. Enough will to even overpower guns.

"Take it easy." The priest turns his palms down and pumps at the air. "Everything is fine."

Cruz continues to writhe helplessly. He cannot breathe. The muscles around his chest are locked tight with pain.

Father Turney gives the men one final look of warning, then hurries back to the fallen young man. With his giant hands and newfound strength, he effortlessly lifts Cruz to his feet and raises the young man's arms. The rib cage opens. Air flows in. The young man sags with relief. His arms fall around the priest's neck. His body flushes with adrenaline. Typically, that means fight or flight. But there is one other possibility. Cry. The boy sags against the mountainous priest and sobs. Sobs until Father Turney's sweatshirt is stained with tears and snot. Sobs as if there is no one in the world but the two of them. Sobs until the two groups of men can do nothing but look down in embarrassment and pity.

"Lo siento," he cries, over and over. "I'm sorry."

His sorrow is unnamed, but the priest understands. Cruz is sorry for the harm he's caused his family. For the man hurt by his dog. For the dog who bled to death. For the drugs and other trouble. For being who he is. For being.

"God forgives," the priest murmurs, holding tight. "And loves you."

When he is done, the young man pulls away and wipes his nose with the tail of his tee shirt. Only then does he become aware of the others. Both sides standing still. Guns lowered.

Ace advances with a determined look on his face. He's got a duty to uphold.

"I got to take him in, Father."

"Let him go," the priest commands. "He's done nothing wrong."

Ace steps back. Cruz Dominguez heads toward the low-slung Chevy. He is unsteady on his feet but trying to saunter with tough arrogance.

Trying to hold his head high. He pauses at the car door and gives the town one long last look. Poor Stonewall. It has seen better days. He spits in contempt, then climbs in the back seat. The other two get in the front. The Chevy pulls away slowly, as if to show that they are in no hurry. They have chosen to leave of their own volition. And at their own cool pace.

The broken muffler rattles windows all down the street.

<>

The little crayon girl comes in from the playroom and climbs on Ayesha's lap. She is no more than three. Tiny and joyful with black eyes and gold studs in her ear lobes. She stares shyly at the stranger.

"Say hello to Sheriff Spire, Nina."

Too bashful to speak, Nina hops down and heads back to from where she came.

"Cute," Billy says.

"Yes," Ayesha agrees, watching the child toddle away. "She is adorable."

"Is there some place we can talk?"

Ayesha speaks to the older woman who is still reading. Asks if there is anything she can bring back. Donuts. Everybody wants a donut.

"I'm buying," Billy offers.

"You got that right," Perez replies.

Inside the gas station across the street, it is very bright. Even brighter than the neon and sheet-metal exterior. Perez grabs a tall plastic cup, fills it with ice, and places it beneath the diet cola spigot. It's late morning. But morning, nonetheless. Spire watches in astonishment. She's completely at ease. Not one hint of embarrassment over her beverage preference. He grabs a cup of his own.

"I admire your self-confidence," he says.

She watches the level of liquid rise and has no idea what he's talking about.

"You must be deeply insecure," she speculates.

"I must," he agrees.

They take a small booth by the window, near a newspaper rack. Spire takes out his spiral notebook, clicks his pen, and starts to write.

"Name? Address? Phone? Social Security number?"

"Are you investigating me?"

"It's just in case there is more than one Ayesha Perez."

"There isn't," she states.

He moves to the next set of questions.

"What did you see? What did you do? Who were you with? Anything else come to mind?"

Perez recounts details to the best of her memory. Flipping back to his field notes, the sheriff finds no inconsistencies. The prosecutor ought to be satisfied. They are done, but the cups are still half full. Perez stares over the top of her drink and studies the sheriff. Billy Spire knows how he looks.

"A woman once accused Abraham Lincoln of being two-faced," the sheriff launches. "He said 'Ma'am, if that was true, why would I wear this one?'"

"Is that your version of small talk?"

"It's the best I got."

Perez can't help but laugh. She sees something beyond his sallow skin and small, flinty eyes. Something of decency and caring. She wonders what else is in there.

"Why do you do this?" he asks. "La Buena Familia?"

"That's a rather personal question, don't you think?"

"It's easy for cops to lose touch with human decency. Helps to be reminded once in a while."

"Okay." She makes a loose fist. Taps her chest three times, then points at the sky. She is a person of abiding faith trying with all her heart to alter a trajectory or two. "It's that simple."

Billy Spire feels pressure behind his eyes and has to clear his throat. Perez sees his emotions and misinterprets. Men. They fall in love so easily. So stupidly. Especially the ugly ones.

"Time to go," she says to break the spell.

"Simple goodness kills me," Spire explains. He jokingly uses his index fingers like windshield wipers across his eyes. "It's worse the older I get."

"I'm not as good as you think."

"It doesn't take much," he confesses. "A TV commercial can bring me to tears."

"Well, I might be as good as laundry detergent," she smiles.

It's a smile containing equal portions of kindness and sorrow. Ayesha wonders if she will ever be at one with herself. If she will ever reconcile her sexual yearnings with a deep love of God. If she will ever be able to accept the entirety of her being.

"It's a terrible thing, being uncomfortable in your own skin," she says of herself.

"I try to avoid mirrors," the sheriff replies in misunderstanding. Billy Spire knows how he looks through eyes of others, but he is often less perceptive as to how others see themselves.

In the quiet that follows, Spire scans the room for distraction, for something to pull his emotions back. The newspapers in the nearby rack are weeks behind. Faded headlines still scream about the riot in Topeka. Perez follows his eyes.

"I was there, you know," she says, eager to move the conversation along.

Spire thinks for a moment.

"Well, you do seem quite the vicious criminal."

"So say the newspapers."

"But not you?"

"The reports are accurate, unless you happened to be there."

"What's the difference?" he asks.

"Difference is, we didn't start it."

"Who did?"

"Your guy, Representative McQuitty."

"That's the second time today he's been called my guy," Billy scowls.

He opens the spiral notebook and writes "Melvin" in the margin. Recording oddities is standard practice in Spire's investigations. Oddities sometimes lead to clues. And clues sometimes solve crimes.

"You're not friends?" she asks.

"No. Not at all."

The sheriff gets up to top his soda and think. Comes back and sits down.

"So, how did McQuitty start a riot?" he asks.

"Stood in a window and flashed his gun."

Perez fans her fingers open and draws them in a slow arc around her waist, exposing an imaginary pistol.

"So, he carries now?"

"He did that night."

Spire shakes his head. Peggy Palmer is right. Melvin has fallen in with the wrong crowd.

"Someone threw a rock at the window," Perez continues. She makes a rock of her fist. Sends it on a short flight, then explodes it with a pop of her fingers.

"And then?"

"You might ask your friend."

"I told you. Melvin McQuitty is not my friend."

"No. Your other friend. Senator Middleton."

"Owen?" Billy asks. "What does Owen have to do with this?"

"He was right in the middle."

"Owen would never be caught in something like that," Spire insists. "He always steers clear of trouble. Always."

"If you say so."

Perez recalls a less careful Owen Middleton. The one with Muriel in his arms. Protecting her, cradling her, comforting her while another man, injured on the floor, gapes at their embrace. A man whose face registers far more than physical pain. If that doesn't spell trouble, then Ayesha Perez doesn't know what trouble is.

Billy is puzzled. It's the second oddity of the day. The second linking of Middleton and McQuitty. He flips open the notebook. Scribbles "Owen" next to "Melvin."

"Are you sure?" Spire examines her face the way cops do when searching for tell-tale signs of a lie.

"Believe what you want."

Ayesha Perez will not have her credibility questioned, nor waste her breath on a sheriff unwilling to hear the truth. She stands up, signaling time to go. Opening a glass case, she uses plastic tongs to snatch out donut after donut. Two full bags.

"Who's paying?" the clerk asks rhetorically. This is not the first time he's seen Ayesha Perez hustle a benefactor.

"The man with the star," she replies.

<>

Three mornings later, a young man appears at the Ewing County courthouse. He has a large head and close-set eyes that twinkle as bright as his smile. He wears a K-State golf shirt. Purple is the ubiquitous color of western Kansas, where the football coach is a god and EMAW. Every Man a Wildcat. Nobody has seen the young man before but, hey, he's K-State. Must be all right. In fact, the young man went to college in Minnesota. MBA from the Wharton School.

"We're here to pay off some taxes," he says, leaning on the counter. "Take possession of a property."

The county treasurer, mother of the two bicycle kids from the outhouse caper, is country nice. Tart tongued and observant, bordering on downright nosey. Not a lot gets past her, especially when it comes to land and indebtedness.

"What property? And who are we?" she practically shouts. She has one of those voices.

"McQuitty's Feedlot. And we are New Frontier Investments."

"New Frontier?" She rummages through a drawer for forms and a pen. "Don't think I've heard of you."

"Oil and gas investments," he chirps, flashing his sunniest smile.

"You think there's oil and gas under McQuitty's?" she snorts while testing a couple of pens on a yellow pad.

"We hope."

"You hope?" Her inquisitiveness is exceeded only by her readiness to offer unsolicited opinions. "This New Frontier won't be in business long if hope is all you got."

"Tell you the truth?" He leans over the counter, so she reciprocates. "I'm new with the company. Assigned to property acquisition. Corporate has this computerized system on worker productivity. Every worker, every day. I'm struggling. My metrics look bad. My boss told me to buy something. Anything. If there's oil and gas, great. If not, we can use it for staging."

The treasurer's sympathies are aroused by a K-State kid in trouble. The young man knew they would be. He has been well briefed by Owen Middleton.

"Listen," she confides, "all you're going to find under that property is dead cattle and dirty water."

"But it gives me time. I got better irons in the fire."

"If you're sure," she answers with a look of motherly concern.

He signs some papers. Pays taxes with a New Frontier check, and registers McQuitty's Feedlot under its new ownership.

"Hey," the young man leans in again, "could you keep this between us? New Frontier likes to fly under the radar, if you know what I mean."

She does know. Oil and gas companies are obsessively secretive. Like there's a claim jumper hidden behind every rock.

"It's between us. And lots of luck." The treasurer watches out the window as he gets in his car, then mutters, "Because Wildcat or not, you're gonna need it."

The young man drives straight to Kansas City International. Returns his rental car and boards a plane to Atlanta. Goes directly to the bank where he works and gives his boss a thumbs-up. Boss dials the phone.

"The eagle has landed," he says.

"Thank you," the senator replies.

It wouldn't do to have the state purchase land directly from a sitting legislator. Especially one with the reputation of Melvin McQuitty. It would draw too much attention, too many questions. With attention and questions, comes jeopardy. Owen Middleton is never clumsy in the handling of details. Not in deals he wants to make happen. And he wants to make this one happen. Bad.

<>

At ten o'clock the next morning, Owen dials up the Kansas Secretary of Administration, a stuffy bald fellow with a squeaky voice. The senator explains how much is to be taken and from what quiet little fund earmarked for equipment, capital improvement, or training. The senator pauses to make sure the secretary is tracking.

"That's all you need?" the squeaky voice asks sarcastically.

The secretary does not approve. But then, he never approves of anything. Oftentimes, when meeting with his cabinet, the governor will begin with "Pat, you go ahead and say no, so we can get that out of the way." Always gets a laugh, never works. The secretary is an indefatigable bobblehead of no. But he understands who he works for and how to follow orders.

"The governor is a go on this," Middleton declares.

"Mind if I double check?"

"Would you mind if I minded?"

"No."

It's a little dance Owen and the secretary go through. A politician's version of playing the dozens. Verbal duels, chest thumping, displays of power. In actuality, the senator and secretary are good friends and highly cooperative. Within the context of politics, of course.

"Send it to the Kansas Commerce Commission," Owen adds, going over that detail one more time.

"You mean *through* don't you? The KCC will never touch it, will they? Not even a quick kiss."

"There's enough love to pay some bills," Owen laughs. "Administrative overhead, you know."

"And what do I say to department heads when I take their money?"

"That we'll pay them back."

Middleton has every intention of doing so. Nobody better appreciates good management. Nor more highly values a positive relationship with the bureaucracy.

"By 'we' you mean the secretary of administration, don't you?" The bobblehead often refers to himself in the third person.

"Hey buddy," Owen agrees.

"I'll see what I can do," the bald man replies acidly.

In fact, the secretary of administration can do pretty much anything he wants. His is a powerful position. He can sweep money without legislative action or professional explanation. And he can do so with impunity, as is his style. All state funds flow through administration and no agency head would dare challenge him. He answers only to one, the governor. A man who readily hides behind the secretary's bellicose reputation. If harm needs doing, let it be done by administration. That way, the governor can preserve his image as a nice guy with good hair.

The secretary hangs up and scurries down the marble halls of the Statehouse second floor. There is a long line of groups winding through the rotunda. It's signing day. One proclamation after another. Mothers Against Drunk Driving. State championship girls' gymnastic team from Girard. Barbers and beauticians for National Scalp Health Month. Intensive Groundwater Use Control Areas. Save the Prairie Chicken. Fort Hays/China collaborative in online education program. Check Before You Dig poster winners. On and on and on. The walls ring with excited voices.

One by one, the groups are ushered into the ceremonial office, where the governor sits behind his ornate signing desk. He is flanked by two flags, US and Kansas, and backed by the enormous stuffed head of an American bison. The governor picked that one out himself. What's more representative of America? The governor greets each group with a glorious smile and friendly banter.

"My goodness, Joe," he says to someone he recognizes. "You should be a candidate for Kansan of the Year. Really, you should."

Joe beams. As do all the other barbers and beauticians bathing in Joe's reflected glory. Nobody takes it seriously, except maybe Joe. But both Joe and the possibility will be forgotten by the time the next group settles in for their photo.

"Say whiskey," the photographer coaxes. He snaps one, then another to be safe.

"Thank you all for coming," the governor cheers in parting. "And God bless Kansas."

"Next," say the staff.

The secretary of administration pushes to the front of the line. Other than a few agency people, nobody knows who he is. But he seems important, so the celebrants let him pass. He steps behind the photographer and catches the governor's eye. Security knows to hold the next group at the door during the whispered exchange.

"Senator Middleton owes us big time for this one," the governor concludes with a slight grin.

"I won't forget," the secretary hisses back. He never does.

"My goodness, Nancy," the governor chirps at the leader of the Prairie Chicken brigade. "You should be a candidate for Kansan of the Year. Really, you should."

<>

After ending his call with the secretary, Middleton readies for another. He sits in his home office, wearing blue jeans and a flannel shirt. Pine bookshelves sag with historical biographies and his economics texts from college. He consults his watch, then dials the designated phone number.

The Kansas Commerce Commission will consider a single item. Recommendations from the Interim Committee on Rural Economic Development. Owen is the first online. He mutes the phone as other members join in. Small talk is small talk. Which he prefers to avoid, in person or by wire.

At the far end of the house, the garage door opens. LeeAnn is home from Denver. He hears her go into the kitchen and rummage around the refrigerator. She doesn't call his name. There is no singing. Could be a bad sign.

The operator takes roll and announces that all conferees are present.

"So, who called this meeting?" the chair joshes. "Senator Middleton, you out there?"

Owen unmutes.

"Yes sir," he says.

"Then the floor is yours."

Owen holds powerful ground as co-chair of the Interim Committee and immediate past president of the commission. He could normally gain passage just by indicating his support. But this deal has some sticking points and the politics are less than certain. So, he will carefully go through detail after detail and hope Melvin McQuitty has done his job.

He explains the governor's charge and the committee's process. Like all good pols, he puts human faces on policy discourse. This is about money, sure, but it's more about people. Like the mayor of Atwood tearfully advising her own children to quit the dying town. The new jail that

Kingman County cannot afford but clings to as its hope for survival. Imagine that. Placing all hope in a jail. That's how desperate the struggle has become. Middleton digresses to mock an anthropologist couple who argue that western Kansas might best be turned into an American Serengeti. A travel destination and hunter's paradise.

"I don't even know where to start with that kind of thinking," Owen says bitterly, theatrically. He understands that an us-against-them dynamic will help overcome any lingering doubts.

The senator sets it out masterfully. He includes all angles and information. All humanity and costs. Others on the conference call listen very carefully. Some take notes on how Owen makes the argument. And how they will, in turn, explain to constituencies of their own. It all leads up to the Interim Committee's recommendations. The senator feels anticipation rise through the jittery static of telephone lines. He consults papers spread across his desk, so as not to misspeak. As if there is any chance of that.

"The committee recommends three projects that budget up to fifteen million."

Someone whistles. The amount is larger than they imagined. Owen forges ahead.

"Southeast Kansas gets five million for gaming."

There was testimony about gambling money going to Oklahoma. To tribal casinos operated by the Cherokee, Wyandotte, and Quapaw. If Kansans are intent on throwing their greenbacks away, better they should do so in their own state. Topeka needs the tax revenues. Besides, we call it "gaming" now. So much more wholesome than "gambling."

"Excuse me, Owen," crackles a distant voice. "Where in southeast Kansas?"

"Excellent question." Like a first-year college professor, the senator flatters every inquiry.

"The committee believes in local decision-making," he explains. "There are details to follow. But I assure you, southeast Kansas will be in charge every step of the way."

They all understand the senator's inexactness. Political Strategy 101. Blurry geography lets every nearby legislator think they have a chance at winning. The southeast is Kansas's poorest quadrant. Beset by meth kitchens and suicide. A place where wins are few and chances are rare.

"Johnson County gets five million for agricultural research, to be divided between K-State . . ."

"EMAW!" a Wildcat interjects.

". . . and Johnson County Community College."

Johnson County, in northeast Kansas, rose in prominence after *Brown v. Board of Education* of May 17, 1954. Filled with whites fleeing Kansas City, Missouri's mixed-race schools via Eisenhower's commuter highways, JoCo expanded to become one of the richest counties in America. Thick with tract houses, corporate headquarters, and strip malls. Because it is affluent and growing, absorbing many displaced rurals, JoCo contributes the lion's share of revenues in a state that is otherwise economically stagnant. Its wealth translates to great political leverage. Nothing happens in the Statehouse unless JoCo gets its cut. Rural commission members understand and ruefully accept. At least the money will fund ag research.

"The final five million will support a new warehousing operation in western Kansas. Involves a large online retailer. The state will offer land, road and rail improvements, and technical grants. The retailer will provide the building, hi-tech machinery, and jobs."

"How many jobs?"

"We're still in negotiation."

"Any location on that?"

"Not yet," Owen answers.

"Hmmm," a disembodied voice drawls. "You know about land, a building, roads, and rail. But not location?"

It's the Wing whose bushy eyebrows are thicker than his mustache. The one who stirred up trouble at the "Mythmakers" exhibit.

Senator Middleton does not answer. The Wings don't have enough votes to defeat the recommendation package. But they can sure cause trouble by asking questions the senator hopes to avoid. Sowing doubts among the press and their talk-show constituency. Representative McQuitty was supposed to take care of this. It was his job to muffle any Wing resistance.

Senator Middleton still does not answer. The extended pause is revealing to the conferees. Of course he knows the location. It's in his district. Were it anyplace else, he would be waxing poetic about selflessness and helping those most in need. Instead, he is tell-tale mute. The senator has scratched a lot of backs in his day, now comes his turn to receive favor.

The silence continues.

"Any other questions?" the chair finally asks, ignoring the one remaining unanswered. He waits one heartbeat, then pushes ahead. "If not, the chair will entertain a motion."

Normally, this is where the Wings would flap and flutter. Refusing to be ignored. Calling point of order over and over, voices rising in frustration. But the difficult Wing seeks no further clarification. He didn't really expect his question to be answered. He just wanted to kick a little and get some skepticism on the record in case the whole project goes south.

One of the senator's allies jumps in. He has the exact words in front of him, thanks to an earlier email from Ewing County.

"Mr. Chairman, I move that the Kansas Commerce Commission endorse findings of the Interim Committee on Rural Economic Development. And further direct the KCC to receive dedicated funding from the Kansas Secretary of State and disperse those monies on a timely basis and as needed for the completion of recommended projects."

"Do we have a second?"

"Second," someone shouts, eager to have his name in the meeting's minutes.

"We have a motion and a second. All in favor say 'aye.'"

There are a lot of "ayes."

"Nays?"

Owen is not sure all the Wings said yes, but neither did they say no. A wink is as good as a nod to a blind horse.

"Thank you all for calling in," the chair finishes, graciously. "Oh, one more thing. Will the KCC issue a press release on this? Let's get good news out the door."

"We'll get right on it," says the agency director. In fact, the senator sent a draft press release earlier that morning. Not soaring poetry, but close. Full of hope and responsibility, deliberation and process, avowals of transparency. Third-party analysis. Returns on investment.

"Anything else for the good of the order?" the chair cheerfully concludes.

"EMAW!" the Wildcat repeats.

Across Kansas telephone lines go dead. One by one.

Owen exhales in relief. Melvin has delivered, following a strategy devised by the senator. Arguing the folly of attacking too many fronts simultaneously, McQuitty convinced the Wings to take a pass on battling rural eco-devo. Sure it's market tampering, but better to focus on satanic urban liberalism. McQuitty even hinted that the powerful Senator Middleton might take an interest in their cause. "After all, didn't he stand with me at the committee hearing? Big as life and right there in the old Supreme Court chambers for everyone to see? If that don't mean something, I don't know what does."

"Honey, that you?" Owen calls. His wife does not answer. Definitely a bad sign.

He pats his papers into a neat stack on his desktop and goes down the hall. The walls are covered with photographs of family and reunions. Hers on the left, his on the right.

LeeAnn has made herself a slice of toast and cup of tea. She sits by the window, gazing out onto a bright winter day. While rummaging around the refrigerator for fizzy water, the senator assesses his wife out of the corner of his eye. She is stiff, formal.

"So, how was Denver?"

"Denver was great, fine," she sniffs. "And how was Topeka?"

"Same as it ever is."

"How long has it been the same?"

"What?"

"I heard you had some trouble Saturday night."

"It was nothing." He waves as if the riot were a bad odor. Then, caught by surprise, the banker peeks around the refrigerator door. "It made the news in Denver?"

"Anybody get hurt?" she continues, ignoring his question.

"A few nicks and scrapes. Goddamn Melvin McQuitty started it. He . . ."

The senator stops. His wife is blowing steam from the cup of tea. Pointedly disinterested in what he is saying.

"What's with the attitude?"

"I got a fascinating phone call a couple of days ago."

Hairs rise on Owen's neck.

"From whom?"

"Apparently, someone you know. At least he claims to know you."

"And who is that?"

"Derek Kovak."

Owen Middleton shatters inside, the way only a compartmentalized man can shatter. The discrete walls of his existence tumble down. The membranes of division. The steady, meticulous construction and containment. The intricate work of an entire life. All shattered, leaving every edge and shade of himself revealed. Naked.

"What did he want?" he asks calmly. His fingers have turned icy. He closes the refrigerator door.

"That's a good question." She sips. "Revenge on you? To get his wife back? To humiliate me?"

"What did he say?"

"Why don't you call him and ask? Maybe you can smooth talk the man. Suggest he has the wrong person. That somebody else is screwing his wife."

"Jesus." Owen leans back against the sink and runs his fingers through his hair.

"Funny," she muses, still gazing out the window. "He never told me her name."

"Jesus," he repeats.

"What's her name, Owen?"

"Does it matter?"

"It does to me. Say it."

"Her name is Muriel."

"Muriel," LeeAnn repeats. "Not very pretty, is it?"

There is nothing he can say in defense of the name. Not because he thinks it ugly, but because every vestige of fantasy has been exposed. And none of it is very pretty. This is no longer a charmed dance of erudite lovers trysting in a Diamond. It is an organic mess of deceit. By people who are old enough to know better.

"What did he say?" Owen asks.

Contempt radiates from LeeAnn.

"Don't worry. He wants to save his marriage. It's not in his interest to take this any further."

"That's not what I'm worried about. Did he frighten you? Did he threaten?"

"Really, Owen? You think I'm that simple?"

LeeAnn has known her husband too long, too well, to be so easily thrown off track. To allow him to cast himself as any kind of protective hero. She gets up to refill her cup from the steaming teakettle.

"It doesn't matter what he said. All that matters is what I say. And you goddamn well better listen."

Middleton tries to hide the trembling of his hands.

"I give you a lot of freedom," she continues, "but I will not be humiliated. Do you understand?"

He nods.

"And that means never."

The sunny, cheerful woman who loves to sing, tops her cup with scalding hot water. Then pours it on her husband. He yelps, quickly pulling the shirt away from the burnt skin of his chest. LeeAnn does not move.

She watches Owen with hard, flat eyes, then carefully sets the empty cup on the counter. She disappears down the hall. The one covered with photographs of family and reunions.

"This is over, Senator Middleton," LeeAnn concludes from a distance.

"Okay," he surrenders. In the way only a compartmentalized man can surrender.

<>

Somewhere deep, deep in the bowels of the Kansas Department of Administration, a mid-level clerk strokes the keys of a computer. His boss looks over his shoulder, just to be sure. It wouldn't do to fumble the secretary's explicit directions.

"Hit 'enter,'" the senior bureaucrat directs.

Numbers flicker across a screen. And just like that, fifteen million dollars moves into play.

<>

Heavy clouds gather. The late morning is so dense and gray it seems the sun might never find its way back into the sky.

Billy is in his office, reading a bulletin from the Kansas Sheriff's Association. It tells of crime trends and pending legislation. The phone rings.

"We have results for you."

When he hears Peggy Palmer's voice, Spire sits up and sets both feet flat on the ground. One is attentive to the KBI.

"Go ahead."

"There's the standard B.S.," she says. He can hear her riffling through pages of methodology, boilerplate, conditions, and limitations. Then she stops. "Okay. Findings and discussion. Got something to write with?"

"Yes." He holds up a pencil as if she can see.

"Death caused by gunshot. High-power and close range. Projectile cut through the wrist . . . probably a defensive gesture by the deceased . . . glanced off radius . . . deflected the pathway downward just a few degrees . . . bullet nicked the aorta . . . exited through his back. He died within seconds."

"How close is close range?"

"Says one and a half to two meters."

"Meters," he sighs while writing. "Whatever happened to feet and yards?"

"Get with the technology, dude."

Billy grunts his disapproval.

"So that eliminates one possibility," he surmises.

"Which is?"

"That he was walking along the highway. Shot from a passing car."

"No. That did not happen. And by the way, did you know the body had been moved?"

"Kind of thought so."

"You might have said something."

"The technology never asked me."

"Fine," she gripes, trying to sound irritated. "From the bloodstains and settling of fluids, he was moved immediately after being shot. There for ten to twelve hours. With as much traffic as the highway gets, wonder how it went unseen?"

"They hid the body pretty carefully."

"Who's they?"

"Your guess is as good as mine."

"I doubt that," she grumbles. Then sits silent. Cat and mouse.

Caught again, Billy must concede.

"Might be someone from around here, someone who knows the highway. The place where we found him has a long view in either direction. Long enough to dump the body, move the truck, and let air out of the tire without being seen."

"They let air out?"

"Yes," Billy replies. "Tried cutting through the tread but snapped the knife tip on steel belting. Had to loosen the valve stem instead. Made it look like Haycock had a flat and started walking."

"That so?" Palmer says.

Spire listens. He can hear the special agent thinking.

"What?" he asks.

"It's interesting. The victim's wounds have the feel of a fight. Close and violent. After something like that, most people tend to panic. Act irrationally. But your killer comes up with a plan to fake the victim's death. Picks the perfect spot and hides the evidence. Hot and cold at the same time."

"What do you make of that?" Billy asks as he writes down "hot and cold."

"Very different temperaments and reactions. I'd bet more than one person was involved."

"Huh," Billy grunts. "Anything else?"

"Well," she says, riffling through the report's last pages. "Mud on the boots is standard Kansas clay. But a lot of cattle feces, mixed with oil and grease. Any of that make sense?"

"Haycock pretty much lived in a junkyard. Oil and grease all over the place. But cattle? Not that I ever saw."

"Well, that's what we got. I'll send the original to you."

"Okay," he says. "Thanks for the help."

"No problem," she replies. "In fact, why don't I bring it over myself. Lend you a hand."

Spire considers the offer. KBI would love to get involved. A solved murder is good for the agency. The stuff of reputations and increased budgets. And he admires Peggy Palmer. But she wouldn't come alone. KBI never comes alone. Bureau men would crawl all over the town, stern faced and asking a lot of dopey questions. Suggesting a predator on the loose. Causing people to lock their doors and distrust their neighbors. Heating up racial tensions that need to be cooled. Maybe even digging up the Haycock property and disturbing the grave of a poor woman who had suffered enough. The sheriff considers. He might need KBI before it's all over. But only as a last resort.

"Let me do a little legwork and get back to you," he replies.

"A-OK, sheriff. Just say when." Her voice is bright and disappointed.

"Got you on speed dial," he promises.

<>

Billy Spire hangs up the telephone, leans back in his chair, and takes a deep swallow of diet cola. Somehow, conversation with Special Agent Palmer has made the murder real. It was real before, of course. But at arm's length. Hidden in the shadows of a drive-by shooting that might have been. Unlikely, sure, but still possible. Not so much a murder as malignancy out on the highway. But now Palmer has confirmed that his hopes are mistaken. Much more is involved. "They" are involved. "They" killed the man. "They" moved the body. "They" who are hot and cold. "They" meaning more than one person.

Murder is not common in Ewing County. Only two in his long tenure as sheriff. And those were acts of simple heat. Domestic violence and a drunken poker game. Heat he can stand. It's the cold part in this situation that disorients him. The self-control. The calculation. He thinks of Ewing County as a place of good people. It is his job to maintain that goodness to the best of his ability. It is his purpose, the light and the length of his days. Now there are icy questions as to whether his meaning is self-delusion. A crushing sense of fault that he had failed to keep the peace. He massages his brow. The irrational angels of a lost boy's soul.

Eventually and with an act of will, he stands up to leave the office. He looks around at the comfortable clutter, the dated furniture, and the lifeless fluorescent lights. He wishes he could stay. But there are killers to be found. Billy walks out to the parking lot and climbs into the Ram 1500.

"I'm sick of this weather," he says of the low, dreary sky.

A little sunshine would make all the difference. But there is no sun and won't be for a while. He starts the engine and begins an aimless cruise around town. Time to think.

There are quite a few cars downtown at Effie's. This is cinnamon roll day. Always draws a crowd. Through the diner window, he sees a booth full of the baby bird old ladies. They are laughing wildly, jacked up on sugar and stories they've told each other a hundred times. Driving slowly, Billy can see the youth in them, the beauty of young girls. They look out and wave. He waves back.

At Stonewall Elementary, kids are out for lunch recess. They are a riot of bright colors. A flat rainbow of stocking caps, quilted coats, and calf-high galoshes. They pump the swings and crawl over a plastic contraption of slides and stairs, all purchased with Duane McQuitty community funds. They scramble up platforms and pipes to conquer imagined castles or perilous mountains. They huddle beneath a plastic jungle canopy. They gambol in flocks, scattering from one spot to another. Stopping and panting and then racing off again. Compelled by reasons only they can perceive.

One child is alone at the fence. Fingers laced through chain links, leaning back and pulling close like standing pushups in reverse. Judging from the clothes, it is a girl. Maybe even Luciana Dominguez. But there is too much bundling to know for sure. It doesn't matter. Billy Spire hates to see a kid alone. Makes him feel sad. Even sadder today. He lowers the passenger-side window and leans across.

"You have a good day in school, okay?"

"Okay," the child responds, startled out of her imagined world. By the time the window is back up, the child has run to one of the playground teachers. She gathers close for comfort and points. Billy waves. The teacher waves back.

"Why, honey, that's just the sheriff."

"He looks scary."

"I guess he does," she answers, recognizing a teaching moment. "But we don't get to choose how we look, do we? Just how we behave."

Billy makes a slow loop past the churches. Methodist, Lutheran, Baptist, Catholic. Way more pews than needed for this diminished town. He wonders which will survive another generation.

The light is on in Farther Turney's rectory office. It glows warm and inviting against the gloomy weather. The priest is sitting at a computer. Billy tries to imagine. Is he writing sermons? Filling out paperwork? Preparing for the betrothed, the bereaved, or those whose faith hangs by a thread?

Guessing makes the sheriff feel less alone. It's almost like being with someone. Almost like friendship. His mind drifts and recalls the sweet-smelling ink, the cylinder and crank of mimeography in the church office. Once, he snuck in and stole some of the other kids' weekly offerings. He still sees the small manila envelopes with signed names and included amounts.

"Jesus," he says in renewed pain over a decades-old crime.

Though he has atoned a hundred times over with anonymous donations, he can never really forgive himself. It's a sin that hides in his soul and comes out to kick his psyche when it's down. The sheriff is not Catholic. But he wonders about confession. Might confessing take away the sin and its kicking? Maybe he'll talk to Father Turney someday. When the giant priest isn't too busy ministering to the betrothed, the bereaved, or those whose faith falters.

In fact, Father Turney is doing none of those things. He is watching a game show on his computer. During commercials, he goes to the stairs and picks up two old paint cans that are packed with dirt. One in each hand, he carries them up and down the stairs until the program comes back on. Thirty, sixty, sometimes ninety seconds at a time. First floor to second, then second to first. In the beginning it was hard. Very hard. But with time, he got stronger, then strong. Now he charges up the stairs. Two at a time.

Out at the Middletons, LeeAnn's car is in the driveway. The brightly lit kitchen shimmers with polished wooden cabinets and Mexican splash tiles. She stands with her back to the window, leaning against the counter and talking on the telephone. She twirls her hair, gestures and primps like a sunny young girl. A few blocks away is the bank where Billy slept, and Russ Haycock killed a lamb. Owen's red Lincoln is not there. It rarely is these days, given the demands of Topeka and various branch offices.

Billy cruises by the Haycock place. He tore away the caution tape when he took the box of hate literature to Great Bend. Now someone has screwed a two-by-four across the door and secured the basement house in the same manner. Must have been Emma Ace. Dutifully safeguarding what little there was, pending whatever fate it awaits. The ground is still discolored over Russ's unmarked grave and will be so until summer. When harsh sunlight will bleach away the upturned darkness of rich soil.

Farther out in the country, Billy drives past his own home. Though it is mid-morning, there are no signs of life. Nadine is not yet up. Won't be for a while.

Farther yet out of town, the sheriff finds himself at the Stonewall Cemetery. A slim gravel road weaves through obelisks and tablets. Statues of waiting dogs and weeping angels. Engraved poems of love and loss and mortality. Prepare for death and follow me. The cemetery sits on a rise that slopes gradually down to the Arkansas River. Overlooking the spot where Russ Haycock's hand was found.

He gets out of the pickup and hears whistles and shouts.

At a nearby farmstead, an old man is working a team of miniature donkeys. Harnessed as a pair, they are beautiful little animals. Not stubby and disproportionate but slim, long-legged, and perfect in their smallness. The farmer walks them in a wide circle, easing up on a weighted sled. At just the right second, he drops a metal hoop onto the sled's hook and snaps the reins. He whistles and hollers. The donkeys drive their shoulders into the harness. Their hooves cut the ground and throw clods of dirt. In thirty grueling seconds, they move the sled twenty feet.

The farmer calls them off. When the animals relax, he lifts the metal hoop and starts them on another wide circle. Their ribcages heave. Their breath comes as bursts of frost. The farmer sees Spire. He waves his hand high and regal, like the Queen of England.

"Best dinky donks in Kansas, don't you know?" The heavy sky serves as a parabola. The farmer's shout carries with perfect clarity.

"Hey buddy!" Billy waves back.

"Looks like we got weather coming," the farmer says, pointing at the sky. "Better stable these two."

The donkeys turn toward their barn. Spire steps through the cemetery, careful to not disrespect any graves. He stops in front of a rectangular granite marker bordered with carved lilies. The beveled top is slightly arched. The sheriff doesn't come here often. It seems intrusive. After all,

Matthew Middleton was not his father. But sometimes Billy just needs to talk to his old mentor. To gain his counsel. To find his way back to the best parts of himself.

〈〉

Owen Middleton is not at any of his branch offices this morning. He is in a conference room of the Kansas Commerce Commission offices on the west edge of Topeka, doing business and avoiding his wife back home. With him are attorneys representing state agencies. They are dressed business casual, working through papers piled high on a circular table.

"The state agrees to acquire an abandoned feedlot in Stonewall, Kansas," one attorney reads. "From New Frontier Investments for a sum of seven hundred fifty thousand dollars."

"Know anything about this New Frontier?" an agency attorney asks.

Middleton pretends not to hear. He remains absorbed in his work. Initialing yellow sticky notes and pressing them in place. His silence is their answer. Ask only what you need to know.

Companion documents transfer ownership of said property to an internet retailer for the price of one dollar. The compensatory obligation is to build a warehouse and automated distribution system that will carry packages from train to truck over endless loops of conveyer belts, clattering wheels, and spinning ball bearings. Each package will be identified, stamped, and routed out the door faster than a fast man can run.

Owen scans the contract. Initials and presses on another sticky note.

The contract's fine print includes progress markers, jobs commitments, minimum length of occupancy, and claw-back provisions meant to salve the concerns of eco-devo skeptics. In fact, no penalties will ever be applied. No matter how miserable the failure to comply. No matter how deep the state's losses.

Owen scans and sticks.

"This set of papers commits nearly half a million for brownfield restoration," the attorney drones mechanically.

Cleaning up the old feedlot. Tearing down grain elevators, offices, storage buildings, and metal fencing. Scraping the topsoil and capping it with an impermeable surface. Providing pumps, pipes, and pits to remediate contaminated groundwater.

Scan. Stick.

"This final contract covers infrastructure for the new warehouse. Water, wastewater, and parking. Upgrades and improvements to the rail spur."

Owen affixes his last sticky note. He is done.

The great thing about sticky notes is that they can be pulled off and disavowed, should any reporter or auditor ever get nosy. Owen doesn't expect any trouble, but his are the habits of a cautious man.

Approved and signed, or in Owen's case sticky-noted, all the papers go into an accordion file that, in turn, goes into KCC archives. One set of documents, minus the sticky notes, is placed in a handsome leather briefcase the senator brought from home.

"Been a pleasure, gentlemen," Owen says, fastening the briefcase latches.

"More than ninety jobs," says one of the state attorneys. "That means a lot out there."

"For Ewing County, it means survival," Owen corrects.

The state attorney who asked about New Frontier runs numbers in his head. Five million dollars for ninety jobs. Fifty-five thousand each.

"Oofta," he exclaims unintentionally. Drawing a glance from Owen, the lawyer quickly looks out a window at the western horizon. "That's a bad sky."

"Yes," the senator agrees. "Let's get out of here before it starts coming down."

‹ ›

Billy Spire sits cross-legged next to Matthew Middleton's grave. He pulls his parka tight, to ward off the spitting snow. He opens the spiral notebook and begins drawing a diagram. At least he intends to draw a diagram. Something linear and clarifying of Russ Haycock's death. But what emerges is free-form design. Wiggly lines. Stars and arrows. Serrations and whorls. The opposite of linear. He is lost.

"McQuitty links to extremism," he explains to his dead friend.

The tiny donkeys trudge back to their barn. They are weary and edged with white lather. Snow begins to stick to their backs.

"Perez has McQuitty with a gun. Right after Peggy Palmer mentioned Owen and Melvin in the same breath."

The neighbor puts his shoulder to a barn door and slides it open. The perfect little draught animals walk in and stop. Exactly where they have stopped for years. Waiting patiently to be detached from harness straps and buckles.

The sheriff recalls something said when they were searching Haycock's home and shed. When the senator was there because he couldn't sleep. When they discovered the barrel full of hate material.

"Owen wished Haycock had stopped that extremist crap. But how could he have known? You told me not to tell anyone." Billy reminds Matthew Middleton of the Haycock incident. Of the slaughtered lamb, the music stand, and the Dodge ER doc washing blindness from the banker's damaged eyes. "I never said a word. Did you?"

Matthew Middleton doesn't answer. It's okay. Billy is used to quiet. He's been married to Nadine for a long time. Still, it helps to talk things through. To say the words out loud.

The farmer puts his animals in their stalls, then ladles grain into feed buckets. They nose in, greedy and self-absorbed. With a powerful shove, the man slides the barn door shut. He heads for the house, giving Billy one last holler from the doorstep.

"You okay?"

"Fine," the sheriff yells back. "Just thinking."

"I thought I smelled something burning," the neighbor jokes. Then goes inside.

By now, the snow sifts down in wide, beautiful flakes. Big as a dime. In some ways, Billy feels better being here with Matthew Middleton. Reminded that the world remains mostly gentle and affirming. A place of familiar greetings, lively children, and simple goodness.

"Thank you," Billy says with an affectionate pat on the grave marker. Mr. Middleton still puts Billy in touch with his best. Even six feet under and mute as stone.

But in other ways, the sheriff feels worse. Much worse.

Someone else has recently visited the grave. There are flowers in the tombstone's brass well. The stems are wrapped in green tissue and bound with ribbon. The blush of color yet remains. Billy knows of only one other person who would seek comfort at Matthew's grave.

"Owen, where are you?" he asks.

<>

Normally, the senator would have waited out a storm at the Diamond. With Muriel. But she is gone, and he has a morning appointment in Liberal. Snow falls heavier and the highway gets slushy, as he noses the red Lincoln behind a lumbering KDOT snowplow and follows carefully. It will be a long drive home. His cell phone rings.

"Well?" a voice drawls.

"It's done."

"Good. That's good." Melvin McQuitty tries to seem cool and unconcerned. But he has big plans for the windfall. Double and triple returns dance in his head. He cannot restrain himself. "So, when do I get the money?"

"Should show up in your account in a few days. A week at the most."

"Excellent."

Owen imagines the lanky representative rubbing his hands. Angular and greedy as a praying mantis.

"Now listen to me," the senator says. "When the announcement comes, we might have news people out there."

"To see what? Dirt and old buildings?"

"It's television, Melvin," Owen explains. "No visuals. No story."

"And so?"

"And so, you need to take down the signs. Anything with 'McQuitty' on it."

"Why? Everyone knows I owned the feedlot."

"It's one thing to know, another thing to advertise."

This is like talking to a child. And exactly why Middleton has not told the representative about tomorrow's visitors from the internet retailer. He would want to meet them. Shake their hands. Talk big. And God knows what he might say.

"Fine. Whatever," Melvin dismisses. "I'll get someone out there in the next few days."

"Not days. Tomorrow. First thing in the morning."

"Fine," the representative intones like an insolent teenager asked to take out the trash. "Anything else, your majesty?"

"Now that you ask," Owen adds with an edge to his voice. "Take them down yourself. The fewer people involved, the better."

"Yes, sir!"

"First thing," the senator repeats.

<>

That night, Billy Spire gets home late.

He spent the evening in his office, expecting to be called out for some sort of weather-related car crash. While waiting, he cleaned off his cluttered table.

The sheriff has a process. Anything that's new but he doesn't feel like reading is stacked on the table's back corner. If nobody asks about it for a couple of weeks, it goes into a box on the floor. If still unasked after six months, the box's contents are emptied into the courthouse's recycling bin. It works brilliantly. He could write an article for *Better Homes and Sheriff's Magazine*, if there were such a thing. In spite of the storm, there are no accidents. The weather has chased everyone indoors. The banality of cleaning his office leaves plenty of room for thinking. For mulling and fretting.

When he gets home, Nadine is watching TV in her sewing room. He listens at the door and can tell that she is deep into her cups. The inhalations are unsteady. The exhalations have a breathy edge of hostility. Without saying a word, he goes into the bedroom. Strips down to his underwear and climbs into bed. Tosses and turns. Roughs up his pillow. Tries to find a way to lay his head that will quiet his thoughts.

In that fitful place between consciousness and dreams, the sheriff half sees it. Someone walking from their car to the grave. Placing the bouquet on Matthew Middleton's grave. Someone also seeking tenderness and guidance. It has to be Owen. It has to be, Billy concludes as he drifts away.

In fact, it was not Owen. Major Harold LaVoy made a quick stop at the cemetery on his way out of town after Effie's.

"I don't know why you did what you did," he said, arranging the flowers with military attentiveness. "But thank you, sir."

The major then left. His visit advancing fate without either intent or awareness.

Just before dawn, Nadine puts her ear to the bedroom door and listens to Billy's breathing. It is deep and steady, with just a tick of snore. Certain that he is asleep, she wanders into the kitchen wearing a short robe and slippers. She pours herself another vodka. Careful not to clink the bottle against her glass. She sits down in the living room, wondering if the sun will fight its way through the clouds and come out today.

In the silver of pre-dawn, their nearest neighbor is already at it. Clearing ten inches of snow from his driveway, shovel scraping across the concrete surface. He stops and stretches his back. Kids from the family down the road pass by. Bundled and hurrying to school. They are poor and eager for the free breakfast.

Nadine lights a cigarette. Its glowing orange tip the only illumination in the room. She feels as empty as her side of the bed. Whatever once mattered to her has been lost. For years. Now, all she knows for sure is the bottle.

The sun finally breaks through the gloomy sky, casting its glow through the living room window. A shaft of light inches toward her. Across the braided rug. Over the coffee table's glass top. Up her ankles to her bare knees. When the warmth touches her fingertips, Nadine rises. She pours herself a little more vodka. Goes back to her room and shuts the door.

<>

Within a few hours, the sun is high, and Ewing County shimmers bright beneath a deep layer of new snow. The sheriff is in his office. When there is no answer on Owen's cell, he calls the Middleton house.

"Well, Billy Spire," LeeAnn shrieks gleefully into the phone. "How's your ugly old self?"

"One of these days, LeeAnn, you're going to hurt my feelings."

"Now Billy, you know I love you."

"Yes, I do know that," the sheriff concedes. "But where is Owen?"

"That's a good question. He drove through that storm and got in late last night. Left early this morning. What's up?"

"Heard he got caught in a little mess the other night."

"What do you mean?" LeeAnn's friendly country twang goes flat and serious. "Is it that Kovak fella?"

"What Kovak fella?"

"Well he . . ." LeeAnn catches herself and regroups. "What mess are you talking about?"

"About the incident at the West exhibit. The riot. Someone told me Owen was there."

"Oh. *That* mess. He hasn't said much about it. Other than blaming Melvin McQuitty."

"That's what I want to talk to him about."

"Well, I don't know where he is. But if you hear from him, say hello for me."

"I'll do that. One other thing."

"What's that?"

"Who is this Kovak fella?"

There is a slight pause. Then LeeAnn reverts to her country voice. The one that's loud and happy.

"Just some customer he pissed off," she says. "Been calling here acting all rude. You know how people are these days."

"That's it?"

"That's it."

"Well, give me his address and I'll go shoot him for you."

"Oh, Billy," LeeAnn coos. "You sure know how to sweet talk a girl."

The senator is at the Liberal Mid-America Air Museum, which is housed in a metal hangar next to a vast vintage runway. Kansas was a great place to train World War II pilots. A flat, spare place with little for a fledgling pilot to crash into, other than the ground. All manner of aircraft is displayed in the massive steel building. Posed on the polished concrete floor, as if springing into liftoff. Or hanging from I-beams at angles that swoop and soar.

Snowplows rake the runway, clearing a long, skinny landing strip. No lesser person than Owen Middleton could have activated the airport on a day like this. The senator burst through the doors bright and early, cheerful and clapping, declaring that a small corporate jet is coming in and everybody needs to get cracking. Workers grumbled, set aside their coffee, pulled on insulated orange coveralls, and fired up grading machines with whirling yellow lights.

Waiting alone in the museum, Owen entertains himself with a depth-perception game set up for kids. It features two cards, each pinned to a nylon line that slides back and forth. Owen stands at one end, adjusting the lines, the goal being perfect side-by-side alignment. Owen's cards keep ending up inches apart. He wouldn't be a good pilot. His perspective is askew.

His phone rings. It's Billy Spire. Middleton does not answer. The corporate jet has just appeared.

It buzzes the runway, low enough to check conditions. Sleek and silver, it has swept-back wings and the familiar corporate logo of an internet retailer. Apparently, the strip meets the pilot's approval, for the plane circles and touches down on its stiff little running gear. A door swings open and stairs fold out. A man and woman descend. She's in her late twenties. He's a decade older.

They are very attractive and smartly, if not sensibly, dressed. The internet retail founder is famous for his casual attire of tee shirt and jeans. Very expensive and tailored, of course. But, still, tee shirt and jeans. His people are held to a more conventional standard. She's in a fitted, pinstriped business suit. He's in gray slacks and navy-blue blazer. No tie, as is the fashion these days. They look straight out of the centerfold of corporate ambition magazine. They also look very, very cold. One of the coverall fellows helps them into the cab of a dump truck. As it grinds through the snow drifts, spewing a fantail of ice, the passengers bounce up and down. When they get out, the man looks rattled. The woman, annoyed.

"Welcome to Kansas," Owen beams.

"I'm freezing," the woman chatters.

Owen hurries them to the red Lincoln. It is warm and idling, the leather seat warmers dialed up high.

The man is with company finance. Trained in accountancy and the law. Owen reaches into the back seat for the handsome leather briefcase.

"This is for you," he says.

"Nice bag," the woman notes. Owen is not sure of her sincerity. The bag is of a distinctly western style and perhaps not to her taste.

"Thought he could use something to carry all those papers."

"Thank you very much," Finance answers as he removes the documents. "But we have a strict policy against gifts."

"O-kay," the senator replies, emphasizing both syllables. It's rude to not accept a gift. Even worse, to make hospitality feel corrupt.

"Paperless is something of a necessity," Finance tries to soften his refusal. "We move around a lot."

"Well then, this will help." Owen reaches into the glove compartment for a thumb drive. He thinks of everything.

"Perfect," Finance exclaims. He sets the bag behind Owen's seat, where it will remain.

The woman is in corporate imaging. Staging and opticals. Determining precisely when, where, and how the new internet warehousing operation will be announced. Middleton hands her a single page of text.

"I threw this together."

She peels off her black boots with metal eyelets. Footwear that looks far more formidable and insulated than it really is. She sits on her feet to warm them up.

"It's going to be a beautiful drive." Owen smiles at the highway's challenging conditions. A smile that says hardship forms character.

"Let's go," Finance answers, manfully. His feet are also cold, but he's not one to give an inch to discomfort. He is an accomplished cyclist and hits the gym at least three times a week. An urban commando. Gritty and stoic.

When Imaging's feet reach some tolerable degree of warmth, she starts in on Owen's paper. Moving her lips as she reads.

"Not too bad," she reports after the first paragraph. "Language could use another polish."

"I'm not much of a writer," Owen lies. "It's just something to kick around."

The senator has dealt with her kind before. Imaging is young. Imaging is hip. Imaging is from the coast. Of course, she will want to polish. He purposely left in a few rough passages for her to revise.

Owen and Finance squint through the windshield as the red Lincoln hums along. Strong light reflecting off new snow is almost unbearably bright, even with sunglasses. KDOT has shoved slush and ice into four-foot berms on either side of the highway, but the asphalt remains packed with snow. Adjacent farm fields are broad and pristine, marred by neither vehicle track nor footprint. From each farmhouse rises a tendril of smoke. Blue icicles dangle from sagging powerlines. Red-tailed hawks, puffed three times their normal size, sit atop telephone poles. Searching for motion in the snow.

"You must be tough people," Finance observes with a deferential shake of his head. "It's so barren."

"Barren?"

"I don't mean to be rude. But just look."

Owen looks.

"It's my home," he observes. "I think it's beautiful."

"Or not," mutters the woman in the back seat. Owen checks the mirror. She is still marking up his paper.

"You a mountains kind of guy?" the senator asks.

"I am," Finance replies. He rocks his shoulders, like someone racing down moguls. "Love to ski. We have a condo in Mammoth."

"People seem to think mountains are full of life," Owen says. "But compared to the plains, they are quite sterile."

"Is that right?" Finance peeks at his watch. It is as broad as his wrist and contains about a hundred dials.

"It might be a different kind of beauty than you're used to," Owen gestures through the windshield. "But this is not barren. Not at all."

"Too subtle for me," Imaging interjects.

"Maybe so," the senator agrees.

It takes ninety minutes to get to Stonewall. They stop at the Gas-N-Go for restrooms and something to drink. As Finance and Imaging wander up and down the aisles, Owen waits at the cash register, money clip in hand. He will not let his guests pay. Not one penny. Company policy and blindness to subtle beauty be damned.

The owner lumbers in from the gas pump, where he was filling the tank for one of the baby bird old ladies. He has a huge belly and hair that stands up like the hackles of an angry rooster.

"Morning, Hugh," the senator chirps.

Hugh gives Owen an exaggerated stink eye. Kind of joking, but kind of not.

"Why don't you mind your own damn business?" he says.

"What?"

"Best employee I ever had. Practically raised that girl. Now she's off to Colby, because some busybody filled her head with foolishness about college."

"Really? Becca went back to school?"

"Yes, she did. And ain't it just grand."

"It is. It truly is," Owen smiles. It is a smile of pure joy. Untroubled by compromise or compartmentalization.

"Glad you're so pleased with yourself," Hugh grumbles. But it's obvious that he, too, is pleased. Kind of. And kind of pissed off. "You got any scholarship money in that bank of yours?"

"I might," Owen muses. "I just might."

"Good," Hugh growls. "I'll be by to talk."

"I know you will."

"And from now on. Keep your damn nose out of my business."

"Just trying to serve the public." Owen holds his palms out. The very picture of saintly innocence.

Imaging and Finance pile bottles of sugary juice and packets of salty nuts onto the counter.

"Not big into healthy eating around here?" Imaging asks, in a way that is more accusatory than inquiring.

She and her partner practically radiate disapproval. Not out of selfishness, of course. Out of concern about food deserts and the epidemic of American obesity, as evidenced by the senator and his friend.

"You work out?" Hugh asks, looking at the man.

"I do," Finance answers. "Spin class. CrossFit."

Hugh nods. Pats the fifty extra pounds of his stomach.

"I do, too," he says, winking at Owen. "Being pallbearer for my friends who exercise."

Owen laughs out loud. Finance and Imaging are less amused.

<>

"Who is that?" Finance asks as the red Lincoln pulls off the highway. He points at the McQuitty sign on the feedlot gate.

"I told him first thing in the morning," Middleton mutters under his breath.

231

"Excuse me?"

"Nothing," Owen replies with a quick shake of his head.

The senator proceeds carefully. The snow is deep but manageable. The icy crust crackles beneath the tires.

"You're not going to get us stuck, are you?" Imaging asks.

"This is nothing," Finance jumps in. "Much worse at our condo in Mammoth. The Land Rover rolls through like a tank. Kids think it's great fun."

"Land Rover," Owen says. "That's British?"

"Sure is," Finance answers with his first real smile. "Amazing machine."

"Well, this old clunker is American made," Owen drawls. "But I imagine we'll be okay." In addition to Lincolns, Middleton family tradition includes economic patriotism. In the rearview mirror, he catches Imaging rolling her eyes.

"So, who is that?" Finance asks again.

"Was and he."

"Okay, who *was he*?"

"Duane McQuitty was the good old boy who owned this place. Been dead for years."

Owen never lies. Lies have a way of catching up to people. But that doesn't mean he always tells the whole truth. Such as mentioning an interim owner. Imaging holds up her cell phone, frames a shot or two, then lowers it without taking any pictures.

"There's not much to see, is there?"

"Maybe not," the senator answers. "But we'll probably get a TV crew from Wichita for the groundbreaking. That's big news out here."

"Really? Amazing."

"Depends on what a person is used to."

"Guess I'm used to more," she says.

"What about those?" Finance points again.

Grain elevators tower against the bright blue sky.

"They're coming down. All of them."

"Out with the old, in with the new," Finance says with an approving nod. He is an urban commando on the bleeding edge of progress. His salary seriously into six figures. He is scornful of those who cannot adjust and embrace changing times.

Middleton snorts in a way that might be interpreted as agreement. But it is disdain. Those who fly over can never understand the life and vitality that once was McQuitty's Feedlot. That once was Ewing County.

They know nothing of this community, or hundreds more just like it. Nothing of the desperation that rises when nothing is all that remains. Where shadows cry in the wind and ghosts dance in the sun.

Middleton makes a slow circle around the office building and workshops. Deciding, for the sake of the deal, that small talk is better than no talk at all, he explains some of the operation's pieces. Augurs, chutes, and pens. They ask questions to be polite.

A vehicle swings around from the opposite direction. A Ram 1500 with a sheriff's insignia on the door. It stops nose-to-nose with the red Lincoln.

"Whoa!" Imaging yelps as the bumpers almost kiss.

Owen's heart sinks.

Billy gets out of the pickup. The senator lowers his window.

"Saw your tracks," Spire says, leaning down to look inside. "Wondered who was driving around in here."

"This is our sheriff, Billy Spire," Owen announces.

Imaging almost gasps. *This man needs to spend serious time with an aesthetician*, she thinks to herself. Years, if not decades. Drink more water. Eat a salad once in a while. Find some thick-framed glasses to hide those awful bags under his eyes. In fact, maybe a full-face welding mask would be best. Doesn't anyone around here care about their appearance?

"Pleased to meet you," Finance says, reaching over Owen's belly to shake hands.

Finance is always eager to schmooze local officials. He will send the sheriff a note thanking him for the nice visit, brief as it might be, and include a gift coupon.

"This place is going to be jumping soon," Owen gushes to preempt Billy from saying the wrong thing. The senator can't afford a scene. "More than ninety jobs. Stonewall is coming back."

Billy Spire has no idea what Owen is talking about. Or why the huckster tone.

"Ninety jobs," he repeats slowly. "That's a lot."

Finance and Imaging smile. It's nice to be the savior. Even if neither can imagine anything in western Kansas worth saving.

"Will you excuse us?" Billy asks.

"Of course," Finance answers.

"This won't take long," the senator assures. He closes his door to keep the warmth in, and the conversation out.

Finance immediately goes to his cell phone. Imaging opines as to where the stage might go. There with farm fields as background. "Not much, but it's the best we got," she says quietly, almost to herself. "God knows where we'll find a riser, chairs, and catering."

"Let's make that the senator's problem," Finance counsels.

"Best thing," she says, "is that after today, we will never have to come back to Ewing County, Kansas."

Finance, still scrolling his text messages, chuckles in agreement.

In bitter cold outside the car, the two men stand face to face.

"Is everything okay?" Owen asks.

"That's what I want to ask you," the sheriff answers.

"Billy, I don't know what this about, but now is not a good time."

In fact, the senator knows perfectly well what this is about. Russ Haycock died just a few feet from where they stand. But he needs time to take his guests back to Liberal. To close the deal. To think through his next steps.

Spire is distracted by laughter from the Lincoln. The woman seems to have said something funny. Both passengers are laughing. The sheriff turns his eyes to the ground, studying tire tracks in the snow as he gathers his thoughts. Good cops hang on to loose details. They throw out left-handed questions just to see what happens. There was something wrong with what LeeAnn told him this morning. Owen would never piss off a customer. It's bad politics. He pays people good money to do his dirty work for him. Something else is going on.

"Who is Kovak?" he ventures.

"Kovak?"

The sheriff nods, not looking up. Repeating words is how perpetrators stall for time.

"I don't recognize that name," Middleton lies.

"That's interesting, because . . ."

Spire stops, finally seeing that which is before his eyes. His focus becomes so intense that the senator looks down as well. There is nothing but tire tracks and snow.

"Cattle feces, mixed with oil and grease," Billy mutters.

"What are you talking about?

Billy looks up. Squares himself to his old friend. His expression has changed. He looks full-on cruel. Dangerous. Heartbroken. Middleton doesn't understand how Billy figured it out. But he did. Haycock died right here, and the sheriff knows it.

"I need to take these people back to Liberal, Billy. It means everything to Ewing County."

"Ninety jobs."

"Ninety jobs means survival."

"I can't let you go."

"I'll be back this evening."

Billy says nothing.

"What? Think I'm going to run off to Peru?"

Billy places his hand on Owen's shoulder in a way that is both gentle and threatening.

"Call when you get close," the sheriff says. "I'll meet you right here."

<>

On the other side of Stonewall, Father Turney is visiting the Engels. Roy has taken a bit of a downturn. The wound in his arm is infected.

"He'll be okay," says Doc Howard. "But until then, there'll be fever, pain."

"And a little ooze," Mama Doc says to the priest. "You might want to look away."

"We'll be brave together, won't we?" Father Turney winks at Roy, then grips the arms of his chair. He doesn't like gore.

Mama Doc unwraps a gauze bandage that's moist with yellowish discharge and drops it into a red bag labeled "biohazard." Roy watches intently as she rakes her thumbnail along an angry red line of stitches. An ooze flows out the end, like toothpaste from a tube. A malodorous compote of disease and coagulation. The priest's smile and courage fade.

"You look a little green," Roy says.

"I'm fine." Father Turney's words are consoling, but his eyes speak of panic.

Mama Doc applies a greasy antibiotic wrap. Roy falls back on his pillow. The old man is in pain. He shuts his eyes, trying to regain his cranky good nature. It's a long and visible battle.

"You seen Luciana do her flash cards?" he eventually croaks.

"No, I have not."

"She's a bright girl, that one." He flicks his hand toward the door as if shooing a fly. "Go see if she isn't something. And let me rest, now."

"I'll come back tomorrow."

The priest kisses the top of the injured man's head. The old man's hair is matted and sour.

"Oh, now," Roy fusses, embarrassed. He uses his fingers like a comb.

"You look beautiful to God."

"Well, next time you talk to Him," Roy snaps, "tell him to do something about that goddamn dog, pardon my French."

"I'll pass along the word."

At the kitchen table, Judy Engel is testing Luciana with flash cards. The subject is math. The little girl's responses are quick and correct.

"She's just as good at science," Judy beams.

Mrs. Dominguez is boning a chicken in the sink. She keeps her head down, but Father Turney can tell she's suppressing a smile, proud of her daughter. Her husband, too. Thanks to one of Eli's parishioners Mr. Dominguez is roofing a hog factory near Dodge. It's hard work. And cold up there, with nothing to buffer the north wind. But, so far, it's going well. The bosses like him and he likes being liked. He has signed up for the next project. Doing the work no white man will do.

The little girl in smudged pink glasses takes a break from her flash cards. She takes her mother's apron strings like the arms of an imagined dance partner. Then rocks back and forth, humming and practicing an intricate series of steps.

"They're having a party at school," Judy explains, her eyes bright with mirth.

"Peace be with you," says the priest.

"And with you, Father," all three reply in unison.

Back at the rectory, Eli puts on his workout clothes, picks up the paint cans, and starts running the stairs. Usually exercise brings him calm. But today, after seeing Roy Engel and how much he hurts, the priest's anger rises with his pulse rate. It wasn't the dog's fault. An animal like that, abused and tortured to meanness, deserves pity. And he should be compassionate, as the church teaches. But right now, pumping his knees and feeling the power in his shoulders. Right now, he is furious. If that dog were here right now, Father Turney believes, he would throw it against the wall as many times as it takes.

And just this once, leave it to others to bow their heads and pray.

<>

On the drive back to Liberal, Owen Middleton is quiet and distracted.

Worried that a lack of appreciation has offended the senator, Finance asks a steady stream of polite questions. He inquires after windmills and tumbleweeds. Rainfall and evaporation rates. Asks if horses really do break their legs in prairie dog holes. Owen responds like a pond turtle surfacing for air. He comes up slowly and answers in deep, patient gulps.

236

Then immediately floats back down to the murky world of his preoccupations. When they arrive back at the Liberal airfield, Finance gives graciousness one last try. Hoping to depart on a friendly note.

"Senator Middleton," he says, extending his hand. "Thank you so much for showing us around."

Normally, Owen would unveil himself, just a little, in a moment like this. He would offer some pithy insight about finance or politics. Enough to hint at the depth of his quiet intelligence, and set the teeth of smugness on edge. But today, Middleton is lost to weariness and concern. He doesn't even have the energy to be falsely convivial.

"I'm sorry western Kansas isn't to your liking," he says.

Finance is taken aback. He prides himself on winning others over.

"No, no. We found this very interesting. Didn't we?"

"Oh, yes!" Imaging's things are bundled in her arms. She is eager to climb in the jet and be gone.

"Next time we fly over," Finance says, "I'll look down and remember all the things I learned today."

"Thank you for looking down on us," the senator says, shaking Finance's hand.

<>

As dusk closes in on Ewing County, an old Jeep pulls up at the McQuitty gate. Way past the demanded "first thing in the morning."

He's wearing jeans, boots, and a jacket with quilted insulation. The snub-nosed thirty-eight with faux-antler grip rests on his hip. He carries the gun as a security measure. It's spooky being alone at the feedlot after dark. Plus, no self-respecting Wing would dare be caught unarmed.

He climbs out of the Jeep and leaves the engine running. He carries a fencing tool, a blue-handled combination of pliers, hammer, nail puller, and wire cutter. Illuminated by headlights, he picks at the curlicued wires that fix the McQuitty sign to the gate. The loops are tight, and his fingers are cold. He hacks and twists and strains and curses. It takes him thirty minutes to loosen one side. By then, it's completely dark.

From down the road, a large car approaches. Lumbering and uncertain. Well below the speed limit.

It is the Hammerschmidts. Kathleen is driving. Going slow because she is scared of the road conditions and doesn't see as well in the dark as she used to. As a rule, she and Larry only go out during daylight hours. But there is no drug store in Ewing County. Hasn't been for years. And the one in Dodge is so busy that it takes forever to fill a prescription. They sat there for two hours. Waiting. With each passing minute, Kathleen became more anxious. She begged Larry, let's come back tomorrow. But he was having none of it. Gasoline costs money, besides the roads are fine.

"Great, you drive," she sniffed.

Larry tugged off his oxygen cannula and snapped back at her.

"All right, I will."

They both knew that would never happen. But Larry had his heels dug in, and they weren't going home empty handed. It's what a man must do. So, Kathleen proceeds at a slow crawl. As if even the slightest touch of the steering wheel might skid them into a snowbank. Where they would surely freeze and die.

"What is that?" Kathleen cries with alarm.

A Jeep is sitting off the road more than a hundred yards ahead. A tall man awash in its headlights. Despite the distance, she eases up on the gas even more.

"Jesus, Kathleen," Larry gasps. "If you go any slower, we'll be backing up."

Representative McQuitty squints and watches the headlights creep closer. Kathleen taps the brakes and the car slides about eight feet. She was right. The roads are bad. The old woman exhales as if she has narrowly escaped death and rests her head on the steering wheel. Larry rolls down his window.

"Melvin McQuitty?" he rasps.

"Who's there?" Melvin shifts the fencing tool to his left hand. Rests his right palm on the pistol.

"It's the Hammerschmidts." The old man turns on the dome light.

"How are you this evening?" McQuitty clomps through the snow and leans down at the window.

"Aw, hell," Larry begins, ever eager to share his complaints. "We got held up at the drug store. The way they treat people these days, why . . ."

"What are you doing out here?" Kathleen cuts off her husband. "And with that?"

She is looking at the gun in its tooled-leather holster.

Owen swore him to secrecy. Grasping for some kind of explanation, the tall man draws inspiration from Mrs. Hammerschmidt's eyes. He pats the revolver on his hip.

"Someone reported stray dogs out here," he says. "After what happened to Roy Engel . . ." He leaves the rest to their imaginations.

"You need help?" Larry Hammerschmidt speaks as if he's ready to fetch his shotgun. Kathleen rolls her eyes. He wouldn't make it ten feet, even if she carried the twelve-gauge and pushed his wheelchair.

"Naw," Melvin replies. "I'm better off alone. That way, if I accidentally shoot someone, it'll only be me."

"If you're sure," Larry replies warily.

"I'm sure," the tall man answers with the Virginian's countenance of grim but brave determination.

"Okay, then," the old man says. He nods at Kathleen and they slowly roll down the highway.

Melvin goes back to work with his fence tool and icy fingers.

A short time later at home, Kathleen helps Larry to his recliner and oxygen tank. Feeling revived, the old man begins to worry.

"I should have stayed with him. What if he gets knocked down? That's what happened to Roy."

"Melvin is half Roy's age."

"And twice as stupid!"

It doesn't take much for Larry Hammerschmidt to get himself into trouble these days. His circulatory system goes haywire at the slightest agitation. The more he frets over the tall legislator, the more he twists uncomfortably in his chair and beads of sweat dampen his hairline. Kathleen attaches a device to his fingertip. A white plastic clip with a red light in its teeth. His blood pressure and pulse rate are dangerously high.

"I shouldn't have left," he moans.

"I'll call Father Turney," she soothes, petting the back of her husband's hand. "He'll know what to do."

Larry closes his eyes and nods. Of course, a priest will know what to do. She dials the phone. It rings twice.

"Why, yes," Father Turney responds. "I'll go out and check myself. You tell Larry to rest easy."

"Did you hear?" Kathleen sniffs as she hangs up. "Father will go himself to make sure Melvin is okay."

Larry Hammerschmidt sags in his chair with a faint smile. The monitor registers an immediate improvement in the numbers of his vitality.

<>

Melvin snips the last wire holding the McQuitty sign in place. The sheet of metal slices down into the snow, narrowly missing his foot. As he is wrestling it to the Jeep, a Ram 1500 pulls off the highway. Billy Spire remains in his truck, considering the scene.

"Did Owen tell you to come here?"

"Owen? No. I was just taking down this sign."

"And why are you taking a sign down out here in the dark?"

"That's a good question," Melvin admits. His mind was never lightning quick.

"What's a good answer?"

"You're right. It's cold. Guess I'll load up and go."

"You're not going anywhere," the sheriff replies.

"Why not?"

"That's what we're going to find out. You just sit and wait."

Melvin drops the sign and slides behind the steering wheel of his Jeep. The night is frigid, but he is hot with fear that the sheriff knows something about Haycock. It's all he can do to keep from running away. If he had any place to go and a faster vehicle to go in, he might have done just that. But he doesn't, and he hasn't. So, he waits. Struggling with what to say and how to say it. It's a fractured process. Fear shatters his concentration again and again.

Another vehicle approaches. The red Lincoln stops beside Spire's truck. Owen scowls at McQuitty and the sign.

"He was supposed to take that down this morning."

"Why do you care?" Billy asks.

"Because it needs to be gone," Middleton answers.

"Why?"

"To keep the McQuitty name out of this."

Spire does not understand. But he nods and jots a couple of words in his spiral notebook. Another loose end.

"You two follow me." He drops the pickup into gear and pulls into the feedlot. McQuitty hurries over to the red Lincoln.

"What does he know?"

"I'm not sure."

"What are you going to tell him?"

"The truth."

"That's your plan?"

"It's the only thing that will work."

"Oh my God," the tall man cries as he starts toward his Jeep.

"And Melvin, you leave that gun in the glove box. Hear me? It's caused enough trouble already."

Owen follows Billy. When the Lincoln's taillights disappear, Melvin pulls the Jeep inside the fence, hops out, and locks the gate. Not to keep anyone out, but to keep Billy Spire in. Long enough to listen to all the reasons he and the senator can concoct.

Spire parks in front of the abandoned office. He turns off the engine and headlights. He can see well enough by the full moon and it might work better to talk in pale light. Where faces are half-hidden and truths flow easier. The other two vehicles arrive. Billy swings down from the 1500. True to the habit of professional toughness, he does not put on his coat. The other two are bundled in jackets and silence.

"Melvin, you start." Billy holds a notebook and ballpoint pen. "Tell me what happened."

"What happened?" McQuitty asks in puffed annoyance. "I don't know what you're talking about?"

"I'm talking about Russ Haycock."

"Russ Haycock?" Melvin rattles his head as though dosed with smelling salts.

"Okay," the sheriff says with the patience of an experienced investigator. "Let me know when you're ready." He jots down a note and moves on. "Owen?"

"Tell me what you need, Billy." The senator speaks in the soft, kind voice he uses to console those denied loans or facing inescapable foreclosure.

The sheriff wonders at the comment. As if his friend is offering a favor. Owen stares right back. Steady and certain.

"I think Russ Haycock was killed here." Billy points at the ground. "Am I right?"

"Yes," Middleton answers. "You are."

<>

Father Turney stops his Honda Fit at the gate where Larry and Kathleen Hammerschmidt last saw Melvin McQuitty. There are several sets of tire tracks, and a fallen McQuitty sign in the snow, but no sign of the representative. Eli grabs the car roof and pulls himself out. He yanks on the gate's padlock. It's secure.

"Melvin must have gone home," he concludes.

Perhaps there were no vicious dogs, or maybe it's just too damn cold. Either way, Larry Hammerschmidt has nothing to worry about. The priest will call and reassure as soon as he gets back to the rectory.

He is dressed in fleece pants, a wool sweater, quilted jacket, and an insulated hat with ear flaps. Every stitch he's wearing is black. Black as night. Black as a Catholic ninja. Still seething with rage at Roy Engel's pain

241

and that "goddamned dog, pardon my French," Father Turney decides to look around. To make sure there is no vicious animal to be found. Half hoping there is.

He checks up and down the highway. Not a vehicle in sight. He hides the Fit behind a mound of snow. No need drawing attention to late night escapades of an archer-priest. Eli takes his bow and quiver from the car and tosses them over the fence. He remembers, then takes a package from the glove box. Climbing the gate, Eli is pleased at how nimble he has become. He jumps down the other side, lands heavily, and falls face first into a drift of snow. Well, maybe not that nimble. Ice sticks to his cheeks and eyelashes. It makes him laugh. To feel like a child. Flush and alive.

He picks up the Razorback and shakes it clean. There are six arrows in the quiver. Each thick as a child's first pencil, with shafts of neon orange. He unscrews the field points, stubby silver cones meant for target practice. Then he tears open the remembered package from the glove box. Free gift from the sporting goods store in Garden City. Out spill six hunting arrowheads with blades flaring back from the point. Sleek and swept, like wings of a jet. Razor-sharp and perforated to encourage bleeding.

After screwing the new points in place, the priest is ready.

<>

"Owen?" Melvin cries. He crowds the senator, trying to intimidate him into silence. Billy Spire steps between the two men and sets his palm against McQuitty's chest. Pushes him back eighteen inches. Melvin is a large man. But against Spire's low gravity and strength, he is nothing.

"How did it happen?" the sheriff asks.

"Haycock attacked Melvin," Owen says in a steady voice. "Melvin pulled his pistol. The damn thing went off."

Spire turns on the tall man with hard, searching eyes. He wants answers. Now. Melvin throws up his hands, unsure of what to say or do.

"Just tell him the truth," Middleton commands.

"But . . ."

"You are going to tell me the truth," Spire warns, edging a little closer. "One way or another."

"Okay," McQuitty surrenders. He gestures at the office building. The one with chicken-wire windows and working doors. "We met here."

"We?"

"A political group."

The sheriff recalls Haycock's literature and the warning words of Peggy

Palmer—"'Therefore, be as shrewd as snakes. And innocent as doves.'
But they usually ignore that part."

"Political? Like the KKK?"

"No," McQuitty huffs. "Just some people who care about Kansas."

"KKK is close enough," Owen interjects.

"Your daddy would be proud," Spire says to the representative.

"I wouldn't talk about daddies, if I were you," Melvin spits back.

Billy takes a moment to write something. At least it appears that way.
In truth, he is deciding whether to continue the interview or knock the
son-of-a-bitch flat on his ass. But the first pulse to take is your own. He
breathes deep.

"Go on, Melvin."

"There were maybe thirty of us. Talking about this and that."

"This and that?" Spire holds out his pen and spiral notebook. His
gesture says, can't you see I'm taking notes? Give me the details.

"Just educating ourselves," McQuitty hedges.

Billy stops writing, considers, then sneers at the man.

"Like conjugating verbs or making a potholder for your mother?"

"Like camouflage, munitions, ambushes, and killer teams," Senator
Middleton offers, voice dripping with acid. "Like hit and run harassment,
movement, and detection."

"All the manly arts," Spire notes, then turns back to McQuitty. "And
just who exactly is the 'we'?"

"I'd rather not say."

"Wings?" Billy parrots the name used by Peggy Palmer, even though
he does not know its meaning.

Owen Middleton nods. He's impressed. It seems the sheriff has been
doing his homework.

"Them and others," the representative mutters. "You'd be surprised."

"I already am." Spire glares at Middleton.

"Not me." The senator holds out his hands. The very picture of innocence. "I have nothing to do with them."

"You just happened to be there?"

"Thanks to him," Owen says of McQuitty.

"We'll get back to that," Spire says to his friend, then returns to Melvin.
"So, you met here. Then what happened?"

"He shows up," the representative answers.

"Haycock?"

"Yes."

"He was part of the group?"

"Not really. Nobody took him serious and it made him sore. But every once in a while, he would show up. Rant a few minutes then leave."

"And he showed up that night."

"Yes."

"And?"

"And we were talking about the things that are happening. To white people, you know. The trouble with . . ." The representative hesitates to say the next words.

"Trouble with what?" Spire demands.

Middleton fills in the blanks, voice dripping with disgust for McQuitty and all things Wing. "Jews, Blacks, Mexicans, Muslims, Asians."

"That's when Haycock went off," Melvin resumes.

"When you were talking about Asians?"

"He started yelling that they were different from the others. How we're being disrespectful of his wife. Then he broke down. Started crying that he loved her. Missed her. I guess that's what he said. Hard to understand through all that blubbering."

"What did you do?"

"We ignored him. Until he stormed out the door and drove away."

"To where?"

"Behind the grain elevators," Owen interjects.

"This is where you enter the picture?" Spire asks.

"As I drove in, I saw his truck sitting in the dark." Middleton's demeanor is calm and precise. "Didn't give it a second thought."

"You came late to the meeting?"

"I didn't know about any meeting."

"You just happened to be visiting the feedlot?"

"Melvin and I had some business to discuss. He asked me to meet him here. Wanted to show off. The representative likes to be seen with people more powerful than himself."

"That right?"

Melvin shuffles his feet but does not answer. Which is answer enough.

"Were you seen?"

"No. The representative is never as clever as he thinks. I waited until the last car was gone. Or what I thought was the last car."

"What happened then, Melvin?"

"Me and Owen were right there." A spot no more than twenty feet away. "Haycock roars up. Jumps out of his truck, waving his arms and yelling."

"Right there?" Spire is keeping notes.

"Yes. Hollering that we shamed his wife. That he won't stand for it. I tried to talk some sense. But you know Russ Haycock. He got crazier and crazier. Finally, he lunged at me."

McQuitty pantomimes the action. He stumbles backward and reaches down. Demonstrates how he grabbed the thirty-eight.

"Next thing I know, he's down. And there is a gun in my hand." McQuitty sounds surprised. As if the accident just happened.

"Was he armed in any way?"

"Well, I didn't know but . . ."

"No," Owen declares. "He was not."

<>

As Father Turney trudges through deep snow, the only sounds he can hear are of his own making. Heavy breathing and the crunch of boots breaking through an icy glaze. Then there is a foreign noise. Scratching. From a mound of household trash thrown off the highway. A black plastic bag is ripped open. Orange peels, coffee grounds, and meat trays spill onto the snow.

There is more scratching. Seems too small for a dog. Still, Eli nocks an arrow. A head emerges from the bag. It is black, with a thin white line running straight back from its nose. The body follows, black with two white bands that run from head to tail. The priest freezes. A striped skunk pauses, chewing thoughtfully on an eggshell, then moves on.

"Glory to God," Eli chuckles and relaxes his bow. "This must be my lucky night."

<>

"It was an accident," Melvin protests. "And I got a right to stand my ground."

"That's for a court to decide." The sheriff has heard this before. Uttered by fools who shot first and thought later, held out as a constitutional incantation that precludes any further discussion. He looks back and forth, his brutal face etched with contempt. "There were two of you. Both younger. Bigger. Stronger."

"I've never seen a person die," McQuitty moans.

"You won't have to worry about that," Billy promises. "You'll see it over and over. For the rest of your life."

The man sags, as if someone has cut the string of his towering height. Owen looks on, unmoved.

"You'll see it, too," the sheriff snaps at his friend.

"I already do," says the haunted senator who wakes up to his own sobs.

"It was your idea to move the body," Billy realizes.

"Obviously, Melvin doesn't show a lot of grace under fire."

"Hot and cold." Spire recalls Peggy Palmer's description of the dynamic.

"Pardon?"

"You should have called me," Billy says, shaking his head in dismay.

"Russ Haycock was dead when he hit the ground. There was no changing that," Middleton explains. "And we can't afford bad publicity right now."

"Right now?"

"The people you met this morning. They're from one of the biggest internet retailers in the country. They're going to build a new warehouse over the feedlot. Ninety new jobs. Enough to keep Stonewall alive."

"And this was the business you were discussing that night? A new warehouse over McQuitty's Feedlot?"

"That's right," Owen says. "Deals like this don't stand up well to loud-mouth opposition, which is pretty much all Wings ever bring to the table. I needed Melvin to hold them at bay."

The sheriff pauses to connect dots.

"Haycock's death would lead to bad publicity. And bad publicity would screw up the deal. So, you moved the body."

"The company we're bringing in doesn't like controversy," Owen explains. "So yes, to save Stonewall, we moved the body."

"It was an accident," the representative wails.

"Melvin, get yourself under control," Spire warns. "Or I'm going to take away that pistol."

"I told him to leave it in his glove box."

McQuitty's voice drops to a whimper.

"And the sign?" Spire asks.

"Melvin landed a little kickback for what he done."

"And you don't want to draw attention to his name."

"Would you?"

The sheriff opens to a new page and raises his pen. The senator interrupts.

"Billy, you don't want to write this down."

"I don't?"

"It's not good to build an extensive record," Middleton suggests, as if discussing the fine print in a loan contract. "That you're just going to have to destroy later."

〈〉

A few minutes later, the priest pauses again. He listens. This time there are voices. Maybe three, on the far side of the grain elevator.

"Who would be out here? And what would they be doing?"

Eli can think of no good reason. So, he concludes the reason must be bad.

His first inclination is to turn around and retreat to the car. Like any sensible grownup would do. But the bow is like a gun. It pulls him. As do all those hours of sit-ups and climbing stairs. His weapon and body urge him to forge ahead. They whisper that he has nothing to fear. In fact, if anyone should be afraid, it's those on the other side.

Slightly crouching, he sneaks forward. With all the stealth a trimmed-down, three hundred-pound man can bring to a snowy, moonlit terrain.

〈〉

"You picked the spot."

"Well, it wasn't him." Owen's expression is smug, dismissive.

"I didn't . . ." McQuitty stammers in protest.

"And the knife tip?" Billy continues.

"You found that?"

"Is that such a surprise?"

"Not at all," the senator dodges. He hopes Billy Spire does not fully grasp the truth. But Billy does grasp. Fully. They may be old friends, but they were never equals. Not when it came to intelligence. Not in the estimation of Owen Middleton.

"I told Melvin to flatten the tire. Make it look like a breakdown. But he screwed that up, too. Broke his knife on the steel belt. Had to let the air out myself."

The sheriff starts writing again. The senator reaches up and gently clamps his hand around the spiral pad.

"Please stop," he says. "You'll just make this harder on yourself."

"I didn't mean to!" McQuitty howls, unable to bear the tension of wealth slipping away, of jail, of killing a man.

"He's right, you know." Owen persists. Kansas is a Stand Your Ground state. Law allows a man to defend himself.

Spire pulls his notebook free of the banker's grip.

247

"We'll let the county prosecutor decide that."

"Our county prosecutor?" Owen asks, eyebrows raised. Of the man who sits on pins and needles, and fixates on anything that might go wrong.

〈〉

Hiding in shadow, Eli slides around the grain elevator. His back presses against its concrete curvature, Razorback half drawn with an arrow in place. Three men come into sight. He doesn't recognize the tall fellow, who seems very upset, nor the one who is calm and common in build. But Billy Spire's profile is distinctive. Low slung and powerful.

"You think this is just going away?" the sheriff asks.

"The county prosecutor is scared of his own shadow. He would never take me on."

"You tampered with evidence."

"Evidence of what? An accidental shooting? Stand Your Ground?" The senator hates to do this, but Billy needs to be realistic. "And even if the prosecutor filed, which he won't, what jury is going to convict us? We're talking about Russ Haycock, after all."

"Even Russ Haycock gets protection under the law."

"Law exists to serve humanity, not the other way around." Owen raises his hands with fingers spread, appealing to reason. "Look, the only thing you're going to accomplish is destroying Stonewall's best chance at a future."

"Along with Melvin's big payoff. Yours, too?"

"I get nothing," the senator snaps. "You, of all people, should understand. The Middletons take care of Ewing County. Not the other way around."

"Goddamn!" McQuitty shouts.

Flooded with adrenaline, he shifts from foot to foot. Arms waving wildly, as if desperate to do something but uncertain as to what. It is then, in the glint of moonlight, that Father Turney sees a pistol on the hysterical man's belt. He shouts.

"Watch out! He has a gun!"

The huge man rushes from the shadows, kicking up sprays of snow with every step. McQuitty panics and pulls the thirty-eight, his finger in the trigger guard. The muzzle explodes. Bullet hits the red Lincoln. Enters the rear fender, exits the back door.

Startled by gunfire, Father Turney stumbles and his fingers slip from the bowstring. The thick orange arrow flies. Undulating in moonshine like a fish swimming upstream, it lands and skitters over the crust of ice. Stopping at Melvin McQuitty's right boot, razor points embedded in his ankle. The representative falls on his side, shrieking in pain and clutching the shaft. The arrowhead's blood-letting perforations work brilliantly. A red stain rises in his sock. Eli scrambles to his knees, face covered with snow.

"Jesus, God, what have I done?" he cries.

Amid the gunshot, hollering with fright and pain, Owen Middleton remains fully mindful. As always. He glares at the priest and rages.

"How long have you been listening?"

In the face of imperious disdain, the giant priest diminishes. He is, again and always, that awkward oaf who broke everything he ever touched. Spilled everything he ever consumed.

The senator never hears the answer to his question.

Sheriff Billy Spire, guardian of the scared and hurt, whips a left hook into his best friend's right cheek. It is a massive blow. Owen is out before he hits the ground.

For Spire, the world disappears. There is nothing. No Melvin. No arrow. No priest. No screaming. No feedlot. There is only Owen Middleton. And a betrayed brotherhood. Worse, a brotherhood that never really was. And there is a sheriff's folly. The senator is right. The prosecutor will never press charges. Russ Haycock will never have justice. Betrayal and bitterness revive in him that simple, urgent, undivided capacity for violence. The sheriff has lost touch with his own pulse.

He straddles the senator's chest, knee on either side, pumping his fists. Cutting and bruising with every blow. Like Joe Spire said, anyone worth hitting once is worth hitting ten times.

Billy's body begins to levitate. He floats six, eight, then twelve inches above the unconscious Owen Middleton. The world comes back to him. He feels the night's cold. Hears Melvin's distant wailing. He sees what he is doing and has already done. The senator is bleeding from the nose and lips. His jaw is discolored and swelling. Father Turney is over him shouting "Stop it!" Over and over.

The massive priest has Billy by the collar and belt of his pants. Straightening to full height, he has lifted all two hundred forty pounds of the sheriff like a bale of hay. In any other moment, Spire would have fought back. Twisted, thrown an elbow at the knees. But there is something safe in the power above him. He relaxes and lets himself be carried away.

The priest drops Spire into a drift of snow. The sheriff rolls over, sits up, and wipes ice off his face. Eli is next to him, hands on his knees.

"Stop it," he says once more, his breathing labored and frantic.

"I'm stopped." Billy looks up at Father Turney who is coughing, sobbing, trying to catch his breath. Magnificent against the starry sky.

"I hate funerals," the priest gasps.

⟨⟩

Father Turney and Billy Spire load Owen into the back of the bullet-damaged red Lincoln. He is unresponsive but breathing. They put Melvin in the passenger seat of the Jeep. The sheriff uses McQuitty's fence tool to cut the arrow shaft. Leaving a few inches protruding from the representative's boot. Melvin has stopped screaming. He sits stiff with pain, agony etched at the corners of his eyes.

Spire drives the Jeep. It takes about thirty minutes to get to McQuitty's house. When they arrive at the line of snow-dappled junipers, Billy turns off the headlights and advances slowly.

"It was an accident," he says once more. "I was never here."

"I understand," Melvin whines. Half in shock. Pale and mumbling.

Inside the house, the blue shadow of a TV set dances on the walls. Billy goes around to the passenger door.

"Not a sound," he warns. "I don't care how much it hurts."

The powerful sheriff lifts the tall man like a child and carries him to the front porch. They hear canned laughter from some sitcom.

"Thank you," Melvin starts.

"I was never here. You drove yourself home," the sheriff repeats, then takes off toward the highway at a slow jog.

Melvin counts to one hundred, then pounds the door. The front light comes on. The lanky, dark-haired girlfriend looks through the peep hole. She cannot see Melvin sitting below. He pounds again. The door opens slowly.

"I'm hurt," he gasps.

She looks down, still holding her glass of wine. Her eyes go from his anguished face to the blood-soaked boot and stump of orange arrow shaft.

"Men," she says scornfully. Then juts out her lower lip and blows her bangs with a puff of breath.

⟨⟩

Billy Spire trudges two miles through snow to an intersection of township roads. Gravel stretches that know little traffic, even in the middle of the day. Ace is waiting in the wrecker, expecting the sheriff to arrive by pickup.

"Jesus!" the mechanic starts when the sheriff appears at his window. "Where did you come from?"

"Don't ask." The sheriff settles onto the bench seat and warms his hands under a heater vent. "Not now. Not ever."

"Well, okay then, princess," Ace snaps. "And thanks for getting me out in this weather at all hours."

"You're welcome."

"You know, Billy," Ace scolds. "Sometimes you take yourself and that badge a little too serious."

The sheriff stares through the windshield and sighs.

"Yeah, well. Sometimes, maybe not serious enough."

<>

Father Turney watches Doc Howard work on Owen Middleton. The senator is lying on a hospital bed beneath a bank of intense lights. Mama Doc hands her husband suturing kits in wax paper packets and dabs sweat off his brow.

"In front of the bank?" Doc's voice is muffled behind the surgical mask. "That's where you found him?"

"Yes," the priest replies. "He must have slipped on ice. Hit the concrete planter."

Middleton groans and reaches toward his damaged face.

"Dammit, Owen! Be still!" Doc commands.

The senator regained consciousness en route to the hospital. He can hear, but Doc has placed gauze bandages over his blackened eyes to protect them from bright illumination.

"Honey, would you hand me that hemostat?" Doc puts in a couple more stitches. He stops, rearranges freeze packs around Middleton's swollen jaw, then stretches his back.

"Lucky you happened by," the doctor observes.

"Bad indigestion. Went to buy antacids."

"I could use one of those right now," Doc says. "Would you mind?"

The priest makes a show of checking his pockets.

"Must've dropped them somewhere."

"Must have," the doctor notes.

When his wife returns with the hemostat, the physician goes back to work. Closing gashes. Medicating against potential infection. Reducing swelling. When all is done, he tosses a handful of blood-stained instruments into a stainless-steel basin. As he peels off surgical gloves, Doc Howard talks to himself.

"This makes no sense, given the kinds and extent of injuries."

Eli starts to reply. Doc waves him off.

"But who am I to question a senator and priest? One holds the keys to hospital subsidies. The other, to the Kingdom. Still, hope I don't ever see anything like this again."

"You won't," Father Turney promises.

Owen Middleton weakly taps the doctor's leg in agreement.

‹›

At two o'clock in the morning, as a Dodge City ER doc is extracting an arrowhead from Melvin McQuitty, Billy Spire sits in the kitchen of the Ewing County prosecutor. Roused from sleep, the man is in his bathrobe and pajamas, uncombed hair poking in all directions. He lights a cigarette and absent-mindedly strokes the little dog nestled on his lap.

"You're saying Russ Haycock died an accidental death," he repeats, struggling with slumber and disbelief. "He accidentally shot himself. Drove his truck several miles the wrong direction, heading away from town. Had a flat tire. Got out and walked another quarter mile. Fell down dead and some animal stole his hand."

"Stranger things have happened," the sheriff insists.

"Not in Ewing County."

Billy Spire doesn't respond. He sits in stony silence, watching the prosecutor anxiously shift things around the kitchen table.

"And why, exactly, did you need to tell me all this in the middle of the night?"

"Because I just finished writing up the case and thought you should know." In fact, the sheriff was afraid he might lose his resolve to choose mercy over the law. The survival of Stonewall over justice for Russ Haycock.

The prosecutor shakes his head. Gets up to pour more coffee and discovers that his cup is already full. He pats the pockets of his bathrobe, then disappears down the hall in search of a cigarette. When he returns to his chair, the little dog jumps back on his lap.

"Sheriff Spire, can you tell me exactly what's going on?"

"A case is being closed."

"Well, Billy." He lights a cigarette and shoots a smoke ring toward the ceiling. "They say smoking gives a thoughtful man time to think and a fool something to do with his mouth. I'm not sure which I am right now."

"Law enforcement involves discretion."

"And discretion is needed in this case?"

"Discretion is always needed," Spire answers, then gets up to leave.

"This makes me very itchy."

"You're never eager to file," Spire observes. "Now when I make it easy, you start to itch?"

"That's not fair," the prosecutor complains.

"You want me to drum up some charges?"

"Certainly not," he replies. He takes a deep drag and decides to follow his natural inclinations. The prosecutor may turn a blind eye toward many things, including suspicious behavior. But he never neglects to cover his own ass. "You'll write up something for me to sign?"

"Of course," the sheriff says.

The nervous man in pajamas watches the Ram 1500 pull out of sight. He stubs his cigarette and goes back to bed. The little dog curls around his feet and the two of them sleep just fine. Ignorance is such bliss.

<>

LeeAnn gasps when she sees her husband's face. Or at least the parts of his face that are visible beneath a thick wrapping of bandage. The priest helps Owen to his bed. Heavily sedated and anxious to avoid her questions, he falls upon his pillow and drifts away.

Father Turney sticks with the same story he told Doc Howard. Involving antacids, Gas-N-Go, and a fall at the bank. But LeeAnn Middleton has none of the doctor's restraint, in either self-interest or temperament. She sets her fists on her hips, arches her eyebrows, and starts digging.

"That wall must be ten feet from the sidewalk."

"Gas-N-Go is in the other direction."

"You're not aware that head or neck injuries shouldn't be moved?"

Father Turney fends the best he can, but the senator's wife is nobody's fool. The priest, finally beaten into submission, says he is exhausted and needs to go home. LeeAnn slams the door behind him. Priest or no priest, someone must answer for hurting her man.

Just after noon the next day, Owen wakes. LeeAnn is next to the bed, reading in a rocking chair.

"How do you feel?" she asks.

Jaw too sore to work, he hisses through his teeth. "What time is it?"

"Almost lunch. Are you hungry?"

"No. I just hurt."

"Doc sent painkillers." She leaves the room and returns with oblong white tablets and a glass of cranberry juice. Using two spoons, she mashes the pills into powder, dissolves them into the drink, and adds a straw.

"Thanks," he says.

"Who did this to you?"

"It's nothing."

"Would you like me to get a mirror?"

"No."

"It was Kovak, wasn't it?"

For a moment, Owen Middleton lies very still. It is hard to concentrate in an opioid haze. But slowly, he grasps what she's talking about. He forces himself to think. To calculate the best play.

"It's nothing," he repeats, certain that dismissal will simply confirm her suspicions. "This is not the kind of publicity we need. Not the bank. Not us."

"I'm calling Billy Spire."

"He already knows," Owen mutters. "And has taken care of it."

"If he hasn't, I will."

"Billy has made sure that Kovak won't ever bother us again. Went a little beyond the law to do it. If you want to protect him, don't say another word. Ever."

She goes back to her reading. Or tries, that is. Owen can hear the rocker creaking back and forth at a furious pace. He knows a storm is gathering. Finally, the rocking stops.

"You're a fine man," she begins.

"I try," he answers. Wary of the more that is coming.

"You do good for so many people."

"I try."

"Still, it's a curious thing."

"What?"

"That you're so generous to the public. And so careless about the people who love you most."

Middleton sighs with relief. She believes this is about Kovak. About a stupid affair. She loves Billy enough to remain quiet forever, if that's what it takes to protect him. All is well. As the dose of opiates takes effect, Owen Middleton slides back into his dreams. His nightmares.

◇

The next week, Billy receives two pieces of mail at the county courthouse.

The first is from the internet Finance. Never one to miss a connection, he sent the sheriff a handwritten note.

Dear Sheriff Spire:

We enjoyed meeting you and look forward to a long, prosperous partnership with Ewing County. Please don't hesitate to contact me if I can, in any way, be helpful in advancing that promise. Until then, thank you for your service to the community.

Smart. Efficient. Fawning, yet dignified. Included in the envelope is a plastic card that carries fifty dollars in credit.

The sheriff puts the plastic card in a plain envelope along with the seven hundred eighty dollars he confiscated from Cruz Dominguez. He prints "La Familia Buena" and its address on the front, then adds "care of Ms. Ayesha Perez." It will go in the mail with no return address, nor any other clues of identity.

The second piece of mail is on legislative stationery, a folded note featuring a pastoral scene of Kansas winter wheat. The distant copse of trees is a leafless brown. The bordering sedge is yellow. The sky is vivid blue. It, too, carries a handwritten message.

Billy, please call me. Owen.

The sheriff tears the note in half and drops it in the trash.

‹ ›

Six weeks later, groundbreaking for the internet retailer is a grand affair.

Even the winter weather seems inclined to celebrate. A dry wind has wicked away recent snow and mud. Temperature is in the balmy sixties. No trace of McQuitty's Feedlot remains. Earth movers have scoured away the grain elevators, buildings, pipe fencing, and run-off lagoon. Nor does anything remain of the violence that occurred there. Only ground. Clean, flat, and innocent as a sheet of paper.

A flatbed truck serves as the stage, complete with a sound system and folding chairs for the dignitaries. Picnic tables have been hauled in from the fairground for general seating. The high school pep club has fixed crepe paper and Mylar balloons to every attachable surface.

The crowd begins to arrive an hour early, giddy with excitement. The groundbreaking promises to be glorious, with free apple cider and pop-corn. But more importantly, it is a rare opportunity to rejoice in this place of dim hopes.

The baby birds take a prominent place at the front table. The Stonewall marching band, a dozen ragtag kids in faux-military uniforms, plays a shaky medley of songs about patriotism and Kansas. The funeral trou-badour directs the band, nodding and gesturing with his head even as he fingers the accordion. Every instrument is needed, especially those in talented hands.

The Hammerschmidts are also among the first to show up. They are determined to avoid a repeat of late-arrival embarrassment. But it's another bad day and Larry needs his wheelchair. Three young men come to help. The brown boy, white nerd, and jock. In a wicked nod toward rehabilitation, the principal required the three to work as a unit. Not surprisingly, the two white kids find they like the brown boy best, for he is smart and tough. They vie for his attention. When the wheezing old man is well positioned, Kathleen offers the boys a tip. Which they refuse. The principal said he would throttle anyone who took so much as a nickel. Kathleen is relieved. She has no more money for tipping than tithing.

The Engels arrive with the Dominguez family in tow. Roy's arm is in a sling, but he's feeling much better. That's made apparent by his energetic orneriness. He issues a volume of loud complaints about every-thing from the placement of the stage—"looking right into the sun"—to fashions of the day—"why don't those boys pull up their pants?" Judy shushes. Luciana giggles. She thinks the old man is hilarious and he likes her right back. Mr. and Mrs. Dominguez stand a little apart. Shy of the spectacle Roy makes. Ever wary of drawing attention. And the trouble that might follow.

The trickle of celebrants becomes a stream as almost every living soul in Ewing County hurries to attend. Every struggling businessman and farmer. Every brave housewife. Every pert Girl Scout and gray-haired retiree. Every tawdry gossip and member of the clergy. Everyone who has fought against cattle disease, sung a funeral hymn, stared wide-eyed at a park privy, or witnessed flames at night. Everyone. Nearly.

Then, led by a highway patrol car with flashing lights, a fleet of white state vans rolls slowly off the highway. They loop around to the back of the stage and unload their passengers. Delegates from various agencies, a regional manager from the internet retailer, and Owen Middleton. The swelling in his face has gone down, though his head remains bruised and misshapen. His jaw is still tight and painful. But not nearly so sore as he pretends. Struggling to speak is a perfect excuse for avoiding small talk.

Dignitaries mount the stage and take their chairs amid good-natured confusion about who is supposed to sit where. The master of ceremonies, director of the Kansas Commerce Commission, signals the troubadour, who rises to the tips of his toes. When he drops to his heels, the band plays "God Bless America." Everyone rises, even Larry Hammerschmidt, who almost pulls Kathleen down as he lifts himself up. It is what a man must do.

The speeches begin. They will not end until every person has said everything at least twice and more effusively than the one before. The message is simple. Hope, at last. Hooray for the internet retailer. And hooray for Owen Middleton, patron saint of Ewing County, for making a miracle happen.

When it's the senator's turn to speak, there is a standing ovation. Somehow, and despite lingering discoloration, Owen manages to absolutely beam. He leans close to the microphone. The audience quiets.

"Lordy," cackles one of the baby bird ladies. Hard of hearing, she speaks too loud. "An ugly race between him and Billy Spire would end in a flat tie."

The crowd is taken aback. The dignitaries squirm in their folding chairs. At one of the far tables, LeeAnn Middleton stands up and glares.

"Who would say such a thing?" she asks.

The senator stares down from the lectern for the longest time. Finally, a crooked smile crosses his even crookeder face.

"I have always been much uglier than Billy Spire," he declares, then chuckles. Relieved and wildly amused at the notion that anyone could be uglier than the sheriff of Ewing County, the crowd roars.

"Between the two of us," he continues, "we'd make a bulldog break its chain."

The laughter doubles. It is a day to rejoice and Kansans love "uglier than" jokes. The celebrants join in.

"Make a freight train take the dirt road," someone yells.

"Make medicine sick," adds another.

"Stop." The senator pleads. "Laughing makes my face hurt."

"Your face has been hurting me for years," shouts Leo Ace, launching a new wave of hysteria.

Senator Middleton allows the laughter to continue for just the right amount of time, then flaps his hands to calm things down.

"No, I love Billy Spire. I really do." He shades his eyes and scans the crowd. "Sheriff, where are you?"

Heads turn to search. Palms rise in dismay. It seems Billy Spire is the only resident of Ewing County not in attendance.

"Must be on duty," Owen excuses. But every trace of amusement has left his bruised, misshapen face.

<>

It is a ceremony nobody wants to leave. The day is too beautiful. The conversation too lively. The hope too intoxicating. The crowd lingers, drinking apple cider and eating popcorn by the handful.

Amid all the bright cheer, there is none so luminous as LeeAnn Middleton. Whatever might be happening behind closed doors, she loves a party. Seeing old friends and catching up on gossip, her blue eyes wide with impish amazement. She gushes over all the young girls, congratulating their mamas as if beauty were a thing of accomplishment. She comforts the frail, whose number grows every year. Fussing over their clothes, whining how much she misses them, making them promise to come over soon for a piece of pie or glass of wine. Some of them will show up. To be greeted with squeals of joy, a big hug, and something delicious from the refrigerator. They will have LeeAnn's undivided attention for as long as they want to stay. In a small Kansas town and with LeeAnn Middleton, there is always time enough.

Two heads loom so high above the crowd that they can't help but see each other. Starting from opposite sides, Ayesha Perez and Father Turney meet in the middle.

"Father." She extends her hand. "You probably don't remember me."

"Remember you?" he winks. "Why I think about you all the time."

It is a canned joke, but Ayesha laughs. It pleases the priest that his tiny flirtation made her smile.

"We witnessed a fire together," he says to prove that he really does remember.

"We did. And I want to thank you."

"For what?"

"For what you did that night. And later for the family."

"It was nothing, I just made some phone calls."

"You sheltered the Dominguez family."

"Oh well," he blushes in embarrassment.

It's one thing to listen and take confessions. To serve as a minor deity, a man of the cloth. It's another thing altogether to accept honest praise from a lovely young woman. The giant priest finds it intimate, human, and unsettling.

"And you saved the life of their son," she continues. "Maybe a few others."

The priest's massive heart surges with emotions, which quickly morph into embarrassment.

"Let's pray those lives stay turned toward the good," he answers gruffly.

It would take some time for Ayesha's comment to sink in. For Eli Turney to fully accept that he did save a life, maybe a few. When it did, the realization brought him peace. From that moment on, ministering to the grief of others would be less cynical, less void. For Father Turney would no longer contemplate death without recalling the lives he had protected. He would no longer regard himself as a huckster who dizzied and spun. Instead, he found within himself a life force, a protective vitality. Ayesha Perez's comment refilled the empty words he had uttered for decades. Death, especially death avoided, affirms life.

A woman arrives and stands closely at Ayesha's side. She is also striking in appearance, but in a different way. Periwinkle blue eyes and the kind of alabaster skin that radiates good health. They are wearing identical tee shirts that call for fair wages. Ayesha looks upon her friend with warm affection, then back at Father Turney. She doesn't have to name what's going on. The priest understands. The companion is obviously bored, eager to move on.

"God loves you," Eli concludes in his fitting, priestly way.

"Not according to the church," Ayesha says in her forthright manner, which is equally fitting.

Eli Turney scans the crowd as he frames his response. Then he locks his eyes upon hers.

"Well, Dr. King said the arc of the moral universe is long but it bends toward justice," Turney says. "Church is the same. But slower."

"I think we've made our point," notes the second woman, becoming more fidgety.

"What point?" the priest asks.

"This company has a reputation for exploiting part-time workers," Ayesha explains. "We want them to know we're watching."

"Keep fighting the good fight," Eli encourages, then shifts his weight and winces.

"You all right, Father?"

"Ingrown toenail," he dismisses.

It is, in fact, an early indicator of diabetes. The priest will eventually lose that toe. But he will accept his fate as gracefully as one can. Fortified in knowing that he was once fit and strong. Could put an arrow through a bull's-eye at ninety feet.

<>

Eli Turney is not the only one limping around after the ground has been broken.

Owen Middleton told Melvin McQuitty to stay away. In part, because the senator didn't want any dots connected. In part, because he couldn't stand the sight of the man. But someone else told the representative, in no uncertain terms, that he damn well better make an appearance.

The day after being shot with an arrow, as he lay in the Dodge City hospital, a woman with short-cropped hair and square-framed glasses walked into his room.

"You're McQuitty," she stated, as if clearing up any uncertainty about his identity.

"Yes?" He sat up in his bed and smoothed his mullet.

"I'm Special Agent Peggy Palmer from the Kansas Bureau of Investigation. I understand that you know something about extremism."

"Says who?"

"We don't reveal our sources."

"You been talking to Billy Spire?"

"I said we don't reveal."

"Well, did he tell you I'm done and over with that?"

Special Agent Palmer wordlessly went over and closed the door.

"That's what I'm here to talk to you about, sir. I'm afraid you're a long way from done and over. Not far as the KBI is concerned."

From that day forward, the representative and the special agent talk once a week. Thursday mornings at nine o'clock. He goes over his calendar and tells her with whom he has met, and with whom he is going to meet. At her direction, he rubs elbows with angry men and women on the fringes. She coaches him on the right questions to ask and how to ask them. Afterward, he sits in his car and makes careful notes. For the sake of appearance, she lets him continue carrying the thirty-eight. No self-respecting Wing would be caught without a Second Amendment solution. But for the sake of safety, his and others, she forbids him from loading it with bullets.

The result of this collaboration is knocks on doors in the middle of the night. Across western Kansas, men and a few women are led away in handcuffs. Charged with illegal weapons and conspiracy. They curse and vow to kill whoever has betrayed them. But they will never find out. KBI protects its confidential sources.

Of course, there is a payoff for McQuitty's cooperation. Special Agent Peggy Palmer keeps secret whatever it is she knows. Melvin often wonders. Is it Haycock or New Frontier? But he cannot figure a way to inquire that does not risk self-incrimination. So, he does what she asks, knowing only that there is plenty for the agent to know.

In fact, Peggy Palmer is only aware of what Billy Spire told her. That the representative knows quite a bit about extremist activities and might be willing to cooperate. She is pretty sure the sheriff knows more than he's telling. But in the cat-and-mouse relationships of local law enforcement and the KBI, it would be rude to simply ask.

Besides, the Kansas Bureau of Investigation never asks unless it already knows the answer.

<>

It was never determined who set fire to the Dominguez trailer. Not exactly.

Peggy Palmer guessed it was part of a larger conspiracy, based on chatter among supremacist groups. There had been an uptick in reported incidents. Vague references to the day of the rope.

Billy Spire wasn't so sure. He had his eye on a local crank. The grandpa of the white nerd. The one who had kind words for Russ Haycock and also carried a "Posse Comitatus" decal in the back window of the truck. A couple days after the fire, the old man abruptly moved to Amarillo, Texas. Told people he was going to look after an ailing brother. But Spire could find no similar surnames in the Amarillo phone book.

He thought about bringing Palmer into the arson investigation. But what good would come of it? The trailer, now a heap of scorched metal and debris, needed to be gone. The Dominguez family was better off. And in all likelihood, the geriatric culprit was now a problem of the Lone Star State.

Still, there remained loose ends that would not tie. More than one person set the fire. Who else was angry or bigoted enough to join into arson? When Billy started considering the possibilities he came to a sad realization. There were more than he cared to count. In Ewing County, Kansas, perspectives and alignments change. Spinning neutrons and protons of identity. Sometimes in frictionless orbits. Sometimes in rude explosions.

Billy hopes things get better. That the internet retailer will raise Stonewall's fortunes. That spirits will improve. Angers subside. That, in seeing how much hurt they caused, whoever helped set the fire will never do anything like that again.

The sheriff is willing to leave it at hope. For now. But if there is even a whiff of more racist crap in Ewing County, Billy Spire will make sure all involved learn the true meaning of fear.

⟨⟩

Owen wanders around, accepting congratulations on the wonderful groundbreaking and his fine speech. He nods and points to his jaw as an excuse to not stop and chat. He keeps moving until he finds who he's looking for.

"I tell you I'm going to do it!" Leo Ace screeches to a conclave of the usual gang.

The men hoot and wave at him like a bad stink.

"I'd be better than the mayor we got!"

"With that mouth of yours, you'd last about ten minutes."

"What did I ever say that was bad?" the mechanic protests, unleashing an even greater barrage of hoots and stink waves.

"Leo," Owen interrupts. "Where's Billy?"

"I'm not sure," Ace answers. The other men lean in to eavesdrop.

"Where is he?"

The lanky man with greasy hair gives the senator a pleading look.

"He's at the Haycock place," he confesses. "But he said don't tell anyone."

"Especially me?"

"I don't recall his exact words," Ace lies.

"I understand," Middleton replies. As he walks away, the conversation heats back up. The old boys have plenty of evidence to offer.

"You once said that if Mama Cass and Karen Carpenter split that last ham sandwich, they would both be alive today."

Everyone groans, but Ace. He slaps his thigh and roars. He loves his own jokes best of all.

"Well, it's true," he howls. "And that's what we need around here. More common sense."

Billy Spire drags a wheelbarrow from the back of the Ram 1500 and sets it on the ground. Pours in a sack of Quikrete and water from a five-gallon plastic container. He stirs with a hoe, dragging the blade back and forth in long, meditative strokes. Soon there comes a heavy mixture, thick and gray. He tips the wheelbarrow and pours its contents into a two-by-three-foot wooden frame atop Russ Haycock's grave. Then levels it out with a garden trowel. As the batch cures, the sheriff picks through boxes provided by Emma Ace.

She and other of the town's women rummaged through the basement house before it was demolished. Clothes, kitchenware, and firearms went to church bazaars. Western novels, condensed books, and even *The Naked Communist* went to the library's fundraising bin. Photographs were added to stacks of ephemera at the Ewing County Historical Society. It didn't seem right to throw them out at the time, although that would certainly come later. Really, who cares about the Haycock family? With special care and her curious sense of beauty, Emma Ace gathered knick-knacks and put them in a cardboard box. Russ's military medals, tiny pot-metal representations of very large things, foreign coins, buttons, Honey's cheap jewelry, a few fancy fountain pens.

"Would you like to have these?" she asked Sheriff Spire.

"What for?"

"The way science changes, with DNA and all that, maybe they'll be of use one day."

"The case is closed."

"I know," she replied, setting the box on his desk. "But just in case."

Emma Ace was saying what a lot of people thought. That the facts around Russ Haycock's death just didn't add up. But then, neither did anything else about that man. His death was just as senseless and mysterious as his life.

Owen Middleton was right. Billy understood that. Any case he had made would have faltered under faint-hearted prosecution, Stand Your Ground, and political realities. In the end, only Ewing County would have suffered. But being sensible is not the same as accepting. The injustice troubled Billy Spire. So did the box full of reminders that Emma Ace left on his desk. So, he decided to do something kind for Russ Haycock. And for whatever atonement an act of kindness might hold.

As the concrete cures, Spire selects pieces from the cardboard box and arranges them across a piece of plywood on the tailgate of this truck.

A car comes up the gravel road. The red Lincoln stops at the edge of Haycock's property. It is a different red Lincoln. Brand new. No bullet holes. LeeAnn thought nothing of the upgrade; fine new cars are a Middleton legacy. Owen gets out but does not approach. He keeps his distance out of respect. Or maybe apprehension.

"Billy, look at me," the senator mumbles. "Say something."

The sheriff does neither. He bends down and touches the concrete, testing to see if it is ready, firm but yielding to his fingertips. None of this is Owen's fault. Not really. He was just doing what he thought best for Stonewall, for Ewing County. And who could have guessed the trouble Melvin McQuitty would bring?

As Owen waits, he formulates his comments. He will tell his friend that he misses him. That there is much remaining to be done together. New projects to be completed. New hopes to be realized. He will offer to forgive, to shake hands, and move on.

Billy respects Owen for his efficiency and intelligence. But his is a cold benevolence that holds itself apart. With rules of its own invention. Justified by legacy and logic. Offered to humanity en masse but wanting at the individual level. Never understanding that other people's small talk was not small to them.

Five minutes pass.

Billy realizes that for his own sake, the friendship must end. Just as surely as Matthew Middleton had put him in touch with the best parts of himself, Owen moved him in the other direction. Toward the compromise of principles. Toward haunting memories. Toward a sense of lostness so profound that familiar streets seemed lonely and strange. The sheriff understands that none of this is Owen's fault. Not really. The senator was simply being who he was bred to be. Still, Billy Spire will be better off apart from his old friend.

One thing for certain, Owen Middleton isn't like his father. Matthew was a great man. His son is only a man of great aspirations.

The senator shakes his head and gets back into the Lincoln. He'll be okay, he thinks to himself. He is not the type to dwell on regret. There is work waiting in Topeka. Some of it involving the League of Municipalities, whose general counsel is an attractive woman. Sexy, in a bookish way. He honestly believes Billy Spire will come around, in time. It never occurs to him that he will miss this friend more than he can imagine.

That there is something foundational in being known and loved for a very long time. And that a person, even a patron saint, is diminished when such familiarity is lost.

Spire hears the Lincoln depart. But he does not look. He sets the decorated plywood atop the empty wheelbarrow, then gets down on hands and knees. Carefully transferring the design, piece by piece, he sets about completing the grave marker he has made.

He makes a border of Lincoln-head pennies and old keys. In the top right corner, he fashions a sun from an oversized commemorative coin and rays of fountain pen barrels. At the bottom edge, he presses in a pot-metal Minute Man to stand guard over Honey's jewels and Russ's medals, including a Purple Heart. He studies his work for a couple of minutes, then adds an Eiffel Tower, a broken gold watchband, and a flourish of curled copper wire. Finally, he spells "RAH" in the center with letters made of drill bits and jackknives.

When it is done, Billy Spire stands to admire his work. The primitive effect is comic and sweet. The shiny elements glisten against a dull gray substrate. Russ and Honey are together again. Beneath matching markers.

Movement catches the sheriff's eye. A red-tailed hawk rises from a fencepost, catches an updraft, and effortlessly ascends into the sky. From down the gravel road, there comes a second vehicle. When it arrives, it is all Billy Spire can do to keep from crying.

Nadine climbs out of the car. She takes a long, weary drag from her cigarette and crushes the butt beneath her heel. Emma Ace, one of those people who do all the heavy lifting, had called. Told her where her husband was. Said he might could use some company. Wordlessly, the sheriff's wife walks over and sits on the tailgate. Looking around and waiting. Waiting in a way that suggests she would wait forever.

Billy starts to say something.

"Don't talk," she says without looking at him. "Just let me be here with you."

"Thanks," Billy answers softly.

"It's the best I can do, you know. Maybe ever."

"I know," he replies.

He wants to touch her, but he knows she would shy away. He understands, but it makes him feel lonely. And in Billy Spire, loneliness always brings memories of youth, followed by shame. About where he came from, who he was, and who he sometimes still believes he is.

Nadine sees the hurt in her husband.

"It's beautiful," she says of her husband's handiwork.

Spire grunts in doubt.

"Don't do that," she scolds. "It's beautiful."

Billy studies the grave markers. His and hers. He sees himself in one of Honey's embedded shards of mirror. Strong sunlight cuts harsh shadows into every deep wrinkle, every crevice of his brutal face. The bags under his eyes are purple and swollen. The bristles of his red crew cut shimmer with sweat. The small eyes all but disappear, as if they have turned inward.

Nadine speaks. "You're more than how you look, you know."

"I hope you're right," he answers.

It is a hope Billy Spire will always carry. And a certainty he will never hold.

The red-tailed hawk rises higher and higher until it is lost in the sky. Beyond the capacities of eyesight. Alone and unseen, it dances on the thermals and spring breezes of Ewing County, Kansas. Far above the rolling hills, greening fields, human geometries, and simple concerns of that place and season.

Acknowledgments

THE AUTHOR IS deeply grateful to Isabelle Bleecker, Nordlyset Literary Agency; James McCoy and the University of Iowa Press; dear friends who read and commented on the manuscript; and his beloved mentors—Floyd, George, and Frances.